Lone Star

Lone Star

An Edna Ferber Mystery

Ed Ifkovic

Poisoned Pen Press

First Edition 2009

10 9 8 7 6 5 4 3 2 1

Library of Congress Catalog Card Number: 2008931506

ISBN: 978-1-59058-587-0 Hardcover

Poisoned Pen Press
6962 E. First Ave., Ste. 103
Scottsdale, AZ 85251
www.poisonedpenpress.com
info@poisonedpenpress.com

Printed in the United States of America

For my mother

"The atrocious crime of being a young man."
—William Pitt to Horace Walpole,
in Boswell's *Life of Johnson*,
March 6, 1741

Chapter One

"No one flies to L.A. in July," I mumbled as the driver opened the door of the limo and helped me in.

I heard someone laughing. "Edna, welcome to L.A."

I'd just stepped off the eight-and-a-half-hour United Airlines flight from Idlewild. "I need a year to recover," I muttered. I'd slept but a few fitful hours, fidgeted in my tight seat, and was happy to see the limo that Jack Warner had waiting for me. How insane to fly to the West Coast in summer. But business beckoned. After all, Warner Bros. Studio was filming *Giant*, my massive bestseller about Texas, and I was a co-producer. This was my baby, really, and when it comes to money, I cast a jaundiced eye on how others jostle my cash. And, though I was loath to admit it, the pulse and verve of Hollywood glamour excited me.

I smiled. "Tansi, honey, you're a tonic after the abominable red eye, but even you can't redeem California."

Tansi Rowland gave a shrill laugh I assumed she'd acquired from years of living in L.A. She reached out and touched my arm. "You look tired, Edna. We'll get you to the Ambassador and let you nap."

I fell back against the soft cushions. "Lovely to see you, Tansi."

Decades back, Tansi's laugh was robust, a chubby girl's rich contralto. Now it was thin and metallic. It had been over twenty years since we'd seen each other, of course. I narrowed my eyes.

Tansi, a thin, wiry woman in her forties, seemed all nerve and hot wire. Where was the vivacious, bubbly twenty-year-old I knew in New York, the roly-poly girl with the apple-cheeks and the unruly hair? Tansi still spoke with a trace of her mother's rich British accent, albeit now flattened by a lethal amalgam of deadened New York vowels and California linguistic breeziness.

I hugged her. "Your mother says hello."

Tansi frowned. Her mother, of course, was one of my oldest friends and the legendary Broadway actress, Bea Pritchard, transported from the London stage in the twenties and the short-lived wife of Wall Street financier Howard Rowland—one of her many moneyed marriages. Tansi, an only child who trailed after her mother from one brownstone to the next, had never married and often seemed embarrassed by her mother's public-house risqué manner. She'd drifted to Hollywood after overachieving at Barnard, but not to be an actress—she had a healthy distrust of performers, given her view of her mother's bedroom. She was Jack Warner's assistant.

Tansi became all business. "Tonight you'll be dining at Romanoff's on Rodeo Drive. Very posh, Edna. With Henry Ginsburg, Jack Warner, and George Stevens—the trinity of *Giant*." She grinned. "The giant trinity."

"So the film is going fine?" I asked, unsure.

"Marvelous." She sounded like a Warner publicist. "You'll want to meet Liz Taylor and Rock Hudson." She paused. "And James Dean."

"The *wunderkind*?"

"He's a little unpredictable." Again, that high-pitched laugh; a nervous sound. "He told me he's scared of you."

"What? I've never met him. Does he think I'll bite his head off?" I shook my head. "I've been known to be a little tart-tongued and…and…"

"Withering?"

"Only with fools, my dear."

"He's afraid you'll ask if he's read *Giant*."

"And he hasn't?"

"No, he refuses to."

I clicked my tongue. "Then I'll show him no mercy."

"That's what he's afraid of."

Both of us looked at each other. Only I was smiling.

That evening I dined at Romanoff's with the battalion of men who were translating my Midas-touch brainchild into film epic. They also seemed scared of me. I like that in a man. But, of course, Henry Ginsburg was an old friend, and, as such, he understood how to handle me—no servile deprecation, no fawning, and, best of all, a witty regard for my place in the world. A large, overflowing man, nattily attired in a pin-striped Brooks Brothers suit, with bland business tie, Ginsburg was a contrast to the wiry, compact Jack Warner with his Parisian gigolo sliver of a moustache; a tidy man in an expensive, though rumpled, suit. George Stevens cultivated a casual Hollywood demeanor, a beefy man with pitch-black hair swept back from his forehead, all open dress shirt and Bwana-of-the-jungle khaki. I had a lot invested in these three men. Hence my friendly trek westward: checking in on the troops.

But I was weary. Red-jacketed waiters swooped down on me when I took a sip of water, and Mike Romanoff, the self-styled prince with the blustery manner, insisted on shaking my hand. Flashbulbs blinded me. Jack Benny and Mary Livingston, seated nearby, waved. I waved back. Sleep, I thought. I want sleep. My afternoon nap (a rarity for me, since I consider such indulgence a sign of weakness) had been unpleasant, disturbed by noises from the hallway. A girl's flirtatious note, a man's throaty roar.

So I thanked the three men, announced that I'd gladly view the dailies in the morning, and was escorted to the hotel and to my suite—too many rooms for one old lady. As I readied for bed, I stared down onto Wilshire Boulevard, then found myself gazing at the enormous vase of lush, perfumed yellow roses I'd discovered when I'd checked in. Already the petals were falling onto the floor. In California nothing stays intact for very long.

◇◇◇

The next morning, Tansi greeted me in the lobby and led me to the studio car. A good nine hours of blissful rest behind me, I felt ready to tackle the day. Tansi was in a spirited mood, and I recalled a carefree walk through Central Park with a giddy sixteen-year-old Tansi and her regal mother—a woman who became furious when a passerby asked me for an autograph and not her. Now, all these years later, Tansi had metamorphosed into an assured self. You saw a woman with a drab flat face and a thin body, with conservative flared white-linen skirt and tame Peter-Pan collared blue blouse, her abundantly permed hair pulled back into a Gibson girl pompadour. All this was offset by bright scarlet lipstick and glistening red nails. A marvelous contradiction, really. Well, I thought, an actress' daughter—the one who ran away to Hollywood to escape the imperial Bea. No mother to guide her, as they said in Victorian novels.

Tansi confided, "Everyone at the studio is nervous about you looking at the dailies."

"Why, for heaven's sake?"

"Think about it, Edna. *Giant* is your property. Hollywood is simply borrowing it, remaking it. What if you don't like it?"

"I don't expect I shall, truth to tell."

Tansi, wide eyed: "Really?" The grin gone, she ran her tongue over glossy crimson lips.

"Because when I told Stevens that the script Ivan Moffat and that other fellow…"

"Fred Guiol."

"I never can remember that name. It's so…weak. Ghoulish. Very Vincent Price. Anyway, I informed them all that the script was illiterate."

"So I recall."

"As it was," I said, sharply. "But when those boys learned to listen to my book they got better." I paused, thinking of changes to my plot, particularly the reinvention of the relationship of the spinster Luz and Jett Rink. That had not pleased me.

I tucked my hands into my lap, waited. I felt warm in the rose-colored cotton dress with the cinch belt, bought especially for this first day at the Burbank studio. But we just sat there. Impatient: "Tansi, dear, is there a reason the car isn't moving? Do I have to fork over a dollar for gas?"

The driver suddenly opened the rear door of the limo and a man slid in, settled himself next to me, too close, I thought, and extended his hand. "Jake Geyser, Miss Ferber. I wrote you."

Humorless, a little boisterous, hail-fellow-well-met. A Rotarian, I concluded, giving him a grim nod.

Tansi looked none too happy. "I forgot to mention that Jake was coming with us, Edna."

I surveyed the new arrival: fiftyish, tall and lanky with a bony, vaguely patrician face, all angle and jut, razor sharp—and an alpine Adam's apple, very mobile. It was the face of a man born to ease and minor gastrological irritation.

"Jack Warner personally assigned me to steer the production of *Giant* to a smooth conclusion. I'm a trouble-shooter, really. I'm the one who has to anticipate sudden disaster."

"Do you expect me to be one of the disasters, Mr. Geyser?"

For a second he seemed flustered, glancing at Tansi, as if, somehow, this were her fault. "Ah no, Miss Ferber. I'm just along for the ride."

But I immediately understood that this was not true. His forced jocularity, his physical proximity, his narrow-slatted glance—the eyes held too short a time, then focused elsewhere—suggested there was a problem in paradise. I wondered when I'd discover it. Jake Geyser leaned back, fumbled with a worn leather portfolio, and stared straight ahead. A cigarette smoker, I realized, given the pungent scent off the English tweed sports jacket and the artfully creased flannel trousers. An affected man, but not people smart. A dangerous man because he'd been given the job of gatekeeper.

And something else. As the limo cruised down Wilshire, along the Strip, through the wide, palm-fringed avenues, out to Burbank, Tansi got noticeably quiet, her body hugging the doorframe, her head tucked in, reminding me of a frightened wren. She seemed taken with the landscape, a tourist in town. The climate of the car sobered, chilled, with me watching them both and realizing—with some fascination—the deep dislike the one had for the other. The spinster Tansi with the Hollywood glitter eye shadow at odds with the servile factotum with the graying temples and the lacrosse-player profile, a man whose duty it was to keep things kosher.

But what *things?* His presence in the sleek car suggested a problem. *Two* guides? Who was I—an Eisenhower cabinet member? Or was his presence a reminder to Tansi to keep still? A problem—I smelled it. I knew it to my marrow.

Tansi and Jake positioned themselves on either side of me in the hot projection room, beseeching me to take coffee, a Danish, some water, maybe tea, an avocado salad, anything, everything. Tansi lost all humor, ill tempered now. Jake Geyser kept clearing his throat.

I leaned into Tansi and whispered, "What aren't you telling me?"

The remark caught her off guard. Without thinking, her eyes staring at the as-yet blank screen, she whispered back, "I can't tell you." She realized she'd slipped and started stammering.

I shifted to Jake, rigid beside me. He'd overheard my off-hand remark to Tansi. Still looking straight ahead, he declared, "I think you'll enjoy this. I…"

"Mr. Geyser…"

For a reason unbeknownst to me—had there been a transition I'd somehow missed?—he began rambling about his ivy-covered undergraduate days, his merry hours on the Princeton fencing team, varsity, summers at his grandparents' beach house in Tidewater, Virginia, something that connected to a scene I'd be watching: Rock Hudson as the Texan Bick Benedict wooing the feisty Liz Taylor as Leslie, in ole Virginny. When the lights suddenly dimmed, he shut up as though slapped.

I got caught up in the flickering images—and, with a tightness at my throat, I heard Liz and Rock mouthing *my* words, albeit bowdlerized by Moffat and what's-his-name. I found them satisfying, a little like a gentle wash of warm water over the body. Rock seemed wooden, almost freakishly large, but then—that *was* my Bick Benedict, a man who comes to understand his inner power and beauty only with decades of living behind him. And Liz Taylor, luminous with those violet eyes and that aristocratic chin, well, she filled the screen with the resolve, grit, and ferocity of coquette-cum-steel woman. I closed my eyes for a second: this was good stuff, truly.

But I was not prepared, not really, for the footage of the young James Dean—the rebellious, moody Jett Rink, the desperate wildcatter, the driven boy. That is, *my* Jett Rink. The way he cocked his head, brought his hand to his brow, and the walk—a strut that was still somehow a slouching glide. This was ballet. This was a new man, light years from John Wayne or Gary Cooper. This was—I remembered a statue of a young wrestler I'd seen in a museum in Naples, a Pompeiian boy, tight, tense, ready to pounce. Somehow, watching him now, I forgot that I had not written James Dean's life—only Jett's. But it was as though he'd entered my book before I'd written it—and told me what to say. I fairly lost my breath. Tears came to my eyes and I fluttered, a little foolish and unhappy. Liz Taylor stood on a stretch of arid land and then, suddenly, James Dean filled the screen, and he mumbled. I had no idea what he said.

Jake Geyser grunted, almost involuntarily, and what registered was his dislike of Dean. Tansi, on the other hand, seemed to hold her breath, fearful of moving. She gripped the back of the seat in front of her.

When it was all over, I said aloud in the sudden brightness of the room, "I didn't expect James Dean to be..." I stopped, the writer suddenly wordless.

Tansi breathed in. "I know, I know. There ought to be a law."

I turned to Jake. "But, Mr. Geyser, I sense something in you..."

"Not really." He turned away.

"I read character for a living, sir." I was furious at his dismissal.

He looked back. "My job is to honor Warner Bros. Studio, Miss Ferber. Not to denigrate its stars."

I rolled my tongue into a cheek. "You let your body do that for you."

Tansi savored the exchange, emboldened by my comments. "Jake is a stickler for punctuality, cleanliness, and law and order, I'm afraid. Jimmy Dean is usually late if he arrives at all. He doesn't shave, he doesn't bathe, he's disorderly. Some days he's the opposite of everything I've just said. Charming, funny…"

"I can't wait to meet him," I said.

Jake, I noticed, was drumming his index finger on the chair rail.

I'd my doubts about casting the feckless, untested Dean as the destructive Jett Rink, until Gadge Kazan arranged a private showing of his unreleased *East of Eden*. I'd left the projection room convinced in the rightness of George Stevens' move, mesmerized by the darkswept performance. And when *East of Eden* opened, and James Dean suddenly—overnight, as it were—emerged as a movie sensation, the new image of Hollywood, the face on the cover of *Photoplay* and *Movie Screen*, the mumbling, plaintive voice of the lost and wayward youth, well, I knew he'd bring his peculiar stamp to the part with the authority of the branding of a prize steer at Reata Ranch. But I hadn't expected the sheer translucence—yes, that was the word—of his performance.

Both guides now closed in on me, grasped my elbows, and squired me out.

"Could you two please let me do my own walking?" I said, annoyed. "I've managed to go from point A to point B in this lifetime without bouncing off the walls like a drunken sailor on leave."

Both mumbled apologies, but each still tried to edge in.

Day two, I thought, of what already seemed like the one-hundred-year war.

◇◇◇

Later that afternoon, happily abandoned for a couple hours by Tansi and Jake, I sat in an easy chair in the Warner Blue Room. Idly, I leafed through the movie script. I was not happy with the considerable changes to my plot, and now there was talk of major shifts in the climactic gala celebration near the end of the movie. Jett Rink, the brutal oillionaire, drunk and spiraling toward his ugly end. The studio was going for over-the-top melodrama. Character, I kept telling myself, is more important than plot.

"Edna, I've been looking for you." A deep voice from the doorway. Flat, brusque, gravelly, but oddly melodic and filled with laughter.

I looked up, smiled. "I was wondering where you were."

I'd met Mercedes McCambridge in New York, a few summers back. The two of us immediately liked each other. Three, maybe four scintillating lunches in New York that summer. A Broadway matinee, a dinner. I'd sent her flowers when she won her Oscar for *All the King's Men*. Now Mercedes played the ill-fated Luz Benedict, Bick's unmarried older sister—a feisty, no-nonsense, rough-and-tumble Texas woman whose sudden death inevitably leads to Jett's great fortune…and the beginning of his fall from grace. The veteran actress—"Call me Mercy, for mercy's sake"—was a look-straight-in-your-eye woman, the only women I can tolerate. A woman cut from my own precious cloth. Other women, the coy, flirtatious, frothy girls—especially the weak and martyred patient Griseldas, mooning and hoping for favor, a man's nod—well, I spit them out like so much bile.

Now Mercy, pushing a youthful forty, reached over to hug me. Dressed in a dull calico flare skirt and a muslin blouse with a corduroy vest ("I'm in costume for still photographs"), she struck me as Annie Oakley, with fierce, intelligent eyes. You saw the wide Midwestern face, the strong carriage, and the nervous gesture of slender fingers casually pushing through uncombed hair. Pioneer woman, with Max Factor rouge and the vaudevillian laugh.

We chatted like old coffee chums, leaning in, small talk about New York friends and acquaintances. Mercy asked about Kitty Carlyle, Bennett Cerf, Dorothy and Dick Rodgers, others. Theater folks, fine people, all. Though I always maintain that I loathe gossip, I yammered on about dinner parties where all the wrong stuff was served—and said. Faux pas among the four hundred, as it were. Mercy also knew Tansi's mother, Bea Pritchard, who'd once upstaged Mercy in a Broadway outing.

"How is the battle-ax?" she asked me.

I grinned. "Looking for her next husband."

"It's hard to believe she's Tansi's mother."

I shook my head. "Oh, but of course, Mercy. The wilder the mother got—remember when she wore that revealing gown to the White House and Hoover got the hiccoughs?—anyway, the more *outré* her mother got, the more puritanical Tansi became."

"But she and Jake Geyser will be the death of you," Mercy said. "Jake is Warner's menacing bull dog in Oxford camouflage."

"Which leads me to ask you, Mercy, what's going on? Jake Geyser and Tansi hinted at some problem that I'm not supposed to know about. Why on earth does Warner have Jake hovering around me like a dazed summer moth?"

"I'm not supposed to tell you. We have orders."

"But of course you will."

Mercy's mouth drew into a thin line, but the corners suddenly turned up, a timid smile, and the eyes had a glint in them. "Of course."

But we both stopped, almost on cue, and turned to the open doorway. James Dean stood there, leaning against the doorframe in costume: the tight worn jeans, the ten-gallon Stetson on his head, wisps of almond-blond hair over his ears, an unlit cigarette in his mouth. A cocky stance, practiced. Yet on his nose horn-rimmed glasses, incongruous, but oddly appealing. His fingers drummed on the wood frame.

I stared, mute. It was, I suppose, when I thought about it later, a little like looking into the sun, or a cup of cold spring water that slackens a desert thirst. He was, quite frankly, a calculated presence, a deliberate act of utter coolness: the wrestler's body, so muscular and taut, sinewy through faded denim; and the face—that hint of boyish hair, the strong chin, the half-closed eyes, and the impossible sensual lips. This was either an actor at his craft or, truthfully, the sudden shift of seismic current. Calm down, Edna, I told myself. He's a boy. He's an actor.

And short. I'd thought him taller, I'd thought him towering. I was a tiny woman myself, barely five feet, with a big head. He was a small man with a big head. I knew him.

"Jimmy." Mercy waved at him. "Come and meet Edna Ferber."

"Madama," he said to Mercy, using the name he called her in the film. He didn't look at me.

"Come in," Mercy motioned.

He seemed as though he intended to walk in, in fact, his feet seemed to move, but oddly his hand rested on the doorframe, a statue, all angle and graceful line. The cigarette twitched in his mouth. He bent in, mumbled.

"What?" Mercy asked.

"I got another letter," he said, the words clipped, loud and spaced out. He sounded surprised at his own voice, but there was anger there, too. And frustration. The eyes closed, then popped open, and I thought of boys caught stealing apples from a greengrocer's stand. I expected him to run away. And now he seemed to see me for the first time. "Miss Edna," he said, slurring the words and half-bowing, the cigarette bobbing.

I didn't know what to say. "Mr. Dean…" I began.

"Jimmy, ma'am."

"I saw you on Broadway in *The Immoralist*."

He twisted his head, intrigued. "And?"

"You were sadly miscast as the effeminate Arab boy Bachar." Flat out. Challenging, in control.

He pulled in his cheeks, making his face look hollow, and held my eye. "Which part of me was miscast, would you say? The effeminate part or the Arab or the boy?"

I paused. I had no idea what I wanted to say. I recalled the provocative scissors dance the homosexual houseboy Bachar had performed onstage, a seduction of an ambivalent Michel—a stage bit that garnered him incredible praise. But he had seemed so *wrong* as the weak, ineffectual but manipulative street urchin. In slippers and nightgown, doing a ballet, flitting and snipping the air with a pair of shiny silver scissors. He was too masculine, I'd thought. But what I wanted to say now was that he'd redeemed himself in *East of Eden,* that his depiction of the troubled Cal Trask, the bad seed Cain of Steinbeck's Eden, had been mesmerizing. *That* was believable—and thrilling. But my throat was dry, and my head throbbed. And by the time I opened my mouth to praise him, he had walked out of the room, just turned and walked away.

When I looked back at Mercy, the woman was laughing softly, and I had trouble looking into her face.

Chapter Two

Mercy told me that Jimmy had received a troublesome letter a week before. "Troublesome?"

She nodded. "Scary."

And now, she gathered, a new one. All the studio execs, from Jack Warner down, were nervous, though tight-lipped. Mercy had overheard Rock Hudson thundering about it to George Stevens, though he'd looked sheepish when he realized Mercy was nearby. Curious, I began asking questions. I'd always be the insatiable girl reporter from Appleton, Wisconsin. But Mercy just mumbled.

"What?" I implored.

Mercy thrust up her hand, traffic-cop style, and said, "I don't like to gossip, Edna. It's some matter with a girl in trouble." She shrugged. "Young people." She sighed. "You know."

No, I didn't, but I was intrigued, and Mercy seemed on the verge of saying something else, leaning forward. But there was bustling at the door and Tansi, for some reason holding an enormous bouquet of flowers—garish hibiscus at that, a purple so dark I thought of blood clots—sailed in, out of breath, and said they were from a friend's garden. She'd driven there to pick them. For a second she buried her face in the bouquet, inhaling the heady aroma. I didn't want them, but Tansi said someone would deliver them to my rooms at the Ambassador. Good, I thought, more dead flowers on my carpet. Browning, curling petals underfoot. The end of a long day at a funeral parlor. I expected a competitive Jake Geyser to march in, maneuvering a wobbly wheelbarrow of bougainvillea, the blossoms bleeding onto his tweedy attire.

Instead, Tansi said, "I saw Jimmy in the hallway…leaving. Did you meet him, Edna? He didn't even say hello to me."

"He stopped in," Mercy said.

Tansi glanced quickly at me, then at Mercy: "Did he bother you about that thing?"

Mercy was quiet.

I raised my eyebrows and craned back my neck, deliberately letting Tansi see. That *thing*? "Tansi, my dear, you seem to be doing a lot of talking about a subject you're trying to avoid letting me in on."

"I'm sorry." She glanced at the heap of hibiscus she'd deposited at my elbow. One gaudy blossom had broken free and toppled to the floor. "I'm sorry," she said again. "It's just that I get so protective of Jimmy. You've seen the dailies, Edna. My God, Warner has a goldmine in him."

"But what's going on?"

Mercy smiled. "Edna, all of us here are a little gaga over Jimmy, I must tell you. Not only those gangly, teenaged girls out there seeing *East of Eden* for the twentieth time, but middle-aged women and—well, all women. There's something about the boy. And Tansi here, she's his guardian angel on the back lot."

Tansi grinned. "I don't exactly *swoon*, Mercy."

"Admit it, Tansi, come on. It feels good to confess infatuation."

Tansi shook her head. "I'm forty-five years old."

I interrupted. "And I'm nearly seventy. And I still couldn't find the words to *talk* to him."

Tansi pulled up a chair, as though ready to share sophomoric James Dean stories. But Mercy cleared her throat and whispered, "Tansi, Jimmy just told us he got another letter."

Tansi jumped, as though stung. "From Carisa?"

"I assume so. He left without saying."

"Could someone please tell me what's going on?" I begged, helpless.

Tansi got serious. "We're on orders from Jake Geyser, supposedly via Jack Warner, to keep the news from you, Edna. Jake's as adamant as Warner is skittish. No one's talking so far, and Jake's hinting that the release of the film might be in jeopardy." She shook her head. "It's all crazy, really."

Mercy leaned over the table and covered one of my hands with one of hers. Yet she was looking at Tansi. "I think Edna has a right to know what's going on."

Tansi fumed. "No, please, Edna, stay away from this. Mr. Warner warned us."

Mercy looked at her. "Tansi, last night Jimmy stopped by my apartment and asked me to talk to Carisa, because, as you know, I was friendly with her a while back and…"

Tansi's voice rose. "Impossible. This has gotten to the point of sheer madness, really. Carisa Krausse is a two-bit washed-up actress who got fired for laziness and…and…Jimmy never did what she said…and…"

Mercy held up her hand. "I told him no, Tansi. I'm not talking to Carisa. I don't think it's a good idea for me to get in the middle of studio business. Warner can handle this."

Tansi flicked her head back, nervous. "I can't believe he asked you to visit her."

"He thinks he can charm me into doing his business," Mercy said, shrugging her shoulders.

"And can he?" I asked.

A trace of a smile. "Probably." Mercy glanced at her watch. "Lord, I'm late." She stood up. "Edna, dinner tonight?"

I nodded.

"I'll invite Jimmy."

I noticed Tansi staring into Mercy's face.

"Will you join us, Tansi?"

Tansi was nodding.

I looked at my watch. Jimmy was late. Tansi was late. I wasn't happy. Idly, I munched on a breadstick that tasted like sesame-studded cardboard.

"Jimmy is something new," Mercy was saying, "the teenager as hero—all those aching children in the darkened theaters relating to him."

We were sitting at the Villa Capri, a place Jimmy suggested for our eight o'clock dinner. He was already a half hour late. I made a gulping sound. "Sounds like another *Sorrows of Werther* spectacle. All angst and no depth."

"Well, Edna, angst is the new attitude."

"We'll see." I was old enough to have witnessed countless generations of young folks who maintained they owned the world, but somehow lost it in a late-night crap shoot with younger pretenders to the dubious throne. James Dean—well, I meant it. We'd see.

Mercy ran her fingers through her hair. "Somehow Jimmy seems different, which is why everyone at the studio is nervous. He has to be guarded."

"Guarded from what?" I asked.

"Jimmy likes to lead a sort of mysterious life, a little on the edge," Mercy said, cryptically.

Driving me to the restaurant, Mercy had discussed the growing panic at the studio: some fired actress was insisting Jimmy had gotten her pregnant. "I don't believe it," she confided. "Jimmy's foolish, but not that foolish. His career comes first." Mercy's fingers drummed on the steering wheel. She glanced at me. "Let's see what you think, Edna. After you talk to him."

I looked around, impatient, unhappy. Overdressed in a shimmering silk dress, with fitted bodice and generous full skirt, a creamy shawl over my shoulders, and wearing my best rope of pearls, I felt grand duchess, intimidating, imperious: the woman of means who means what she says. But the place didn't suit me, and I'd groaned as Mercy turned into the tiny parking lot, just off Hollywood Boulevard. The drab adobe-style restaurant seemed attached to a seedy, rundown hotel, obviously for transients and miscreants—those drifters who flocked to Hollywood and lost their way. The restaurant itself seemed a mere step up from a highway hash house. Once inside, the owner, Patsy D'Amore, seated us with a flourish, having got a call from Jimmy himself, who, I gathered, was the darling of the eatery.

"Jimmy. He come here before he's famous," the man announced, so loud that other diners looked at us. "He come here all the time now."

"It's his hangout," Mercy added. She smiled, her voice deepening on the word as though she were pointing out an opium den.

Mercy, I noted, had dressed more casually, fittingly: a wrinkled gray circle skirt, a wrinkled muslin blouse, a charcoal-gray sweater buttoned at the neck. She looked like she'd just stepped off a bus.

I didn't like the place, but I hadn't expected to. Frankly, this wasn't the Upper East Side, and the cluttered tables, the dripping red candles stuck into Chianti bottles, the obligatory red-and-white checkered tablecloths (stained—at least ours was), and the sentimental Blue Grotto art work dotting the walls like panels from a stereopticon, all suggested one more cheap Hollywood backdrop for a second-rate Anna Magnani movie. I'd have a lettuce salad, perhaps. Maybe a glass of red wine. No, a martini. No vagrant vermin could survive in that alcoholic concoction.

"He's late," I said again, checking my watch. I was ready to leave.

Mercy buttered a breadstick. "Of course. It's part of the new young-actor mystique, really. How to out-Brando Brando. But he'll come, Edna. I know he wants you to hear his side of the story. You *have* to, he told me. He knows I told you about Carisa."

"Me?" I exclaimed, too loudly. "Everyone is trying to keep me from learning this shocking and sordid tale, and he wants me part of it?"

"He tells people things all the time. Some people."

"Who?"

"People he trusts." She munched on the breadstick. "He wants you on his side against Warner and Stevens—the studio."

"Me? A woman he's never met?"

"He knows exactly who you are: a writer from New York. That means something to him. He's a little bit of a poseur, trying to be a Bohemian intellectual out here in this sterile land, walking around with a Zen Buddhist paperback in his back pocket, sitting in the commissary with *War and Peace*. That sort of thing. But whole other parts of him are genuine, truly. You'll learn that. He likes older women as—well, confidantes. He trusts them—*us*. Well, *me*. In Marfa, Texas, he hung out with me in my hotel room when I was sick; he called me 'Mom' when I wasn't 'Madama' to him. Surrogate mothers, all of us. I gather he got close to Geraldine Page when he did *The Immoralist* on Broadway."

"So we're supposed to sooth his fragile ego? I'm one more older woman sucked into his..." I stopped.

Mercy looked serious. "He *is* fragile—and aggressive and rude. And often cruel. But I'll tell you, Edna, I got to know him in the ugly dead world of Marfa, a place that hadn't seen rain in seven years. At night you could hear your life leaving you. He was like a little lost lamb, shivering under the shadow of Liz Taylor's beauty and Rock Hudson's aggressive presence. *They* were the names. Filming *Giant* there with these three young stars—well, it brought out something in each of them."

"Like what?"

"In Marfa, pettiness, vanity, and fear took over. Liz had to have someone fanning her ego, Rock kept trying to convince us all he was the Texas he-man. And Jimmy—well, he was the untried scared boy, frankly." She paused, leaned in. "I'll tell you, Edna, there were times when the sadness was so raw in him, so deep, I couldn't look into that handsome face. He kept hiding from everyone. I've never met anyone so...lonely."

"And it's not a pose?"

"Maybe a fraction of it is, but no, it's there. It used to frighten me. It's like he doesn't care if he lives or dies. You should see the way he races around in those cars, like a demon. If I live, I live. If I die, I choose it. You don't meet people like that. They crave life so much that they cultivate dying for it." She smiled. "Enough of this. We spend all our time talking about Jimmy Dean."

"Well," I said, grinning, "there's something about that mouth."

Mercy laughed. "Everyone says that. It's a woman's mouth. Someone in makeup called it a whore's generous mouth. Everyone wants to watch those lips move."

"Perhaps that's why he mumbles, barely opening that mouth. He's rationing its pleasure for us mere mortals."

Mercy agreed. "So we mother him."

I bit the end of a breadstick, chewed it. "I'll not be a mother, thank you. I've managed to survive that trap for sixty-odd years."

"You may have no choice."

I looked at my watch and fretted. "I have little patience with lateness, Mercy. And I'm surprised about Tansi." I looked to the doorway, where some other diners waited to be seated.

"Don't look there," Mercy said. "He comes in through the kitchen."

Before long, I heard a *brum brum brum*, too close to the building, the grunt of shifted gears, the rat-a-tat dying of a loud, intrusive motor. Mercy rolled her eyes. Within seconds, the swinging doors of the kitchen clattered and Jimmy flew in, pausing a moment to look around. Spotting us, he strode across the room.

"You're late," I fumed. I eyed his uniform: the smudged jeans—an oil slick on his thigh—the worn biker boots, the white T-shirt barely visible under a shiny red nylon jacket, collar turned up. His hair was uncombed, looking like damp straw over a creased forehead.

He slipped into a seat, leaned his elbows on the table, and hunched forward. "Had some trouble with my cycle."

"Your what?" I asked. Because, if I heard correctly, Jimmy pronounced the word *cycle* as *sickle*.

"My motorsickle." Or so I spelled it in my head.

I grinned. "You from the Midwest?"

"Fairmount, Indiana, ma'am," he said in a drawling, lazy voice. "Cows and corn and religious copulation."

He began fiddling with the breadbasket, spinning it around, extracting the thick breadsticks, lining them up, log-cabin style, crisscrossing them, using every piece in the wicker basket. I stared at the construction, expecting disaster. Jimmy flicked it with a finger and the makeshift pile shifted, but didn't topple. Boorish, I thought, and childish.

"I understand you've not read my *Giant*," I said, purposely, looking into his face.

Jimmy looked at Mercy, half-smiled, rubbed one of his eyes with a grimy finger, and turned to me: "Rumor has it I haven't even read the screenplay."

"What?"

"If you listen to dictator Stevens who calls himself my director."

"Don't you think…"

"I think I understand Jett Rink the way you want me to. He's a hungry boy who becomes a hungry man. He gets what he dreams of, but it ain't ever enough." He pushed the breadsticks, and they scattered across the table. He gazed around the room. "Sometimes when I come here nights, I sit in a little supply room right beside those kitchen doors. I sit on an orange crate, and munch on antipasto Patsy makes for me. And nobody knows I'm there. No one. My own little room, a closet with boxes filled with cans and jars and God knows what else. The problem with L.A. is that everyone is always expecting you to say something."

"And you'd rather be quiet?" I asked.

He shrugged his shoulders. "I refuse to sit over there." He pointed to a booth across the room.

I pulled in my cheeks. "Too far to walk?"

Jimmy giggled. Actually giggled, full-throated and rich, and we all smiled. He pointed a finger at me and shook it, as if to say: "Good one, Miss Edna." Then, serious, "No, that's where Pier and I always sat. Unlucky number six."

"I have no idea what you're talking about," I said. "You've been here two minutes and you're talking to yourself." I wasn't happy.

Mercy interrupted. "Edna, Jimmy dated Pier Angeli for a long time. You know, *The Silver Chalice*, with Paul Newman. Didn't you read about it in the papers?"

"The gossipy sheets? Hollywood blather and bilge? Not even with a decree from Caesar himself would I…"

Jimmy spoke over my declaration. "You know, I asked her to marry me. But I'm not the kind of good boy her mustached Italian Catholic mama wanted, so she forced Pier to marry that empty shell Vic Damone. You know how Italian mothers believe their pretty daughters are all virgins, which is why they all try to become whores as fast as possible…"

Mercy reached over and touched him on the wrist. "Jimmy, enough." Emphatic, but motherly, I thought.

Jimmy gathered up the breadsticks and tossed them back into the basket. The table was strewn with crumbs, flecks of sesame seeds.

For a while, we sat there, a frozen tableau, and I felt the room moving around me. Dishes rattled, glasses clinked, a waiter mumbled in angry Italian to another waiter. Silence at the table. A waiter gave us menus, then left. Jimmy drummed on the edge of the table with a breadstick, and the tip snapped off, toppling to the carpet. I heard his boot heel grind it. He hadn't removed his dazzling red windbreaker, unbuttoned over the T-shirt. The brilliant red against the ivory white, sharp enough against his fresh blond looks. Very dramatic, I thought.

He clicked his tongue. "Miss Edna, can I give you a ride on my cycle sometime?" There was a mischievous gleam in his eye.

"I'm afraid I'd fall off the back."

"Not if you hold onto me tightly. I'll take you for a spin out to Laurel Canyon, all narrow roads and hairpin turns, up into the Hollywood Hills where you can look down on a different L.A." He squinted his eyes. "Unless you want to do the driving. I'll hold onto you."

I realized he was flirting with me. Oddly, I was enjoying it. "The problem is that I'd travel so slowly you'd fall off for sheer boredom."

"Jimmy likes speed," Mercy said.

"If you can see where you're going, then there's no use in heading there." He looked at Mercy. "Tell Miss Edna about the time I gave you a spin in my MG."

Mercy laughed. "I can't remember because I was unconscious for most of it."

We were interrupted by Tansi's arrival. She rushed to the table, apologizing for lateness, blaming it on the garage that serviced her new car. Tansi pulled up a chair, repositioned it, twisting her body this way and that, sputtering, taking over the conversation. We sat there, waiting. "A scratch, mind you, on a new car." Jimmy, car *aficionado*, immediately began a barrage of questions about the Chevy Bel Air she'd purchased. Shoptalk, the two of them. I lost interest, then became angry at the inane exchange, Tansi talking of engine size, accessories, tire sizes.

"Can I drive it?" Jimmy asked.

Tansi balked. "But you *speed*, Jimmy."

He turned away, bored now. He lit a cigarette, blew smoke across the table, and Tansi reached into her purse for a cigarette. I watched the two of them smoking, and was momentarily enthralled: Jimmy's careful, deliberate playing with the cigarette, the long Chesterfields moving and sliding as he inhaled, or said a few words. Tansi, however, worked at the cigarette, as though it required calculation. The thin shaft was unnecessary and a little irksome, but part of a picture she was setting up in the eyes of someone watching. One was total seamlessness; the other artifice; one, syncopated rhythm, the other, a pesky protuberance.

Jimmy offered me a cigarette. I debated taking one but finally shook my head. "Now and then, with a cocktail. At the end of a day's work."

"When I wake in the morning," Jimmy said, "I usually find I already have one in my mouth."

"I find it relaxes me," Tansi volunteered, and Mercy and I both started to laugh.

Mercy tapped her on the wrist. "Tansi, it actually seems to make you a bundle of nerves."

But Tansi was in a good mood now. "You know, I learned to smoke from Bette Davis movies. You know how she leans in to light cigarettes, bringing the cigarette to the match?"

"Is that what you were doing?" I asked, smiling. "I thought you were trying to set yourself on fire."

Jimmy drank wine spritzers, finished the first one in a couple of gulps, and immediately signaled for another. I sipped my martini, very acceptable—and picked at an antipasto. Suddenly Jimmy stood up, stopping the conversation. Then he slumped back down, dug into the pocket of his jeans and extracted a piece of paper, which he tossed, carelessly, onto the table. It lay there, crumpled, like a wasted napkin; but, I noted, it held all of our eyes; some unearthed runic tablet, magical now, and powerful.

"The new letter," Jimmy said.

I reached for it, but Jimmy put his hand on it. My fingers collided with his. "What Jack Warner didn't want you to know, Miss Edna, is that a girl I dated while we were on location in hellish Marfa, Texas, has sent me this letter and one before it, claiming I'm the daddy of her unborn bastard baby." He waited, watching me. Tansi made a gargling sound, throaty and harsh. But Jimmy never looked at her.

I stared. "And, I gather, you're not?"

Jimmy howled, stretched out his arms and threw back his head. "You're something else, Miss Edna."

I was frowning. "I'm serious."

"No, it ain't true. I swear. And she's crazy."

"Just what does she want?"

Mercy spoke up. "It's hard to say. In the first letter she said she wants marriage, that Jimmy be a real husband and father, as he's supposed to, but she ends by saying she wants money so she can go away. Two different messages."

"And in this new one she hints she'll tell the world my dark secrets to that rag *Confidential* and ruin my career."

Tansi was rattled. "Good God. That's what Mr. Warner is afraid of."

Mercy turned to me. "Jimmy gave Warner the first letter…"

"My mistake! I never learn."

"You *had* to. You *had* to," Tansi said.

Jimmy ignored her. "Carisa's just plain crazy."

"Warner is afraid any negative publicity will hurt the movie," Mercy noted. "Maybe even sink it. America in these blacklist Commie days is not too forgiving of Hollywood and its sins. Careers lost, lives ruined."

Jimmy stretched out his arms again. "I'm innocent," he said, staring at the ceiling, looking bored.

I grunted. "So are those sad souls condemned by Senator McCarthy, now begging for jobs from friends who turn their backs on them."

Mercy spoke softly, "I really thought it would go away, Edna. A stupid, desperate girl who's misguided. Talked to by the studio. But now," she turned to Jimmy, "a second letter."

"This one is plain crazy, folks. My deep dark secrets. 'You think you're a big movie star now.' That sort of thing. 'I'll take care of *that*. Marry me. You promised.'"

Tansi was surprisingly blunt. "Well, did you promise her?"

Jimmy shook his head. "I never promise women things."

"What does that mean?" I asked.

He didn't answer. He finished his drink, smacked his lips, and signaled the waiter for another. I didn't like this. I'd been sipping my cocktail slowly.

I waited a moment. "Tell me, do you have dark secrets she can tell the world, Jimmy?"

Jimmy closed his eyes for a second. "We all have dark secrets we don't want the world to have."

I pontificated. "I don't."

Jimmy narrowed his eyes. "You're a downright fibber, Miss Edna."

I drew in my breath. I didn't like this. This young man was hard to read. Talented, maybe—probably. But foolish, impetuous, foolhardy. Like most young men, a blunderer, if not a downright bounder.

He seemed to read my mind. "I'm not a cad."

"Just what happened in Marfa?" I asked. *Giant* was my gold-mine. Visions of studio hesitation, delayed openings, audience boycotts, a callow but censorious press, nasty accusation, deadly scandal. My mind reeled.

Mercy began, "There was nothing to do in Marfa. For six long, long weeks. Nothing. Except for stars like Jimmy and Rock and Liz, who lived in houses, we stayed in the one hotel, the Presidio, three or four to a room, while Jimmy shot jackrabbits at night, riding in a Jeep out over the white buffalo grass."

Jimmy didn't seem to be listening. He spoke over her words. "Mercy came down with sun poisoning."

"Jimmy was the ringleader of a bunch of young people, like his friend Tommy and some other bit players, including Carisa. They hung out at the Old Borunda Café on San Antonio Street and drank Lone Star beer..."

"And died from the heat," Tansi added.

Mercy kept going. "But Jimmy started seeing Carisa Krausse who, despite her name, played a Mexican girl in the film. I was surprised to see her there because, well, I'd worked with her before in *All the King's Men*, and no one liked her. Something was wrong with her. She'd become peculiar, quirky, talked too much, accused."

"And no one warned me," Jimmy said.

"Anyway, her behavior became so erratic and unprofessional, a malingerer, that Stevens fired her, shipped her back to L.A., and when we all got back here, she wrote that first letter."

"And now a second," Jimmy said, shaking his head.

"And this is the news Jack Warner wants me shielded from?"

Jimmy grinned. "Everybody, well...ah...is scared of you."

"So what's the answer?"

I noticed, sadly, that Jimmy was tipsy, though it was easy to miss, given his slurred, inarticulate speech, half-spoken sentences, grunting, and his slouching. I caught Mercy's eye, and then turned to Tansi, who looked bothered, casting sidelong glances at Jimmy, watching. Eyes half shut, lips drawn into a drunkard's bemused smirk, Jimmy seemed ready to fall asleep.

Good Lord, I thought, this is like a rehearsal for the final scene of *Giant*, with Jett Rink collapsing onto the banquet table in a drunken stupor. The inevitable final act of a story that began when a lonely boy fell in love with another man's wife.

My question hung in the air.

"Madama can help." He raised his glass to her.

But Mercy shook her head. "Just because I met Carisa at an earlier shoot—we actually rehearsed together one day—Jimmy thinks I can talk sense to her, make her see how…" She trailed off, shrugged her shoulders, punctuating the moment with her deep sigh. "You can't talk to an irrational woman, Jimmy. She has problems…"

He cocked his head to the side. "Come on, Madama. You can talk some sense into her. People *like* you."

"Not everyone. And I have a poor track record with deranged women. Some of your other friends know her better. Lydia, for one."

"God, no," Jimmy moaned.

Tansi turned to me. "Jimmy just broke up with Lydia, also in the movie. Lydia Plummer."

I smiled, "You certainly do move through a crowd, Jimmy."

He didn't answer. "Madama…"

Mercy, firm, rigid. "Jimmy, if talking to Carisa would help, I would. But she's obviously got some obsession here. And what if there really is a baby?" Jimmy shook his head, denying the possibility. "Let Jake Geyser and Jack Warner take care of this. They have experience with this kind of tomfoolery. After all, need I point out, Hollywood is built on blackmail and threats and rumor? They must have ideas, no?"

Tansi lit a cigarette. "I agree. Stay away from her. If the press got wind of this, my God! It'll go away. It *has* to. Jimmy's name must be kept—well, pure."

Jimmy's eyes got wide. "Pure?" Sarcasm in his voice; bewilderment. He looked at Tansi, and I realized he didn't care for her. Worse, he probably rarely knew she was in the room, this drab, pencil-thin woman with fluttery nerves and bird-like gestures.

"Yes, pure. Like it or not. My job is to secure your image."

Jimmy made a sudden click-click-click sound, his tongue against the roof of his mouth. "Madama," he pleaded.

I looked at her. "Mercy, you seem so set in this matter. Is there something you're not saying?"

Mercy just shook her head.

"But if this—this Carisa knows you…"

Tansi looked horrified. "Edna, my God. I can't believe you'd suggest talking to this woman. This is like stoking a fire. Making her think we're taking this seriously."

"We have to take it seriously," I insisted.

Tansi wasn't happy. "She's a failed actress living in tenement in the worst neighborhood in L.A. Out of a job, nothing. Should we send a Warner Bros. limo to her doorstep?"

Jimmy, restless, zipped up the red jacket to his neck, stood and looked down at us. A little unsteadily, he backed up, toppling a chair, and, in a melodramatic gesture, he moved his hand out toward us, a slicing gesture, cutting—a signal of leaving. He backed off, and disappeared through the kitchen.

In my darkened suite at the Ambassador, I lay in bed, unable to sleep. This was to have been a celebratory visit to Hollywood. My arrival during the final days of shooting, the ceremonial gesture of Jack Warner and George Stevens, who'd already confided that the film was wonderful—a blockbuster, they promised. A Hollywood high mark; enduring, legendary. But now this. I closed my eyes. Images of Jimmy Dean at the dinner table, the swagger, the pouting, the enigmatic shifts in conversation. My God, this debacle of the poison letters. Probably a cavalier Casanova violating this poor woman's trust. A gigolo. A failed actress with the impossible name of Carisa Krausse playing a sullen Mexican servant in my movie. Jimmy Dean, this girl and that. Kiss this girl, hug that one. Leave them behind. The pretty boy hero, girls strewn at his ankles like leaves swirling at the base of an autumn tree. Look at Tansi, wormwood spinster with crimson nail polish, eyes aflutter; that sensible woman I'd known as a young girl. Even Mercy, another smiling supplicant. Even me. Caught by him, fascinated by the enigma, entangled now. Something wrong about the boy. Whole parts of him left untouched, ignored, avoided. Well, it was Jack Warner's problem, and that toady Jake Geyser—another simpering fool. Let…

The phone rang. I jumped, glanced at the clock. Midnight. Twelve o'clock. Three a.m. back in New York, where I belonged among the cosmopolites. In my own bed on the Upper East Side. I fumbled at the nightstand.

"Hello."

Silence.

Louder. "Hello."

A sputter. "Well, I was telling you the truth, Miss Edna."

My head cleared. "Jimmy?"

I heard him clear his throat, then a stifled snort. "I'm sorry," he said.

"It's all right."

"Do you believe me?"

In the darkness of the room, everything around me unfamiliar, I listened to the tinny, faraway voice. For a second I imagined I was hearing a little boy's voice, so high and breaking; wavering, pleading. Startled, I found myself breathing hard. "Jimmy."

"Something horrible is gonna happen, Miss Edna."

"Like what?"

Silence. "When people push me, things happen."

I felt a chill up my spine.

"You know, I don't know how I'm supposed to take care of things by myself. Everybody expects me to make it on my own. I can't do this on my own. They don't realize…" The words stopped abruptly. I heard noise behind him, not too far away— drunken revelry, shrill laughter, a snatch of jukebox music. *Papa loves mambo. Mama loves mambo.* Bar noises.

"Jimmy…"

Then I realized the line was dead.

Chapter Three

As I sipped tepid coffee and munched on dry cinnamon toast in the coffee shop the next morning, I was paged and found myself talking to Jack Warner. Idly, I'd been reviewing the breakfast served me at the posh Ambassador. I'd already returned the pancakes, deeming them desiccated shoulder pads from an abandoned Joan Crawford dress. I'd maintained the milk for the coffee had turned, the butter clotted, lumpy and discolored. I'd resigned myself to anemic toast and decided breakfast would have to wait until New York—Molly's toothsome French toast, made from thick slabs of homemade bread, with real maple syrup the color of precious amber. Out of season strawberries, plump and scarlet and juicy, probably flown in from California. All my life, I thought suddenly, I travel, travel, travel; all my life I want to hurry back to New York City, where, staring out from the fifteenth floor, I announce royally that I despise it to the marrow of my being. Well, we always hate the thing we love too much.

Jack Warner, crisp and authoritarian on the phone, said there was a meeting at ten. His office. He said he'd provide breakfast. I winced.

"Something's come up," he said.

"I know about the letters to Jimmy Dean."

"I know you do," he said, flatly. "I'm sorry, Edna. It'll be handled promptly."

Promptly? The first letter arrived three or four days earlier. What passes for promptitude out here in the land of lights, camera, inaction? "Jimmy says she's lying about the..." I looked around, glancing at the other diners, themselves intent on wolfing down indigestible and sickly gray eggs..."matter. At hand."

I could almost hear Warner smoking—the intake of cigarette smoke, the raspy cough. "Things are different now. I got a letter yesterday," he said. "This one was addressed to *me*."

Back in my room I dialed Mercy's number. Though she lived with her husband outside L.A., Mercy was subletting a small efficiency near the Burbank studios. A convenience, she said. She despised the expansive L.A. freeways, jumbled with traffic most mornings and afternoons; she dreaded the dreary fogs that sometimes settled in during the late summers, a haze that covered the steamy avenues. She liked her hideaway, a stone's throw from the soundstage. She answered on the first ring, and I told her about Warner's call. "I'm not surprised Carisa has the nerve to include Warner in her scheme," Mercy said. "One night, after sipping too much brandy at some party, she told me the only way to make it in this business was to get to know Jack Warner himself. She said she had his private home number, but was saving it. She had big plans."

"She was already an actress."

Mercy scoffed. "You're using the word generously, Edna."

"But she got roles."

"No, Edna, like most bit players, she was just there—like a newspaper left on a breakfast table."

"So she thought she had a future?"

"What bit player doesn't? She said all she had to do was fall into his path, and he'd spot her talent." Mercy chortled. "She thought discovery was the art of timing."

"These letters seem to be her new exercise in bad timing." I paused. "Come to the meeting with me," I said, abruptly.

Mercy laughed. "No, no, no. Oh Lord no. Old Man Warner would flip to see me, a supporting actress, at his table uninvited. You know, when he calls meetings in his own bungalow, no one sits to his immediate left or right, fearful he might ask a question they can't answer. Sorry, Edna, report back to this private citizen when you leave." She laughed again, enjoying the moment.

That didn't make me happy. "Will you be at the studio later today?"

"Yes. Late morning. No shooting today. You're scheduled to do photo sessions with journalists. Smiling with Rock, schmoozing with Liz, dancing with Jimmy, philosophizing with little old homespun me."

I groaned. "A wasted day."

"Don't you like to have your picture taken?"

Sitting in Warner's conference room, a Spartan arrangement of long table and straight-backed chairs, with grainy photographs of forgotten movies on one of the walls, I surveyed the group of officious men gathered around me. The War Council, I deemed them: perfunctory, dull-eyed men, in crisp seersucker suits, some with barricades of briefcases and derby hats situated before them. Each man rigid of spine—faces cleared of liveliness, blood. Men who looked like front-office accountants or junior-level bankers; men who looked as though they desired to be elsewhere. Glancing at his wristwatch, one man flicked a piece of inconvenient lint from a sleeve; another seemingly developed an early tic; another man, as round as a bowling ball, with rubicund face, scratched a red, balding, flaked scalp. And the one other woman, Tansi, seated at my right, sprightly this morning in a pastel print dress, white daisies against a light blue cloth, with a string of tiny pearls choking her neck. She looked ready for a picnic.

She nodded at the men, like a hand puppet with loose wiring at the neck. They ignored her. And I suddenly understood Tansi's nervousness, her twitching. The lone woman in the den of dismissive, self-important men, a woman who'd gained a modicum of Hollywood power, but would never be given equal billing in any of these men's worlds. I certainly understood that deplorable state: all my life I'd battled the disregard of unimaginative men in power, grotesque lumpen souls who guffawed at their own unfunny lines, who thought their tired insights original. Tansi, when I knew her in New York, the fresh young Barnard graduate, was delightfully cynical, witty, downright funny. So the world of men had hammered that out of her, obviously. On the quicksand battlefield she'd floundered, surrendered. She wasn't a Dorothy Parker who could best the men she encountered. She wasn't Jane Addams or Eleanor Roosevelt. She wasn't, well, Edna Ferber, who brooked no attitude from these lesser lights. I'd have to talk to Tansi about that. Men could be beaten at their own game—you just had to tell yourself it was easy to win.

Seated next to George Stevens, Jake Geyser was speaking, his public voice not East Coast Princeton now but, jumping the Atlantic, decidedly British aristocracy. I concluded he'd been an actor as a young man, probably a servant in those tiresome, English drawing-room comedies. Jake was reviewing the letters, and Warner watched him closely.

"Mr. Warner," he said, nodding to the boss, "wants to review what we know—have done. About this mess." He hung on the words, as though they were an unwelcome sentence come down from the Spanish Inquisition. "I've telephoned Carisa Krausse again, but the conversation was…unsuccessful."

"What the hell does that mean?" said Warner. Everyone jumped.

Jake kept going, feebly. "I've visited her." He grinned. "She doesn't live in a desirable neighborhood. We all know Skid Row—at least from the newscasts—all the drunks, the prostitutes, the pawnshops. I was afraid to park my car." Kaaaah, he said. Beacon Hill Boston now, perhaps. Lord, he was a smorgasbord of dictions.

"And?" Prompting from Warner.

"Frankly, sir, she's hard to read. I think a little mad." Uncomfortable, he looked around the room, as though for support. Nothing, obviously, had been done. "I'm trying to understand what she wants."

George Stevens thundered, "She wants to sink my movie!" He actually leaned into Jake, who inclined his body away.

"I'm not so sure. I get the sense she'll go away if she gets what she wants."

"What, marriage to James Dean?" Tansi offered timidly.

Jake ran his tongue over his lower lip. "She's hard to read, as I say. She...her conversation is all over the place. I was uncomfortable sitting in her rooms. She lives like a packrat, papers everywhere, clothing strewn about. I felt at one point she'd attack me. I'd have to call the police, but you said," to Warner, "whatever I do, keep the cops away from this."

Back and forth. Balderdash, rehashing familiar ground, struggling to find an answer. The toady as purveyor of codswallop.

I interrupted, impatient. "Your letter, Jack?"

Warner looked at me, and seemed surprised I'd spoken—and didn't look pleased. "Largely illiterate scribbling. I'd like to know who hired her for Marfa, frankly. She doesn't even punctuate her sentences."

"I don't think parsing sentences is why we're here." Folderol, I thought, a waste of time.

He held up his hand. "Carisa's letter to me, like her new letter to Jimmy, outside of its ebb-and-flow grammar, threatens exposure to *Confidential* magazine. Just an off-hand threat so far, no contact with those bastards. It seems *Confidential* has tired of beating the Hollywood blacklist to death and even all those racial scandals—what Negro is wooing what white beauty, what blond starlet Sammy Davis is bedding at the moment—and is going after other sordid indiscretion. So I guess Carisa knows that. And, I gather, Jimmy likes to..." he glanced at me, then Tansi, himself now the decorous, polite gentleman..."have his fun."

Nincompoopism, Hollywood style, dictatorship masquerading as consensus, ending an hour later. "Edna has to meet the press," Warner announced. Staring at Jake, he told him to take care of business. Jake, his diction suddenly sounding more South Jersey shore than Oxford, sputtered, "I'll do my best." The wrong answer, surely, for Warner squinted his eyes and his face got red. I knew Jake's next job would be waiting tables at Don the Beachcomber, dishing out the moo shoo pork.

As the room cleared out, Warner signaled me to stay. He wanted a "quick word." He confided, "A bump in the road, Edna, really." Then Stevens and Warner both spoke at me, edgy, trying to play down the incident. I wanted to get away, frankly. Warner grumbled, "I gave orders for everyone to keep their mouths shut." Emphatic, deliberate.

I found myself contrasting the two important men. The first time I'd met them, that dinner at Romanoff's, I'd been intrigued: Stevens, the beefy, affable sort, and Warner, the slender, controlled businessman. They seemed to circle around each other, like cobra and mongoose, respectful but aware that life shifts in a flash. Stevens, for all his blustery confidence, struck me as an overgrown schoolboy, happy with a camera he got for Christmas. Warner, keeping his distance, appeared the grammar-school principal, watching, wary. When he moved, he always seemed to be positioning himself. He's the director here, I thought. The man conscious of angle and perspective.

Now, both men leaned into me, anxious. Stevens bristled, then blustered, talking loudly, and seemed intimidated by me. But Warner fascinated me, unhappily so; he seemed to speak in a deadly, unlovely drone, matter-of-fact, and, for some reason, he spoke over my shoulder, as to a person behind me. Worse, his eyes suddenly focused—drilling into me—when the subject was the bottom line, the money I'd invested in the movie. Oddly, I thought of a villain out of a nineteenth-century stage melodrama. I sighed. These two men would never be friends in any world other than Hollywood.

When Warner stopped talking, Stevens started to say something, but Warner cut him off. "Edna has to meet the press."

◇◇◇

Soundstage B, where *Giant* was being filmed, buzzed that afternoon, not with assistant directors and best boys and costume girls, but with reporters and photographers, led by a fussy

Hedda Hopper. The set itself was properly movieland: carefully positioned props, bits of Texas gimmicky, weathered lariats and saddles, even the vintage 1924 Rolls Royce touring car used in the movie. Flashbulbs popped, blinding. Photographers screamed requests, one more shot, just one. Hedda Hopper chatted with Chill Wills. Jane Withers leaned in to kiss her. I sat in a canvas-backed chair, gaudily stenciled with my name in blocky black letters: EDNA FERBER. I wondered, idly, if I could cram it into my suitcase. It would be quite the conversation piece at one of my dinners. Edna on set. The novelist on location. Noel Coward would hoot. George Kaufman would snicker; he'd quip that I was the Rita Hayworth of bestsellerdom. Dick Rodgers would steal it, hold it for ransom. Someone snapped my picture, and, trancelike, I muttered, "Yes, I love what they've done to my novel." Yes, yes, of course. I posed and smiled, a wide-eyed Mary Pickford agog at the Hollywood fuss and frenzy.

Jack Warner introduced me to the press as "the little lady who started the new civil war in Texas," alluding to the fury my novel had caused, with its view of Texas smugness, shallowness, and intolerance. Now, aptly, he quoted my favorite line. "What littleness is all this bigness hiding?" Everyone laughed. Score one for Warner. But I wondered at the irony of his using the sentence.

Rock Hudson, I decided, was trying hard to impress me. Not only that, he was too tall. Surely over six feet four, and broad-shouldered, a stone wall. Wisconsin lumberjack, with that granite chin and those long arms, but the manner was too obsequious, too slick. After all, I was but five feet tall, tiny— maybe tinier than ever, as age stooped me—so now I had to look way up, since he made no effort to dip down to me. The effort was a little like a tourist looking up at the Empire State Building and realizing, finally, it wasn't worth the neck strain. When I called him "Sonny," he seemed shocked. Maybe he was savvy enough to realize that the epithet was my name for all young men in disfavor.

"Miss Ferber," he said, still not stooping, "an honor."

I bit my tongue. "The honor is all yours," I said. He chuckled.

I heard someone muttering that Jimmy was late, and I saw Rock twist his head, eavesdropping. The smile disappeared. Stevens had demanded the major cast be there—in full regalia, head-to-toe costume and makeup. Mercy had told me that Jimmy often balked at Stevens' demands, disliking the man's dictatorial manner. He was used to the free-flowing, Method-acting any-way-you-feel style of Nick Ray, the Bohemian director of *Rebel Without a Cause*, whose own mumbling speech and desultory direction appealed to Jimmy. Now, lamentably, Jimmy hadn't bothered to show up. Stevens, hovering nearby, spat out under-his-breath commands to his aides, who scurried off like hyperventilating mice. Rock Hudson, still standing next to me—the tallest schoolboy at the birthday party—narrowed his eyes. "We're not all so professional," he confided to me.

I smiled, as a camera popped in my eyes. "Meaning what?"

"Jimmy doesn't take some things seriously."

I felt the need to defend the boy I scarcely knew. "Jimmy seems to listen to his own clock."

Rock widened his eyes. "He's...unreliable." Again, the flirtatious smile. "Such boys are dangerous."

I stared up at him: the stone-carved face, cynosure of millions, *Modern Screen*'s actor of the year, the all-American male, so emphatically wrought he seemed almost a façade of a building. Dressed as a rich ranch baron, with pristine white linen suit and ten-gallon white hat, he seemed a statue in a public park. Soon a flock of pigeons would discover him. "Ma'am," he was saying, oddly speaking in his Texas drawl, in character, "in Marfa, Jimmy and I shared a house. Days would go by and he wouldn't say a single word to me."

"Well..."

"He never smiled."

I'd heard the stories. Jimmy and Rock, water and electricity. Norman Rockwell and a Village Beatnik poet, co-habitating. Deadly.

"It's a new generation," I said, a little lamely.

Rock would have none of it. "I've seen the future, then, and it doesn't take a bath."

I sidled away, my back to him. Luckily Liz Taylor, herself late from makeup, rushed in, smiling. Tansi waved to her, as to an old friend. Rock, doubtless staring at my small but iron-rod back (though, I believed, neatly attired in a polka dot blue-and-white flare dress, clutch bag, and three-stranded pearls), mumbled something about wardrobe, and disappeared. One last camera pop made him turn and look, a rigid line of gleaming teeth. But the photographer was focused on the radiant Liz.

Arriving with two assistants pecking at her, Liz Taylor sallied up to me, took my hand, and thanked me for the role of Leslie Benedict. I smiled, a little flabbergasted. How beautiful the woman was. How stunning. A woman whose tinkling, nervous laugh and melodic timbre seemed perfect for her patrician, girlish beauty. And those violet eyes, riveting as cut gemstone. A raving beauty, reminding me of Lillian Russell, a beauty of another century—and more buxom. A different standard of beauty then, but compelling and magnetic. But Liz had a way of charming, tucking herself into me. When the photographers finished, we sat in a corner next to the out-of-place Rolls Royce, gabbing like sorority sisters, with me oddly at ease.

The subject turned to Jimmy. Liz pointed at George Stevens, conferring with some lackey, both their faces crimson. "George isn't happy," Liz said. "Jimmy is supposed to be here, of course. I know he wants to meet you…"

"I've met him," I said, grandly. "Quite the original."

Liz laughed. "He's quite wonderful. He has a wonderful laugh and a warm heart, really."

I cut in. "Rock Hudson doesn't like him."

Liz pooh-poohed the rivalry. "Oh, Rock, he's wonderful, too. But he's from another era of acting: study your lines as written, stand on your mark, just follow the director. Rock's afraid people won't like him. Jimmy doesn't care. Jimmy likes to…well…

improvise. A script is just a suggestion. Rock can't do that. And that's what Jimmy does best."

"Yet you get along with both of them?"

"Well, yes, of course." It dawned on me that most people got along with Liz. "In Marfa, Jimmy clung to me. Like he was an orphan. We're about the same age—what is he? Twenty-four or so? But he looked at me as, like, a mother or an older sister. Can you imagine that? At first disconcerting, but then I realized what he needed from me. Other men woo me, shamelessly, fawningly, promising me anything. I'm used to people flattering me. Jimmy demanded I flatter him. You know, he never made…advances. Ever. Jimmy just wanted a shoulder to cry on."

Mercy McCambridge had said much the same thing. "Mercy," I said, baiting, "said he saw *her* as a mother…"

"The both of us, really. Once he even stumbled, called her 'Mom' on the set. Usually it was 'Madama' because Jimmy always stays in character. It was so charming. When everyone laughed, he pouted and stormed away. Mercy and I didn't laugh. Jimmy disappeared for hours." Liz shook her head. "Jimmy's a strange boy. Rock's a strange man. That's the difference. Boy and man: both rivals for Mom's affection."

I wondered if Liz knew of the dangerous letters, but decided not to ask. Mercy would know. Maybe Jimmy (and the studio) shielded Liz from that nonsense.

"Do you know about his Siamese cat?"

"What?"

She smiled. "You know, he was so alone that when we got back here I got him a kitten, which he named Marcus after his nephew in Indiana. Edna, he dotes on that kitten. It's funny. He's out speeding around at night, tearing up the hills. You hear about him in the nightclubs with Pier Angeli or with Lydia Plummer or these days Ursula Andress, and then you see him scurrying home to feed Marcus. It's quite…" she paused, "quaint. Endearing, really."

Liz was eventually whisked away, waving goodbye, as cameras popped. Then everyone waited, impatient. Mercy brought me coffee, sitting with me and chatting. George Stevens appeared and disappeared, in doorways and out. Hedda Hopper said she had to leave; another engagement called. This was not good news. She was just too powerful a woman to insult. Her gossip columns could make or break a career. I looked up and pointed. "Well, here he is, finally." I was relieved, as though Jimmy could now escape Stevens' wrath.

Mercy shook her head. "No, that's Tommy Dwyer, his buddy."

The young man neared, a young girl on his arm, the two of them trailed by another young woman. Both women were dressed in evening gowns with ostentatious necklaces, bracelets. Texas gaudy, I figured. Oil money Baroque. Bit players in the Jett Rink banquet scene. Tommy, I realized, was a painstaking carbon copy of Jimmy, albeit a slightly chubby version, his hair blonder, his carriage too precise, with none of Jimmy's insolent slouching. Tommy was dressed in a red-nylon jacket similar to the one I had seen on Jimmy. Reading my perplexed expression, Mercy explained that it was a uniform Jimmy established in the soon-to-be-released *Rebel Without a Cause*: the T-shirt, the black penny loafers, the swept back hair, the cigarette, and that glorious red windbreaker. Tommy now puffed himself up like a carnival huckster, yelled hellos to other actors. Leaving the two women, he walked up to Mercy. "Jimmy didn't show?"

"Not yet."

Mercy introduced him to me. "Tommy grew up with Jimmy in Fairmount, Indiana."

Tommy beamed. "A year behind him in high school. Knew him to say hello to. I bumped into him in New York when I moved there. He was trying to be an actor. Me, too. Everybody in New York wants to be an actor. We spent the whole of one long afternoon watching Monty Clift in *A Place in the Sun* in Times Square. Over and over. I couldn't get him to leave. We had the best time. Then, you know, Jimmy came out here for *East of Eden*." It had a rehearsed, rushed sound to it. He seemed ready to add to the dreary biography, but the look on my face stopped him.

I didn't like his voice—cracking, flat, boring. Worse, the eyes now darted, furtive, from me to Mercy, then to the whole room, squinting, watching. For Jimmy? Close up, he was a pale reflection of Jimmy. He was just there, like a potted plant. "I stopped in to see Jimmy," Tommy said, "but, well, Jimmy is Jimmy." He looked back and motioned to the young woman he'd walked in with. "That's Polly, my girlfriend. From New York, too. I trailed Jimmy out here, and she trailed me." He laughed, waved at her. "She's in for a costume fitting."

Polly seemed content to stay back with the other woman, both standing with folded arms. I found myself wondering about the second woman, who looked peevish. "And who is that other girl, who looks so unhappy?"

Tommy chuckled a little too long, ending with a rough phlegmatic cigarette cough. "That's Lydia Plummer, who was Jimmy's girl for about a month. She wanted to make it last forever. She's got a speaking line in the banquet scene. Two words." He motioned both women over, but George Stevens was suddenly back in the room, thundering. The two women hugged the back wall, uncomfortable, anxious to leave. Tommy, a little nervous, excused himself. He said to Mercy, "We don't belong here today. Tell Jimmy I'm looking for him. He ain't answering the phone."

When Tommy left, I asked Mercy, "Why does he dress like Jimmy?"

"Because, sadly, he wants to be Jimmy. He thinks he can be the next James Dean."

"And how does Jimmy feel about that?"

"Hard to say. He's gone out of his way to plead for parts for Tommy and Polly. They're like leeches. He got him to play a ranch hand in Marfa, but Tommy couldn't stay on a horse. Still, you see him in a couple scenes. Polly was there, playing one of Bick's party guests. She had a line, but lost it in a script edit."

"So what does he do?"

"When he's not making believe he's an actor, he parks cars in the lot across the street from the CBS Radio Studios on Sunset. The same lot where Jimmy parked cars before he went to New York."

"And they've remained friends?"

"Sort of."

"That's not really a testimonial."

"Something's been happening with Jimmy's crowd," she said, slowly.

"New faces?"

"Not so much new, but old ones disappearing."

"And that includes Tommy and Polly? And, I gather, this Lydia Plummer, who seems to have come here today to look distraught."

Mercy nodded. "Exactly. Jimmy seems to be trying to get distance from Tommy. Jimmy is on the verge of being the next major star. He knows it. He wants it. He's gonna have to leave people behind."

"That sounds cruel, though perhaps necessary."

"Very necessary, so far as Jimmy is concerned. Look, Edna, Tommy's a drain. And this red nylon jacket is the last straw. Pathetic copycat. But Jimmy's been leaving people behind for years. He stops thinking about people he's friendly with, and then they're gone. Jimmy's loyalty takes him only so far."

I looked to the doorway. I wanted to see Jimmy walk in.

The news people and the photographers were packing up, and George Stevens stormed around, a big, blustery heap of a man, shaking with fury. "I sent a car to his new apartment in Sherman Oaks. No Jimmy. No one has seen him."

I kept my mouth shut. Stevens apologized to me, gallantly, but I waved my hand. But clearly it did matter to the officious Stevens, a taskmaster, a man who approached his movies with a sense of sheer professionalism, everything in place, no room for moodiness or spurts of juvenile behavior. Jimmy was a schoolyard bully making his own rules. I touched him on his sleeve. "The film is important, George, not a picture of me with James Dean."

Stevens spoke too loudly. "But that's what I ordered."

I shrugged.

Stevens leaned in. "You know, I've written a memo listing every late or missed shot, every sullen remark, even his stupid rudeness to a crew member. And I'll tell you, Edna. I'll never make another movie with him. Never." He half-bowed, a sort of Prussian stiffness that struck me as anachronistic—I'd seen silent-era German directors do likewise, Josef von Sternberg, for one—and left the room.

Tansi watched him leave. She came over to me, hurt in her voice. "No, he'll never make another movie with *you*," she whispered to his retreating back. "I'll be *his* choice *not* to."

Chapter Four

"Miss Edna." A voice boomed behind me. Jimmy arrived two hours later. I'd just returned from lunch with Mercy and Tansi.

"Of course," Tansi mumbled. "Now he arrives."

Jimmy stood there, nonplussed, inhaling a cigarette, while Tansi, frantically dialing numbers from a book she carried, managed to get some photographers and reporters, lingering on the lot, back into the room. Jimmy was at his most gracious, greeting me as though he'd never met me before, then smiling for the cameras, flirtatious, mischievous, circling me like I was a delightful prey, putting his arms around my shoulders, whispering. The photographers loved it.

I loved it. In spite of myself.

Jimmy had arrived as Jett Rink—the young wildcatter, worn denims and scuffed boots and ten-gallon hat, dipped low on his forehead. He was the rangy, belligerent ranch hand, seething with resentments, falling in love with Bick's wife, and not yet the cruel and despotic oillionaire of JetTexas Oil.

As the photographers snapped pictures, Jimmy charmed and insinuated. He danced on chairs, he whooped and hollered. He sang a cowboy tune in the twangy, nasal Texas accent he'd mastered for the role. Everyone grinned. At first, I was alarmed by his manic performance, but finally I relaxed. This was no errant schoolboy, some Peck's Bad Boy for a disaffected generation of post-war lost teenaged children. This was a self-absorbed lad, himself his best and most tantalizing subject. True, his moods were explosive and extreme. A troubled boy, certainly. But watching him unfold himself, like a tentative flower, petal by petal, unsure but seeking the overhead noontime sun, I realized there had to be a strain of purposeful scheming in him, a force that competed with some natural orneriness, some tractor-pull stubbornness. This boy of the Midwest soil, this dervish, this carnival showman, this brilliant hayseed.

He was playing to the camera, swinging me around like some dosie-do barn dancer. I let him, intoxicated, but wary.

"Rope tricks," he announced, laughing, as he proceeded to twirl a lariat, rodeo style, the sloppy ovals he created lingering in the air like dusty rings blown by cigarette smokers. "I learned this in Marfa. That, and the insatiable mating habits of jackrabbits."

He insisted on teaching me to twirl a lariat, standing behind me, holding my elbow and wrist, spinning out the thick rope like a spider launching a filament. I was awkward and a little embarrassed. I'd not even told my own doctor about the growing weakness in my shoulders, those sharp pains, but I played along, gamely. Under his tutelage, I actually hurled out the rope, and Jimmy yelled, "Whoa, little doggie." Which made everyone, including me, howl. The photographers were savoring this. Exhausted, I begged respite, and Jimmy, the cavalier gentleman with an arm around my waist, led me to a chair, the one marked EDNA FERBER, in fact.

"You're a real cowgirl." He politely kissed my hand.

"Sure, Annie Oakley with a blue rinse and rhinestone brooch." Though, I admit, my heart raced. I was loving this.

Flushed, I surveyed the room. Rock Hudson, standing in a doorway, was frowning. Behind him, George Stevens, arms folded, watched, quiet—his face set. Rock leaned into Stevens, who nodded up and down. Again, I told myself that *they* were right. Of course they were right. Jimmy *was* impossible. A boy so easy to condemn, yet so easy to forgive.

Frankly, I was baffled by my own behavior here. This was not like me. I'd long ago dismissed frivolous behavior from my life, and there were days I felt I'd even relinquished my sense of humor. There were days when everything bothered me, made me testy. There were weeks when I was filled with nameless rages, feuding with my old friends, with family. I wrote damning letters to people who once loved me. Well, I didn't like being old, old. I didn't like the fact that my New York friends were all old, old. Now—here was this Jimmy, a wood sprite, Ariel, genie in a bottle. He got me laughing, stupidly, unexpected, and from the depths, and I was out of practice. The muscles at the corners of my mouth ached.

After the press disappeared—oddly, they'd all forgiven Jimmy for being late, backslapping, making wild promises to him, one even promising to accompany him to a car race—the room went quiet. Suddenly Jimmy started walking in circles; fretful, nervous, unable to settle. Tansi and I sat, like jurors in a box, as Jimmy hummed and grumbled, yet could not stop moving. He looked unhappy.

Jake Geyser had monitored the brilliant spectacle from a distance. He glowered like Cotton Mather wagging a bony, blackened finger at the depraved souls of Salem. He strode across the room. A man used to compliance, he'd been given a task he never sought: herding in the recalcitrant actor and, worse, dealing with blackmail, threats, and vitriolic letters. His was probably a world of brandy snifter decorum, golf engagements on forest-green courses, of Sundays in the park with a tweedy wife and a passel of obedient, if stymied, children. Not in the job description—this—this rebel. Hollywood, as he knew it from the star-system days of the forties, was Clark Gable or Humphrey Bogart or Joan Crawford or Katherine Hepburn—as efficient as office machinery.

He spoke through gritted teeth. "Jimmy, your lateness throws off a whole schedule." He waited. "Mr. Stevens is fit to be tied."

Jimmy was quiet too long, and everyone waited. Standing a couple of feet away from the steel-jawed Jake, the slovenly Jimmy seemed to coil downward, a spring unhinged, and the lariat he still gripped floated menacingly in the space between them.

Jimmy looked into the stern, unyielding face. A half-smile. "Well," he slurred, in an exaggerated Texas drawl, "if he's fit to be tied, I got me here a right appropriate lasso." He spun the rope outward, and it brushed Jake's jacket. Jake jerked back. Jimmy squinted. "You know, as an Indiana farm boy, used to the smells and mayhem of barnyards and hen coops, I'd have to say that you are easily recognizable as a horse's ass."

The two men stood there, hating each other. Those nearby squirmed, uncomfortable. Fascinated, I watched the dynamic, though I was unhappy with this ridiculous Mexican standoff. Men at their silly games. *You* first. No, *you* first. Come outside and I'll…

Jake, the unpracticed combatant, sputtered, turned and fled the room; Jimmy threw out the lariat, high above his head, floating the ropes, attempting some exquisite and perfect circle. It fell to the ground. He looked at me. "I read that DaVinci could draw a perfect geometric circle freehand, without a compass. Tell me I can't make this rope do the same." Again, he hurled the lariat pell mell over his head, but the circle he created was lopsided, sloppy, and the rope fell onto his shoulders, so he stood there, perplexed, looking like a man who'd just failed to hang himself.

I kept glancing at Tansi, who had positioned herself on my left, her elbow bumping mine. She was breathing hard, and I marveled at the spectrum of shifting emotions that glided across her features. The eyes that followed the crestfallen and embittered Jake to the door were triumphant, her enemy bested. Her lips were drawn into a tight, compressed line, but there was glee in her eyes—a shimmering that scared me. But when Tansi looked back at Jimmy, standing there like a dumbfounded circus clown, the rope looped over his neck, Tansi's eyes glazed over, and she looked like she was afraid. Not of him, but for him. She made a *tsk*ing sound, and I caught her eye.

"Nobody understands him," she said.

"I believe I do," I answered.

The air went out of the room. Mercy insisted we needed coffee. "I'm from Kinsman, Illinois. Population 164. In my blessed Papist household we addressed any problem with pots of hot, brewed coffee, so strong it corroded our Catholic soul. That was, of course, before I discovered liquor." She squired us out of the building, across the cement walkways that connected the various soundstages, and out the front entrance, to the Smoke House, a sandwich-and-coffee eatery by the front gates that served as a hangout for the Warner crew and performers. "This is where we live," Mercy told me. Tansi, like an obedient dog, followed, unhappy. Leaving, we spotted Jake on the telephone, and, looking at the taut tendons in his beet-red neck, I understood how furious he was.

Seated, with coffee, I said, "That was not a good moment."

"Honestly," Tansi fumed, sitting back, "Jake is so…"

Mercy interrupted, "Tansi, you have to stop apologizing for Jimmy."

"I'm not. It's just that Jack Warner told me…"

"Tansi, Jimmy was wrong this afternoon. Plain wrong."

Tansi stared into her lap.

Silence. I examined a mountainous cheesecake under glass, dripping with glazed strawberries. In a frosted glass case a stainless steel bowl contained wavy whipped cream, stung by the cold. Perhaps a nibble, a taste. I stopped looking.

Staring at Tansi's stricken face, Mercy changed the subject, talking about her husband Fletcher, a weekend trip they were planning to San Francisco—a brief respite to see friends. Tansi relaxed, and I decided I would have the cheesecake. Tansi lit a cigarette, expelled the smoke, and I surprised myself. I craved a cigarette. Tansi made a joke when Mercy said her husband, though tolerant of her being an actress and gone for weeks at a time, often told strangers she was a cruise ship entertainer. "At least," Tansi quipped, "he didn't say you were the beleaguered assistant to a tight-fisted film mogul. That's one more euphemism for the oldest profession on earth allowed a woman."

"Tansi!" I yelled, shocked. But we all started laughing, and Tansi couldn't seem to stop.

The eatery was largely empty at that hour, but Mercy nodded to some newcomers who strolled in, ordering coffee to go, and I realized one of the two women had been with Tommy Dwyer earlier. What was her name? The one with two words in *Giant*. Mercy waved them over, but both seemed a little reluctant, looking at each other.

Lydia, I recalled, Jimmy's most recent girlfriend; that is, his most recently discarded flame. Yes. Lydia Plummer, hovering back in the shadows with Tommy Dwyer's girlfriend, Polly. Now the women slipped into chairs opposite us, and Mercy made the introductions. "Edna, meet two of the satellites that revolve around Jimmy Dean. Lydia Plummer, still in costume— will they ever film that banquet scene?—and Nell Meyers, who works in the script department." Both women nodded, then looked at each other. I could see that Lydia did not appreciate Mercy's comment about her being another moon in Jimmy's peculiar solar system.

"I can't stay," Lydia said, looking at no one. "I'm supposed to be there. They're reshooting a scene. I have one line and I don't want to tempt the cutting room floor." She seemed to be speaking to the far wall, and her eyes looked teary.

Curious, I studied both women. So this was Jimmy's last girlfriend—this bit player, Lydia Plummer. You saw an eye-catching girl, slender of frame though oddly fleshy, the mouth too large and too pouty, robust painted lips, the eyes already lost in wrinkling, bunching skin. It was hard to read her features, covered as she was in her screen makeup. But I thought her coarse—a roadhouse waitress, perhaps, a buxom Tom Jones barmaid. A little too vacant-eyed. That bothered me. The eyes glassy, perhaps a drinker's eyes, dim, washed out. I wondered what she looked like without the elegant costume, the trumpery, but I supposed Lydia a prosaic beauty, maybe a high-school belle who was told too often she should be in Hollywood. Stupidly, she bought that Greyhound ticket.

"So you have a speaking line?" My words seemed to startle her. She actually jumped.

Lydia ran her tongue over her lips, moistening them. "One line in *Giant*, tomorrow a leading role. Look how fast it happened to Jimmy." The words stretched out, labored over. But she said Jimmy's name with an icy sarcasm, spitting out the word, and the name hung in the air like a black mark.

Mercy shook her head. "Edna, Jimmy is not one of Lydia's favorite people these days."

Lydia grunted. "Swine." She tossed back her head, and the light caught the gold necklace around her neck. Then, in a quiet confessional tone, the voice now soft and fuzzy, "I just don't understand why he stopped caring." Again, she stared at the far wall. Following her gaze, I was intrigued by the sight of the cheesecake.

Nell spoke for the first time. "Lydia, you know how things *are*."

A flash of anger. "No, I don't. Not actually. Only someone who's never been in love can say *that*."

Nell turned red. The two women, I noticed, were a contrast: Lydia, fleshy, grossly sensual, perhaps; a little raw at the edges; a strawberry blonde; and Nell, short, squat really, round like a fur ball, a roly-poly frame that seemed, somehow, block-like, stolid. Perhaps it was the look in her eyes that suggested immobility, a marble glare, humorless. And yet she seemed to be smiling, like she was constantly telling herself a joke she expected no one else to get. A girl perhaps twenty, unpretty in a land where beauty was the name of the game. So she slapped on makeup, heavily so, a feeble attempt to enliven that dull face with powder and eyeliner. The general effect was of a chestnut burr slathered in confectionary sugar. You saw a girl all in black, a beret on her head—eyes darkened with kohl-chalk. She was very Greenwich Village transported to California, land of sunshine. A girl dropped into the wrong geography. No—some ersatz replica of Greta Garbo, an exaggerated approximation of the mysterious Swedish actress. Nell Meyers, script girl as seductress, playing an exotic chanteuse, maybe, waiting to be famously alone. If Lydia seemed garish and effusive, a pretty woman spilling out of her sexuality, then the younger Nell was a shadow, a hidden corner. Lydia was a bar girl with too many drunken nights at gin mills under her girdle. Lydia at middle age would be a Botticelli slattern, all rolling bulge and generous lipstick and five-and-dime perfume. Nell at forty would be a rotund sorcerer with a mosquito-thin voice, sitting on a bar stool saying, "Don't come near me."

"What exactly do you do?" I asked her, ignoring Lydia who suddenly seemed lost in her own thoughts.

Nell sighed, "I file scripts." But she said it with a Garboesque flurry, the lacquered nails fluttering around her face, like wild birds.

Tansi spoke up. "I got Nell the job."

Nell looked at her, still smiling. "Yeah," she admitted, "I never *ever* wanted to work for a studio. My mom and I lived next door to Tansi, before Mom moved back home. I was taking classes at UCLA, aimless, you know. Tansi and Mom played—what?— bridge? Canasta? I never paid attention. So here I am."

"Nell's mother is so sweet," Tansi said. "I miss her."

"Well, I don't."

Lydia looked bored and stood up. "Let's go." She turned, forgot to say goodbye.

Tansi spoke up. "Stay a bit, Nell."

"Love to, but I'm on the clock, you know." She caught up with Lydia, who was already heading toward the door.

Mercy said to me, "You'll find this interesting, Edna. Lydia was Carisa Krausse's roommate a while back, before she moved to her new place. They had a falling out."

"Over Jimmy?"

"Who knows?"

"And how does Nell fit into all this?"

Mercy shrugged. "Acolytes at Jimmy's shrine, all of them."

Tansi interrupted. "Nell met Lydia and Jimmy at a party, and that was the beginning."

"You don't sound glad," I said.

"I don't like Lydia."

"Why?"

"There are rumors of drug use, Edna. Her *and* Carisa, in fact."

"Tansi, don't tell tales out of school," Mercy sharply replied.

"I don't care. A drinker, too."

"Stop it, Tansi." Mercy looked peeved. "You're not being very nice."

"I just don't like her friendship with Nell. Nell is, well, an innocent. I know she's playing some role in her head. Look at the dumb makeup. But she's a child. I told her mother I'd look out for her. You know, I got her into the Studio Club on Lodi Street, near Sunset. Edna, it's a hotel for young girls in entertainment, very safe and protected. One hundred girls, with references. Men can't get past the lobby. But would you believe dumb fate—her roommate is Lydia, of all people. I want her to move out of the place."

"That's her choice," Mercy insisted, pushing her coffee cup away from her.

Tansi's voice was too loud. "Lydia is not a good role model."

Mercy frowned. "Let Nell make her own choices, Tansi."

"I know. But I promised her mother…"

"I had a mother who tried to run my life for decades," I declared.

"And what did you do?" Mercy asked.

"Rattled my chains."

Tansi spoke up. "Okay, okay, I won't gossip, but I *know* things. I know that Carisa and Lydia had a fight, and Nell told me she herself was afraid of Carisa's mouth."

"Why?" I asked.

"Carisa took a dislike to Nell."

"Because of Jimmy?"

"According to Nell, yes."

"You don't believe her?"

Tansi breathed in. "Jimmy doesn't chase *every* girl. He's not interested in Nell. Men don't notice Nell, you know. She's, well, short and..." She stopped.

I sipped cold coffee, placed the cup on the saucer. "Why did Jimmy break up with Lydia?"

Mercy answered quickly. "I'll tell you what I think. The studio thought he'd look better with Ursula Andress, her in a gown, him in a tuxedo. The two of them having dinner with Bogart and Bacall up in their Benedict Canyon home, Jimmy petting their two boxer dogs. Good camera shot. It's all publicity."

"What does that mean?"

"It means a lot of Jimmy's dating is programmed by the studio. Jimmy also likes to keep his real life private, do things his own way. He seems to have overnight infatuations with each new girl, and sort of sees her for a while."

"Sort of?" I asked.

"Yes, exactly. Sort of. Once or twice. Lydia for a week or two. Pier a lot longer—and more heartfelt, that one. Maybe a real love there. Maybe not. But yes, sort of. When they call him back, hungry for his love, he's never home. Out on his infernal bike in the hills. Jimmy is a little confused about things." She shrugged her shoulders.

"I'm not following this." I found it difficult to understand the dating patterns of these odd young folks. It was all a tedious muddle to me. But I asked Mercy, "Is Tansi right? Is Lydia on drugs?"

Mercy pursed her lips into a thin line. "Probably."

"But this is not the reason he left her?"

"Probably not."

"Then why?" I begged.

Mercy shrugged her shoulders again.

Tansi was frowning. "And you call me a gossip?"

Mercy spoke coolly. "I don't gossip, Tansi. I just insinuate facts."

Chapter Five

Tansi insisted on driving me back to the Ambassador and seemed thrilled with me as her sole passenger. Her car, she said, was brand-new. Look, look at it, she insisted. What do you think? Bored, I looked. A spotless Chevy Bel Air, sparkling and shiny. "Everyone in L.A. has a new car," I said, joking.

Tansi nodded. "Well, you have to."

"How sad!"

"Why?" Tansi asked.

I chose not to answer, finding the subject tedious, but finally said, "I felt Mercy was being evasive. She was holding something back."

Tansi pulled out into traffic. "You mean about his going out with Lydia?"

"And others. How he treats the girls he sees."

A stretched out response. "Noooo…not really."

"And now you're doing it, too. Mercy strikes me as a forthright woman, and you're an old friend, but everyone seems to deal with Jimmy gingerly, only comfortable on the fringes. No one wants to get to the heart of him."

"Maybe because we don't know how to talk about him."

"Or," I said, "maybe everyone is nervous about actually getting to the heart of him."

"No, Jimmy is just a sweet guy who…"

That surprised me. "I'd never call him sweet, Tansi. Brooding, rude, sullen, yes. At times happy, joking, frivolous, funny. Sweet, no."

"Charming, then."

"All right, charming, if you will."

But the conversation made Tansi uncomfortable. She started pointing out local landmarks to me, like a guide, cutting across boulevards, weaving her way through the city. Pershing Square, where soapbox orators declaimed their madness all hours of the night. Grauman's Chinese Theater. The Moulin Rouge. The Egyptian Theater, where *East of Eden* was still playing. "Jimmy comes to stare at the marquee," Tansi told me.

I kept repeating, "I've been here before, Tansi. Before you were born, in fact. The palm trees were smaller, but looked about the same. The buildings were still ugly and on the verge of being replaced with newer, uglier, shinier ones. And the stars were too clear in the sky, with too much space below. The mountains were still over there." I pointed, dramatically.

Tansi laughed. "I'm sorry." She turned onto Sunset Boulevard.

I pointed. "And that's Schwab's. We can sit at the counter and be discovered like Lana Turner."

"They say that never happened." Tansi pointed at a building and grinned. "But you don't know about Googie's."

I eyed the eatery next to Schwab's. "And I choose not to." An odd-looking restaurant, with its grotesque architecture: upswept roof, diagonal glass panels, zigzag markings on the boomerang-looking signs, a nightmare clash of blue and orange, a matchbox construction, pieces of building dropped willy-nilly and then glued together.

"That's a Jimmy hangout, a coffee shop. He used to live nearby."

"Let's stop in," I said suddenly.

Tansi kept driving. "Oh no. I've never been there."

"Come on, Tansi, let's stop. I want to get a feel of the place. When I come to L.A., I'm squired to the Cocoanut Grove for drinks, to Don Roper's on Rodeo Drive for fittings to make me look like Ginger Rogers, to the Mocambo to see Theresa Brewer or some other screeching singer I can't stand. No one ever thinks to take me to a coffee shop."

"There must be a reason for that. Googie's is for young people."

"Good. Then we'll fit right in."

Tansi swung her car around, a little too dramatically, so that I slid in my seat, held onto the dashboard. "I learned my driving maneuvers trying to follow Jimmy to events. He doesn't believe in speed limits."

"But I do, Tansi. My remaining hair is white. Please don't make it fall out." I patted my careful perm. "More than it already does."

Standing in the doorway, a tiny woman dwarfed by the soaring archway, I waited and considered the place no country for me. Tansi, uncomfortable, hovered behind me. I surveyed the sleek, polished eatery, as crisp inside as a deco highway diner: the stark, high-backed booths and the chrome-and-glass tables, the cluttered geometric glass tiers suspended behind the counter, jam-packed with cobalt-blue soda glasses and rose-colored plates. Diagonal floor tiles, alternating black and white, gave the floor a dizzy, schizoid feel. The whole place seemed taken with itself, smart and trendy, and I thought of the hipster word I never employed—cool. But what made the small place bounce, even hum, was the energy, the sense that something was happening, something contagious and electric. Late afternoon in L.A.: freeways cluttered with honking, desperate cars, but, inside, a cavern of muted voices. Not quiet—there was too much talk going on, but it was like an interplay of piano notes, the one echoing off the other. Half of the tables were filled, perhaps. But the occupants sailed back and forth, young men and women, talking, laughing, backslapping, confiding. Everyone seemed to know everyone, and everyone seemed, to my jaundiced eye, eighteen years old.

"Tommy and Polly are here," Tansi whispered.

I looked. Tommy and Polly stood near a booth, chatting with friends, watching Tansi and me settle into our chairs. I muttered under my breath, "Does he ever take off the red jacket?"

Tansi grinned. "Then he wouldn't be James Dean."

"But he's *not* Jimmy."

"And then his girlfriend Polly would leave him."

I stared at the young woman I'd seen on Tommy's arm. "What's her story?"

"Polly Dunne?" Tansi glanced back at the couple, both of whom had stopped talking, simply watching us. I saw a willowy girl, tall and slender—a sapling leaning back to earth. I supposed it had to do with her being a half-foot taller than her boyfriend, some way of making them seem more a couple. Tommy, on the other hand, seemed to be craning his neck upward, arching back, reminding me of a baby bird stretching for nourishment. An odd couple, really. Yet they touched a lot, seemed to bump into each other, as though to make sure the other was still there. I thought Polly's look bizarre. For such a tall girl, she was almost all bone and no flesh, with a shock of brilliant auburn hair on her head—a crown of sudden sunset. She wore clothes I considered the stuff of thrift store backrooms: a lacy crinoline skirt that flared out, way below the knee, a puffy lace blouse that I thought had disappeared with Lillian Gish silents. A modern girl clothed in some ensemble more applicable to a barn dance in rural Kansas, circa 1900. Rebecca of Sunnybrook farm with garden spade, stopping for an egg cream in an American café.

"Well," Tansi said, "she's sort of hard to get to know. She clings to Tommy like he's the last piece of floating driftwood. She spends much of the time berating him for his lack of ambition. Tommy believes fate will pluck him from the dailies and make him the next Brando. But Tommy's lazy. Jimmy got him a bit part in *Giant*, as you know. Before that, he had an audition for a speaking role in *Rebel*, but he came late. Polly almost killed him."

"Why doesn't she leave him?" I eyed the staring couple, watching Polly fluff her head of red curls and Tommy pull on the cuffs of the jacket.

"I think she believes his friendship with Jimmy will get *her* a place in Hollywood."

"Another ambitious actress?"

"They all are, his crew. She's in *Giant* in a dinner scene. Stevens needed what he called a 'statuesque beauty.' Nell Meyers is the only one not infected with the acting bug—just yet. Though I'm afraid Lydia has put ideas in her head, too."

I nodded. "Jimmy's assembly of bit players."

"Exactly. And the only one with any talent, clearly, is Jimmy."

"Mercy says he's trying to distance himself from them."

"He already has. Lydia Plummer got on his nerves right away. We all saw it, but not her. Jimmy told me, I guess confidentially, that she wanted him to get her a juicy part in his next picture."

"Rather brazen, no?"

"I suppose so, but not surprising. Very Hollywood, once you've been here for a while. Hollywood is the land of make-believe. Everyone makes believe they're talented. At parties, the only refrain you hear over and over is, 'I'm waiting for my break.'"

I bit my lip. "Most probably don't realize the word 'break' should be used in the past tense. Polly doesn't look very happy. And for some reason they're still staring at us."

"I hope you don't get to know her, Edna. Despite her weird look, she's known for her rude mouth. She can be harsh with folks."

I was curious. "How does Jimmy deal with her?"

She shrugged. "You know Jimmy. He flirts with her, he ignores her, he makes fun of her—he can be a deadly mimic. When he knew you were coming west, he did one of you..."

"Me!"

"Of course, he didn't *know* you, but he knew we were friends. So he'd arch his voice, piercing Margaret Dumont falsetto out of some Marx Brothers routine—with you wanting to rename the movie *Gigantic* because it made you rich."

I grinned. "I love it. I do." I glanced at the frozen, staring couple. "But Tommy Dwyer intrigues me, a boy who unashamedly takes his coloration from another, and isn't afraid to be mocked. By God, he even does his hair like Jimmy's."

"What else does he have? Parking cars? Weekend auditions at the Beverly Hills Playhouse? He wants to stay in the sunshiny world of L.A., and, if he can be Jimmy's occasional understudy or stand-in, so be it. It buys cheap red wine and Mexican food and New Year's Eve, maybe, at LaRue's on the Strip."

"And they all know this *femme fatale* Carisa Krausse?"

Tansi glanced at the couple, then back at me. "I don't think she was ever close to Tommy or Polly. More Lydia's friend. Polly is close to no one. The girls don't like her. But I'm invisible to her. Too old. I'm not a rival."

I made a face. "One thing I've learned is that women become invisible quicker than men."

"Some women are born invisible."

I recalled Tansi's lonely, solitary childhood under the care of this nanny or that one, sent to a Swiss boarding school where no one liked her, dragged from one New York apartment to another by an effervescent, much-marrying famous mother.

We ordered sodas from a waitress who never looked at us.

Then Tansi nudged me, and I jumped. I found myself staring at a couple of gangly teenagers, perhaps eighteen or nineteen. The boy and girl were identical twins, with small mooncalf eyes set too far apart in round, expansive faces, with stringy arms out of place on such rotund frames, with corn-fed, slapdash grins on splotchy, acned faces. A strange couple, the two, standing there, shoulders touching, blocking the doorway, and vacantly grinning like gassed fugitives from a dentist's chair. Worse, both were dressed identically in T-shirts, penny loafers, and red nylon jackets.

"Good Lord," I exclaimed. "The Katzejammer Kids are back in town."

Tansi laughed. "Welcome to the sideshow. You're looking at Alyce and Alva Strand."

Eyes wide. "You *know* them, Tansi? They look like they've toppled from a hay wagon."

The twins sauntered over, their heads swiveling left and right, as though on ball bearings, looking, looking. They stopped at

Tansi's table, though they first waved to Tommy and Polly, who immediately looked away. "Is he here?" one said, and I wasn't sure which one spoke. The voice, garbled as though impeded by a mouth of marbles, was neither male nor female.

Tansi said no.

They looked at me, as if they should know me, and then silently turned and found seats on the counter stools, twisting left and right, facing each other, then shifting back and forth, scanning the crowd.

"Jimmy's fan club," Tansi remarked.

I raised my eyebrows. "My God."

"They're harmless. They follow Jimmy *everywhere*. He doesn't know what to make of them."

"And *you* do?"

"They're Jimmy's oldest fans. We're talking 1951 now, a lifetime ago, Hollywood years. Jimmy got his first break on TV, playing John the Baptist in *Hill Number One*, an Easter pageant on Father Peyton's Family Theater. Jimmy in a white toga and sandals, devastatingly handsome and sexy. The nuns at a California girls' school assigned it as homework." She chuckled. "The girls fell in love with Jimmy and formed the Immaculate Heart James Dean Appreciation Society. I'm not making this up, Edna, I swear. They held meetings, wrote letters—all the sheltered Catholic girls going crazy. One of the girls, Alyce Strand," Tansi pointed to the ditzy girl, then sitting with an index finger tucked into her cheek, "became his devoted fan. And somehow her brother, he of the singular brain cell, became enamored of Jimmy, too. Jimmy has a legion of male fans now, though they're the tough high-school misfits, the kind with the slicked-back Brylcream hair and the biker boots. Not so Alva. He's an oddball who…"

"I don't understand." I was bewildered. "For what—four years—they follow Jimmy?"

"Yes, and after *East of Eden* and Jimmy's spectacular celebrity, they ratcheted up their obsession. They feel they *own* him. They *follow* him."

I was furious. "They are sick."

"Harmless, Edna."

"Oh, no, no, Tansi, I don't think so."

"Edna, you seem to give them more worth than they deserve. Stars need their fans."

"Tansi, you seem to believe Hollywood is a land removed from the rest of America."

"And it isn't?"

I paused. "They're like Tommy—living no life but Jimmy's. They can't *have* his life, you know."

"They don't work or anything. They live at home, and indulgent parents let them play out their bit parts."

"I suppose it's cheaper than the cost of an asylum."

"Edna!"

Tommy and Polly, unhappy with the sudden proliferation of red-nylon jackets in Googie's, left, nodding to Tansi and me as they passed. I noticed they purposely avoided looking at the Strand twins, who'd been facing each other, but then swiveled on the seats, facing out, grins plastered on faces. Their eyes never left Tommy. After all, Tommy Dwyer was a James Dean friend.

Tansi was telling me how the Strand twins amused her, but she stopped.

James Dean was standing just inside the front door. Oddly, he just seemed to *appear*: an apparition materializing from another world. But, of course, he'd strolled in, in a leather jacket and biker boots. He sat across the room, but didn't acknowledge us, and I watched his profile: rigid, the flexible mouth, the cigarette dangling. He noticed me watching him, but turned away, looking away, too, from Alva and Alyce Strand. I saw him suck in his breath.

Clearing her throat, Tansi yelled across the tables: "Jimmy, here."

He shook his head. No.

Jimmy's presence compelled the eatery into an awkward paralysis. People stopped talking and watched him. Looking up, Jimmy caught my eye. Sheepishly, I smiled. Jimmy narrowed his eyes, tucked his head into his chest like a bantam cock, and

turned away. I felt foolish, rebuffed, the slight acknowledge-
ment I'd offered rejected. For a second, I was furious. How dare
he? I was *Giant*; I was *Show Boat*; I was—I stopped. I had no
idea *what* I was to boys of his generation. I wrote words down
and sometimes actors read them into cameras. Suddenly, I felt
ancient—an attitude I never allowed myself. The dowager in
the diner. The waitress had placed two sodas on the table, and
I pushed mine to the side. Tansi, I noted, quickly drained her
glass and was now munching on an ice cube.

Tansi looked flustered. "It isn't personal, Edna. He's moody
sometimes."

"He's downright rude."

"Oh, Edna, no."

"He's a brat." I paused. "And stop defending him, Tansi."

"I'm not…"

"He's allowed to get away with boorish behavior because
you *let* him."

"Talent has its entitlements."

"Nonsense. I've been talented all my life, and I…"

Tansi cut me off. "And you've been known to be imperious.
Even rude sometimes. I mean no offense, I…"

I pulled back, smiled. Good for you, Tansi, I thought. "None
taken. But I'm that way with fools. Jimmy has to learn to sort
out his rudeness."

Tansi shook her head. "Maybe you should give him lessons."
She meant it humorously—even her eyes got bright—but the
line came out too quickly, too strident.

I glared.

When I turned to look at Jimmy, he was gone. I hadn't
even heard the chimes over the door ring. Maybe he *was* an
apparition.

Late that night, in my hotel suite, settling into my pillows with
tea and a Mary Roberts Rinehart mystery I had trouble following, my phone rang.

"I'm in the lobby," Jimmy said.

"And?"

"Invite me up."

I glanced at the clock. "Jimmy, it's after ten."

"So?"

"For a minute."

Within seconds he was there, slumped into a chair by the window, his leather jacket still zipped up, looking around the room. "They're really scared of you, Miss Edna, if you get all these rooms for yourself."

"I'm famous."

"So am I."

"What do you want, Jimmy?"

He shrugged his shoulders and mumbled.

"You're going to have to be more articulate with me. I'm old, hard of hearing, and I value oratory as a lost art."

"You know, in high school I won the Indiana state competition for oratory."

"And as a prize, they took away your need for future clarity?"

He laughed. "I love it. You won't let me win."

"I didn't know we were in a contest."

"Everything is a contest in life."

"And you have to win?"

"Of course. I always do."

"And you need to do battle with old ladies in sensible shoes and beauty-parlor perms?"

His eyes widened. "Everybody lets me win these days. It ain't fun."

"Maybe you need new combatants."

"That may be so. I got no one to fight with."

"You seem to have your crew—Tommy, Polly, Lydia, Nell…"

He cut me off. "Miss Edna, I've come here to beg and plead."

"I don't know you, Jimmy."

"Yes, you do." He looked toward the window, out into the black night. "I got famous too fast."

I had no idea what he was talking about. "I heard about your *Hill Number One* TV show."

He shook his head. "Oh, *that*. The Strand twins. They'll disappear."

"Like Carisa Krausse?" I wanted to challenge him.

Jimmy slumped back, folded and unfolded his arms. He started to speak, then stopped, stammered. Grunted. "What?" I asked.

"Sort of why I'm here."

"Jimmy, you were rude to us at Googie's."

He looked surprised. "How so?"

"You enter, I assume through the front door, although legions of fans may ascribe other powers to you, and you ignore civilized nods of hello."

He didn't answer.

"I don't like rudeness." My voice was a little too strident. I was surprised that I was nervous.

"I wasn't being rude."

"Perhaps we'd both better consult the same dictionary then."

"You do got a way about you, Miss Edna." He sat up, grinning. "I wanna be like you when I grow up." He tilted his head and looked at me, as though expecting a laugh. But I sat there, lips pursed. "Look," he said, "rude is not ignoring you in a dumb diner. That's just—just, well, nothing. It's, it's, like, well, nothing. Rudeness, if you think about it, is barging in here late at night, uninvited, and jostling with you, working myself up to asking a favor of you. That's the real rudeness."

I fell under his spell, a little intoxicated by his hazy, narcotic drawl. I sat back, relaxed. "Tell me about Carisa Krausse."

"Hey, we had an idle fling in Marfa. I was bored, there was nothing to do. She was pretty, she was always around me, Pier Angeli had just left me, and, well, nothing happened. A couple late-night rides in a car I borrowed from Mercy. They took my car away so I wouldn't kill myself. Suddenly, I see she's falling for me. Before Marfa, back here, in rehearsals, she was around, and I'd sensed her…well…instability. But sometimes I lack common sense. I swear we never…we…there is no way any baby is mine, Miss Edna. Not with her."

"What about other women?" He was sitting up now, the sober schoolboy before the demanding teacher.

"That's mostly PR. Like Terry White, that pretty vacuum. You know, the studio had me and Terry go to a movie. So the limo pulls up, she says not one damn word to me, not one, but the minute we get out of the limo and the reporters are there, the big smile comes on, she grabs my arm, and acts like we're lovey-dovey boyfriend-girlfriend. Not a word the whole time." He sighed. "Sometimes I actually like the girls they hand me. Most times I don't."

"But your reputation?"

His eyebrows raised, the eyes unblinking. "I don't know what reputation I have."

"Mercy says you 'sort of' go through women."

Jimmy looked at the ceiling, then burst into laughter. "Love that Madama. So…so…"

"Truthful?"

"Maybe so." He crossed and uncrossed his denim-clad legs, stared at his boots. "I'm not sure what to do around women," he said, suddenly.

"What does that mean?"

He shrugged his shoulders. "I just got some questions I gotta answer."

Now I was confused. "About what? Marriage?"

He opened and closed his eyes, blinking wildly. "Well, sex, frankly."

Not a subject I was comfortable with, truly. I winced. Birds and bees may indeed do it, but not on my watch. I'm almost seventy, and I stare like a deer in the headlights at the mention of that monumental and ferocious three-letter word.

"I'm not following you." And I wasn't.

"Forget it." He stood up and walked to the window, looking down into the street. "You got some good view of an empty city here." He pointed. "Somewhere over there is Chinatown. The

street of the Golden Palace. You can get your fortune told there."
He looked back at me. "You know, L.A. has a real different energy
than New York. New York is pulsating and real nervous-like. It's
jumpy and feverish. It's all throb and burst. That's where artists
can *grow*. You know that. You *live* there. L.A. is emptiness. So
much room to wait things out, to dream and not to do. People,
you know, float from one exhibitionist outpost to another,
grasping for ideas that are best left untouched." Most of what
he'd just said was mumbled, and he seemed to laugh at the end
of each line, as though embarrassed by the sentiment.

"What are you talking about?"

"I want you to talk to Mercy. That's why I'm here. Convince
her to talk to Carisa. Mercy was the *only* person Carisa liked. She
told me that. She said Mercy reminded her of an older sister who
died of some disease or something. And that fool Jake Geyser
called me again tonight, and asked me if I had any idea how to
shut Carisa up. This is all beyond him, though he won't admit
it. He's panicking. Unwed mothers, Jimmy Dean's love child,
forbidden passion, God know what other lies. They're pressuring
me. What am I supposed to do?"

I nodded. And then kept nodding. Even after he left, backing
his way out like a servant in some costume drama, bowing and
shuffling, I sat there nodding. Then I got angry with myself. I
felt, suddenly, that he'd charmed me, wooed me, reeled me in
like an available (and not very challenging) fish. I glanced at
the clock. After eleven. I didn't care. I dialed Mercy's number,
knowing she'd be up. I apologized, but Mercy was delighted to
hear my voice. I filled her in on Jimmy's visit, even the earlier
encounter at Googie's, and Mercy chortled. "Did he tell you
about his mother?"

"No."

"He's saving that story for you. It starts out, 'I was nine
when my mother died.'" She stopped, and seemed sorry she
was making light of his story. "But it's real. His pain is worn
like a coat he can't take off. But let me guess. He wants you as
intercessor with me."

"Yes, he wants you to talk to Carisa."

"I've already told him no."

"Why not, Mercy? I don't understand."

"I don't know, really. Like Tansi, I just assumed it would go away. I don't believe Carisa is pregnant. She's just a melodramatic and misguided girl…"

I closed my eyes. "I promised him I'd convince you otherwise."

Mercy laughed. "I knew it." Then I heard her sigh. "You know, after that last letter to Warner, I've been thinking maybe I should step in." A pause. "If I go there, you have to go with me."

"I don't think…"

"I'm not giving you a choice. Good night, Edna."

That night I dreamed of towering, pitch-black oil rigs, a line of them punctuating the parched yellow land, strung out like telephone poles. Rhythmic drilling in the arid Texas landscape, monotonous and steady and thunderous. All night long the clamorous cacophony of cold steel and taut wire and oily rod against caked, clay-packed dirt—pounding, pounding, pounding. I woke with a headache.

Chapter Six

Los Angeles lay, at midafternoon, under a heavy sun, like a blister erupting on the skin. A film of dry heat covered the sidewalks and buildings, and everything struck me as sere or lemon yellow; dried skin, flaking, dissolving into dust. I'd spent late morning and early afternoon in meetings with studio execs. Stevens, rushing in from shooting for five minutes of comment, made an off-hand remark about Jimmy's annoying tardiness, but then qualified it—after all, he was talking to the money men—remarking that Jimmy's performance was nothing short of glorious. I nodded. I'd seen an hour of dailies that morning and was pleased. When the meeting finally broke, I went for a walk. But not very far. Under a nickel-gray sky with that lazy sun behind wispy clouds, the heat exhausted me. And besides, people in L.A. didn't walk. They only moved on wheels. My beloved Manhattan pastime was taboo here. An old lady tottering along hot sidewalks in expensive shoes, I fully expected a benevolent passerby to offer smelling salts or a free ride to a mental ward.

Back at the hotel, I napped, a brief uncomfortable sleep, fraught with Gothic visions of screaming children impaled on wrought-iron fences. It startled me awake, that ugly nightmare. Children? Fences? Impalement? I lay there, a bead of sweat on my brow, and suddenly remembered last night's equally disturbing dream—all those oil rigs on endless Texas plains, pounding, pounding. L.A., I told myself, sitting up and preparing to put a cold compress on my forehead, was a place conducive to jolting nightmare. Only in murderous and serendipitous New York City could a soul find comfort—so long as you were fifteen floors above the city, tucked into an Upper East Side doorman building, away from the slapdash West Side and cacophonous Lower Manhattan. Frontier lands, both places, wild west shows, noisy and grimy.

Promptly at five I left my suite, headed downstairs to the Cocoanut Grove, where Warner was hosting a cocktail party. The one formal-attire event of my visit. Posh, posh. Men in rented tuxedos and women in ostrich plumes, doubtless. I was guest of honor, the invitation said, but so was producer Henry Ginsburg and director George Stevens. So, I joked, were Liz and Rock and Jimmy. And Chill Wills and Jane Withers. Maybe even Lydia Plummer with her two-word moment. Oh well. Five to seven. Two hours of stilted chatter, indigestible food, and expensive but warm champagne. I'd dressed appropriately, as indicated by the invitation. The creamy off-white silk flared dress with swirls of silver piping around the clinched belted waist, a lace bodice (a nod to my Victorian birth, I told myself), the rope of cultured pearls I felt naked without, and the black patent-leather clutch containing nothing but a hairbrush, faint red lipstick, perfume, and a mirror. This was as regal as I'd ever look: the novelist dowager, the first lady of American literature, taking on Hollywood.

Closing the door behind me, I paused, and remembered the elbow-length white gloves I'd specifically bought, obligatory at such formal occasions. A woman without gloves is a social misfit, I knew, recalling my forgetting to wear gloves to the Hoover White House and the looks I'd garnered, my escort into the room taking my bare forearm as though touching poison ivy.

I met Mercy in the hallway outside the Cocoanut Grove and apologized for last night's telephone call. She shrugged it off. "Actually, you got me to agree to something I was trying to convince myself to do anyway. I was able to sleep well."

And I dreamed of grimy oil wells and disemboweled, impaled children.

Mercy was in a shimmering blue cocktail dress with a band of rainbow-tinted sequins accenting the scalloped neckline, very nice, indeed. And a single gold heart around her neck. Simple, but elegant. A rhinestone clip in her hair, almost lost in the curls. I suddenly thought myself dowdy, drab, the old prune with the pearls.

She nudged me, pointing. "Sal Mineo."

I turned to see a slight, dark boy passing by, looking straight ahead, dressed in a grownup tuxedo. "He looks like he's twelve."

Mercy leaned in. "He's part of Jimmy's fan club. Ever since *Rebel.* By the way, did they screen the movie for you? You have to see that red jacket you've come to love. Anyway, Sal's been emulating Jimmy, the preening walk, the insolent glare, the clothing, even the haircut. In Marfa, he stared at Jimmy all the time."

Tansi joined us. "My, my, Tansi," I said. "You really do go all out for cocktail hour."

For a second Tansi looked unsure of herself, but she noticed I was smiling, my eyes appreciative. "I try."

"Very…fetching." And, I told myself, it was, this metamorphosis in Tansi. The awkward angular figure with the unruly hair was transformed by a pencil-shaped velvet dress, teal blue, with black satin stripes running down the sides, up around the high collar, lace trimmed. Very proper, yet oddly sensual. She'd had her hair done, not the usual assembly of bobby pins and helter-skelter baubles, with vagrant wisps of runaway hair escaping. No. Tansi had spent time at a salon—"The one on Rodeo Drive," she informed, "you know, Duarte's"—and the effect was, indeed, arresting. The pointed plain face was softened by cascading curls, and she wore a pillbox hat, with pinned-back veil. Unlike mine, her gloves were wrist length, and looked more appropriate. Mercy, too, wore such gloves. As did all the women walking by, I noticed. Only I wore gloves that encased my arms to the elbow. But I didn't care for Tansi's makeup—shrill whore's lipstick, fire-alarm red. She did love that red. She saw me looking. "It's called Ever-So-Red," she said. "From Pond's. All the starlets wear it." She twirled around, happy, and the satin stripes caught the overhead light, spotlighting her. She whispered to me, "Maybe this will get me married."

Tansi's remark surprised me. So she still entertained the idea of marriage, this middle-aged woman? Good God. Why? The maiden lady as temptress; the hideaway virgin as vamp; oxymorons for the dreaded cocktail hour. Why would she *want* to be married? She'd made it forty-five years without male interruption. Frankly, I cherished my own much-touted spinsterhood, embraced it like an anthem, a badge of arrival.

Inside, I let myself be squired to this gaggle of important souls, then to that one. The mayor. The lieutenant governor. Betty Grable. Lex Baxter. Ricardo Montaban. I drank champagne, only one; just one. My habit, for many years now. Souls nodded at me, some virtually genuflected so I assumed I was somehow their paycheck, and I smiled and resisted the urge to hiccough. Photographers circled, bumping and questioning, following Rock or Liz or Mercy or Sal. But not Jimmy, who hadn't arrived. "He *told* me he'd be here," Tansi pouted. "I *begged* him."

And then he was there. A group of men moved, and there was Jimmy, sitting on a side chair, a drink in his hand. No tuxedo on him, to be sure, but a black turtleneck, very tight, and he'd shaved. Creased blue linen slacks, falling just right over black penny loafers. I thought he looked collegiate, a little East Coast preppie, a runaway from Phillips Exeter.

But he also looked tired, droopy. Perhaps the need to select appropriate clothing for the formal affair had exhausted him, I mused. I headed over, but found it difficult to maneuver my tiny self through well-wishers and progressively drunker and drunker guests. Japanese waiters floated by with huge trays of drinks and platters of *hors d'oeuvres*. I glimpsed assortments of caviar, shrimp, wedges of cheese, shimmering yellow and white under the lights; diced avocados on bits of toast slivers; even a cascade of white-hazed deep purple grapes, looking individually polished. I wondered why it all looked so unappetizing, this cornucopia of spoils. And then it hit me. It looked like a movie set prop, a plaster of Paris construction, fake food arranged and painted and shellacked. Nothing looked savory, tempting—a culinary landscape that seemed paste and sawdust and sprayed-on enamel. You weren't supposed to eat it—just admire.

I spotted Lydia, standing nearby, watching Jimmy but not approaching him. She looked pale and shaky, and at one point Jimmy glanced her way, frowned, and Lydia, panicking, rushed out of the room.

A photographer asked Jimmy to stand for a photo; he didn't answer. The man, his burdensome camera pressed against his chest, repeated the request, probably believing Jimmy didn't hear him over the din. A chamber ensemble to his left was playing Chopin, and not very well. No response. Jimmy stared at the floor, his fingers drumming the arm of the chair. But he did extract a Chesterfield from a pack, flipped open a matchbook, and lit it. He expelled smoke into the air, in the direction of the photographer. I realized he *had* heard the request. The photographer, unhappy, was already moving away.

"Jimmy," I said, approaching. "You were rude to him."

He smiled thinly. "I guess I'm rude a lot lately."

"Why?"

He shrugged his shoulders. "I've made three movies in about a year. I'm losing my energy."

I tried unsuccessfully to avoid the obsequious Jake, who more than once sidled up to me, smiling, asking irksome questions: "Can I do anything for you?" "Is Tansi taking good care of you?" "Do you know you can call me?" "You're not using the car the studio has made available to you?" Then, finally, "You haven't spoken to anyone in New York about the…the Jimmy matter?" Everything seemed to lead up to that last question, and he waited, pensive as a schoolboy caught cheating at multiplication tables.

"Well," I said to him, "I did speak to a close friend at *The New York Times*."

A gasp, a bubble forming at the corner of the mouth. "Miss Ferber."

"Mr. Geyser, I'm jesting. My lips are sealed." Nodding, he hurried away.

Then Tansi was at my side, bustling, nervous. Unfortunately a few strands of her careful coiffure were breaking free, and I realized Tansi, antsy as a barnyard hen, couldn't help picking at her hairdo. "Edna, come with me." I followed. In the hallway we spotted Mercy, who was sneaking out, a sheepish grin on her face, and Tansi fumbled for her cigarettes. She had trouble striking a match. "You're not going to believe this," she said to both of us, "but Jack Warner just told me he got a second letter from Carisa this afternoon." She paused, inhaled, coughed, and waited.

"What did the new letter say?" Mercy asked.

"Just one line." Tansi took a deep breath. "It said, 'Tomorrow nothing will be confidential—or will it?'"

"What?" I asked.

"The scandal magazine. She's definitely going to that slime bag Robert Harrison of *Confidential* to expose Jimmy."

"Expose what?" I asked, exasperated.

"Does it matter? Lies, innuendo, misconceptions. Once rumor is out there the damage is done."

I was naïve. "Just how important is this *Confidential*? I've never read it."

Tansi started to explain, but was a little frenzied, and she sputtered to a stop. Mercy, coolly, "It's a sleazy pulp that thrives on gossip and sin, appealing to America's prurient interests. I've read some copies left in dressing rooms. Titillation, suggestion. Cruel and deliberate. Big-bosomed girls like Jayne Mansfield. Adultery among the stars, unwed mothers, fornication; you name it. Their current crusade is the lavender crowd."

"The what?"

"Homosexuals. Like 'The Lavender Closet,' that sort of thing." She paused. "They call them the hands-on-hips boys. Girly men. It's gutter stuff."

Tansi found her voice. "They don't like Liberace with his red-ruffled shirts and all that gold and black brocade he sports."

I smiled. "Well, then they have a modicum of taste, despite their scandal-mongering. But is there more to the Jimmy story than the allegation of an unwed baby with Carisa?"

Silence. Tansi and Mercy looked at each other. Mercy cleared her throat. "Jimmy has done some indiscreet things."

"Like what?"

Mercy sideswiped the question, lowering her voice as some people passed by, leaving the party. "America is a scary place these days. Hollywood is a whipping boy for old-style Aimee Semple McPherson evangelists—den of iniquity, sin city, you name it. Eisenhower blandness covers us. McCarthy and his witch hunt. The infernal black list."

"And," said Tansi, "it's like everyone is waiting for the next explosive scandal."

"And that might be Jimmy," I said, flat out.

A bustle behind us, as Jimmy flew out of the room. He said nothing, though we stared, expectant. His face was scarlet, and from where I stood, I could see the veins in his neck, swollen and purple.

"Warner must have told him about the new letter," Tansi said, scared.

"Party's over," Mercy said.

"Jimmy," I called out to him.

He bumped into some men smoking cigarettes, and then, almost blindly, he rushed out of the hallway, headed to the street.

"My God," Tansi said, edgy. "I've never seen him like this." She turned. "I need to get inside. I have to powwow with Warner and Jake." She hurried away.

Mercy's eyes followed Tansi. "Edna, I'm worried about Jimmy." I shook my head. I was thinking about *Confidential*, and the vague, amorphous accusations. What was I missing here? "I don't want to go back in there," Mercy added. "Not now. Jimmy took the party with him. What do you say you and I grab a bite at Jack's Drive-in on the Strip? The food is wonderful and we're way overdressed, although on occasion I've seen some Beverly

Hills matrons there in mink coats ordering hot dogs with chili sauce." She hesitated. "Unless you have obligations in there."

"No, I'm ready. But I sense you have an agenda, Mercy."

"Of course. You and I, I've decided, need to plan our visit to Carisa. That new letter is too scary."

I returned to the party to say my goodbyes, but I couldn't locate Stevens or Warner. Even Henry Ginsburg, I discovered, had left. Tansi was walking in circles. When I saw Jake approaching me, I fled, but I realized he was also sneaking out, maneuvering himself toward a side door. That made me smile. Mercy waited in the lobby, and then, with me as a passenger, we drove to the eatery to plan our assault on the hapless Carisa Krausse. "Our commando raid," Mercy termed it.

"More like," I countered, wryly, "the charge of the frightened brigade."

I savored a massive hamburger slathered in avocado and mayonnaise; the bun crisp and chewy; and fried potatoes cut so slender I thought them wood shavings, with a trace of sea salt, perhaps; and a dish of peach ice cream, speckled with huge chunks of red-gold fruit the color of a good sunset. Good food at last, I told Mercy. "In California most food, I've found, is filtered through sunshine and dabbled with greasepaint."

Mercy laughed. "Edna, you have to come to my home for a home-cooked meal."

"Well, this is a good start." I bit into the hamburger.

"So," Mercy began, "let's talk about Carisa."

Suddenly, I blanched. I'd just been thinking how restful I felt, tucked into the booth, when the image of Jimmy and his mountainous rage flooded me. "Oh, Mercy," I cried out.

"What?" Alarmed.

"I just had a horrible thought. You don't think Jimmy would go there *now*—to Carisa's. He's in such a foul mood. You don't think…"

Mercy covered her mouth for a second, looked scared.

"We're going there." I stood up.

"It's a dreadful neighborhood," Mercy said, hesitating. "Skid Row. And it's late."

"It's barely," I glanced at my wristwatch, "eight o'clock. Civilized people are just sitting down to dinner."

But Carisa's neighborhood silenced me—blocks of sad, dilapidated buildings, seedy, ill kept. I'd glimpsed New York's Bowery over the years, shook my head over the vacant-eyed winos bundled in mission-house overcoats. But this Skid Row was numbing, block after block of what looked like sagging flophouses, shanty hotels, pawnshops with weathered signs. As Mercy's car cruised into the area, I observed panhandlers, hookers, lost souls leaning against walls, or hunched over. "It's really called Skid Row, this area," Mercy told me. "Or the Nickel, because much of it centers on Fifth Street. Los Angelinos avoid the area—notorious for crime, drugs. Look." She pointed to a man staggering off a sidewalk. "It's like a big stereotype," she said. "A Warner backlot for a James Cagney movie. Angels with dirty faces."

I frowned. "A stereotype is sometimes nothing more than the redundancy of truth." Mercy looked at me. Third Street. Fourth Street. Street after street, fading daylight, shadows settling in.

Flickering neon sign on a corner bar: H RRYs, the A missing. That alarmed me. A cardboard sidewalk shelter, a man's feet visible. Eight-thirty at night, the streets eerily still, souls shuffling along, trancelike; yet the night seemed noisy, violent. The echoey tintinnabulation of jukebox music from deep inside a tavern. Then, as we idled at a light, snatches of a fierce husband-wife spat filtered through thin walls. The sobbing of a child—or maybe it was an alley cat in heat, hidden behind a shabby fence. The clamoring of a distant late-night freight train; a truck bumping over a broken street, headed to the warehouse district. Mercy parked her car in front of a three-story building, and we sat there. An old man staggered by, bumped into her fender, and I started. Not the brightest of ideas, this.

Gathering my voice, "You've been here before, right?"

"In daylight," Mercy said, faltering. "High noon."

"It must look better then."

"Well, it looked safer, shops open, traffic, you know, cops."

"This is what Tansi warned me about?"

Mercy frowned. "Tansi wasn't built for this patch of God's earth."

"And we are?"

I surveyed the adjacent buildings. A pawnshop with oversized signs: CALL ME LARRY! RADIOS & TOOLS HIGH PRICES PAID! BUY & SELL. PH. MI 2021. A storefront window cluttered with motley goods. LUCKY BOY HAMBURGERS. RUTH'S GRILL COCKTAILS.

"Well, what should we do?" Mercy asked.

I caught my breath. "Which apartment?"

Mercy pointed up. "In front. The second floor. The one with the lights on. She's home."

"How do we know she's alone?"

"God, I never thought about that. I just hope Jimmy's not there." Mercy looked at me. "You want to leave?"

I shook my head, resolute. "I'm never coming back to this neighborhood after tonight."

Mercy smiled. "It's not, I suppose, dangerous. It's just…poor."

"Not much consolation, I fear. And we're really not dressed for this." We looked at our fancy dresses, the jewelry. "We look all wrong."

"Maybe they'll think we're working girls."

"We are working girls." I grinned. "I look like an aged madam out on the town." A pause. "Let's go."

"You want to stay in the car?"

"No, I wouldn't miss this conversation. Carisa Krausse has loomed a little too large in my imagination these past couple days. I need to place a face to—to the madness."

The building was quiet. On the first floor, a radio blared from a back apartment. A Spanish station, a soap opera perhaps, with slammed doors and breaking glass. Then a male voice, a tenant's gruff baritone. But I was confused by the interior: the hardswept foyer, the polished but discolored old ceramic tile, with long-abused art-nouveau designs; the nicely lighted hallway, old wallpaper but clean, stairs swept and scrubbed; railings worn but glistening. The stink of old varnish and countless tenants, but also the astringent odor of lye soap, diligent cleaning, a battle against grime and decay and mites and spilled lives. I walked slowly up the stairs, holding onto Mercy's arm.

There was music coming from Carisa's apartment, not loud but wafting gently into the hallway. Lavish violin strings, the thump of piano keys, the light air of a girl singer. Rosemary Clooney? The Boswell Sisters? I had no idea. Music from radios, especially the plaintive crooning of adenoidal female singers, always irritates me. I consider the sentimental slurring of the Andrews Sisters tantamount to treason during the last world war. But I keep such sentiments to myself. Jerome Kern, yes; Cole Porter, certainly. Witty men, clever lyricists, jaunty confections, the Broadway ditties. Yes, I thought, Rosemary Clooney. Or maybe Kate Smith?

I didn't like the fact that Mercy, unconsciously, was humming the tune.

When Mercy gently rapped on the door—a little too softly, I thought—the door flew open because it had not been latched, and we stood there, staring at the body of a young girl, sprawled indecorously on the floor, her head resting in a pool of blood, her body twisted.

I looked at Mercy, Mercy at me.

"Is it…?" I gasped.

Mercy nodded.

I stepped into the room. "This is not going to make anyone happy."

Mercy frowned. "But maybe it solves somebody's problem."

For a second I closed my eyes. In the darkness I saw zigzag, shooting shafts of bright light, and I felt the rush of blood to my temples, throbbing, throbbing. "So it begins," I said, my voice scratchy. "So it begins."

Chapter Seven

Late that night, long after midnight, I lay in my bed, unable to sleep. I was trying to place events in order, categorizing, shifting the facts. I sorted through the last, horrendous hours, from the moment of awful discovery of the body to our dismissal by the police, with Mercy dropping me back at the Ambassador.

I wondered how I'd managed to stagger to the elevator, make it into my suite. In my room I'd slipped into a chair and sobbed for a half hour.

The police: Detective Cotton. What was his first name? Xavier. Detective Xavier Cotton rushed in a half hour after the beat cops arrived, Mercy having knocked on the superintendent's first floor apartment door, startling the old Spanish man, and sputtering: Call the cops. Then everything happened so fast. Looking back, it seemed but a matter of scant minutes before the two fat, balding cops and then Detective Cotton rushed up those stairs.

I marveled at the detective, frankly. You saw a trim man in his late thirties, dark and wiry, short, a pointy ferret face; with weary dark brown eyes, dull and a little washed out. Baked-bean eyes, I considered them. Eyes that looked like they hid everything, the surface glazed over, disarmingly. That made me nervous. When he spotted Mercy and me waiting in the upstairs hallway, his eyes got large, as though trying to focus. That razor-lipped mouth was suddenly agape, reminding me of farcical cartoon characters registering shock. Of course, he was surprised, really. Here in this tenderloin building, this bitter, noisome outpost of Hollywood's glitter-dome world, here stood these imposing and improbable women—both decked out in elegant silk dresses and pearls and diamond bracelets. Cotton stared at me as though I were Ma Barker dressed for a cotillion. Mercy stood at the top of the stairs, with arms folded, waiting, head down; and I stood near her, grande dame with my mane of white hair, my quizzical stare, my eyes darting, my curiosity volcanic. And wearing an over-sized sapphire-studded pin on my dress (a gift, I reminded myself, from Erle Stanley Gardner—and thus amazingly perfect). Two escapees from a decadent Hollywood party, detoured somehow into a Dickensian corner of the globe.

Detective Cotton nodded at us, entered the apartment, and I watched him approach the sprawled-out body and stare down at it, all the time nodding his head. He seemed out of focus, in the wrong place. I sized him up immediately: a dullard, a plodder, and therefore dangerous.

Within minutes, Jake Geyser barreled up the stairs. "I called him," Mercy told me. "He'll have to handle *this*." That didn't make me happy. Two clowns for the price of one. Why had Mercy done that? I would have nixed that notion. But Mercy understood the peculiar politics of Hollywood. Movies governed municipal law, perhaps. Oddly, Jake seemed in his element now, leaning into Cotton, whispering, even placing one hand on the detective's shoulder, a fleeting suggestion of camaraderie, though Cotton didn't look too happy being touched. Jake was tall, lanky; Cotton small, compact, runt of the litter. Mutt and Jeff. Jake was dressed in a ratty sweater, torn at the elbows, no socks in his black tie-shoes (very unflattering), and wrinkled pants. Where was he coming from? And so quickly? Both men conferred and looked back at the doorway, where I now stood, watching. Cotton motioned to one of the cops, and we were hustled downstairs to the superintendent's apartment, where, minutes later, Cotton questioned us.

Upstairs, a crime team took over; and just as well. I had no desire to see Carisa's sheet-draped body lifted onto a gurney, shuffled down the stairs, the stench of death already palpable in the apartment. I had little to say to Cotton; and with Jake there, a ghostly shadow against back wall, I believed the less said the better. What could I say? We knocked on her door, it flew open, and Carisa lay there, dead. We backed out of the room. Or, at least, Mercy said she did. I was quiet. But why were we there? To see Carisa, whom Mercy knew. And I? A writer from New York, slumming. Why the finery? Well, post-party wanderings. A visit to Carisa. Cotton eyed me suspiciously. The old lady gussied up in party silk.

"A writer? Like scripts?"

"Like novels," I said, dryly. Curtly.

"You write anything I heard of?" he asked.

"I doubt it."

He turned away for a second, made a note. "Why at this hour?"

Mercy shrugged. "Eight-thirty is hardly late. We left a cocktail party, got a bite at Jack's Drive-in," Cotton widened his eyes, staring at Mercy's dress, "and it seemed a good idea at the time."

"In this neighborhood?"

"We were in the neighborhood."

He clicked his tongue. "I doubt that." He looked at Jake. "So she worked for Warner Bros. Studio?"

"She'd been fired though. A month or so back."

"Then why is everybody here?"

"I came because Mercy called me."

Cynical. "The good citizen."

"She was an employee."

"Then what's this crap you're telling me upstairs about the studio wanting to handle the publicity?"

Jake leaned in. "As we speak, Jack Warner is talking to your chief."

Said matter-of-factly, but deliberately, the line hung in the air: its power obvious, its no-nonsense ultimatum clear-cut. Cotton looked from me to Mercy, back to Jake. So this is what was happening, his disgusted look indicated. Stonewalling, movieland style. This, his narrowed eyes suggested, was no minor-league murder case. "There's a murder here," he said, flatly.

Jake, almost snidely, "And it's your job to solve it." He softened his tone. "And you will."

Detective Cotton, equally snide, "I appreciate the vote of confidence from Howdy Doody."

Then I spoke up. "Just why is Warner involved in this?" I looked at Jake, who stared at his hands.

Cotton looked at me. "Madam, in L. A., you learn that the studios wield a lot of power—even over the police."

Jake cleared his throat. "The studios don't obstruct the police, Detective."

"Maybe not, but they do delay and hinder and…" He shrugged, then shook his head. "Hollywood corrupts."

Mercy had been staring at Cotton intently. "Excuse me, Detective, but you look like you might have been an actor. Once?"

The comment caught him off guard, it seemed—as it did me, I have to admit—for he flipped open his notebook and reached for a pen, as though he'd just had a brainstorm that could solve this murder.

"Just out of college, UCLA, a few attempts. Bit parts." His voice got louder: "And then I realized how—how corrupt it all was."

So, I reasoned, that might explain some of the bitterness, the contempt for Hollywood. One more failed actor. That, and the fact that he probably faced stonewalling often—the long arm of MGM, 20th Century Fox, Warner Bros. Studio. Maybe even Disney. Mickey Mouse as dissembler, Minnie as stonewaller. I stared at his face. The thin manicured moustache, the slicked-back hair, shiny with cream, even the cut of his sports jacket. That was it, I realized. He'd patterned himself on some matinee idol of another decade. John Gilbert, maybe, or John Garfield. Some mannered, stylish notion of metropolitan lover. Or, maybe, an early Clark Gable. Was everyone in L.A. a one-time (or future) bit player? Was that the coin of the kingdom here—actors as loose change? And most of them unhappy. I thought of Tommy Dwyer and Lydia Plummer and even the now-dead Carisa Krausse.

Detective Cotton, noting the hour and my visible fatigue—I sat slumped at the super's kitchen table, my hand around a cup of coffee he'd provided—let us go, but said he'd get statements from both of us later on. "But I have nothing to say," Mercy said.

"Then say that." He turned away.

I kept silent. After all, I'd been left in the apartment while Mercy bounded down the stairs to call the police (and, lamentably, Jake). I'd gingerly stepped into the room, touching nothing, but observing, making an inventory. A glance at the dead woman's face. The familiar grotesquerie of features, a face contorted with surprise and astonishment. But, curiously, the eyes thankfully shut. The pool of blackened blood, swirling away from her twisted head, seeping into ancient floorboards. Short shrift there—instead, I surveyed the room: a tiny apartment, broken down, a cracked window repaired with brown tape, a ceiling molding pulling away from the wall, a cabinet door with loosened hinges. But Carisa had tried to make the place decent, with cheap draperies over the windows, small Montgomery Ward prints of flowers and star-lit fields and New England covered bridges, and a threadbare oriental carpet, ragged at the edges. But she was clearly a packrat, a woman who didn't discard anything, stacks of *L.A. Times*, a neat pile, but ready to topple; movie magazines, too many, *Modern Screen, Movie World, Hollywood Secrets, TV Radio Mirror*, and *Photoplay*, piled everywhere, all looking pristine, unread. Orderly piles, though, the edges evened, if abandoned. But glancing into the small alcove that served as a kitchen, I saw a tiny table with one plate, one fork, one knife, an old cloth napkin, a bottle of opened wine, red. But there was no glass. I looked into the sink. Nothing. Did the woman drink out of the bottle?

Moving back toward the door, I stepped around the statue I'd seen when I first walked in. Lying perhaps four feet from the body was a chunky, weathered-green, stained object, heavy looking but cheap, maybe a foot high, lying face up. A grotesque woman, with an exaggerated protruding stomach. A fertility goddess? What? Mexican or Aztec or Indian? Something from a tourist stand at a desert reservation in Arizona or New Mexico?

Against a back wall there was a small desk with two drawers pulled out, the only sign of disturbance in her apartment—save, of course, the very obvious body. The contents were strewn onto the desktop—piles of letters, shifted through. A letter from someone in San Francisco. I dared not touch them, tempted as I was. But someone had obviously rifled through the pile, looking for something. Some letter? Someone who knew that Carisa Krausse saved everything. And that person wanted something back. One of the drawers was empty, and I surmised that it had contained the scattered letters. I stood there, a little shaky, and stared from the rotund statue to the scattered letters on the wobbly desk. And then, looking into the other open drawer, I spotted what looked like a syringe, resting on a small cloth bag. Drugs? Medicine? That, the murderer had left. Or left behind?

Then I had heard noise in the hallway, and backed myself toward the entrance. And suddenly the music from the radio, a quick-paced jingle, upbeat and advertising Pepsi-Cola, was buried under the swell of rising voices in the stairwell.

When I arrived at the Burbank studios just before noon, dropped by my driver at the *Giant* soundstage—I'd violated my long-standing rule of rising promptly at seven, choosing instead to lie, wide awake, in bed until after nine—I expected frenzy, if not hysteria. A foolish assumption, that. Wandering around, strolling toward dressing rooms, I found calm and silence, an eerie pall covering the conversations and movements. I learned shooting had been suspended for that day, over Stevens' protests. So the vast expanse of Jett Rink's ballroom looked abandoned, but I noticed production teams still fine-tuning the large banquet hall, preparatory to Jett-Jimmy's final disastrous moment, the drunken collapse of the mighty wildcatter. In the cavernous room, an electrician cursed loudly, and his voice echoed off the high ceiling.

Unable to locate Tansi who was, I learned, sequestered with Jack Warner and Jake Geyser, I knocked on Mercy's dressing room door, and was pleased that she was there. She was in a foul mood. "Shooting suspended, but Stevens demands we sit here, in costume. Just sitting. Liz Taylor is sleeping in her dressing room. I heard her yelling at someone. Rock Hudson is God-knows-where. Luckily I have no lines scheduled—I died in Marfa, in more ways than one." She stood up. "I'm sorry, Edna. Come in. I've been itching to yell like a banshee since nine this morning."

"I thought there'd be a flurry of reporters all over the lot today."

Mercy pulled out a chair for me. "God, no. Reporters are only allowed on set at the discretion of Stevens—and Warner. But, Edna, word has come down that the murder is not—repeat, not—to be spoken of. Of course, when I arrived, everyone was buzzing. Lots of folks knew Carisa, and I gather there was a short piece in the press this morning. The Warner PR machinery is already in place: a short squib stating the Carisa Krausse, an actress, was found dead in her apartment last night, apparently a homicide. No mention of her connection to *Giant*. No mention of Warner Bros. Studio. One more *ingénue* going the way of all flesh, fading into the Hollywood Sunset and Vine."

"You're bitter, Mercy."

"I suppose I am." Mercy reached for her coffee. "I knew Carisa. You know, I thought her odd, maybe genuinely crazy, and I came to dislike her. No, I came to a point I thought it best *not* to be with her."

I nodded. "Surely Cotton will do his job?"

"As much as he can, Edna. You don't understand the power of men like Jack Warner. The folks at MGM. At 20th Century. All of them. All branches of government in California are contained in *them*. No, Detective Cotton will investigate, and will probably solve it, but it's going to be done with a low profile."

I rubbed my weary eyes. Last night's sleeplessness still covered me.

Yes, I understand that movies are big business; the bottom line is cold cash, often ugly cash, piles of green moolah. I play at that game myself, having negotiated with musty publishers like the old-time Doubleday crew, often with tart tongue and steely eye. I like to win. I understand money. But I also understand the ethics that, I hope, underlie my reason for living: the life of the decent, socially conscious middle-class Jew that I emphatically am, especially in the post-Nazi era, in the lame-brain Eisenhower malaise that breeds a Joe McCarthy and his nefarious ilk. "I'll speak to Warner."

Mercy chortled. "Edna, Edna."

"I mean it."

"Let me be cynical a moment here. When you're around, they're kowtowing and salaaming and treating you like the High Priestess of God-Almighty Fiction, but Warner is a hard-nosed skinflint with a propensity to believing that folks are born evil."

Sighing, resigned, "So what will happen?"

"First off, you may have noticed the chilly temperature of the soundstage. This morning Tansi assembled the troops, and read—with shaky voice, I might add, unhappy to be designated lackey—a terse memo from Jake Geyser. Why he couldn't do it I don't know, except that it came off as mean-spirited and petty. Leave *that* tone to a woman, right? So Tansi reads the note that we should all cooperate with the police, in particular Detective Xavier Cotton from the Central Detective Bureau, who will be roaming the hallways, questioning folks about Carisa. But there was to be no gossiping at the water cooler and no idle chatting to reporters. Carisa's death was 'unfortunate'—that's the word he used—but it has nothing to do with 'the production of *Giant* or the inner workings of Warner Bros. Studios.' Signed, 'The office of Jack Warner.' Jake couldn't even affix his own weaselly name to it, though I saw him hand it to Tansi, coach her when she sputtered, and even push her out in front of the troops. She wasn't happy."

"So Cotton is around?"

"He's somewhere. I talked to him for a bit, then gave one of his men a statement, and they'll be gunning for you shortly. He's not happy because he knows his hands are tied here, and he can wander the halls all he wants, with his All Access badge on, but it doesn't mean a thing because Jack Warner and the Chief of Police—Jack's golf and charity-function crony, by the way—are his bosses. If he stumbles on a murderer, all well and good, so long as it's low key. Warner Bros. will distance themselves from it." Mercy waved her hand in the air. "Shall we go for fresh coffee? This cup is cold."

"We're avoiding something." I stared into her face.

"He didn't show up," Mercy answered, quietly. "He was supposed to be here and he's not. There's no answer at his place."

"So what's the scuttlebutt?" I asked, nervous. I hadn't stopped thinking about Jimmy since last night—the moment of discovery, my hours awake in bed, and even this morning, having coffee in my room.

"We're not supposed to talk, but here's what everyone is whispering about. Cotton learned that Carisa sent letters to Warner and Jimmy, and had copies in hand when he spoke to me. Warner may logjam the investigation, but he's not a fool. It would get out soon enough. The studio can't seem to be hiding anything. But Cotton is aware of the slippery ground he's on. Jimmy's name is all over this deed, obviously. And so Cotton reads that Carisa has gossip to reveal to *Confidential*, that she's carrying his baby, she wants money and marriage and whatever else she spewed in those insane letters."

"So Jimmy is suspect number one?"

"Our rebel as killer."

"Not good." I shook my head slowly.

Mercy smiled. "You do love the understatement."

"Jimmy ran out of the party early, around six or so." I paused. "Are the police looking for Jimmy?"

"Cotton has been asking, 'Is he here yet? Let me know the minute he shows up.' He's obviously decided Jimmy is the easy answer, so far as a designated murderer is concerned. Though 'easy' is the wrong word here. If Jimmy is the killer, it means trouble for everyone."

"For the studio."

"Everyone. It's sort of hard to release an epic film when the star is being electrocuted at San Quentin."

I felt a chill. My heart beat wildly. "My God, Mercy, no."

"I really don't believe Jimmy killed Carisa, Edna, but what do I know? Even accusation of murder can get the censors in an uproar. My God, remember the uproar two years back when Columbia used the word 'virgin' in *The Moon is Blue?* The Catholic Legion of Decency started speaking in tongues. Walter Winchell turned purple."

"I want to talk to Jimmy," I said.

"Don't we all."

Later Tansi joined us in the commissary, and I asked how she was. "I will never do Jack Geyser's dirty work again," she sputtered. "He *sprang* that on me."

Mercy patted her wrist. "He's a damn coward."

Her hands shook. "It's bad enough I have to be called late at night, told to prepare the dumb press release, then say—no comment, no comment, no comment. I couldn't sleep all night. And Jake pushing me out like that."

"Have you seen Cotton around?" I asked Tansi, interrupting.

"He's blowing hot and cold, frustrated. He's asked me the same questions ten times. What did I think of Carisa? I told him I scarcely knew her. In Marfa I had to deal with her when she was fired—get her out of there. Cotton says to me, 'Was she angry?' I said yes, she seemed angry all the time. I don't remember much about her. Then I hear him asking the same questions of people in lighting and in sound. They stare at him as though he's speaking another language. He shows her picture. They nod. Yes, she was around. No, no, they didn't know her. It's maddening."

"It's police work. Stabs in the dark, looking for a light."

"Well, I have to contend with the slow simmer of Warner and the hiccoughing panic of Jake."

"Scylla and Charybdis," I said.

Tansi smiled. "More like Ma and Pa Kettle, fighting over a chicken bone." But she leaned in. "But he's already asking for Jimmy, who, by the way, I can tell he doesn't like, not even having *met* him."

"Why?"

"He referred to Jimmy and Marlon Brando as the dirt-under-the-fingernails school of acting."

"Who else did he ask about?" I wanted to know.

Tansi whispered. "He asked me if knew Max Kohl." She turned to Mercy. "Do you know a Max Kohl?"

"No." Puzzled. "He didn't ask *me* that. It must be a name he picked up after my conversation with him."

"Let me guess," I said. "A bit player."

Tansi looked confused. "No, I don't think he's ever worked for us. At least I've never seen him on the Warner list. But he was—or is—part of Jimmy's world, I gather. Cotton talked to me right after he talked to Lydia. She cornered me in the hall, panicking, and told me about her talk with Cotton. She mentioned Max to him—that he dated Carisa, disappeared, came back. She says his name just came out because she was nervous. Lydia says he's been seeing *her*, since Jimmy left her. He calls her. She says he scares her."

"What in the world does that mean?" I asked.

"I don't know." She breathed in. "After she was fired, Carisa retreated into that apartment, and Max was seen around town with her. He'd met Lydia through her. But Max had a fight with Jimmy, Lydia said."

"Over what?"

"Nonsense, Lydia said. I don't know." She sighed, weary. "I don't know him. He was Jimmy's motorcycle buddy, I guess. You know, Jimmy has that other life. Late night, riding his bike at breakneck speed into the Hollywood Hills. I saw him tear past, one night, hands in the air, whooping it up. He was with some other guys."

"Is he a suspect, this Max Kohl?"

"Cotton wants to talk to him. Supposedly, he'd been staying with Carisa, but moved out last week. Lydia learned that from Carisa, who was scared of him, too. Lydia told me that once she told Cotton about Max Kohl, she couldn't stop talking. And now she feels guilty. Like she got him in trouble. She's afraid of him."

I nodded. "Lord, a new character in Jimmy's world."

Tansi continued, "When Cotton asked Lydia where to locate Max, she said to ask Jimmy."

"Why?"

"Well, she said she doesn't know where he lives. He showed up one night at her place with Jimmy and then alone. He's stopped in, and they've gone out. He sits in the lobby of her building until she comes down. She's afraid to say no to him. Jimmy would know where he lives. They're buddies." She paused. "Or *were* buddies. I don't know. I don't think Lydia is telling the whole truth. I know she doesn't want Jimmy to know she's seeing Max, so she's lying. She's hoping Jimmy will come back to her. But Lydia just babbles on and on. She said Max was a friend of Jimmy, and then said they had a fight and now hate each other. She told me she'd stopped talking to Carisa, and then said she just spoke to her days ago. I guess she just rambled on to Cotton."

I was impatient. "This is madness. Lydia makes no sense. What does this all mean?"

Tansi shrugged. "Well, Lydia told me she broke down, weeping. Cotton left her alone, but said he'd talk to her later."

I turned to Mercy. "This Max Kohl intrigues me."

Tansi started rustling papers. "I think Lydia's hysteria got Cotton to thinking there's a lot more to this story than he first thought. She couldn't keep her stories straight." She looked at her watch. "I have to get back. Jake is a man possessed today. I heard him tell Warner that Jimmy has been nothing but trouble."

"All geniuses are," I said. "Even those who murder."

Tansi rushed her words. "Oh, Edna, you certainly can't believe Jimmy would hurt anyone?"

"That remains to be seen," I said. "I like the boy, but last night I saw a dead woman lying in a pool of blood."

Tansi gulped. "Oh, God, Edna. Please! I told you not to go there. That neighborhood. Nobody goes *there*."

"It's not the neighborhood that killed her, Tansi."

Tansi whispered, "Yes, you two go there, and you find *bodies*."

I smiled. "Only one, Tansi."

"One is too many."

Mercy looked at Tansi, who looked exhausted. "Granted," Mercy said. "But it wasn't the neighborhood that killed her."

"Edna, my mother would *kill* me if you got *hurt* during my watch."

I stood. "I'm a big girl, Tansi. Have been for many decades, with no complaints. World wars, two of them, haven't done me in. I doubt this will. I don't need attending."

"I didn't mean…"

I softened. "I know what you mean, and, all right, I understand. And thank you, dear. But a woman who can't take care of herself, at any age, is a fool. Trouble for a woman should be, well, temporary."

Mercy was smiling, but Tansi looked offended. Mercy stood. "All our nerves are frayed. Tonight, eight o'clock, my apartment, no refusals from either of you. Wine and a tuna casserole and a loaf of homemade bread. And peach cobbler, from scratch. No refusals. The three of us, relaxing."

Tansi started to beg off, so I asked her, "Can you give me a lift, Tansi? I don't want to ask for the studio car. I'd find Jake in the back seat dictating a memo to me about my errant behavior last night."

Tansi smiled. "Of course."

◇◇◇

Mercy's efficiency scarcely held room for the three of us, much less the bowls of food she spread out. We all ate too much, and I announced that I never ate tuna casserole because it reminded me of church potluck dinners back in Appleton, Wisconsin, but this—this was manna from the gods. "It's because I include almond slivers," Mercy said, "and bits of water chestnut I buy in Chinatown. But I really think it's the wine talking." And the peach cobbler: robust, oversized chunks of deep velvet fruit, banked under waves of thick heavy cream, slathered over a brown-tinged crust of brilliant pastry. "This isn't cobbler," I announced. "It's sin."

On the hi-fi, Mercy played the same record over and over: Frank Sinatra. *Music for Young Lovers.* "Jimmy gave it to me. He loves it."

I noted the look on Tansi's face: surprise, and a little hurt. Tansi was getting tipsy, and at one point asked, "Haven't we heard this song before?" Mercy and I laughed hysterically. We'd heard it a half dozen times.

"More wine, Tansi?" Mercy asked.

A knock on the door. We all jumped, with me spilling wine on my sleeve. Red wine, no less. So much for this new blouse, overpriced at Saks to begin with. Mercy switched off the hi-fi.

When she opened the door, a sheepish Jimmy Dean stood there, head cocked to his chest. "I heard the laughter."

"Jimmy, where have you been?" Mercy said. "Everyone's been looking for you."

"I know, I know. This Cotton guy questioned me at my apartment a few hours ago. Practically called me a murderer to my face. Quoted the letters Carisa wrote and wagged his finger at me." He strode into the room, dropped himself into a chair. "I thought you'd be alone, Madama."

"I'm allowed to have guests."

Jimmy looked at me. "At least they're friendly faces."

I spoke up. "Don't count on it. Jimmy, tell me, what do you know about this?"

He'd been drinking; not much, perhaps, but enough to make his eyes glassy. "Nothing. I rushed over to see her right after I left the stupid cocktail party. Okay, I admit that. Just drove there. But she wouldn't let me in, I swear. We argued. I shouldn't have gone there. But after that new letter…She said she'd see me burn in hell. Slammed the door. So I left."

"How long were you there?" I asked.

"Minutes."

"You tell this to Cotton?"

"Yeah."

"What did he say?"

"He just looked at me like I was a murderer."

"What time were you there?"

"I dunno. Just after six or so. Later. Cotton asked me that."

"And you left—when?"

"I dunno. I'd say minutes later."

"You see anyone?"

"No."

I looked at Mercy. "We were there around eight-thirty. And Carisa was dead."

"I didn't do it."

Tansi, comforting him, "You're not a murderer, Jimmy."

Jimmy seemed just to notice her. "I just assume everyone *knows* that."

"Well, where were you today?" Mercy asked.

"I had to get away."

"You always have to get away," I said. He looked at me.

"Well, I rode my bike into the hills. I couldn't stand to be around people."

"How did you hear about Carisa?" I asked.

"Lydia called me."

"When?"

"This morning. Early. From the studio, I guess. She was hysterical. Cotton told me she blabbed about Max Kohl. I don't know what that's about."

"Who is this Kohl?" I asked.

"A biker guy. We rode together. He stayed with Carisa. Fooled with her. Then he went after Lydia. Not a nice guy."

"And you are?" I asked.

He grinned. "Not all the time." A pause. "I didn't do it, Miss Edna. Do you believe me?"

"I'd like to."

Jimmy turned to Mercy. "Madama, you believe me, no?"

Mercy nodded, kindly.

"Tansi?"

"I believe you." She emphatically nodded her head.

"Miss Edna?"

"Prove to me that you're innocent."

He laughed. "Somehow I knew you'd say that. So how do I do that?"

"By telling the truth, every bit of it."

"I've told you…" He hesitated. "I didn't want Carisa to die. She was making my life hell, but I didn't want her to die."

"So who do you think did it?"

He shrugged his shoulders. "That neighborhood? A robber, maybe. I don't know. She hung out with some bad types lately. Folks on drugs." Another pause. "Help me, then, Miss Edna. You and Madama and Tansi. Help me."

"Jimmy, I don't think the police want our help."

"The police want to railroad me. I could see it in that Cotton's eyes."

We talked more, in circles, the hour getting late, and there seemed nothing left to say. But he lingered, stretched out on the floor, eyes half closed. Then, looking like he was ready to leave, he stood, walked around the room, inches from each of us, almost slow motion. He poured himself a glass of wine and quietly slipped back onto the floor, at the edge of the love seat where Tansi and I sat. He sat there, Buddha-like, swaying back and forth.

"I've never been good solving problems, you know." He half smiled. "Just creating them. Obviously. You know, I can't get away from my mother," he began. I looked at Mercy, who was shaking her head. "When I was nine," Jimmy continued, "she died out here in California. She was my only friend, really, not my father, never my father, and she wanted me to dance, to sing, to talk out loud to people. To be something. She told me I was special—one of a kind. Imagine a mother saying that to a little boy. Not famous or good or rich. But *special*. I felt a glow all over me, like my mother had blessed me. Like I was touched on the head by a hand made of gold. And then she died on me, just left me like that. That cancer eating her away until I had nothing left to hold onto, without a road map. What did she expect, me to do it all by myself? And my father, numbed into silence, sent me back on that long train ride to Fairmount, alone on the Silver Challenger Express, just me. Alone. An orphan now. Me and my mother's coffin. At each station I jumped off and ran up the platform to see that the coffin was still there—to make sure she was safe. I had to protect her, get her home. Me in my little wrinkled suit, running up and down the platform, out of breath, and then back to my seat. Over and over, till I got home. And then I sat there at the depot, me and the coffin, waiting. I was nine years old. Nine. With a cardboard suitcase and a dead mother."

"Jimmy," Mercy whispered.

I sucked in my breath. Was this performance? Or was this real, this bittersweet, sentimental monologue? Rehearsed, said so often, the mother story, Mercy had told me about. Real or not, this moment stopped me, brought me to tears. Either way, I was captivated.

Long silence now. Three women stared down at him, waiting.

Jimmy withdrew a recorder from his back pocket, waved it at us with a sheepish grin, and then, as we watched, began to play a reedy, high-pitched ballad: Sweet Molly Malone. *She wheels her wheelbarrow through streets wide and narrow, crying cockles and mussels alive alive-o!* Plaintive, haunting, utterly perfect. The notes hung in the air, sweet and thin, floated, fell back upon him. Eyes closed, head inclined, he breathed into the instrument, and the song was exact, smooth and seamless. But near the end, inhaling, he missed a note, and the sour note broke the melodic flow. He paused, shook his head angrily, started over. Again the same wrong note. Quietly, he dropped the recorder into his lap, opened his eyes, and started to sob, his body rolling back and forth, his face wet with tears.

Chapter Eight

At the Smoke House the next morning, just outside the studio gates, Mercy and I barely spoke. Jimmy's late-night appearance and the melodramatic air he played on the recorder, and the awful, sloppy breakdown, lingered about us like a fog you couldn't escape. Mercy looked tired. Jimmy, I learned, had stayed at the apartment long after Tansi drove me to the Ambassador. I stared into Mercy's face. I sensed what she was thinking. Jimmy and the dead Carisa. Jimmy and the movie. Jimmy and the bone-marrow-deep sadness. Jimmy and the mother who left him. Jimmy and the unexpected late-night knock on the door. Jimmy, Jimmy, Jimmy. God, how quickly and emphatically that man-boy managed to insinuate himself into all our lives.

"Well," I began, "I gave my statement to Detective Cotton earlier, and he kept saying: Is that it? I finally told him he was getting on my nerves, and he pouted like a brat. What's the requisite for becoming detective in L.A.—imbecility? When I say I've said my say, I assume others will believe me."

Mercy smiled. "Others don't know you, Edna."

"They do now. Or, at least, one quivering soul does. Cotton likes to project a hard edge, a role he's doubtless learned from Edward G. Robinson pictures. Cell block melodramas. Beneath it all, he's a mediocre actor playing a part. It's just that he can't remember the lines."

"That's because he has none. He's an extra." Mercy sounded weary.

We drifted into silence. Gazing out the window at the sunny landscape, I asked when it was going to rain, and Mercy said, "Next year, maybe."

I pointed outside. "Hollywood manufactures everything else. Can't they fabricate rain to break the monotony of endless, clear, and boring days?"

"I don't think you should move here, Edna."

"There'd have to be some climate changes first. I'd have to speak with someone."

We lingered, dawdled, drank more coffee. A lunch crowd was filing in, and I noticed Sal Mineo walking in with another young man. Mercy followed my gaze. "A little boy, no?" she remarked.

"Another Jimmy acolyte, that boy with Sal?"

Mercy flicked her head toward Mineo's friend. "That's Josh MacDowell. He was Jimmy's drinking buddy, but one of the souls discarded along the way."

"Why?"

"I don't know."

"Well, we'll have to find out, won't we?" I insisted. "Do you know him?"

"To nod to. He works in wardrobe. He's not an actor. He knew Carisa, too. I remember she mentioned him to me. Or maybe Jimmy told me something. I can't remember."

The two men were walking by, but I raised my voice: "Hello." Said too loudly, I realized too late, some heads turning. An old lady requesting the popular Mineo's autograph?

Sal stopped. "Miss Ferber," he greeted me. Respectful, nodding; the dutiful polite boy. Nice New York boy, transplanted west. But he seemed ready to keep walking.

Mercy, following my glance, took over. "Hello, Josh."

The young man looked at her, without recognition. Sal glanced at her, then at Josh.

"I was Carisa's friend," Mercy continued. And the young man went ashen, his shoulders sagging. "I remember she mentioned you."

I looked at him. Nearly six feet tall, perhaps, but pencil-thin, raw-limbed, with prominent Adam's apple, high cheekbones and deep-set eye sockets, a cadaver-like face, fairly macabre, with an oversized jutting Roman nose. So fair of skin, parchment-toned, he easily reddened. He mumbled something back, but I couldn't catch the words.

"What?" From Mercy.

He cleared his throat. "I still cannot believe it. When Sal called me…" He looked at Sal who seemed to be picking his nose, absent-mindedly, unhappy to be stopped there.

He reminded me of someone, this loping, giraffe-like young man, with the ladder neck and the exaggerated parts. When he turned to look behind him—for no reason that I discerned—I suddenly thought: Aubrey Beardsley, some *fin de siècle* aesthete. I'd known so many in another world: Paris, Berlin, Vienna, before the war. Not *that* war but the first one, the big one, with the Kaiser. That war.

"Would you like to join us?" I asked.

Sal rushed his words: "No, thank you."

But Josh was already sinking into a chair, his body seeming to unbuckle itself, the joints giving way. Something, indeed, to watch. Sort of like an unglued Houdini.

"I'm Edna Ferber." I held out my hand. He shook it.

"I know. I'm pleased to meet you. I once acted in a high school production of *Dinner at Eight*." He smiled thinly. "A walk on."

"A bit player?"

"Sort of."

"I'm not surprised." He narrowed his eyes, not catching my meaning, but I hadn't intended that he do so.

"You're part of Jimmy Dean's circle?" I asked.

A long pause, Josh frowning. "I didn't know he had a circle. I just know him from, you know, around. I met him when he did some television—the Kraft Playhouse. I was working wardrobe. We'd go out to the clubs. A bunch of us."

"How did you all know Carisa Krausse?"

He cleared his throat, looked at Sal, who was shuffling from one foot to the other but finally sat down. "Well, strangely, I introduced *her* to Jimmy. You see, I went to high school in San Francisco with Carisa. She was Jessica in those days. We drifted down to Hollywood right after high school. She wanted to be in the movies. I just wanted to escape my family. She was escaping into escape." He must have thought his own words clever because he stopped, widened his eyes, and grinned. But then, probably remembering the context, he sobered. "We were best friends for a long time."

"Were you still friends?"

"No. I mean, I stopped in now and then. We'd lived together for a while, but not in that hell hole she moved to a few months back. We sort of drifted apart. But she'd be in for a fitting, and I was in wardrobe and we'd catch up on things."

"So you introduced her to Jimmy?" I said.

"Yes, I told you that," He looked peeved. "I mean, that probably wasn't the best thing I could have done." He looked at his nails, and I noted they were bitten to the quick: a thin line of dried blood on each fingertip.

"Why not?"

"Well, it's hard to talk about. I mean, she's dead and all. I mean, well, Carisa started getting—odd. Frantic, sort of. Jobs not coming her way. No rent money. She was always a little eccentric. You know, saying outlandish things. But then I think she couldn't help herself. Like madness came into her. And she met some bad apples. Drugs and all. That's when I kept away."

"What kind of drugs?"

He looked at Sal. "I don't know much about drugs. Just what people tell me. Like heroin, I guess. I'm not saying for *sure* she did it, but it was *around* the apartment. I saw it. She said it was nothing. It scared me. One night, I bumped into her and Lydia, when they were still talking, and then Jimmy came along. She liked him. He liked her. Sort of."

"Sort of?"

Josh waited a while before he spoke. When he did, his voice was hard. "Miss Ferber, Jimmy likes to play people. Experiment. See what they're about. Push people. He'll do things just to get people to, you know, go to the edge. He fools with their lives. If they fall apart, that can't be helped." The more he spoke the more bitter he sounded.

Mercy said, "That sounds cruel."

"Well, he's a bastard."

"To you?" I asked.

"Yeah, for one."

Sal was edgy. "Josh, this is Jimmy we're talking about."

Josh sneered. "Sal moons over Jimmy. Doesn't know he's in *love* with him." He spat out the word. Sal frowned, looked around, his face becoming flushed, and he seemed ready to bolt. But Josh continued, "I'd seen Jimmy a few times, with his friends. Even at one or two parties. We drank together in bars. But then he started to avoid me. Was rude to me."

"Why?"

Josh groaned. "You wanna know? I'll tell you. I'm too girlish, he said. He actually said that. He's uncomfortable around guys like me." Josh bit his lip. "It's not my being a male that bothers him. It's the kind of male I am."

"I'm not following this," I said, exasperated.

"Jimmy likes more masculine men."

"What are you saying?"

Nasty, his voice purposely loud, "I already told you Jimmy likes to experiment."

Sal jumped up, twisted around. "Josh, please." He looked down at Josh. "I'm sorry." He backed up. "Come on, Josh." Pleading.

Josh seemed hesitant. "You see, I don't *like* Jimmy Dean. *He* does." He pointed to Sal. "I've seen the beast in him, so I regretted that he got involved with Carisa, because I still liked her."

Bluntly, I probed, as Josh stood, "Do you think Jimmy killed her?"

"It wouldn't surprise me."

"That's quite an accusation."

"Well," Josh said, "he once beat her up so bad she hid away for days, black and blue."

I sat up. "Jimmy?" I turned to Mercy. "Do you think that's possible?"

Mercy didn't look surprised. Quietly, "He told me he hit Pier Angeli so hard she passed out."

I slumped back into the seat. "Mercy, what?" Fury, like a wind through me; a knife. "God, no."

"It's what he told me, Edna. He told me he wasn't proud of his temper."

"That's barbaric." I drummed a finger on the table. "Barbaric."

Josh, standing, "No, Miss Ferber, that's James Dean."

When Josh and Sal left, an annoyed Sal muttering into Josh's side and Josh looking oddly triumphant, I spotted Tommy Dwyer sitting by himself at a table, his back to me. I wondered when he'd arrived, and wondered, too, if he'd overheard the conversation with Josh. He seemed *purposely* turned away. I nudged Mercy, who shook her head. "Hard to miss that red jacket and manicured pompadour." As we watched, Tommy scribbled onto a pad, bent over the page intently. Now and then he looked up, drank from a cup, and then resumed writing. "His memoirs?" quipped Mercy.

I mumbled. "My Life as a Shadow Puppet."

While we watched, Tommy's girlfriend Polly walked in, glanced around, spotted him, and rushed over. She looked angry, and he tapped the pad. Don't disturb me, his gesture said. But Polly spotted Mercy and me and, mumbling in his ear, they both turned. Caught watching them, we waved, self-consciously. I motioned them over. Join us, I mouthed. They didn't move. I waved some more. Reluctantly, the couple walked over.

Tommy sat, Polly didn't. The tall redhead was wearing a crimson-colored gingham smock that accented her hair, very Victorian maiden. "Polly, sit," I said. She didn't budge.

"I saw you two when I came in, but I'm working," Tommy said.

"Writing?"

"My screenplay."

Oh Lord, I thought. The dumbbell as diarist. Alphabet soup for the grammar school crowd. Rebel without a dependent clause. I dared *not* ask about it. He might tell me, and I'd have to take to my bed.

"We're concerned about Jimmy," Mercy started.

"Why?" Polly asked.

That remark struck me as unusual. "Well, because of Carisa's death."

"We don't know anything about *that*," Polly said, harshly. Reluctantly, she slipped into a seat.

"You know about the letters she wrote."

Tommy nodded. "Of course. Everybody does."

Polly's voice heavy with anger. "Jimmy was foolish, going out with that nut case."

"You knew her?"

Sarcastic: "We all knew her. No one liked her. Jimmy has his fling, he always has to have his fling, and the rest of us have to dance around the story."

"What does that mean, Polly?"

"I mean, Jimmy *knew* she was crazy. He just liked to see how crazy she was."

Tommy interrupted. "Polly, no. Jimmy liked her. He told me he did."

"She is a pretty girl who made herself available to men. Any man. Of course, he liked her. *You* said she was pretty."

"She was Jimmy's girlfriend." Tommy looked at her. Shut up, his look told her.

"Not girlfriend, Tommy. Quickie partner, tryst, tumble in bed. I'm *your* girlfriend. You're my boyfriend. There's a difference."

"You didn't like her?" I stared into her slender face.

"She ignored me. She saw me as a rival. Not for men, but for *parts*. I'm young, good looking, and ambitious."

"Do you think Jimmy killed her?" I asked Polly.

Tommy answered quickly, nervously. "No, never. Not Jimmy. He's…"

Polly interrupted, matter-of-fact. "Anything is possible, but I'd say no."

"Why not?"

"Jimmy isn't into drugs. One of *those* friends did her in. Everyone is saying that. I know about the letters, but that was stupid stuff. Her drug friends—that's where to look. Miss Ferber, Jimmy's a coward at heart. Talk to Lydia, Jimmy's pre-Ursula Andress, post-Pier Angeli fling. Talk to her when she's not stoned on the ladies room floor. Ask her what she thinks. If anyone knows that crowd, it's Lydia." She sat back.

"Do you think Lydia's connected to the murder?"

Polly opened her mouth to speak, stopped. Then, slowly, "I can't say. I don't like either woman."

Tommy kept looking at her, shaking his head. "Christ, Polly."

I baited her. "It's considered bad taste to speak ill of the dead."

Polly made a fake laugh. "I've never been accused of being society's good girl. Speak ill of the dead? I didn't *like* her. I don't like most people."

Tommy, unhappy, "You're giving Miss Ferber the wrong impression."

"I don't really care, Tommy."

Tommy leaned into me. "Is Jimmy in trouble?"

"Maybe."

He shook his head. "Damn."

I stared from one to the other. Polly, the deliberate harridan, angry, moving the conversation her way; Tommy, meek, Jimmy's slavish lapdog. The two like discordant bookends—almost a vaudeville routine. What was going on here?

Suddenly, I heard Tansi's voice from the entrance. "Edna."
She rushed over. "I heard you were here."

"From whom?"

"Sal Mineo. He's not happy."

"He's a sissy," Tommy noted.

Tansi glared at him.

"What is it, Tansi?"

She drew in her breath. "Jimmy told Warner he wants to
issue a statement to the press, professing his innocence, and
Warner blew a gasket. It seems Sheila Graham called and said
she'd heard that Jimmy had dated Carisa. Hedda Hopper and
Louella Parsons were dealt with, but Graham is another story.
But that's not the real news." She stared at me. "Some reporter
found out that Carisa had been picked up for prostitution when
she first came to Hollywood, a couple years back. Cotton told
Jake the police already knew of it. So Warner's not happy. Some
heads will roll." She paused. "And that's not all. Even though
Jimmy is still Cotton's prime subject, he told Warner that when
they went to question Max Kohl, he ran from the cops. Can you
imagine battling the cops?"

"Is he in jail?" From Tommy.

"Do you know Max Kohl?" I asked, surprised.

"Sort of. He rode bikes with Jimmy. In the hills. Jimmy said
he's a tough customer. A bully."

"Jimmy doesn't ride with him anymore?"

"No."

Polly snickered. "One more person Jimmy abandoned."

"Stop it, Polly."

Polly turned to me, speaking in a mocking tone. "Tommy
is afraid his time is coming. Fairmount loyalty only goes so far
in this land of make-believe. Jimmy is a big star now. Three
big pictures now. Interviews in *Look* and *Life*. *Vogue* says he's
'in' now." She faced her boyfriend. "It's only a matter of time,
Tommy. You're history."

"Stop it." A whine.

"You better finish that goddamn screenplay. You can't park cars all your life."

Tommy stood up, tugged on the red jacket. It seemed too tight for his broad chest, and I thought, darkly, that perhaps it was Jimmy's size, not his. A hand-me-down? Jimmy tossing off bit parts, pieces of clothing. Polly stood now, tucked her arm into his.

I touched Tommy's sleeve. "Would you two like to be my guests for dinner tonight? Someplace nice?"

"No." From Polly.

"Yes." From Tommy.

A pause, uncomfortable. The two looked at each other. Tommy looked back at me.

"Indulge an old lady, please." I smiled.

Polly nodded. "All right. I guess." Her tongue licked her upper lip slowly.

"The Brown Derby at eight?" They nodded.

When they were gone, Mercy seemed tickled. "Dinner with those two?"

"Something bothers me. Is that an act or are they for real?"

"Of course it's an act, Edna," Tansi said, smiling. "You're in Hollywood."

Chapter Nine

The phone was ringing but I didn't pick up. I was weary of people. So I bathed, soaking in lilac bath salts, my eyes closed, and then relaxed with a martini and a forbidden cigarette. The phone rang again. "Edna, I've been *calling*." Tansi sucked in her breath. "My mother, by the way, sends her regards, and says you should convince me to return to New York." A harsh laugh. "Fat chance." I started to say something, but Tansi interrupted. "But I have news, Edna." Again the breathing in. I could tell she was smoking a cigarette. "The studio just learned from Detective Cotton that Carisa was pregnant. Pregnant! Can you believe it?"

Jimmy, you're the father of my unborn baby. I'm gonna tell…

I put out my cigarette: a taste of burnt ash in my mouth.

Tansi repeated her story, but I told her I had to go. When I said goodbye, raising my voice, she was still talking.

I dressed slowly for dinner, my mind dwelling on Carisa and her unborn child. What a horrible ending! Sadness gripped me, and I found myself near tears.

I was still in a daze when the studio car dropped me off at the Brown Derby. Within seconds, Polly and Tommy pulled up in their sputtering, noisy car, a tired convertible, the top down, with Polly driving. Reluctantly, the parking valet assumed possession, receiving the keys from Polly with the attitude of someone acquiring a lethal virus. Polly stood there, looking after the sagging car as though losing a friend, a worried look on her face. Curious, this West Coast car culture. Automobiles attached to lives like love notes worn close to the heart. Did Tommy own a car? True, he parked cars for a living. Maybe, sadly, he couldn't afford one. And, indeed, Polly seemed to be the dominant gene in that sociological construction called the modern couple. The car disappeared behind a bed of Bird-of-Paradise that I thought too garish, indeed—especially under the indigo-black sky, with a line of royal palms nearby, accented with spotlights. El Greco, I decided: a tourist postcard.

I wasn't certain why I wanted to be alone with the couple, other than that earlier intuitive and impulsive moment. I expected a wearisome meal in the company of boors. But I was convinced that they had something to tell me, though I had no idea how it related to the murder and my helping Jimmy clear his name. Because that was exactly what I was doing—helping Jimmy. Yes, he'd pleaded for help that awful night at Mercy's; but, later on, as I soaked in my bath, eyes closed, I'd had an epiphany: Jimmy was innocent. Jimmy, the spoiled brat, the caustic boy, the cooing charmer, the brilliant actor. These were the contradictions that sometimes accompanied genius—and, I liked to believe, similarly defined *myself*. Not that observers could spot them in me, maybe labeling me an aging novelist with a tendency to acerbic comment and a short fuse. No, as the bath salts soothed and swirled, I thought, there may be a lot of the unsavory in the lad but not the stuff of murder.

I was pleased to see that Tommy and Polly had altered their costume for the fancy eatery. Tommy wore a simple black turtleneck and creased trousers, and a somewhat rumpled wheat-colored linen jacket, a little too big and a little too thrift shop. Polly's dress was a marked-down Woolworth's rendering of June Allyson—flair and flourish, faded pink roses on a mauve velveteen cloth. Her face bore just a trace of pink lipstick, becoming on her, and in the shrill light of the restaurant marquee her auburn hair looked like burnt cinnamon.

They were nervous, which is what I wanted. Frankly, I was used to people being nervous around me. Inside, they sat stiffly at the table, waiting.

Polly took the offensive. "I don't know why you wanted to take *us* to dinner." She stared directly into my face, challenging. "Especially a place like this." Tommy watched, with drowsy eyes.

"Why not? I'm a writer. Young people fascinate me." It was a brazen lie. Young people, in the main, were callow, dimensionless; at best, they were static characters in a novel I was living. There were, of course, exceptions, and marvelous ones, but I knew, without a bit of doubt, that these two weren't among them.

Tommy half-bowed. "Thank you."

I stared. What had I said that warranted a thank you?

"You know," I began, "when I saw you sitting by yourself in the Smoke House this afternoon, I thought you were Jimmy."

Polly rolled her eyes. "It's the red jacket."

"Well, I like the look." Idly, he fingered the sleeve of his sports jacket. "Other people besides Jimmy wear red jackets, you know." Said emphatically, he sat back, fumbling for a cigarette.

"What you like is having people think you're Jimmy." Polly glared at him. She turned to me. "Since Jimmy started wearing that red jacket, people associate it with him. It's from *Rebel Without a Cause*, and that's not even *released* yet. There were some photos in fan magazines, and that's all it took. Suddenly, his fans are clamoring for the jacket." Polly went on, her voice weary. "It's the way Jimmy dresses off camera. But now and then. Not every *day*," she emphasized. "Tommy rarely takes his off."

Tommy grunted.

Polly stared into my face. "Jimmy has a powerful hold on Tommy." She looked around the room, then glared at the waiter placing menus before them. She waited until the man left. "Tommy can't get away from Jimmy's influence."

"You're talking like I'm not even in the room," Tommy whined.

Polly spat out the words. "It's hard enough living your own life without copying another person's."

"Actually," I volunteered, "I suppose, it's easier to copy someone else's life. Making your own up is hard work."

"You hear that, Tommy? You've taken the easy way out."

Tommy, sheepish, "I just think that Jimmy is—cool."

My Lord, I thought. We begin with such anger, without even a pleasant preamble to dinner. "Has anything happened today?" I asked them. "You both seem out of sorts."

Polly and Tommy looked at each other, and Polly ran her fingers through her hair. "Of course something happened," she admitted. "It's Jimmy who always sets us off."

So I learned that Jimmy had rebuffed Tommy that afternoon, a phone call that left him hurt and angry. Jimmy hung up on him. He'd done that before, but today it particularly rankled. So they'd been arguing about Jimmy since the insult. I was pleased. Keep arguing, please. I sat back and watched.

Tommy defended himself. "Back in Fairmount, he was real together, you know—acting, basketball, motorcycle racing through the farm fields on the cycle he built himself. Everyone *talked* about him. They *knew* him. He liked that. I wasn't following him to New York City, you know. I just wanted to be an actor. But I—we," he pointed to Polly, "bumped into him one night. He remembered me. He hung out with us. We…"

"Tommy became one more sparkle illuminating Jimmy's star."

"So what? He said I got talent."

"Jimmy tells everyone he has talent. Until he changes his mind."

"Jimmy said I'd go right to the top."

"But Jimmy works at it, day and night, despite what he says. You park cars and wait for someone to tap you on the shoulder."

"Jimmy says…"

"Jimmy says. Jimmy says." Polly imitated his crackling, flat voice. She stopped, looked at me, red-faced. "My God, I'm sorry, ma'am. This is the conversation—the fight—we always end up having lately, and this time we're doing it in front of you." She shook her head. "It doesn't matter."

We ordered. Tommy said he wanted red wine. For once, I was indifferent to the menu, quickly ordering the first chicken dish I'd spotted, and recommending sirloin steak, rare, when they hesitated. Tommy's finger, I noted, had been tapping the steak listing, the priciest item on the menu. He gulped the first glass of wine so quickly the wine steward, taken off guard, had to rush to refill the goblet. Polly eyed Tommy. A warning.

"You're in *Giant* and *Rebel*?" I asked Tommy.

"Not so's you'd notice me." He pointed at Polly. "Both of us." She nodded. He paused. "You know I had the lead in the Fairmount High School production of *The Front Page*. Got a review in the local paper. I showed Jimmy a copy."

"Yellowed and worn at the edges," Polly mocked, cruelly.

"How does it feel to be a part of Jimmy's world?" I asked, knowing it was an explosive line.

Polly spoke and was furious. I noted a trace of lipstick on her front tooth, a spot of pink that looked like a stain. "If Jimmy has a 'crowd' we're *not* part of it."

"Not true, Polly," Tommy bristled. "We do hang out with him."

Polly looked at me, breathed in deeply. "We're on the fringe. Tommy's the snapshot in the high-school yearbook Jimmy keeps opening to by accident. He's looking for other people and Tommy's in the way."

Tommy shook his head. "For Christ's sake, Polly."

"So just who are his friends then?" I asked.

For a moment Polly debated her answer. "Jimmy has circles of friends, some overlapping. Some secret and hidden. Some obvious.

"Meaning?"

"The girls he hangs out with. Dates, maybe. Maybe sleeps with."

Tommy spoke up. "You see, Jimmy can't really settle on a girl. I mean, he seemed serious about Pier Angeli, but her mother stopped that. He wanted to marry her."

Polly smirked. "That was just talk, Miss Ferber. Look, Jimmy's career is what drives him—not marriage. I think ninety per cent of that was PR. Jimmy the lover of the Italian beauty. Great photo shoot stuff. On the set, at clubs, dancing at Trocadero, late night snacks at Barney's Beanery."

Tommy glared at her. "He *did* care for her."

"Jimmy doesn't care for people," Polly said. "Women—girls—are fodder."

"What about Carisa's claims?" I interrupted. "The letters?"

That seemed to stop Polly cold. She looked at Tommy. "Carisa is unstable—*was* unstable, I mean. Sorry. Jimmy said she was—in his cruel phrase—available for lonely nights in Texas. Frivolous. Nothing more. Marfa was boring, over a hundred degrees in the shade. At night you could play Canasta and drink Canada Dry with Jane Withers. Whoop-di-do. So he'd go off. And waiting there was Carisa, smiling and opening her shirt."

"And Lydia? How does she fit into all this?"

"You know, just another actress mooning over Jimmy."

Tommy lowered his voice. "Did you know that Lydia and Carisa were roommates once, a year back, before Carisa had to rent in Skid Row. Lydia moved into the Studio Club to get away from Carisa."

Polly smirked. "Each one blames—blamed—the other for drug use, Miss Ferber."

"Lydia is a sad wreck of a girl," Tommy added.

"And yet Jimmy dated her."

Another shrug of the shoulders. "Well, again, dating," Tommy said. "He rebounded from Carisa and Pier. He finds Lydia waiting in the wings. Calling him. They go out, he gets sick of her, he ignores her. She cries. He sees her again. He leaves. He had to. She's so…clutching. Jimmy doesn't want to be around drug users, you know. He likes to be the only person acting weird in a crowd. Lydia is too much trouble. He dumped her."

Polly added, "She had a falling out with Carisa, real nasty, but I know she'd been to Carisa's apartment lately."

"How do you know that?" Tommy asked, surprised.

"She mumbled it to me one night."

"Where was I?"

"Worshipping at Jimmy's shrine."

He made a clicking sound with his tongue.

"You both are not painting a pretty picture of Jimmy and women here."

"Because there's none to be painted," Polly said. "Jimmy doesn't want anyone to say no to him. He's that insecure. And when anyone *likes* him—truly likes him—he then has to make them hate him."

"Do you hate him, Polly?" I asked, bluntly.

A hesitation, a flicker of the eye. "No, I don't hate him. I'm someone he doesn't even see. 'Tommy's dating a telephone pole with a nest on her head.' That's how he once referred to me."

"I told him that wasn't nice," Tommy mumbled.

"Thanks for the support, lover."

But in that brief moment, staring at Polly's face, I saw something: melancholy, sadness, some regret. Polly, sensing my probing eyes on her, became self-conscious, broke a piece of bread into pieces and scattered the pieces on the tablecloth.

"What about his other circles?" I asked, sitting back. Amazing, I thought, how easy it is to let people talk when you just tap into their anger.

"The bikers," Polly said. "Sometimes Jimmy rides the night away with his motorcycle buddies."

"Like Max Kohl, Carisa's friend?"

"I've only seen him a couple times. A scary guy, built like a longshoreman," stammered Tommy.

"But they had a fight," Polly said. "So I heard from Jimmy. I don't know why."

"He's into race cars. Fast bikes. Like Jimmy."

"I heard that Max Kohl has been calling on Lydia."

Polly spoke up. "Yeah, Lydia told me. She's none too happy."

"But you don't know him?"

Both shook their heads.

"I think he did bit parts for a while, but I'm not sure," said Polly.

"Why am I not surprised?" I smiled. "Hollywood is the land of bit parts."

Tommy's eyes narrowed. "You make it seem like a crime."

"Only if it leads to murder," I said.

Tommy and Polly looked at each other, then back at the tablecloth, suddenly fascinated with the fine linen.

For a while they talked of Jimmy's movie-lot friends, the crew members he associated with, carpenters, best boys, and not so good boys and girls, usually drawn into Jimmy's temporary kingdom by a shared interest in race-car driving, late-night revelry, interest in jazz music or oriental philosophy or bullfighting. Like a shuffled deck of cards, Polly noted. "Each time a new hand is on the table, there are different face cards." She smirked. "And older women. Geraldine Fitzgerald. Mercy McCambridge, and his agent—his 'Moms,' he calls them. The only women that *really* matter to him."

"Why?" I asked, seeing myself in that unwelcome covey.

They both shrugged.

While they talked, Tommy drank. Occasionally Polly glanced at him, tried to get his attention, and, once, nodded at the wine bottle. I ordered a second bottle of my nefarious prop for this one-act play. I barely sipped my drink and scarcely touched my food. But Tommy and Polly ravished theirs. At another time I would have been pleased, for I value souls who understand the delights of the kitchen. I would have routinely condemned Tommy, had I not seen the beneficial results of getting him drunk.

When Tommy excused himself to go to the rest room, I was waiting. "Polly, what's your involvement with Jimmy?"

The question caught the young girl by surprise, for she actually jumped, then looked at Tommy's disappearing back.

"What?"

"I thought I saw something in your eyes when we were discussing Jimmy's less-than-decent relationships with women."

She smiled. "I underestimated you." She sighed. "I could lie to you, Miss Ferber, but I'm not going to. Jimmy and I had a moment—*one* moment, that's all. A moment of weakness on my part, but a moment of sheer cruelty on his. Jimmy takes possession of other people's property. I'm Tommy's, and even though Tommy has *nothing*—no hope, no future, not even *me* some day—Jimmy had to be cock in the hen coop."

"So," I sympathized, "a moment. But you still seem to have a lot of emotion."

"What?" She whispered the word.

"It was more than a moment for you, Polly." The declarative sentence, I thought, more powerful than the interrogative.

Polly started to say something, but then, gulping, started to sob. "I thought I did it for revenge," she mumbled. "You know, Tommy does whatever Jimmy does. Don't get me wrong. I *care* for Tommy. I do. But something was said, an overheard remark, that led me to suspect that Tommy had a…a moment with Carisa Krausse."

"Carisa!"

"She was Jimmy's in Marfa. But Tommy has to have what Jimmy has. A rumor I never mentioned to Tommy. Carisa likes to sleep around with any…" She paused. "I'm not being very nice." She dabbed her moist cheeks. "It's probably something I just imagined."

"But you thought you'd get back at her," I said, focusing.

She ran her tongue over her upper lip. "I'm lying a little. You see, I've always had a sort of crush on Jimmy. Of course, you can't tell him. I just can't shake it. You see, when we first got here, I wanted Tommy to be Jimmy—ambitious, focused, and handsome."

I smiled. "And since that moment with Jimmy, nothing."

"I'm back to being wallpaper."

"Is it possible Carisa's baby was Tommy's?"

Polly blanched. "Oh, my God!"

"And Tommy never…" I stopped. Tommy staggered back to the table. Polly, nervous, started munching on a roll, her tear-strained face turned away.

"Talking about me?" he asked, slurring his words.

"Yes," I confessed. "I've gathered that Jimmy has yet another circle. I talked with this fellow Josh MacDowell today, a friend of Sal Mineo."

Polly shot a quick glance at Tommy, who'd turned pale.

"What did I say?" I asked.

"Josh is very musical." Tommy grinned.

"Stop it." Polly glared at him.

"Musical?"

Polly, confidentially, "In Hollywood when you suspect any man likes, well, other men, you ask if he's…musical. Like a code word for a touchy subject."

Tommy bellowed loudly, "Jimmy doesn't like swishy guys."

"Yet Josh was a drinking buddy."

"For a real short time. Now Josh has his sights on Sal Mineo, who's sixteen and doesn't realize he's musical." Tommy thought his line hilarious, and started laughing, but stopped and said with a sneer, "A bunch of freaks."

Polly turned to me: "The one area Tommy will *not* imitate Jimmy."

"Meaning?"

Tommy announced, "Jimmy's an experimenter. He got all his breaks in California and New York through a sissy named Rogers Brackett, some queer radio producer with connections. Jimmy lived with him in New York. He met other men who got him parts on Broadway. Jimmy did what he had to do."

"So you mean he sleeps with men?"

"Well, somebody hinted him and this Max Kohl had something going on, but maybe not. Because Jimmy likes to hang out with tough guys. He goes to parties in the Valley, homes of movie execs and hot shots who are that way, where there are guys who experiment." Tommy was speaking too loudly, but sloppily, dragging the words out. "But I think Jimmy likes it too much." He waved his hand in the air. "Who knows?" He hiccoughed.

I listened closely, realizing that Josh MacDowell had used the same word: experiment. Jimmy experimented with other worlds. The portrait of a young man in search of…of what?

Polly, glancing at her blotchy face in a compact mirror, left to repair the damage. Tommy stared at me. "So that's our Jimmy," he smirked. "You feed us and we give you his story, at least the part with the warts. Which is why, I guess, you fed us. But he's the biggest star on the lot. Can you believe it?"

"You resent him, Tommy." Another wonderful declarative sentence.

"No, I love him. He's my buddy."

"But I'm thinking maybe it should have been you who plays Jett Rink and Cal Trask and Jim Stark. All the rebels and sad boys."

"I was the lead in *The Front Page.*"

Daggers drawn. "Don't you get tired of being his shadow? Maybe, if James Dean wasn't around, there'd be a Thomas Dwyer, in a red-nylon jacket. Girls asking for your autograph."

Suddenly he looked at me, and his eyes got wet. "When is it *my* turn, Miss Ferber? When?"

I sighed, touched the back of his hand. "He seems to have all the luck."

Tears streamed down his cheeks. "That's it, exactly. Luck. Damn luck, really. That's all it is in this God-awful town. And who you sleep with. Jimmy'll sleep with trolls for a part. He *has*, and look where he is. Ugly old men with potbellies. Women who wear sable coats with nothing on underneath. He *told* me. Christ. Now he's king of the world. Wherever we go, people scrape and bow. In Googie's they sit behind the glass partition and stare. They mob him. One movie. One! And I'm there carrying his coat. Me." He looked at me through sloppy tears. "He's a dirty man, Miss Ferber. Not only that unshaven look, the sticky unwashed hair, Christ, even the dandruff, but inside. Inside." He paused. "But I can't stop loving him…" He trailed off.

Polly returned to the table. She looked at Tommy, whose face was wet with tears.

She looked at me, wonder in her eyes. I sat there nodding.

My God, I thought. I've had them both weeping. She metamorphoses from the witch of the west into a weeping soda-fountain shop girl; he, the meek of the earth, metamorphoses into a barroom drunk, filled with ill-defined anger at his meal ticket.

A successful dinner.

"Are you having dessert?" I asked, cheerily. "I hear the crème brulee is the best in California."

Chapter Ten

The next morning I phoned Mercy. "I need an accomplice."

"Aiding and abetting is a part I've played in many movies."

I was thinking out loud. "Carisa pushed someone too far. Despite her madness and her drug use, if that's to be believed, Carisa seemed to draw people in. What we do know is that different roads led to her—and to Jimmy. Josh a high-school pal of hers. Josh introducing Jimmy to her. Jimmy dating her. Jimmy leaving her for Lydia. Lydia her old roommate and on-again off-again friend. Max Kohl seeing her before and after Jimmy. Max Kohl a biker buddy of Jimmy." I was also thinking about Tommy Dwyer, maybe stepping out on Polly with Carisa. And Polly suspecting their tryst.

Mercy clicked her tongue. "There's too much Jimmy in the picture."

"Mercy, our aim is not to solve the murder, really. That's Detective Cotton's bailiwick, troglodyte though he strikes me. No, I think we have to prove Jimmy's *not* guilty. He's our worst enemy here, of course, hostile to everyone, especially the police."

I could almost hear the smile. "And you need me as an accomplice for what?"

"You can start by being the driver. I don't think Warner wants the studio car idling in questionable neighborhoods."

"We're cruising Rodeo Drive?"

I chuckled. "I vowed never to return to Carisa's apartment after that night, but I'm afraid we have no choice."

"I'll gas up the getaway car."

◇◇◇

By noon Mercy's Ford sedan pulled up in front of Carisa's apartment house, and we surveyed the building in daylight. Still Skid Row. Broad daylight revealed grime and decay and utter disregard. Defeat in the tired buildings; defeat in the struggling, shuffling souls. A man dressed in a winter coat, huddled in a doorway, stared into the street. A rickety car pulled up in front of a pawnshop, and an obese woman in a flowered muumuu and loose sandals started to drag what I thought was a brass coat rack across the sidewalk. I stared, mesmerized. A little girl in shocking pink pedal pushers trailed the large woman. A soiled, used-up street. A hint of naughtiness in the jaunty walk of a couple of spangled girls. It reminded me of Pigalle, touring France one hot, hot summer with Noel Coward and Louis Bromfield. They always insisted on cultivating Parisian life in the grimier, suspect avenues, those wags, dragging me along for shock value. As I stepped out of the car, a young woman, so rail-thin and pale she seemed not even to be there, floated by, smiling, smiling. A haunted, parched face; the hunger of reaching zero.

Rapping on the door of the first-floor apartment, I recalled the superintendent's name from that awful night when I sat in his meticulous kitchen, light-headed from the sickening sight of a dead woman's body. Manuel Vega seemed happy to see us, ushering us in with a cavalier bow. An old-school gentleman, Vega was in his seventies, a tall willowy man with a shock of absolute white hair and, these days at least, a fuzzy white beard stubble. Skin the color of hazy mahogany, he seemed youthful, robust, though he moved carefully and employed a lion's-head cane. He spoke a deep, resonant English, no accent, though I had expected one. He looked a casting department stereotype of the old hidalgo of the hacienda. Instead, he spoke with the spacious, lazy drone of the typical Angelino—a stereotype of another persuasion.

He insisted we drink lemonade, his own creation, a liquid so transparent I thought it water. It had tartness undercut by a surprising sweetness that satisfied. Superb, I told him.

"How may I help you?" he asked, bowing again.

I explained that Mercy and I—I called her Mercedes, and the man nodded—were looking into the death of Carisa, strictly as a favor to a friend who stood accused, a young man in danger of being falsely charged of a murder he didn't commit, a man who...

"James Dean?" He cut me off.

I started. "You know him?"

"My granddaughter is a huge fan. Sitting through *East of Eden* a dozen times. She took me to see it, in fact. She insisted. A marvelous movie."

"Why did his name come to mind?" I asked.

He smiled. "He's famous, and you are here now."

I sipped the lemonade. "Interesting."

"Well, I like the movies now and then, though I'm getting old, ma'am. You see, I was in the movies when I was young, the silents of course, once in a scene with Valentino himself. And in one of Mae Murray's wonderful comedies. With the little money I made, I bought this house of six apartments for a song, and here I am, years later, as the streets get sadder and sadder." He shrugged his shoulders.

"But you know James Dean?" Mercy asked.

"I don't know him. It's my granddaughter who told me he comes here to visit. I didn't pay attention to the comings and goings. In this neighborhood if I get the rent, I'm a happy man."

"Did you ever talk to him?"

"Never." He paused. "Or at least I don't think so. So many young boys and girls come and go, visiting the Krausse girl, that I didn't pay attention, you know. So long as everything was proper. Proper, you know. But Connie, my granddaughter, is here on weekends. She tells me—you know who I saw leaving the second floor apartment? James Dean, she says. I say who? And she shows me his picture in a movie magazine. She wants to ask for his autograph, but doesn't have the courage. And so she takes me to see *East of Eden*, and I say—yes, that's the lad. Looks different, though. That red jacket he wears."

I held my breath. "What can you tell us about him?"

He looked around his small kitchen, seemed to frown at a cobweb he spotted above the sink. "Nothing. He comes and goes."

"Often?"

"Not a lot. I can't say. My granddaughter *watched* for him on weekends. I don't know. I'm old. I nap in the afternoons and go to bed early. I'm up at four, and the apartment building is sleeping. You know, for a long time Carisa's not even here, filming in Texas. She'd only been here a short time before she left for Texas. Then she's back, crazy-like. She said they fired her."

"She have a lot of visitors?" Mercy asked.

"Young people, drinkers, partiers. But so long as everything is quiet and the police stay away, I'm happy."

"The police ever come to her place?" I asked.

"Not till she was dead."

"Did you ever see Jimmy—James and Carisa together? I mean, go out or walk together?"

"No. But I heard them once. Yelling. I knocked on her door. It's late, and then there's quiet. I don't know it's him but Connie says she saw him leave."

"He left then?"

"The next morning." He frowned. "I spoke to her about that. This is a Catholic household, ma'am, a decent place, and I frown on that. She said he fell asleep on the floor, that he was drunk, as if that's supposed to make me happy. But after that, nothing. Silence. Except that she wanders up and down the stairs, by herself, out to the bodega, back with cigarettes, whiskey, and God knows what else. Across the street to the bar and grill where she eats a lot of times. I see her in there, night after night, enchiladas and a beer. A quarter for a meal. A poor man's restaurant."

"Were you surprised she was murdered?" I asked.

He sighed. "You know, I talked about this with Detective Cotton. The same story."

"About James Dean?"

"Of course. It's the police. I'm not looking for trouble."

"What did you tell Cotton?"

"He asked if I was surprised at the murder. Well, yes, it's not an everyday event. Even around here. Only in the movies. I was murdered in a William S. Hart movie. I took a long time to die." He smiled. "I wanted to be on the screen for a long time. But, as I told Cotton, I was going to evict her. She stopped paying the rent. She wasn't working, she said, since they fired her, but I just didn't like some of the crowd that started coming around. Late-at-night crowd. I found a syringe—a needle—in the hallway last week. She said it had nothing to do with her, but I knew."

"So you asked her to leave?" Mercy wondered.

He shook his head. "Not yet. She hid away in the apartment, wouldn't answer the door sometimes. If I saw her on the street, she just nodded at me. There was this creepy guy around for a while—tough, muscles, and a look that could stop you dead. When I found out he'd been staying over nights, I said something to her. He disappeared. On weekends my granddaughter is here. I gotta watch out. I had one daughter and she married a crazy so I know crazies. Drugs, beatings, tough guy stuff, trouble. He's in jail, and my daughter works in a hotel weekends, so Connie stays here with me. Fourteen years old, a beauty, who wants to be in the movies. Big surprise! That's the trouble with living here. Other places your child wants to go into business or, I don't know, school. But here, it's Hollywood all the time, covering you like a cotton-candy dream. I talk to her, but you know how babies are…"

Mercy interrupted. "What about the others who visited her?"

He stopped, waited, reached for cigarettes. He offered them to us, and surprising myself, I was tempted. I shook my head. Thank you, no.

"She got the most visitors, that girl. For a while, before I learned she was an actress, I thought she was a whore. Pardon me. Hard to tell. Lots of young girls look like it. Now and then I get one here, got to boot them out. But she was more… what?…crazy than anything. I don't mean crazy like oddball or, you know, wacky funny. Like Carole Lombard. No, this one was certifiable. All that walking at night, all the wandering in the hallways, unable to sleep, a woman with demons pursuing her. Still, I had to tell her to leave, but I never got around to doing it. Maybe I wouldn't have. I felt sorry for her. A pretty girl and so crazy. Still, people like James Dean came to see her. What does that tell you? She told my granddaughter she was gonna marry James Dean, and my Connie started crying. But I told her that James Dean is not marrying Carisa. Not on this good green earth. Him, up there in the movies. Big time. All la-di-dah in his sunglasses. No way he's marrying her. You know what she was? A failed actress. And let me tell you, there's nothing more pathetic in this town than a failed actress. Pity and *tsk tsk* from everyone. *You* didn't make it. Of course, they think *they* will. This town's bottom heavy with sad lives."

"Mr. Vega." I cut into the monologue. "Someone killed her."

"I know."

"And I don't believe it is James Dean."

He nodded.

"Can you help us?"

He looked into my eyes. "I don't think so. You see, Connie told me—and I told Cotton—that she saw Dean in the apartment the night Carisa died. She was watching for him. I believe what she's told me." He paused. "Connie said she heard yelling and screaming, the two of them. Probably just before she was killed."

"And she told all this to Detective Cotton?"

"Yes, of course."

"Did you recognize anyone else who came lately, a day or so before she died? Anyone who stood out?" Mercy asked.

He paused. "I told you I didn't pay much attention." He took a sip of lemonade. "But one day or so before she died, I was coming back home and Carisa was on the sidewalk talking to a man. Yelling and arguing."

I sat up. "A man?"

"An older man, dressed up like he was going to a play. Tie, jacket. Man in his fifties, say. Very pompous."

Mercy turned to me: "Jake?"

"Probably. Did you hear what they were arguing about?" I asked Vega.

"A little. The man was asking her to do something, and she was saying no. Kept turning away, but then coming back, baiting him. Cat-and-mouse game. He looked angry, I'll tell you. Face all purple."

"What happened?"

"I don't know. I went inside and seconds later I heard her running up the stairs."

"Alone?"

"Alone."

"Anyone else?"

"Lots of people. One guy a lot, back when she first moved in, before Texas. Very effeminate, don't like his kind, to tell you the truth. He came a lot. Lately he stopped in again. One time with a pretty young boy. Maybe Mexican. I don't like that stuff in my building. I say live and let live, but swishy is swishy, you know."

"You talk to him?"

"Of course not."

"Anyone else?"

He shook his head. "Lots. What can I tell you? I can't help you. I hear footsteps up and down. Men, women. I don't know. There was this other girl, an actress, I can tell, laughing too loud. But Carisa was okay until she got back from Texas. The first couple months here she was quiet. After Texas, she started to fall apart." He bit his lip. "You know, one night, I couldn't sleep and heard someone going up to her apartment, around three or four in the morning. A knock, real loud, and then someone running back down the stairs. I don't like that."

"Why?"

"I just felt he was delivering her some drugs. What else could it be at that hour? Not even there long enough, you know, for a—pardon me, ma'am—quickie."

There was a gentle rapping on the door, and an old woman in a sagging housedress, her hair tied up in a kerchief, mumbled something in Spanish. While Mercy and I watched from the kitchen, Vega went into the living room and dialed the phone, speaking with his back to us. When he returned, he looked confused. "I've just called the police. Mrs. Sanchez tells me someone has slipped into Carisa's apartment, past the crime tape that's there." Immediately I stood up and started to move. He waved me down. "No, sit tight," he said. But I had to see. "Please. Would you get yourself hurt?"

Mercy touched my arm. "Let's wait."

But I stood in the outer doorway, door open, facing upstairs, waiting. The hallway was empty now, and I heard nothing from upstairs. All right, I wouldn't tackle the stairs, not with an intruder there, but should anyone leave, I wanted a good view. Interesting, this intrusion; in broad daylight. Someone brazen and most likely desperate; after all, crime scene tape would deter most souls. I waited, impatient. Within minutes, the same two balding, beefy cops who'd come the night Carisa was murdered showed up, and, minutes later, surprisingly, Detective Cotton, out of breath, flew into the hallway. Without pretence I trailed Cotton up the stairs.

The door to Carisa's apartment was wide open, the POLICE DO NOT CROSS tape dangling off the jamb, most of it bunched on the floor.

I stood at the top of the landing, with a skittish Mercy poised halfway up the stairs. Vega and Mrs. Sanchez, more sensible souls, remained in the apartment below.

The cops and Cotton led very boisterous and aggressive Max Kohl into the hallway. At least I assumed the muscular, hirsute man, then struggling with the cops, was the elusive biker. "I got a right to be here, dammit," he was yelling. "I got a key." He tried to show the officers the key in his pocket, but they held his hands pinned behind him.

"You broke into a crime scene."

"I thought you just forgot to take it down."

"What were you after?"

"I left some cash there, and it's mine." Kohl twisted and threw one cop off. Grappling and struggling with him, they managed to handcuff him, pushing him against a wall.

Cotton, perspiring and reaching for a handkerchief, turned and suddenly discovered me standing there. He looked astounded. "Oh my God. What?"

"What?"

Cotton looked from Kohl to me to Mercy, who'd inched up the stairs. "Do you all know each other?"

"I never met him before," I announced.

"Did you come here together?"

"Of course not," I said, indignant. "Do I look like his accomplice?"

"Last time you two looked like prom queens at a hooker convention."

"Sir, you are…"

He cut me off. "And you're in the hallway for what reason?" Perplexed, head shaking. He was not happy.

"We were talking to Mr. Vega about the murder."

"You were what?"

"Unlike you, I'm convinced James Dean did not kill Carisa Krausse, and I'm convinced you'd like to see him charged, so…"

"So you're doing my job?"

"No, only you can do that. Clearly." I looked at the dumbfounded Max Kohl and back at Cotton, who was wiping his brow. "I'm just helping a friend."

"Twice I come upon you," he looked at Mercy now, "and *you* at a murder scene."

I spoke sharply. "Only one murder scene. Mr. Kohl, if that is who I assume this young man is, still looks very much alive—though angry."

Kohl narrowed his eyes. "Who are you? How do you know me?"

"I thought you arrested Mr. Kohl when he tried to escape questioning."

"Bail, lady, bail," he said. "It wasn't a felony."

"Perhaps it should be."

"Write your congressman."

"Aren't you compounding your problems, Mr. Kohl, by breaking into a crime scene?" I asked. He stared at me, open-mouthed.

"Miss Ferber," Cotton said, "I don't need your help."

"I'm curious."

"Save it for another time."

"I need my money," Kohl thundered.

"For what, more bail?" I asked.

Detective Cotton looked at me. "Ma'am, it's not a good idea coming around places like this. Do you know what goes on in this neighborhood? Tourists don't come here."

"I'm not a tourist. I'm a novelist."

"You might end up a dead one."

"Well, Fannie Hurst would be tremendously pleased, then."

"What?" He threw his hands up into the air. "You could get yourself murdered."

"Then you'd have two homicides to solve."

Cotton shook his head, smiled in spite of himself, which caught me by surprise. "Why do you want to make my life difficult, Miss Ferber?"

"I'm just asking questions to help a friend."

"Go home," he said. "Now."

"Detective Cotton…"

"Did you hear me? Go home."

"I happen to live in New York City."

"Perfect. American Airlines has a midnight red-eye."

"Sir."

"I'll even drive you to the airport."

Chapter Eleven

I sat in Mercy's dressing room in Burbank, the two of us sipping tea, my elbows resting on a small table, with Mercy reclining in an easy chair, draping herself over it, legs up on a small wobbly ottoman. She looked serene, eyes dreamy. "Edna, when I travel with you these days, the police tend to show up moments later." She chuckled, almost to herself. "I haven't had this much excitement since Marfa, the night Jane Withers beat me at Monopoly, and, crowing like a strangulated hen, walked into a wall."

I laughed. "Only two times, Mercy. The gods work in mysterious ways."

There was a knock on the door, and Detective Xavier Cotton walked in. Mercy looked at me, eyes bright, and sat up. "Make that three times."

"Ah, Miss Ferber, you're here, too. As I expected, since the two of you seem intent on becoming the Dolly Sisters of Hollywood crime."

"Detective Cotton, I explained why we were there."

He spoke to Mercy. "The studio has given consent," he said it sarcastically, "to have a number of Carisa Krausse's acquaintants fingerprinted. We've lifted some good prints from the crime scene. Sometime this afternoon, if you can make it downtown…"

Mercy nodded. "Gladly."

I smiled. "Me, too?"

He tucked his tongue into the corner of his cheek. "Not yet."

Both Mercy and I laughed. He didn't.

"I've been fingerprinted before," I commented, still smiling.

"Why am I not surprised?" Again, without humor. Cotton said lines that should be accompanied by bursts of hilarity—or at least a smile. Did he have a light side, a moment when he let go, held his sides, rolled from side to side, laughing? I wondered about his home life—marriage, children, mistresses? Hookers? Dogs and cats? Ferret? Something that looked like him? "We've had most of the principals down to the station this morning, quietly, unannounced, but of course you were otherwise engaged."

"Have you spoken to Jimmy?" I asked, curious. "I understand he's shooting today."

"Which is why he can't be disturbed. And no one can see him fingerprinted at the station. We have to come to him, carrying our little kit and talking happy like we're itinerant preachers saving his soul."

"Very funny," I said.

"I'm never funny."

"Sit down, Detective." Mercy pointed to a chair. Surprisingly, he sat. He pulled at the cuffs of his shirt until the edges showed under the sleeves of his sports jacket. He evened them up, flicked a piece of lint from the sleeve, then sat there nodding his head, watching us.

"What?" From me.

"Two nosy women."

"We try."

A sliver of smile, forced, "And what have you learned?"

"Are we sharing information?" I asked.

"You're trying to save James Dean's skin. I'm trying to shore up the evidence against him." He reached into his pocket and extracted copies of Carisa's letters. He fanned them, dramatically. "I've never seen such a fascination with letter writing. You know, Carisa had a bunch of letters on her desk. But some were missing."

"How do you know that?" I probed.

He watched me, eyes narrow. "I suspect you noticed that yourself, Miss Ferber. You were alone in the apartment for some time—you and the body." He glanced at Mercy. "In reconstructing the scene, I surmised that you, Miss Ferber, were alone there for what? Ten minutes? Fifteen? Twenty? What did you do?"

I smiled. "I touched nothing. No prints of mine."

"But I'm supposing you noticed the scattered letters on the table."

"I did."

"What else?"

"Well," I said, "I saw a syringe."

He smiled. "Good. Me, too. Do you know what was in the bag?"

"No."

"Heroin."

"As is rumored," I said.

"In fact, the autopsy showed she had just ingested some into her fragile body. She may have been a little loopy when she let in the murderer."

"Or," I surmised, "she shot up with the murderer who took his own syringe with him."

"Interesting. Maybe. Maybe not. What else did you see? I mean, besides the things you outlined in the thorough statement you've already given us." His tone was sarcastic.

"A neat woman, though a packrat. She saved every scrap of paper."

"True." He nodded. "And what does that mean to you?"

I glanced at Mercy. "Well, it suggests that she might have *saved* something the murderer wanted back, probably a note of some sort. Because…because the only things in disarray were the batch of letters extracted from one of the drawers."

"Exactly. Somebody took a letter or letters."

"And you don't know what letter or letters?" Mercy asked.

"Hard to say," he said. "The letters left behind were family notes, a mother in San Francisco, birthday cards, Christmas cards, junk. She saved everything."

I nodded. "And someone knew that."

"Maybe. Or realized it once he was there with her. She may have mentioned something about it—which led to the murder."

"So," I continued, "if the murderer took a letter, then we have trouble knowing the motive for the killing."

"We?" He raised his eyebrows and frowned. "You mean me—*me*."

"I was using the royal *we*."

He frowned. "In your wanderings have you two ladies found anyone who likes to write letters?"

"All literate people write letters," I noted. "The telephone is for luncheon engagements and to berate shopkeepers."

"Can you imagine Max Kohl writing a letter? Or, say, Josh MacDowell?" He paused. "Maybe James Dean scribbles letters?"

"I can imagine Max Kohl pasting a letter together with words cut from *Coronet* magazine."

Cotton laughed a hearty fake laugh. "Good one."

"I'm being serious."

"You'd like to pin the murder on him."

"I just want to clear Jimmy," I said. "You know, I'd have thought the epistolary tradition had died in an earlier century, but, I gather, it lives abundantly, if absurdly, in modern Hollywood."

He narrowed his eyes. "What?"

"Nothing." I waited. "Did you get anything out of Max Kohl this morning?"

He smirked. "Not that it's any of your business, but no. He's a slippery one. The problem is that he seems to have an alibi for the time Carisa was killed. Or at least he's lined up folks who lie for him. We've learned he knew Carisa a while back, dated her, maybe, and then disappeared. Seems he was in jail in New Jersey for a couple months, a bad check charge, but drifted back here and back into her life about the time James Dean dumped her. A troublemaker, muscle for a local boss for a time, got into a numbers racket, and, I suppose, the source for Carisa's drugs. Biker fanatic. How he met Dean, I understand." He stopped.

"Why are you sharing this information with us?" I asked, finally.

"I suspect you know much of it already. And I'm hoping some of it—something I say—will trigger something in you, something you stumbled on. Either of you."

"I don't stumble onto things," I said emphatically. "I uncover truth."

His tongue rolled over his upper lip, then disappeared back into his mouth. "Manuel Vega says you ask very good questions."

"Well, thank him for me."

Again, the tongue, a wary gesture. "Maybe you'll *hear* something."

"And share it with you?"

"You're a law-abiding citizen. And, so far, the only one here I can say with any certainly is *not* the murderer."

"What about me?" asked Mercy. Cotton didn't answer her.

"Did the autopsy show anything else besides her being pregnant?" I wondered.

He hesitated. "Well, yes. Seems she'd been killed some time just before you gals sauntered in. The M.E. says between seven and eight. You arrived at eight-thirty, just on the heels of the murder."

"Good God," said Mercy.

"Indeed, Miss McCambridge. The body was still warm."

"And was she killed with that statue?" I asked.

He smiled. "Oh, that's right. You were alone in the apartment. You noticed it before the cops got there."

"It's hard not to notice a body and a statue…"

"Lying right nearby. And did you note the kind of statue?"

"It looked like a fertility goddess."

"That's right. Aztlan, in fact. Aztec. Piece of chiseled stone. Weighty. Big bellied woman."

"A good murder weapon."

"But not what killed her, it seems." He stopped, seemed to be waiting for me to say something.

"But…"

"Autopsy shows she died from smashing her head on the metal edge of a table. Looks like, so far's we can reconstruct it, someone hit her with the statue, but it just grazed her shoulder, she fell, hit her head, bled to death in minutes. Being stoned didn't help her. Traces of liquor and heroin in the bloodstream."

"So it may not have been a premeditated murder," I mused.

"Bingo. A fight, tempers flare. Suddenly she's dead." He paused. "And the interesting thing I learned from your favorite boy is that the statue was a gift from Mr. Dean himself. Strange."

"Why is that strange?"

"A fertility statue to a pregnant unwed girl? Very Ellery Queen, no?"

I said nothing.

Cotton went on. "Someone threw the statue that was conveniently there. Then rifled through the drawers for a letter."

"And took it away," said Mercy. "The evidence."

"So," I concluded, "you need to find out which letters were removed."

Cotton took a long time answering. "Or, to make my life easy, which letter was *not* removed by the murderer."

"Meaning?"

Again, the deliberate wait, the calculated staring from me to Mercy. "It seems Carisa did hide *one* letter. One letter she did not, for some reason, keep in that drawer with the others. A letter Carisa Krausse hid under a pillow."

I held my breath. "From?"

"Well." He paused, stretching out the word, and then melodramatically removed a copy from a breast pocket. "From your boy Jimmy. Who, when asked right after the murder, said he *never* wrote any letters to her. None. Zippo. Nada. Who, me? Who, when he finishes shooting, is going to be shown this copy, which seems to contradict his statement to the police. Unless, of course, someone else forged his signature."

Mercy and I stared, uncomfortable. I was tempted to snatch the letter from him, annoyed with his roundabout conversation, his purposeful leading up the revelation of the new letter. Silent now, I waited. After all, this was Cotton's grandiose moment, and he wanted to work it his way. Basil Rathbone as Sherlock Holmes, American style. The debonair Rathbone in pinstriped suit, with carnation in buttonhole. Well, Cotton's sliver of a moustache was in need of a barber's trim: one corner was higher than the other.

"Well…" I began.

"Exactly." He unfolded the sheet of paper. "And let me quote you a line from the newly discovered letter." He skimmed what looked to be a neatly typed copy. "Oh, here it is. 'You know this is a lot of crap from you and no one is going to take your crap seriously, you know.'" He paused. "No, that's not exactly the line I wanted to read to you ladies. Oh, here it is. 'You know, people can get hurt if they get in my way.'" He looked up, made eye contact with me. He echoed. "'Hurt.'"

"I heard you," I said, icily.

A half-hour later, sitting alone in the commissary, nursing coffee—Mercy left for an interview with Louella Parsons whom she deemed "that bastion of bathos"—I was in no mood for Tansi's intense, excited assault.

"Edna," she sputtered, pulling up a chair. "I've been looking for you. Detective Cotton is all over the lot. He's mad because he just found some letter, but Jake won't tell me what's it about." She drew in her breath. "Edna, they fingerprinted me this morning."

I was not in the mood for Nancy Drew. "So?"

Tansi paused for an imperceptible second. "It was so *Public Enemy* or something. James Cagney."

I was still fuming from Cotton's surprise information; more so, his smug delivery, his toying with me.

"I mean, in my lifetime I would not have expected it," Tansi continued. "We all had to go, of course. Warner sent a memo.

Now *that* memo will be omitted from the *Giant* archives, I'm sure. Jake protested, said it was impossible. He hadn't gone to Princeton to be treated like a common criminal. I went with him, but he fussed and fumed. On the way back he kept showing me his stained fingertips until I exploded and said he wasn't Christ revealing some stigmata. You know what he said? 'I'm not made for skullduggery.' I loved it. Then he said: 'All the hugger-mugger stuff is bad for my digestion.'"

I held up a hand to stop the flood. "Tansi, did Jake say anything about the murder investigation?"

"No, why?"

"Just wondering."

"Jake has decided—I guess Warner, too—to ignore me. Everything goes through Jake. The fewer people who know, the fewer the leaks to gossip sheets. Jake did say that some writer at *Confidential* phoned Warner, started asking questions. That threw Warner into a panic."

"Tansi, I just asked you if you'd heard anything, and you said no. And then you share the Jake story and *Confidential*."

"But," Tansi defended herself, "I thought you meant evidence."

I was tired. "Whom did you see at the precinct?"

"Lydia Plummer was leaving, and not happy. She was with Nell Meyers, but they didn't leave there together."

"How do you know?"

"They were both leaving when we arrived. Lydia called a cab and Nell waited at the bus stop. Jake and I watched Lydia get in the cab, and I tell you, she looked like death itself: pale, fluttery, and nervous. Nell's avoiding Lydia now. Afterward, I asked Nell about it. You know, by the way, she's finally listening to me. She's leaving the Studio Club—and Lydia. Since Carisa's death, Lydia is often hysterical, crying jags, whispered nonsense, and imagined horrors. I guess she's told Nell some things about dating Jimmy—but she said she still plans on marrying him. Other girls are the problem, she said. It's crazy, no?"

"Why?"

"Jimmy has already told Lydia to get lost." A pause. "Nell told me she thinks Lydia killed Carisa in an argument."

I sat up. "What? What did you say?"

"Well, Lydia, I guess a little out of it, told Nell that she'd gone to the apartment to see Carisa. Old roommate, you know, though they hadn't talked in a while, some sort of fight. But I guess they started talking again. Anyway, Lydia told Nell they argued about Jimmy. Lydia was jealous. Lydia was angry at Carisa."

"I'm not following this."

"Lydia interpreted those letters Carisa was writing to Jimmy as a personal affront. A slap at her. Carisa, she told Nell, was old news, so she should leave her Jimmy alone. Lydia resented the baby threat. Lydia said *she* was the new girl and thought Carisa's letters were a ploy to get Jimmy back. Nell told me she told Lydia—but now *you're* the old girl. He's got Ursula Andress. Lydia went nuts. Yelled at Nell. Scared her."

"Would Nell actually tell Lydia that to her face?"

"Why not? Nell can't stand Lydia now that I've made her see the light."

I drummed my fingers on the table. "Jimmy has to come clean about a lot of things."

Tansi spoke in a soft voice. "What does that mean?"

"Jimmy hasn't been forthright with the police." I was thinking of Jimmy's newly discovered letter.

"Oh, I'm sure there's a reason, Edna."

"You don't lie to the police."

"He wouldn't lie. Maybe he forgets things."

"No, Tansi, stop this. I like Jimmy. I do, despite some of his childish behavior. And I don't believe he'd kill anyone. But if we're to help him, we have to be realistic. Your idealizing him into junior-grade God is touching, but one of the dangers of elevating men to godhood is that, well, we're forced to stare at them up there. Sometimes, when the light hits the statue, you see the pock marks, the blemishes, the…"

"I'm not a giggly bobby-soxer, Edna," she said, hurt, bewildered, near tears.

"I know you're not, Tansi. And I know you are an intelligent woman. But your protestation of Jimmy's innocence smacks of unexamined devotion."

Tansi stood up, not happy. "Jimmy is the future of Warner Bros.," she said. "And he's a *good* boy."

"He's not a boy. He's a man."

"You know what I mean. He's decent and…and…"

"Then work with me to prove he's innocent."

"How?" Tansi breathed in. "I *want* to."

I shrugged. "I wish I knew."

"He is innocent," Tansi pleaded. "He *has* to be. Maybe Nell is right. Maybe it was Lydia."

"You can't just say that, Tansi, without proof."

"How can anybody prove that? But Nell's convinced Lydia killed Carisa in a fit of anger. They had nasty fights, really. A number of them. And do you know what Nell told me? She says Carisa probably had it coming."

Chapter Twelve

I sat with Detective Cotton the next morning in my suite at the Ambassador. I'd reached him at the precinct the previous afternoon and related Tansi's story of Nell and Lydia, and the accusation of murder. My information wasn't news to him, it seemed. Though I considered the information of little value, I decided to create a bond with him: a mutual sharing. I was convinced he'd held back crucial bits of information, and his candid talk with me was a conscious ploy. Before he hung up, he asked if he could stop by in the morning. Of course I said yes.

I served him coffee, and I noticed he didn't slurp it noisily nor did he overload the hot brew with excessive sugar cubes. I smiled.

"Nice place," he said.

"I don't own it."

"Whenever I stay in a hotel, it's one room." He looked around. "Not a half dozen."

"I sleepwalk and the management is trying to avoid lawsuits."

"Then they should have put you on the ground floor." He smiled.

"You're obviously curious about something. Otherwise we wouldn't be sitting here."

"In fact, yes. For one thing, your obsession with James Dean's innocence."

"It's not an obsession, sir. I've never obsessed about a single thing in my life. But in my scant dealings with him, I sense... well, I sense a certain truth in him."

"My gut tells me he's dirty."

"Proof?"

He shrugged. "Slow train through the alleys of L.A."

"Sounds like a line from an old Wobbly protest song."

He looked baffled, but didn't ask me to explain. "But I've come to believe we're on the same side of the law here..."

"Of course."

"Though your intent is more narrowly defined. And I trust you, Miss Ferber. I asked around about you, even called a cop I know in New York City. He never heard of you. And that can be a good thing. But hereabouts you have a reputation for, well, decency."

I nodded. Thank you.

"So I believe anything *you* uncover that is relevant will come my way."

"Hence my phone call to you yesterday."

"That struck me as a little self-serving."

"Like your being here this morning?"

He nodded.

"Tell me something." He put down the cup he'd been holding. "What do you see in this James Dean? I've talked to him a bunch of times lately, when he's found or available, and he's moody, evasive, downright rude. On top of that he hadn't bathed when we spoke."

"Please, sir." I was munching on a soda cracker.

"Sorry. But I just don't *see* the attraction. They're telling me he's the wave of the future. Clark Gable is passé, and Brando and Dean and Clift are in—people who talk with stones in their mouths and who thumb their noses at...at everything." He looked angry.

"Detective Cotton, I sense you're a well-intended man. I also sense that you were probably happy when Clark Gable was tossing Vivian Leigh around like a sack of potatoes—*that* Hollywood. You have about you a hint of Ronald Coleman."

"I don't like what the Second World War did to America."

"You're blaming this on a war?"

"A slippage of morals. Everything's turned upside down. Teenage drag racing. Rock 'n' roll. Thank God for McCarthy and his ferreting out Commies."

"I don't choose to discuss domestic totalitarianism and rearguard politics with you this morning, sir. It'll only give me indigestion."

"So be it," he conceded. "So be it. But I'm curious. Are you writing a book?"

"I *wrote* a book. It's called *Giant*."

He glanced to the side, as though unwilling to face me. "I mean, you seem to be *intent* on this murder case." Stressing the word.

"Intent?"

"Don't you think it's odd for a little old lady to venture into one of the most depraved parts of L.A., especially at night, looking for a woman she's never met?"

I waited, watched him with cold, cold eyes. When I spoke I knew my tone was peevish, which I despised in myself. "Sir, I didn't get to be a famous and rich writer sitting in a comfortable drawing room sipping tea with pretentious social lionizers." I took a breath. "If you read my work, you'll notice I have written about lumber camps in the wilds of Wisconsin, and truck farms in Connecticut and in Chicago, and interracial love on the Mississippi…"

He held up his hand. "Okay, okay. I just asked a question."

"And, I hope you realize, I have walked streets filled with derelicts, villages where every eye on me is hostile, shacks where depraved girls…" I stopped. I was surprised by the trace of a smile, a genuine one, not the snickering, insulting facial gestures he'd offered earlier. "What?"

"I appreciate honesty," he said. "I almost never encounter it any more."

"Perhaps you need to be honest with yourself first?"

"What does that mean?"

"You're convinced Jimmy is the killer, a bias you've allowed to set in concrete."

"You misread me, Miss Ferber."

"I don't think I do, sir."

"I gather evidence, but I do start with a premise. And my premise, given the scant evidence to date, is that your darling boy is the culprit." He kept going, even though he noticed I was ready to speak. "And the fact that he didn't mention this threatening letter to Carisa is one more piece of bad news for him."

"Bad character, perhaps; faulty judgment, definitely. But not necessarily an indictment of murder."

"I've found that behind most murderers is, oddly, bad character."

"But not all bad or questionable character leads to murder."

"Granted."

"Tell me, Detective Cotton, what was all this foolishness about fingerprints? You've sent everyone into a tizzy."

"We really didn't think there would be any surprises. The apartment is filled with undocumented prints, but I was curious to see who of the Warner's crowd went there—more in terms of print frequency than anything else."

"And you learned?"

"Not much. The usual suspects. What I expected." Again, the sardonic grin. "Lydia Plummer, ex-friend. And I might add, fellow drug abuser big time. There's a secret for you, which everyone freely tells me. And Josh. Even Sal Mineo. James Dean, of course. Indeed, the most telling: there was a thumbprint on the Aztec statue, but it was a gift from him to her. And its base has a bunch of smudges, unreadable, blurry prints. Maybe the killer rubbed the statue quickly with a handkerchief."

"Other prints?"

"Nothing of your Miss McCambridge, even though she said she was in the apartment. She claims she visited once, sat on the sofa and then left, taking Carisa off somewhere. Tansi Rowland, nothing. Oddly, Jake Geyser, all over, excessive, though he claims he dropped off papers one time. And another surprise. Tommy

Dwyer was there though he says he stopped in with Dean. His prints were on an unwashed glass. Dean says no, that Tommy did not go with him. His girlfriend Polly: no prints. What also surprises me is that Lydia's roommate, the script girl…ah…Nell Meyers, who's actually *accused* Lydia, was there."

"But only Jimmy admits to being there that night."

"And he claims she was alive when he left." A pause. "Couldn't you have gotten there earlier, Miss Ferber?"

"Then you'd have had to solve more than one murder."

"Who left the cocktail party early?"

I hesitated. "Well, Jimmy, as you know. Mercy and I. Lydia slipped out early. Jake left. Not everyone was there." Tommy and Polly, I thought. Josh. Nell.

"So we've learned. You know, so many people floated in and out of the apartment of a young girl everyone says was a crazy, a drug user. Lydia hated her, they fought, yet she visits, one time with Josh MacDowell. Josh first denied knowing Lydia, then said it was because Lydia did heroin and he didn't want to be tainted. Nell says that Lydia and Josh talked on the phone a lot. Seemed to be plotting revenge against Jimmy because he dumped them both. Somehow, she thinks, they would *use* Carisa to exact revenge against Jimmy."

"But killing Carisa to implicate Jimmy is rather extreme."

He held up his hand, palms forward, then interlaced his fingers. "Welcome to Hollywood."

"You're being very candid with me, Detective Cotton."

"At this point, I have nothing to lose."

Surprisingly, I noted, he'd seemed to change during our talk, as he abandoned his crusty shell, his testy manner. Sitting with him over coffee, I thought him a curious anachronism, some fugitive from a Charles Laughton movie, cool and aloof. Once he knew his cast of characters, he could soften the edges a little, like a dramatist who, having hammered out her characters, then relaxes, comfortable in the knowledge that her creations will behave as expected.

Detective Cotton was readying to leave, standing up and stretching.

"Detective Cotton." I looked up at him. "There's a danger here that I might start to like you."

"Don't count on it," he said, buttoning his sports jacket. "You'd be one more woman I've failed in my life."

"You're talking like a character in a Dashiell Hammett novel."

"I've got to get my lines from somewhere."

◇◇◇

I could hardly keep my wits about me during a noontime lunch with George Stevens, anxious to get my opinion on some script changes for the penultimate banquet scene with Jett Rink. My mind kept drifting to James Dean and Xavier Cotton and Carisa Krausse. Leaving the meeting, I met Jake and Tansi, sent by Jack Warner himself, the two tugging at my sleeves like I was a coveted chicken wishbone. I dismissed both but, on the spur of the moment, asked Tansi to meet me at the Smoke House at four. I was having coffee with Mercy. Tansi seemed grateful, Jake miffed. But walked to the Blue Room by a chatty Tansi, I immediately regretted my kindness. Full of news, a Homeric Hedda Hopper, Tansi kept up a breezy but tiresome flow of conversation. I did learn that Nell had moved out of the Studio Club, much to Lydia's consternation.

"Nell told me Lydia started screaming at her," Tansi said. "They were having lunch, and Nell waited to the end to tell her. Lydia lost it. She'd just told Nell that she'd had another row with Jimmy, who told her to keep away from him. According to Nell, Jimmy kept saying to her, Lydia, you know I left you weeks ago. Like it was old news."

"Where did Nell go?" I asked.

"I thought I told you."

"No, you didn't."

"She has nowhere to go, really. She makes almost no money at Warner's. So I told her she could stay with me until she gets on her feet. I have that spare room."

"Tansi, is that a good idea?"

"She's a friend, Edna. I had no choice. I'm the one who persuaded her to get away from Lydia."

"But, Tansi…"

"I don't want her to face Lydia's temper. I've *seen* it. In Marfa one night, she and Jimmy got into it, and I was down the hall. It was ugly the things she said to him. Well, him to her, too."

I started to warn Tansi to stay out of peoples' lives, but stopped. I said nothing.

Later, at the Smoke House, sitting with Mercy and Tansi, I was startled to see Sal Mineo and Josh MacDowell walk in, both nodding at us but striding past, taking seats far away. Moments later, to my horror, Max Kohl stormed in, looking beefy and furious in a worn leather motorcycle jacket, with boots and sunglasses, barreling in, scanning the room, then approaching Josh and Sal. We fell silent. Then Tansi, too loudly, said what I was thinking. "Why is Max here?"

"What's going on?" Mercy whispered.

I shrugged it off. "Why is everyone surprised? We all know Max was a friend of Carisa's, dated her——and knew the others. Josh was her old friend and Jimmy's drinking buddy. Maybe Josh rode bikes with Jimmy."

Tansi shook her head. "Max is in a *different* world from Josh and Sal."

"They all have Jimmy in common."

Mercy laughed. "We all have Jimmy in common."

Tansi leaned in. "Such a good-looking man, Max is, but too mean."

"And now Max is seeing Lydia?" I asked.

Tansi nodded. "Supposedly. After Jimmy dumped her. After he dumped Carisa. But Lydia still calls Jimmy. Come back, please."

"It's incestuous," Mercy said, "A small-knit group of young folks—bit players—who go from one to another, looking for love."

"They experiment."

I looked at Tansi. "That's curious. Both Tommy and Josh said that about Jimmy—that he experiments with people. He uses them up."

Mercy added, "Well, in Hollywood people move into your life and then disappear, especially the penny-ante contract players."

I stared at the three men. Sal Mineo, boyish, dark, pretty, always nervous, and a little weary; looking as though he were biding his time, waiting for direction; hanging with friends he'd gladly dismiss when others—livelier, more thrilling—came his way. Josh, effete and pale, as long as a string bean and as supple, eyes darting around the room, searching, resting back possessively on Sal and then, unhappily, on Max. Josh, now smiling through brilliant teeth, then biting a ridge of nail, anxious. And Max Kohl, hairy, bulky, a blunt crew cut; sweaty, undeniably good looking; sensual, fleshy nighttime biker, in love with speed and darkness. Carisa's ex-boyfriend. Lydia's current flame, maybe. A man who, straddling a chair, seemed to be telling Josh and Sal a mesmerizing story, one they weren't happy to hear, because they were rigid, attentive. Then, as abruptly as he entered, Max left, but not before rapping on the table with his knuckles, emphasizing a point. Heads turned to watch the swagger and thrust of his body as it moved out the door.

"Well," I said, finally. "Not happy, that one."

Tansi looked puzzled. "I wonder what…"

Suddenly Josh and Sal were leaving. Mercy spoke up. "Max looked like he was threatening you two."

Sal's voice was breathy. "Scary man. I don't know him."

Josh cleared his throat. "I do, through Carisa. I *warned* her about him. But she liked him. Jimmy liked him. Jimmy didn't *know* him. He just likes anybody who rides a bike."

"What was that all about?" Tansi asked Josh.

Josh was antsy now. "Somehow he heard that I, he says it was me, told the cops he supplied Carisa and Lydia with heroin. Everyone knows about the drugs. I wasn't the only one who knew that. But he thinks Cotton will pin Carisa's murder on him."

"Did he threaten you?"

Josh blanched. "He told me to keep my mouth shut. About the drugs. Cotton's looking to connect Jimmy to the murder, but I guess he'll settle for Max. Max, well…Max never liked me."

"Why?" From Tansi.

Josh arched his eyebrows, shook his head, snickered. He threw back his shoulders, asserting himself, but purposely creating a classic Hollywood gesture of the dandified character. Or an exaggerated Joan Crawford dismissal. "You figure it out, my dear," he said, and walked away. Sal, smiling sheepishly, followed him.

Liz Taylor sent me roses, out of the blue, with a note that simply said thank you for everything. The *everything* was underlined. I wasn't certain what I was being thanked for, though I suspect people generally and routinely thank rich and famous people. Out of habit. People think it's one of the rules. But Liz was rich and famous, so I sought her out to thank her. Frankly, I had the feeling somehow her odd note—I did appreciate the crisp thick cream paper, with the monogram ET embossed in silver—related to Jimmy's dilemma. But Tansi had told me that Liz avoided the topic, uncomfortable. I caught up with her in makeup. A quick touch up, she mumbled, nodding toward the young man working on her eyes. He hovered and bent and squinted and sighed, Leonardo dabbing a miniscule speck of burnt umber on the Mona Lisa. Next to her, reviewing a spiral notebook filled with notes, a young woman was mechanically listing obligations and meetings, photo shoots. Liz seemed to be paying her no mind, smiling at me. I walked near. I thanked her for the flowers.

"Thank *you*," she said, grinning. "You flew all that way to be with us."

I realized I rarely saw her alone—never, really. There was always someone pulling at her sleeve, whispering in her ear, or, in this case, making those violet eyes even more luminous. She turned to the young woman, who was prattling in a singsong tone. "Laura, enough. Later." But Laura, momentarily intoxicated with her recital, kept talking. Liz lost the smile. "Enough, I said. Later." Loud, sharp. Laura faltered, and stood back. Liz looked back at me, the face again wreathed in smiles. "I do hate yelling at people."

I narrowed my eyes. "Oddly, it's what I like doing best."

But I could see her glance at Laura, who stood there, eyes unblinking, waiting to resume her catalogue of activity.

"You're always surrounded by people," I observed.

She shook her head. "I started in this business when I was a child. A danger, really. I learned that pouting got me attention." She grinned. "The truth is that now I'm grown up, and I find it still works. It's hard to let go of something that works." She glanced at Laura. "I can say anything and people accept it. You know how pretty little schoolgirls are." For a second she seemed unhappy with her own words, as if someone suddenly shoved her in front of a mirror and she didn't like what she saw. She shut her eyes. When she opened them, the confusion was gone. "I'm being foolish."

I was impatient. "Have you talked to Jimmy?"

She seemed surprised. "Why?"

I glanced at Laura and the makeup artist, and Liz followed my glance. Worry settled over her features. "Laura, Charles, darlings, a minute alone with Miss Ferber." The two disappeared.

"Miss Ferber, I heard you're working behind the scenes on that unfortunate business."

"The murder?"

Liz squinted and checked her eyes in the mirror. "Of course, Jimmy had nothing to do with that. You really needn't bother yourself."

"How do you know?"

Her face became a canvas of little-girl smugness. "Really, now. Jimmy Dean? He's so…sweet. A little madcap, insane, a little boy jumping up and down and saying look-at-me; but really, it's all foolishness."

"The police might think otherwise."

"Of course, they won't."

"Miss Taylor…"

"Liz…"

"Miss Taylor, you seem sure of this."

"Jack Warner assured me it'll all be okay."

"He did?"

"He takes care of everything. He called and told me not to speak of it with reporters. Well, I've been in this business forever. I wouldn't dare. He talks to me like I'm a scattered child." She dabbed at a hint of powder under her left eye. "Jack is sort of infatuated with me, I'm afraid. And men who are infatuated with me make the mistake of thinking I'm not very bright."

"But you might be a little naïve when it comes to Jimmy."

She held up her hand. "Really, no. Jimmy will be just fine." She stood up. "I have to run." She touched me on the wrist. "Again, thank you."

I still didn't know what I was being thanked for.

I planned on sleeping early that night. Yet I dawdled, sitting by the window in my suite, still dressed in the outfit I'd worn to dinner with a couple of Broadway producers visiting L.A. for a week. They'd insisted on dining with me at La Rue's, followed by a night of Symphonies under the Stars at the Hollywood Bowl. It hadn't been unpleasant, but tiring. So now, dark L.A. beneath me, with streams of headlights on the boulevard, a slight night wind rustling the tops of the palms I looked down on, I resisted bed, because I knew I'd not be able to sleep. A glass of chilled wine, barely touched, and a desire for a cigarette. What was with me? Earlier I'd taken one of Tansi's cigarettes, and then one of Mercy's. I started feeling guilty about appropriating them, and that did not make me happy. I was used to having one rare cigarette, maybe at the end of a good day of writing. A cocktail and one cigarette. One, just one. Maybe once a week. That's it. Now I was plundering Tansi's and Mercy's packs. How ridiculous!

The phone rang.

"It's Jimmy."

"Where are you?"

"In your lobby."

"Why?"

"Come down. Please."

"It's late."

"No, it isn't." A pause. "Come down."

I protested, but emptily. I wanted to see him. I threw on a jacket over my dress, grabbed my clutch, and met him in the lobby. A cigarette in his mouth, the first thing I spotted. *His* image, which he'd never relinquish.

"What is it, Jimmy?"

Surprisingly, he drew his face close to mine, and I smelled the rich tang of tobacco, the trace of whiskey. Not heavy, but there. And something else: a raw, almost earthy smell; sweat, dirt. A farm boy's smell. "Come on. Outside."

"Jimmy," I said, hurriedly, afraid he'd slip away. "I have to ask you something." He looked at me. "Why didn't you tell Detective Cotton you wrote that nasty letter to Carisa? Why did you hide that fact from him? Do you know how it makes you look?"

He didn't answer, just shrugged.

Frustrated, I wanted to ask him again, more loudly this time, but I sensed he wouldn't answer.

Outside he pointed to his fancy sports car. I didn't know cars. What was it? An MG? A Porsche? Some slick little convertible, glistening under the overhead lights. Sitting there, poised, at the ready, a doorman admiring it. He opened the passenger door, bowed. "Please." He motioned me into the car. "See how it feels."

Reluctantly, I slid into the plush, deep seat, sunk in low, felt immediately foolish, and tremendously old. He jumped in, boyish, turned the key, slipped the sleek, expensive vehicle into gear. I tapped him on the wrist. "Wait, Jimmy. I can't do this. Where are we going? Stop." It was night; it was chilly; it was late. I was…well, I was Edna Ferber, septuagenarian, playing sidekick to a hot rodder. Dragster. Rebel. Part of his wolf pack.

He stopped. Reaching behind, he grabbed a thick wool blanket and quietly wrapped it around my shoulders, my neck. I started to say something, but he whispered, "Ssshhh! You'll spoil it." And then he found a scarf, draped it over my hair and around my neck, and tied it snugly under my chin. His deft fingers moved quickly, and I found myself enthralled by his movements, his touch, his gentleness.

"I'm too old for joyriding."

A raspy cigarette voice. "You're not. You know you're not."

Secured, I sat there, and he sailed off. Down the boulevards, around corners, up the steep roads into the Hollywood Hills, speeding, speeding, the car edging near dark borders of eucalyptus, bowers of bougainvillea, boxed hedges. Speeding, speeding; the car sailing into air that seemed blue and smoky, headlights beaming on distant trees and roads that suddenly were behind me. I closed my eyes, frightened, then relaxed. It was as though his body and his mind were part of the well-oiled smooth machine—a oneness, I told myself. Nothing bad would happen to me, impossible. On and on, up into the shadowy hills, blazing around the hairpin corners, the occasional car ahead soon left behind. Approaching cars were small dots of yellow enlarging into moon-wide bursts of light that suddenly disappeared behind us. And then, seeming not to break speed, he stopped, spun the car downward, and we sat on the edge of a hill, a wooded, thick land, and below me spread nighttime L.A., blocks of light and blackness set against low-hung blotchy clouds in an indigo sky. I heard the hum of an airplane, far above, and saw the flickering of some aerial lights in the distance. Down below, L.A. was a gem to be swallowed, white, delicate, awful, yet magnetic.

He pointed, an impish grin on his face. So I looked.

"I wanted to be the one to show you this," he said. "It's the only way to imagine this world."

I started to say something but realized it would come out garbled, gobbledygook from a fairy-tale character. My head swam; my throat was dry. So I just sat there.

He took off his horn-rimmed eyeglasses and stared, and I realized how intense, almost possessed, his face became: a new beauty to him, this squinting myopic boy. "Sometimes the world is better if you can't see it," he whispered.

Still I said nothing.

"You know, Miss Edna, in Beverly Hills there are no cemeteries. None. People there think they're going to live forever."

For a while we sat there, Jimmy without his glasses on, with me staring at his profile. Silence.

Then, nodding, he put the sports car in gear, drove back down the hills, slowly now, as though the thing he'd feared he might lose had been safely won; and the rest was indifference. At the hotel, I uncovered myself from the layers but realized I had not been touched by L.A.'s night chill. Carelessly he tossed the blanket and scarf behind him. I opened my door. He tapped me on the shoulder. When I looked back, still numb and under water—for some reason I found myself crying—he seemed to be muttering something, but it was his familiar halting, stumbling talk.

"What?" my mouth said, though I knew I vocalized no words.

"You only get to do most things once."

Chapter Thirteen

The next day, spent on the arm of Jack Warner who rushed me through some meetings and *tête-à-têtes* with Very Important People (I capitalized the phrase in my mind, though, I told myself grimly, they were decidedly lower-case people), I'd nodded, smiled, bowed, and babbled thank you, yes, very nice, quite, lovely lovely lovely, so many times that I thought I was nineteen again, and begging for employment in Appleton, Wisconsin. Finally, I retreated to my hotel, where, within minutes, Jimmy called me, his voice light and airy, boyish.

"Where were you? I've been calling all day." He paused. "Breakfast tomorrow at Googie's, at eight. Meet me there. Please." The line went dead.

So the following morning, still basking in the glow of that delicious climb into the Hollywood Hills, I had the studio car drop me outside the busy eatery, filled at that hour with sloe-eyed locals. I paused, tentative, on the threshold, a clanging bell announcing my arrival; but no one took notice of the matronly woman standing there, dressed that morning in a youthful sun dress, daffodil yellow, with a rhinestone brooch suitably placed over my heart. I thought I looked, well, twenty years younger.

Already there, surprising me, Jimmy rose, rushed over, and squired me back to a booth, where a cup of coffee rested on my side of the table. He ordered food, and I chose an English muffin with boysenberry jam and more coffee, please, and piping hot, if possible. Jimmy smiled. "You don't eat enough."

"And you, so slender."

"The camera puts weight on me."

I breathed in. "And you wanted to see me for what reason?"

He laughed. "Right to the heart of things." He sat back. "Actually, Miss Edna, no reason. I'm treating you to breakfast. My spies in the house of Hollywood report that you and Mercy have chosen my cause. The maiden taking over the quest from the knight."

I pursed my lips together. "I seem to recall a young knight making a heartfelt request for assistance one grim, heavy night."

There was a twinkle in his eyes. Really, I thought, a twinkle. Strangely, I'd heard that tired expression all my life—indeed, had employed it generously in my fiction—but now, perforce, I seemed to experience it for the first time. Twinkle in the eye: a brightness, a sparkle, a flash that suggests life unsullied by nagging worry, and, truth to tell, a world away from murder.

"Then," I said, "if my purpose here is to consume ham and eggs, let me play interlocutor."

"A minstrel show, and me in it."

"Tell me, Jimmy, why did you hold back information from the police?"

He made a clicking sound. "I never really thought about the letter to Carisa. I didn't *forget* it, but it just seemed unimportant."

"Come on, Jimmy. Really? With all the scuttlebutt about *her* letters to you and Warner?"

He shrugged.

"But Jimmy, Detective Cotton *asked* you if you wrote to her."

"How do you know that?"

"He told me."

"Whose side are you on?" But he was smiling.

"Yours, and you know it. Sooner or later, everyone is on your side. It's a dangerous talent you have, young man."

"I lied to him. The question took me by surprise. Police make me nervous."

"What else have you lied about?"

"Nothing, I swear. I wouldn't lie to you." He took a sip of coffee.

"You'd better not." I knew I sounded schoolmarmish, a little arch and pompous, but I didn't care. Murder it is, I thought, and I'll say what I damn well like. In fact, I say what I like, no matter what. I don't need a murder to make me blunt.

"You know, Miss Edna, I'll tell you something. I find that I don't even think much about the murder. I think about *her* all the time, but not the murder. Carisa *alive* and laughing and saying weird stuff. To me she's still alive. It's like, well, it's over—a scene shot, in the can, edited. The film over. I've done three movies in about a year, more or less, and everything I do is filtered through this phony prism of celluloid."

"But you were close to her."

"We did go out, for a moment. It was nothing. You know, dating. Christ. I'd stop at her place. Yes, I know, I gave her that cheap statue because when she was at my place she liked it, but it was just having fun, you know, going out, the way young people do. It's what young people *do*."

"Did you know she was crazy and maybe on drugs?"

"The craziness I spotted right away, hard not to. But I'm drawn to crazy types, oddball characters, you know. I like those souls that teeter totter on the rim of the universe."

"But drugs?"

"That I learned right after Marfa. I don't mean marijuana. Reefer. That's not drugs. I mean that stuff she did. I think it escalated when the studio axed her. It was Lydia Plummer, oddly, who told me. And then she, too, confessed to sticking the old needle in her pretty flesh. Freaked me out. Not reefer, that's nothing. That's not a scene I like, heroin. Back in New York, that café on Bleecker at MacDougal, you know, the Zigzag Cafe, the beatniks smoked, the poet and painters, even the Stalinists, you know, maybe, we all did reefer but not the needle crap. I ran away. My vices are…otherwise."

"But then you dated Lydia?"

"Miss Edna, I drift from girl to girl. She…like pursued me. We're talking a couple of weekends. That ain't a life contract. That's dating. But girls seemed to go too deep with me. I swear I didn't promise anybody anything. And they want so much. Everybody wants so much from me." He suddenly seemed to freeze up. "I look in the mirror and hate what I see. I don't see what others see." He paused. "I just don't like myself."

"That's foolish, Jimmy."

"I'm not saying this to make you feel sorry for me." He looked into my eyes.

"But people do feel sorry for you, Jimmy, especially when you talk like this."

"It's the only way I know how to talk. You know, all my life I've tried to fit in, though I know I don't. I never *tried* to be different. I just was. So I jump at the world, fight with it."

"Maybe that's why you're a fine actor. You lose yourself in the role."

"No, I don't lose myself. That person is *me*. I'm only myself playing the rebels. They're typecasting me. I get nervous about next year. Can I play the rebel for years to come?"

"You'll grow."

"Miss Edna, I'm losing my hair even now."

"You'll still be James Dean."

"I think I'll be dead by thirty."

I got chilled. "Don't say that."

He withdrew a pack of king-size Chesterfields from a breast pocket, offered me one. I shook my head. "Too early in the morning. My vices are reserved for evenings." I watched him light one, take a puff, put the cigarette on the table, upended, balancing it, watching it. Then he picked it up, took a drag, put it down, and balanced it vertically again. I watched, enthralled. Neither of us spoke. When the ash was long and wispy, ready to fall, Jimmy picked up the cigarette, stared at the long ash, and looked for an ashtray. There was none on the table, so he stood, let the ash fall onto the linoleum floor. He sat back down, smiled. "I never can seem to find the ashtray."

I said nothing. Each movement he made seemed as if he just invented it.

The boyish gleam he'd shown when I'd first sat down was gone now, replaced by melancholia, as he tucked his head into his chest. I've lost him again, I thought. I felt tightness in my chest. When I reached out and touched the back of his hand, he recoiled, as from an electric shook, and the touch seemed to startle him awake. "I'm doing it again," he said. "I'm begging for love from you."

"It's all right to want people to love you," I said, and the line surprised me. It didn't sound like me.

"I used to own a .22 automatic but the studio took it away from me."

"What?"

He stood up, embarrassed, and flicked a bunch of singles on the table. "You know, there was that cool line from that Bogart movie. 'Live fast, die young, and leave a good-looking corpse.'"

"Jimmy."

Within hours I was sitting with Jake Geyser at the Smoke House, having an unwelcome lunch, and immediately I contrasted the studio functionary with the mercurial Jimmy. Jake looked officious in a casual tan summer suit, with an apparently trendy narrow tie. He sported a fresh haircut, shorn close, military style. I noted something else. He looked away from me when he spoke, his eyes returning only when I responded. Evasiveness, perhaps; or a mannerism. Nevertheless, it was off-putting and irksome.

Jack Warner, learning through office scuttlebutt that I was often in the company of the hirelings, was concerned. I'd been spotted at Googie's and elsewhere, even Carisa's tenderloin flat. "Mr. Warner wonders if you're all right."

"All right?" I echoed.

"Are you bored?"

"Because of the company I keep?"

"You have an inordinate fascination with the death of Carisa Krausse?"

"And shouldn't we all? Until it is solved?"

He whispered, through compressed lips, "There are people who do this for a living."

"No matter." I wanted to be away from him. "Tell me, Jake," I said, stabbing a piece of wilted lettuce on my plate, "Detective Cotton tells me your prints were all over Carisa's apartment."

He turned his head, as though slapped. What a dreadful man, I thought. Had he ever been attractive? I had no idea why I thought that, other than the perverse sensation of realizing his life was probably spent in the shadow of better looking, huskier boys, athletes, prep school Princetonian pampered heroes. A hanger-on, a Uriah Heap. Now, water boy to the stars.

"Well," he got defensive, "hardly all over."

"How did that happen?"

"I stopped in once, to *plead* with her. Warner *told* me to go. Do you think I'd drive there? I told him to ask Tansi, you know, woman to woman, but Warner said no. Tansi, though obedient to a fault, made it clear she would not do that. And Warner, old school gentleman, believes you don't ask ladies to do dirty work."

"How noble," I said. I meant it as a throwaway line, but it came out harsh, unfunny. "But *you* went."

"Once, I swear." He looked at his uneaten sandwich, mayonnaise oozing onto the plate. "Once. Inside that hell hole, moving through stacks of magazines. She either read a lot or someone mistook her apartment for a town dump." His eyes flickered; he looked pleased with his own observation.

"Had *you* sent her a letter?" I asked, suddenly thinking of it.

"Of course not."

"Everyone else seems to have."

"Detective Cotton probably told you about the papers he found there."

That stopped me cold. "What?"

"Oh!" Silence. "Oh well. Just before she died—was killed—that's when I went there. Warner's people made me offer her some money, but she had to sign a sheet disavowing any connection with Jimmy or the studio. Promise not to talk to *Confidential*. To the gossip columnists."

"And she agreed?"

"Almost. I left the papers with her, and she promised to contact me. She had conditions."

"Did she?"

"No."

"Did you go there the day of the murder?"

"I swear I didn't."

"Maybe you did, and she had conditions you couldn't accept."

"And so I killed her? Good God!"

"How much money?"

He hedged. "Enough so that she could move out of that rattrap. Move on. Resettle. I knew she'd take it. She was…joyous."

"The super, Mr. Vega, saw her arguing with an older man on the sidewalk."

He squinted his eyes. "Good God. Yes, that was me. A few days before my visit. She was coming out of her apartment, and I pulled in front. She got frightened, and we screamed at each other. Or, rather, she screamed at me. I thought she'd hit me. She kept saying that Jimmy sent me."

"So it wasn't just one visit, as you've said. It was at least two."

He looked at me. "I don't consider that street scene a visit."

"You're playing games, sir."

"No, I'm not."

"Who did you think killed her?"

He shrugged.

I smiled. "You're a good company man. You want to believe it's Jimmy, but your job demands that it not be him." I glanced toward the doorway.

Jimmy stood there, watching, and seemed angry to see me with Jake. Then, hovering a moment near our table, he slid into the seat next to Jake, uninvited, and smiled at me. "In the course of a given day, Miss Edna, you go from the sublime," he bowed, "to the ridiculous." He indicated Jake, but didn't look his way.

"Now, Jimmy," I began.

Jake fumed. "You know, Jimmy, you may be the studio darling, but your manners are questionable."

"Oh, my manners are just fine."

"Boorish, rude…"

"Jake, I don't like you." Blunt, heavy duty, flat out.

"And I don't like you."

"You *have* to. Warner ordered you to."

"I'll do anything in my earthly power to help you in your career, but that doesn't mean I have to…"

"Yes, you do."

"Come on, Jimmy," I pleaded.

"You know, Warner knows what I think of you," Jake said. "I've told him. He just nods and tells me to do my job. Frankly, a lot of people don't care for you. I know Miss Ferber thinks you're," he paused, searching for a phrase but could only bring up an ancient one, "the bee's knees, but I think you're a slovenly, ill-kept brat."

Jimmy shot back, lamely, "And you're a hack."

Fascinated, I sat back now, observing the exchange of pepper-shot vitriol, and realized, suddenly, that both men were enjoying themselves on some atavistic level. Clearly despising each other, they still delighted in some crude ritual. I imagined a schoolyard where, finally, fisticuffs would end this verbal assault. Or an irate teacher would drag the errant boys into the principal's office. My, my, I thought. Boys will be boys.

They were tiring. "The only comfort I have is knowing that you will be named a murderer by Detective Cotton."

Jimmy paused, cut to the quick. He recovered. "Interesting. You didn't say you thought I did it, just that I'd be *charged* with it."

"I meant…"

"Which suggests that you know I didn't do it." He smiled. "Because, I suppose, you're running from the truth."

"And what is that?" Smug, an old British public-school demeanor asserting itself.

"That you're the *real* killer."

Jake, stunned, stood, mumbled something about a meeting, and left. Jimmy yelled after him. "You gonna make Miss Ferber pay for her own lunch?" Jake never looked back.

"Quite the show, Jimmy."

"Everything is rehearsal for me."

"You were rude."

"Yeah, I suppose so. That's what I do. You know, I'm not the nicest guy, Miss Edna. People tell me that I'm gauche—I love that word—and I gotta agree. Sometimes I wonder how people can actually stay in the same room with me. Frankly, I wouldn't put up with my antics. I can't tolerate myself."

I shook my head. "I can't tell if you're serious."

"I am."

"Why are you here?" I asked nervously.

"I'm meeting Tommy. He thinks I've been avoiding him and Polly."

"Have you?"

"Yes. Tommy is too…clinging. If I want to see myself, I'll look in a mirror. I don't need to see *him* as me."

Within minutes Tommy arrived, out of breath, and Jimmy motioned him to sit down. I looked at my watch, stood up, ready to leave, but Jimmy shook his head. "Wait a bit." I slipped back into my seat.

Tommy was in a tizzy. He'd come from a fight with Polly. He was used to their spitfire battles about his future, their freakish love, his notorious lack of ambition, his life as a shadow, but, he confessed, near tears, this time something was different. Polly seemed to want to *leave* him. For good. Not the sporadic running away to stay with a girlfriend over night, only to return, penitent, giddy, in love again.

What happened, I learned, since Tommy began talking almost immediately, without so much as a howdy ma'am (he obviously learned his manners at the James Dean academy of social decorum) was that Detective Cotton had told Polly that Tommy's fingerprints were found in Carisa's apartment and that angered her.

"Why would Cotton tell her that?" Tommy whined.

"It seems to be his way," I said. "Tell everyone bits and pieces of evidence and hope someone reacts. He's tried it with me."

Tommy frowned.

"You hadn't told her you were there?" Jimmy said.

"I'd told her I went with you."

"You didn't."

"Oh, I did. Remember. That one time?"

"No, Tommy."

"You forget. Most of the time I waited in the car but I did stop in…"

"You waited in the car one time, Tommy."

Tommy seemed annoyed now, petulant. "She thinks I," he glanced at me, "you know, slept with Carisa. I mean, she's had suspicions, even accused me of it once or twice. But Cotton's comments, like, made her nuts."

Jimmy's voice was edgy. "But you did sleep with her."

"No."

"Of course you did. Carisa told me—couldn't wait to tell me. Lorded it over me, in fact. 'Your boy picks up your leftovers like a street Arab plucks coal from train tracks' was how she put it."

Tommy blushed and stammered. "One time."

I interrupted. "Seems to me, if I can judge by what folks are telling me, everyone visited Carisa just once. People in Hollywood seem to do things only once."

Jimmy grinned. "We're easily bored here, we box-office wonders."

"So I accused Polly of sleeping with *you*," Tommy said, emphasizing the last word.

I thought Jimmy might react, but he simply sat there, unperturbed, it seemed, relishing the moment. "I don't need your girlfriends, Tommy."

I could see that Tommy was testing Jimmy, watching, hoping for something. But then he backed off, saying with a half-hearted giggle, "I knew it was nonsense. Sorry, Jimmy. I shouldn't have said that."

I expected Jimmy, the troublemaker, to announce, "Yes, I did. I admit it. And Polly has a crush on me." But Jimmy, looking a little sad, seemed suddenly to pity the sycophantic boy from his hometown. "Tommy, don't worry. Polly'll get over it. She always does. She loves you." Said, it was a wistful, almost melancholic line, with Jimmy lingering on the word *loves* as though he'd discovered a new sensation, a wet confection that warmed the mouth. Our boy of perpetual surprises.

Jimmy purposely changed the subject and chatted about Lydia who, he announced, had called him the night before, somnambulant, in a narcotic haze.

"What did she say?" I asked at the same moment Tommy did. We waited.

"It was hard to understand her, you know. She said she was alone. She felt that Nell leaving her without warning, roommates and friends no more, was too much."

"What do you do when someone you know is taking narcotics?" Vaguely, I thought of a Chicago jazz saxophonist I once befriended, who died one night at the apartment of a friend. And a book I'd read as a young woman: Thomas DeQuincey's *Confessions of an Opium Eater*. And Coleridge's "Kubla Khan." That's it. My knowledge of drugs is literary. Sometimes it's safer that way.

Both men stared at me, and neither answered.

Jimmy went on. "She said she was scared. Really frightened."

"Of what?"

"She didn't say. I think because Carisa was murdered, and they were friends. After a while I realized she was still on the line but saying nothing." He shrugged his shoulders. "So I hung up."

"That's it?" I asked.

Jimmy smiled. "I had to go to bed."

◇◇◇

Late that afternoon I sat with Jack Warner in his office, and I was certain I knew why. Tansi had cornered me, predictably frantic, saying Jack requested a brief meeting. "Of course, I told him you'd be there," she said, overlapping my stuttered one word "Why?" But I dutifully went, and sat there, uncomfortable in a straight-backed chair, while he fiddled with a stack of memos on his desk. I cleared my throat. "Tansi's tone suggested some immediacy."

He looked up, but didn't smile. "Tansi assumes everything I say is urgent."

"And it isn't?"

For a second I saw wariness in his eyes. That thin sinister moustache twitched. This dapper man in the pristine blue suit, with the sensible no-nonsense haircut, the manicured hands idly leafing through the memos, didn't know how to read me. A humorless man, unfortunately; a man who decided comedy had no rewards. "It is the way I run my business." Said levelly; matter-of-fact, with the slightest of edges.

"Well…" I began.

"Jimmy," he said, and the slender fingers stopped drumming the memos.

I waited.

"Well?" he asked, tilting his head.

"I didn't realize it was a question."

He leaned back in his chair, swiveled left and right, folded his hands behind his head, and contemplated me. "I'm assuming you know, deep down, that he probably killed that woman."

"I know no such thing, Jack." I sat up, rail stiff. "And she had a name. Carisa Krausse."

He shook his head back and forth, impatient. "This has to go away, Edna."

"But a murder…"

"It has to go away. Look, I don't know if Jimmy Dean killed her—Carisa—but you're a little too close to the fire, Edna."

"What does that mean?"

Cloudy, unblinking eyes: "I don't care, frankly, about Jimmy's private life because, to tell you the truth, he no longer *has* a private life. None of them do—Jimmy, Liz, Rock. All of them."

"We all have private lives."

"Not stars like those three. Jimmy is young. He doesn't understand what's at stake here. Maybe he killed her, maybe he didn't. It has to go away. You don't understand…"

I interrupted. "You think I'm meddling? That's why I'm here?"

He sat forward. "We can't have you traipsing around Skid Row." He stopped. "Look, Edna, we're friends, the two of us. We've put in place a vast ungainly machinery, you and I. *Giant* is a huge bestseller and soon to be a blockbuster movie. An epic. It's what Hollywood does best. Romance, up there on the screen. It's beyond private lives now. This isn't just James Dean here, some haywire hayseed messing up. James Dean is a creation, a slick glossy face that looks good on the cover of *Photoplay*. Rock Hudson—last year *Magnificent Obsession*. This year's most popular man in Hollywood. Number one. Liz Taylor, one of the great beauties. My job is to cultivate the dream. In movie houses all over America people stare up at that screen and see a world they'll never have, can only imagine. Bigger than life Texas romance, oil millionaires, furs, cars, beautiful people like Rock and Liz and Jimmy. Real people don't look like that, Edna. Look around you."

"It's all a lie, then?"

"Of course it is. It's the grand illusion. Cinemascope and Technicolor—a moviemaker's palette. We paint dreams."

"And what about the nightmares?"

"You don't understand."

"But I do."

"Edna, it's fantasy writ large." He sighed. "Hollywood is a star factory. Rock and Liz, they understand this. The game. Liz smiles and weeps and flashes her eyes and thinks, I'll be a beauty forever. The world's oldest *ingénue*. The little girl from *National Velvet*. Rock thinks his granite chin and rugged physique will stay chiseled forever. What other choice do they have but to believe this? But Jimmy has to learn that Hollywood is a big fat sow sloshing through the mud, moving, never stopping, effortlessly. And all about her flies swarm and buzz and hum and dip and flutter. Liz and Rock and Jimmy are the flies right now: they get all the attention. But the sow always moves on, plodding, and after a while there are new flies overhead." Suddenly, he stood up. "Enough. I didn't mean to get into all this. It's just that it all," he waved his hand in the air, "has to go away."

I stood up. "I still don't know why you called me in here," I grumbled.

His baffled look suggested I was a slow-witted old lady. "Let me put it this way. We'll handle the Jimmy business."

"Of course." I turned to leave.

"I don't think I've convinced you."

I looked back. "Did you really expect to?"

That surprised him. "Well, actually, no. I don't have *you* under contract."

I fiddled with my purse, a little nervous, and started to walk out.

"Edna." I turned back. He was opening a small jewelry box, tan leather flecked with gold. The overhead light caught the chaotic glint of diamonds on a sleek gold band. Good God, I thought, is the man trying to buy me off with riches?

"Lovely," I said, backing up.

"It's just a bauble," Jack said, flashing it before me. "A present for Liz. She likes presents." He snapped the case shut. "She likes to feel wanted, appreciated."

"Don't we all," I snapped, and left the office.

Chapter Fourteen

That weekend, on a crisp, brassy Saturday afternoon, Mercy and I drove back to Carisa's apartment. I had one purpose in returning: Connie Zuniga, Vega's fourteen-year-old granddaughter.

"But why the need for surprise?" Mercy asked.

"I don't want her rehearsed story. In Hollywood everyone talks like they've memorized a script."

Mercy glanced at me as she pulled up to a light on Fifth Street.

"But she's already told her story to Detective Cotton."

"Yes, right after it all happened. Now, days later, she's got *that* story perhaps, but maybe she can recall some other things."

"Like what?"

"I don't have a clue."

As Mercy's car stopped in front of the apartment building, I spotted Vega at the curb, shuffling garbage cans. Up and down the street, curbs were dotted with broken-up pails, dented tins, lopsided cardboard containers, overflowing with debris. The junk in Carisa's apartment would fill dozens of such containers. But was there one tidbit of useful information in those mountainous stacks of *L.A. Times*, *Collier's*, *Movie Life*, *Stardom Magazine*, movie scripts, rehearsal notes, cards and letters and bills, paid and unpaid? The important letters—maybe just one letter?—were gone, taken by the murderer.

Vega watched us step from the car. He was perspiring, his face flushed; and he wore a stained Hawaiian shirt over white linen trousers, rolled up above his ankles, showing bare feet tucked into sandals, unstrapped, the leather worn.

"Ladies." He bowed, one hand gripping his lion's-head cane. He wiped his brow with a large white handkerchief. "A surprise."

"We apologize for intruding, Mr. Vega," I said, "but we were hoping your granddaughter Connie might talk to us. You said weekends…"

He looked behind him, back to the house. "She's inside, in the kitchen, supposedly peeling avocados, but I suspect her nose is buried in *Modern Screen*." He grinned.

"A favor, sir. Would you mind if we had a word with her?"

"Still the same story?"

"Yes, I'm afraid. Has Detective Cotton been around?"

"Again and again. He has the persistence and stubbornness of a deadly bull dog that keeps coming at you."

Quietly, he led us into the kitchen. With the curtains drawn over tattered blinds and the only light coming from a dim-watt bulb over a table, the room was a surprise: cool, serene, monastery-like, the street noise distant, not even a ticking clock. I heard the rhythmic scraping of a knife against avocados, each lifted from a wicker basket and then sliced into, the rough-knotty green skin deftly peeled back, and the lush, overripe green meat turned quickly into an earthenware bowl, and another lifted up. Green, slimy fingers attached to a skinny little girl who sat at the table, her eyes faraway, her movements mechanical. At the other end of the table, pristine and untouched, a copy of *Photoplay*, unopened.

"Connie," her grandfather said, rousing her. "Will you please share your story with these two fine ladies?"

"Story?"

"The day Carisa Krausse died." He paused. "They've come just to see you."

The young girl nodded, stood, wiped her stained hands on a towel, and then sat back down, facing us, hands folded on the table. She smiled.

Vega set glasses of lemonade before us, and I was pleased. I remembered the exquisite drink. I sipped mine, and resisted the temptation to smack my lips.

Connie was a beautiful child, with something of her grand-father's rich mocha coloration; the high cheekbones, the slender nose, the round black eyes, deep and clear; the long straight black hair, so shiny it looked greased, touched with abundant and rich oils. Aztec girl, I thought. Mexican girl. Oddly, I thought of the statue that had been hurled at Carisa: that grotesque green replica of an Aztec girl, with protruding belly and flattened features. A far cry from this ravishing girl; this untouched girl, so innocent, sitting among avocados and kitchen shadow; yet overwhelmingly exotic, sensual. Handmaiden at some ancient shrine.

"Thank you, Connie." I stopped, looking at the girl's moving lips. "What?"

"Have they caught the murderer?"

I realized the girl was afraid, living there in the house. "No, not yet."

Mercy said, quietly, "Did you like Carisa Krausse?"

The girl shook her head slowly. "Not really. Abuelo," she pointed to Vega, "doesn't want me to bother the tenants." He nodded at her. "But we'd say hello. I always wanted to ask her questions because she's like an actress, and I wanna be in the movies someday. Only one time I saw her after James Dean left, and I had to say something. She said she was gonna marry him. But after that, well, she didn't talk to me. She was, you know, strange."

"Strange?"

"She'd yell at nothing, like a little wild, she'd..." Her voice trailed off.

"You ever see who visited her?"

She nodded. "Sometimes lots of people. Movie people. I figured. Some not so nice."

"Why?" From Mercy.

"Loud, rough. Scary."

"But not all."

"No." Her face brightened. "I started watching the first time I saw James Dean come in. I couldn't believe it."

"How did you know him?"

She shifted in the chair, got up and poured herself lemonade. She was wearing a simple blouse, but she had on a poodle skirt lacking the appliquéd poodle at the hem. Instead she had a hot rod car embroidered there. A long skirt, neat and pressed, over saddle shoes with bobby socks. I smiled. I could be looking at a girl in New York City or Tampa or Keokuk, Iowa.

"Maybe he came before but a lot of good looking, you know, guys came to see her. But then I saw *East of Eden* and he was in the movie magazines and suddenly everybody is talking about him. And then he was here. Here!"

"You talked to him?"

She blushed. "Once. I bumped into him in the hallway, and, and he said, 'How are you?' I didn't say anything except mumble, but he just looked at me, he smiled at me, and I couldn't move."

Vega said, from across the room, "Since then, she has his pictures on the walls of her room, and she buys the magazines, and she waits by the window when she's visiting me…"

"Abuelo!" she blurted out, mortified. "He's a star. All my friends want to hear my story. They ask me *everything*…"

"Was he here the day Carisa died?" Mercy asked softly.

For a moment she seemed confused. "What?" I asked.

"I don't want to get him in trouble. He's not in trouble, is he?"

"No," I answered. "Just tell us what you know."

Warming up, excited: "Well, I *saw* him that afternoon."

"When?"

"I don't remember the time. I told Detective Cotton I couldn't remember the first time but it was late in the day."

"The first time?" That surprised me.

"Yeah, well, he was here twice that day. He came back."

I looked at Mercy. "Early? Late?" From Mercy.

"I told you—the first time was late afternoon."

"Before five?" I asked. The cocktail party, from five to seven. Jimmy's brief appearance, his leaving at—what time? Six or so?

"No, after. I was watching TV before that. I was talking on the phone with my friend, and she was going to the movies."

"What did Jimmy do?" I went on.

The girl grinned. "Jimmy. You call him Jimmy?"

I nodded, feeling schoolgirlish: the president of his fan club.

"I'm afraid so." Mercy caught my eye. She was amused.

"Nothing. I saw him on the sidewalk, coming onto the stoop. So I cracked the door and stared into the hallway. He ran up the stairs."

Vega grumbled. "Connie, I told you not to intrude."

"He never *saw* me."

"He was alone?" I asked.

"Yes."

"In that flashy car of his?"

"Oh, no. I didn't see a car. The only time I saw him in a car, well, he was in a big, like, station wagon. With wood panels on the side. Brand-new."

I turned to Mercy. "Jimmy drives a station wagon?"

Mercy grinned. "A Ford station wagon, designed for the modern family of four. Mommy, Daddy, and the kiddies. It's a side of Jimmy you don't know."

"I gather." I shook my head. "And then what happened?"

"I heard him yelling at her, and she was yelling back. In the hallway. I got scared."

"What did he say?"

"He was swearing, calling her names. She must've done something bad to him."

"Did he go into the apartment?"

"I dunno. He wasn't there long. Yelling like crazy. I just stayed by the door and waited."

"Where was I?" her grandfather interrupted.

"In the garden, I think, out back."

He frowned.

"So how long was he upstairs?" Mercy asked.

"It was like minutes, I guess. Then I heard him on the stairs, and he comes running down, real fast, and out the door."

"Did you see his face?"

"Why?"

"Was he angry?"

"He went by too fast. I couldn't tell. And I jumped back, afraid he'd spot me."

"But," I said, "you said you saw him again. He came back. Later?"

"Yeah, I mean, well, I thought he left for the day so I didn't care. I got ready to go meet my friend, you know, do something. So long's I'm back early, Abuelo doesn't mind. So like fifteen minutes later—I don't know—I left and I waited for the bus on the corner. The bus came and I got on, and, you know, it goes by my house. So I'm staring out the window and then, all of a sudden, there he was again, running out the front door. Like a maniac. But the bus was moving, and I had to crane back my neck. He's running and all, running, like..."

"And you hadn't seen him arrive?"

"No, I was dressing in my room. I never *expected* him back."

Mercy, her voice dark. "And then he was."

"Yeah, I was so angry. Here I was on the bus, and he's running out of my building."

"Alone?"

"Yeah."

"Did you see him get into a car?"

"The bus was moving fast, you know, but, no, but I felt somebody was waiting for him there." She paused, as though conjuring up a picture in her head.

"What?" From Mercy.

"Well, looking back, I saw this car across the street, and there was this lady sitting there, looking out, at him. She was watching him. I could see her right there, but the bus was turning. And I thought, God, he got some girl waiting for him."

"He went to the car?"

"I couldn't tell, but I thought so. Looked like it. He was running in that direction—toward her. Jumping off the stoop, onto the sidewalk."

"So you don't know if he was with her?"

"No, I don't, but I just had that feeling. You know? Like she was waiting."

"Why?"

"Because suddenly I felt that I'd seen her sitting there before. I don't know exactly, but something about her made me remember. Like she'd been one of the people that visited Carisa. One of her actress friends. Maybe with him. I don't know. I mean, you know how it's like in the back of your head, and then it's there, sort of. It all happened so fast. I'm on the bus and it's moving, and so I'm thinking that maybe he dropped something off."

"What did she look like?"

"I dunno. She was just one of the girls that come here. I kept thinking—she's in the movies, maybe. Maybe Julie Harris from *East of Eden*. James Dean and her together."

"You can't describe her?" I asked.

"I thought I just did."

Both of us waited, expectant, but nothing followed. Connie seemed edgy now, as though she'd said something she shouldn't have.

"And you told this to Detective Cotton?" I asked.

She nodded.

I turned to Mercy, who stared back. Cotton hadn't mentioned any of this to me, certainly; but why should he? It was *his* investigation, not mine. He meted out information piecemeal as was his desire, though it bothered me—this sin of omission. Then, like a hot flash, I experienced a wave of fear: yet another block in the wall being built around Jimmy.

Connie was mumbling something else. "I also told him about Alva and Alyce."

"Who?" From Mercy.

"You know," I said, "the twins, the boy and girl who follow Jimmy around." I turned to Connie. "They were here that day?"

She shook her head and rolled her eyes. "Crazy. Those two. They're *always* around. Somehow they learned James Dean comes here and sometimes they wait in the restaurant across the street, watching. I don't know if he even *talks* to them. They are so weird, those two. Always together, running around like maniacs or standing on the sidewalk, staring."

"So they were here that afternoon?"

"Yeah, that's what I told the detective. When the bus stopped at the next stop, I noticed they were running up the street, turning into my block. Almost arm in arm, hurrying, like they knew James Dean was there. A couple times when I talked to them, they're, like, out of breath. Was he here? What's he like? What did he say to you?" She grinned. "I told them he always talks to me, and they go crazy."

Her grandfather interrupted. "Connie, you talk to these crazy people? And you lie to them?"

"It's not, like lying, Abuelo. It's like we're in the movies. Sometimes I imagine whole conversations with James."

"Such foolishness." He shook his head but never took his eyes off her face.

An absolutely beatific look washed over her; a quietude, a softness in her already gentle features. "It's James Dean," she breathed, so reverential that no one said anything. She wrapped her arms around her body, swayed a bit, and closed her eyes. "It's James Dean. Not on the screen. Here. In my hallway. In my house. *Here.* Who else can say that? Not my friend Jennie. The star she's come closest to seeing was Montgomery Clift in a car. Passing by. That doesn't count, if you think about it. James Dean, well, he smiled at me."

Chapter Fifteen

Rock Hudson's publicist had called twice, trying to set up a luncheon. I'd resisted but Tansi, walking in as I was stumbling through an excuse, mumbled in a tinny, schoolmarm voice, "Oh Edna, you have to, it's Rock Hudson." I found myself grinning. And, oddly, I agreed to a hasty lunch in Jack Warner's private dining room. Now, sitting with the brilliantly handsome man in that quiet chamber, platters of untouched food delivered to us by obsequious servers who promptly bowed and disappeared, I stared across the table. I wondered why I'd taken an instant dislike to him. Steely eyed, suspicious, Rock stared back, a sliver of a smile on those beautiful lips.

"You seem uncomfortable." His voice was throaty, a careful mannered drawl, rich and full.

"I've never really liked very, very tall men. You notice I'm very small."

Suddenly he roared, Texas-style gusto, probably learned from my novel, his hand slapping his thigh. "And I thought you didn't like me because of my personality."

"I don't know you, personally, that is," I said evenly. "All I know is the matinee idol up there on the screen."

"And that's not me?"

"Do you believe it is?"

Again, the mesmerizing eyes, the purposely jutting chin, the graceful turn of the long rugged body in the Texas millionaire denim shirt. "There *is* someone called Rock Hudson, you know."

"He's an invention."

He smiled broadly. "True, but I don't remember the other person. That bumbling, frightened, wide-eyed lad from Winnetka, Illinois, named Roy Fitzgerald."

"You like your success?"

"Of course."

"Is that why we're having lunch, so you can assure me that you're happy in your celluloid world?"

A long silence, Rock playing with a fork. He put it down. "Jimmy Dean," he said, finally.

"Magical words, no?"

"Not to me. I hear he's seduced you into his fragile web."

I laughed. "Good God, Rock, give me some credit."

He held up his hand, palm out. "I don't care about Jimmy, Miss Ferber. I care about this movie, and what he's capable of doing to it. Sinking it. *Giant* is a milestone for me, a film that's moving me one more step away from B-movie oblivion. That's where I was three or four years ago. Jimmy's playing fast and loose with *his* fame. I don't. I've worked hard. I've bowed and scraped and played the game. I've totally embraced this invention—as you call it—called Rock Hudson until it's cash at the bank."

"You'll still be a star." My hand dramatically swept from his face down across the table.

"Not if the movie is killed."

"No one is killing the movie. Not on my watch."

Rock sat up, sucked in his breath. When he spoke his words were clipped, his face scarlet, his dark eyes piercing. "I think he's a murderer. I do."

"Rock, for heaven's sake."

"There's something wrong with him. You know, Miss Ferber, in Texas we shared a house. He was a filthy pig, he was brazen, he was purposely rude and foul. Christ, he spit on the floor, he," a pause, "did a lot worse things, I tell you. In Texas, working with George Stevens, we sensed—I sensed, Liz did, so did

others—that here was our future. This movie would always say
something about *us*. But Jimmy acted like it didn't matter."

"Of course it matters to him."

He frowned. "He puts his private life out *there*. Everyone can
talk about it, mangle it."

"And you don't?"

He looked alarmed. "Only I'm in control of my private life."
He drew his lips into a thin line. "That's why it's dangerous to
get close to a guy like Jimmy."

"You might be colored by the same brush?"

He hesitated. "Exactly." Then he smiled. "No chance of that.
He hates me. I hate him. If I have to talk to him, he refuses to
answer me. A baby boy, a slaphappy puppy."

"This doesn't make him a murderer."

"Miss Ferber, one thing I know that some folks around here
don't know is that it can all disappear in a flash." He pointed
around Jack Warner's well-appointed room with the plush gray
carpeting, the cascading draperies. "I fought my way here. I'm not
gonna let it vanish. Warner has to play this murder his way."

"What if Jimmy is innocent?"

That seemed to surprise him. "The Jimmy Deans of this
world are always guilty of something."

"Have you no sins?"

"Rock Hudson is an invention, as you said." He grinned.
"He's been created without sin."

"That's not answering my question."

He faltered. "I just want to do my job, Miss Ferber."

I pushed some food around my plate. Neither of us had
touched the lunch. "Well, I respect that." And my words made
him smile, sit back. "It's how I got where I am, too." We looked
at each other a long time.

For some reason now, idly, he started to ramble on about
acting—*serious* acting, he said—about dreaming. Especially
dreaming, the will-o'-the-wisp vagaries allowed by unpredictable fortune. His early days, waiting for a break, his numbing
work as a truck driver. I sat back, charmed by the warm-water

flow of words. The more he spoke, the more he sounded like a schoolboy—some lonely fourteen-year-old kid, a feckless dreamy kid, cruising down a back lane on a clunky bike, hurling newspapers onto whitewashed porches and emerald-green lawns enclosed in picket fences. The modulated voice disappeared, and what surfaced was a curious mixture of laid-back Midwest twang and jittery teenage angst. I marveled at the transformation. And, emphatically, I liked it.

His stories reminded me of an Appleton, Wisconsin boy I remembered from Ryan High School days—a gangly, long-limbed boy whose name I've forgotten but whose presence has stayed with me. A boy on the high-school stage, acting a piddling role in *A Scrap of Paper*, his quivering voice and jerky body at odds with the ferocious hunger in his eyes, the fire there, the desperate desire to be away from the parochial town, to be out there in the world, magnificent on some city on some hill. So I felt then that I knew Rock in a way he'd probably forgotten. And the more he talked, the more I realized I couldn't dislike him. That was too easy. I didn't want to pity him either because so much of him struck me as so hollow, vain, lost. No, the fragility he refused in himself was what made me smile now.

So we talked about his role as Bick Benedict, about *Giant*, and he talked about *So Big*, which he said he'd read and loved. And when I stood up to leave, he said, "I'll be in New York this fall. Can we have lunch, you and me?"

Standing, facing him, I nodded. "Of course. My pleasure."

"Thank you."

In the hallway I closed my eyes, still thinking of that shy boy from my high school days.

"I may actually learn to like Rock Hudson," I told Mercy when I saw her in her dressing room.

"Oh, no, he charmed you."

"No, Mercy, I just allowed myself to be charmed. That's different."

◇◇◇

Later, resting at my hotel, I opened my door to face a dapper-looking man in formal attire—though the tie was slightly askew—a courtly-looking gentleman, graying at the temples. A sheepish grin on his face. Jimmy bowed to me, in costume as the middle-aged Jett Rink, the oillionaire in decline. They'd shaved his temples to create a receding hairline, and the makeup attempted to suggest a dissipated, unhappy man. I wasn't convinced—he looked vaudevillian stock character, some clown in a monkey suit.

He looked over his shoulder, feigning nervousness. "I escaped for the afternoon. Stevens thinks I'm in my dressing room. My scenes were done this morning, but he likes us to be around in costume to flatter his ego." He handed me a crumpled newspaper. "This is for you."

"Come in," I said. I'd been reading a novel by Sloan Wilson. *The Man in the Gray Flannel Suit*. Annoyed at its prosaic style and its ugly view of the world, I was looking for an escape. "Come in."

He fell into a chair, drew his legs up to his chest, wrapped his arms around them.

I unfolded the paper and found myself staring at a small, amorphous piece of clay, an embryonic torso, clay twisted into arms and legs and a narrow, long protuberance that, perhaps, would become a head. An incomplete body, some surrealistic object, a figure suspended between creation and fruition. I held it, wondering what to say.

"I made it for you," he said, finally. "You like it?"

"Yes. I didn't know you sculpted."

"I do a lot of things." He shrugged his shoulders. "It's, like, anonymous man. You got to do the rest of the work yourself—create a life for it in your head. Like I imagine you do when you write characters like Jett Rink."

"Is that why it has no face?"

"You're missing the point," he said. "Faces get in the way of things. Look at me. Everybody keeps telling me I'm…I'm gorgeous. You don't know how sick that makes me feel."

"It's a gift."

"Or a curse."

"It's your point of view, Jimmy."

A broken smile. "Exactly, I guess. That's the point of my statue there. See? Point of view." He withdrew a folded piece of paper from his breast pocket and handed it to me. I unfolded it and found myself staring at a remarkable likeness of my own head, ancient and large, with a mane of teased white locks, and fiery, hard-as-nails eyes.

I gasped. "My Lord. Me?"

He grinned. "You."

"This is very good. I mean, I don't like any pictures of myself—never have. But this is startlingly true."

"You have a great head on that tiny body. It dominates. It's *there*, like a monument."

"The missing figure from Mount Rushmore."

"It's a sketch I'm doing for a sculpture I'm working on—of you."

"Thank you." I waited. "Jimmy, where do you find the time?"

"I never sleep. I feel like I gotta keep moving. I feel like there's a wall out there and I keep nearing it. It'll stop me."

"Are you talking about fate?"

"Yeah, fate. Maybe." He banged his head, as though rattling his brain. "I read a lot about the Aztecs. I'm a bad reader and I go slow. Like a page a day. But they had this cool sense of doom, you know, from what I've read. Like they tried to make the most of whatever time they had on earth. The Aztecs, well—I want to live my life like they did. Hard driving, filled up."

"You've made a good start. You're young and famous. At what? Twenty-four?"

"It means nothing. I'm not famous *inside*. Movies lie. You ever see *Sunset Boulevard*, when it came out a few years back?" I nodded. "Well, I've seen it over and over. I watch Gloria Swanson, old, you know, and there she is, walking down that final staircase and she says that I'm-ready-for-my-close-up line.

Well, I've already had my close-up scene. At twenty-four." I started to say something, but he held up his hand. "No, let me finish. But the line that always gets me is when she says: 'I'm still big, it's the pictures that got small.' Whenever I hear that, I think, wow. That's *not* me, can never be me." He breathed in, closed his eyes. "So now I'm on the big screen, and I'm big, big, big. So big, you know. But I think, I'm still small, even though my pictures got big." Then, as if jolting himself from a reverie, he sat up. "Enough."

"Jimmy, there's nothing wrong with fame."

"Yeah, I know. It's what I hungered for. How can there be anything wrong with it?" His voice was ironic and slurring. He stood. "I gotta get out of here. I gotta make the scene with Ursula Andress for some photographer."

"I understand she's beautiful."

"Sure is. A hell-fire, too. Studio set us up, originally, one of those phony lovey-dovey things. But we hit it off, strangely, and now we're really *dating*," he stressed the word, "as opposed to being seen together."

"Hell-fire?"

"We do battle, her and me. She's got a temper, like me. I'm learning German so we can fight in her own language."

I waited a second, then said, "You don't hit her, do you?"

Jimmy squinted, interlocked his fingers and stretched out his arms. "People been telling tales about me, Miss Edna?"

"I heard…"

He sucked in his breath, breathed out, making a bubbly sound. "Sometimes things get a little heated, and, like something rises in me, so red-hot I'm about to burst, and I lash out."

"You should never hit a woman."

"They hit me, too, you know."

"Still, a man has an obligation."

"Pier Angeli used to slap my face. I'd slap her back. Lord, Natalie Wood slapped Sal Mineo one afternoon. That surprised the hell out of him."

"Why?"

"He was, I don't know, being a pest and she was having a bad day."

Jimmy got quiet. I watched him wither, sink back into a seat, pull his knees up and wrap his arms around them. I waited. He was staring at his knees.

The phone rang, and I jumped. It had rung a few minutes before Jimmy arrived and I'd ignored it. Now, flummoxed, I went into the bedroom to answer it. It was Tansi, eager to talk. "I'll call you back," I told her. "Jimmy's here."

"There?" Tansi exclaimed. "Why?"

"I'll call you back."

But when I returned to the living room, Jimmy was gone. As I sat down, I glanced at the table where I had laid Jimmy's gift, the statue without a face. It was gone. He'd taken it back.

Tansi, when I reached her—her line was busy, and I got irritated—wanted to know what Jimmy was doing, but I dismissed her curiosity. "He dropped off a drawing he'd made."

"Of what?"

"No matter, Tansi."

"Stevens was looking for him. Everyone made excuses." She waited for me to answer, but I kept quiet. "Edna, I just have to tell you about a lunch I just had. With Nell and Lydia."

"I thought Nell moved in with you, and Lydia was angry, hurt."

"That's it exactly. You see, Nell is a sweetie, a little too young and naïve maybe. So after she moved out and Lydia had that nasty tantrum, Nell started feeling funny about it. She doesn't like to *hurt* people's feelings, of course. So she asked me to help, and I said—how? I didn't know what to do…"

"Tansi, get on with it, please." I was impatient, looking at the spot where the odd statue had rested. He'd even taken the newspaper he'd used to wrap it in.

"So we three had lunch at this jazz club on the Strip. Chatting, clearing the air, Nell apologizing and saying she had to get on with her life. She wanted no hard feelings."

"And how did Lydia take it?"

"Well, that was odd, really. At first she was cold, distant. She even made a crack about how chubby Nell is, how she could never be an actress looking like that. Imagine! Then she seemed to just relax. She said it didn't matter any more. You know what she said? 'We were really never *friends*, just roommates.' That was a little hard, I thought, but Nell just nodded, happy to be forgiven."

None of this was earth-shattering revelation or headline news. Lydia and Nell talk, bold face print. *L.A. Times.* "So they really didn't iron out differences?" I said, bored. "Just quietly walked away from each other."

"I suppose so." I could tell Tansi didn't like my facile summary.

"Seems unnecessary to me."

"I mean—it was a bizarre lunch. I felt I was in the middle of a novel."

The Woman in the Gray Flannel Life.

"Did Lydia talk about the murder?" I interrupted.

"Of course, we all did. But Nell said very little. You know how she told everyone she thought Lydia killed Carisa."

"And yet you had a delightful lunch?"

"Well, she didn't *accuse* her at the table. I know Nell was afraid Lydia might have heard what she'd told people, but Lydia never mentioned it." Tansi quipped, "That would be hard for the digestive system."

"Truly," I agreed. "Murder while the ketchup oozes onto the table."

"Lydia changed at the end, though. Strange. She drank too many cocktails, which I paid for, by the way. Nell and I each had a couple of their famous Manhattans. Lydia kept drinking, and the lunch ended in shambles. I mean, she was the one who brought up the murder, and then she started to sob. But then it was all about Jimmy. And it had nothing to do with Carisa. Once Jimmy entered the conversation, everything was about him. Lydia said she was afraid of Detective Cotton."

"Why?"

"The way he interrogated her, I guess."

"Well, is she hiding something?"

"I don't know. But Nell, I learned, seems to have a crush on Jimmy. It's charming."

"So do you."

Tansi laughed. "Of course, we *all* do, Edna. But I have more of a professional obligation to him. He can be very nice and…" On and on she went. Call it what you will, Tansi Rowland, I thought, but you're as smitten as a love-starved spinster dreaming of Clark Gable sans undershirt in *It Happened One Night.* Which, admittedly, is not hard to do. I'd been there myself, unexpectedly, sitting in a dark movie theater in New York on a chilly fall afternoon. But that was years back. Now, ancient as dust, I could only recollect, albeit faintly. I was the lifetime spinster, by choice.

"So how did it end?" I wanted to hang up the phone.

"Lydia said she was going home to nap. She was weeping at the end but, well, that was because of Jimmy, not us."

I considered that the only ones viewing the lunch as salutary were Nell and Tansi. Lydia, perhaps, had a different slant; a woman driven to despair by their words and their presence.

"But I think she's getting over Jimmy," Tansi said. Over the phone lines I heard Tansi laugh. "The last thing she said was that he's as good an ending as any other man."

"What does that mean?" I asked.

"I took it to mean she was going to forget him."

Yet the Lydia who phoned me later that night was hardly the woman Tansi described. I heard hysteria, sputtering, inarticulate words. At first I had no idea who was calling me, until Lydia, in a moment of lucidity, mentioned that lunch with Tansi and Nell. "We talked of you," Lydia said, "and Tansi said you were a good friend and I thought of you because I had to call someone."

"Tansi told you to call me?"

Slurred speech, rambling. "No, she said *she* calls you. You're always a comfort. Jimmy says he calls you, stops in. He told me. Everybody talks to you. You are the lady novelist." The epithet made me wince. What was going on here? "And I just dialed the Ambassador, and now you're on the phone with me."

My lucky day, I thought. But maybe a good thing. I hadn't really talked to Lydia Plummer, who seemed somehow to figure in the murder. Friend of Carisa, ex-roommate, inheritor of Carisa's two boyfriends, Jimmy and Max Kohl. And, more importantly, famously accused of the murder itself—by Nell, charming luncheon companion. Schemes of revenge (maybe with Josh) against Jimmy.

But Lydia made little sense. I waited, hoping for something lucid to emerge, though, as the minutes went by, I despaired of that random morsel. "Would you believe…a part for me…the…only time…Jimmy said he'll take care of it…and someone… well…just that it was…I don't care…perhaps you know…do you know…" On and on, drunk, most likely; in a narcotic stupor, maybe. "You know…Carisa was my enemy but…but what really gets me…just think about it…Jimmy leaving *me*. *Me*. Leaving *me*." She started to scramble the words, then dissolved into sobbing. "Carisa, yes, doomed…a witch you know…but *me*?"

I got tired of the sloppy emotion. "Lydia, perhaps you need rest. Go away. Go back home."

"Home? I burned those bridges…bridge…Tansi told me to stop blaming Jimmy. But Jimmy *is* to blame…you know… you…behind every bad story in Hollywood sits Jimmy. Carisa told me…"

"What?"

Lydia suddenly seemed to focus. "You know, I thought nobody knew about the letter I wrote to her. All those threats."

"Jimmy's letter?"

"I said mean things about her and Jimmy. Nasty. Those lies Carisa spread. I told her to stop it. About Jimmy and his biker friends. Even Max. All the rumors about Jimmy at strange parties in the Valley. Jimmy is *not* like that. I wanted her to leave me and Jimmy alone."

"*You* sent a letter to Carisa?"

"Max Kohl told me things, and I wanted to hurt…"

"You sent a letter?"

"Carisa kept Jimmy from me. I hated her."

"Lydia, slow down, please. What letter are you talking about?" I was frantic.

"Nobody knew I sent that letter, and now it makes me look like a killer."

"What did Detective Cotton say to you?" Another bit Cotton kept from me. So he'd unearthed another missive. What was with this young crowd, firing off letters like verbose Edwardian correspondents? Jimmy's letter, threatening Carisa; now Lydia's, threatening. They bed one another down, I thought cynically, and then spend hours writing angry letters to one another.

"How was I supposed to know he found that letter? It was my secret. I told no one. Carisa called me and said…" Her voice trailed off.

"What exactly did you say in that letter?"

"I told you…everything." She was fading, drowsy, out of steam.

"How was it a threat?"

"I said I'd hurt her…you know…it's just something you say to scare…"

"What did Cotton tell you?" Obviously more than he told me.

"What?" Out of focus.

"Lydia!"

Silence. A hum. I was listening to a dial tone.

The phone woke me up, and I glanced at the clock. One in the morning. Good grief, what was wrong with these people out here? Back East I got my solid eight hours a night, faithfully; a walk in the morning, maybe one at night, rain or shine. And so to bed. I was not myself without the requisite hours.

But at one a.m. the phone needed to be answered. Groggily, "Yes?"

I heard Tansi's teary voice. "Oh, Edna," she said, "I know it's late but I had to tell someone."

I tried to focus in the dim room. "Tansi, what is it?"

"It's Lydia. She killed herself this evening. Jake Geyser just woke me up and then I told Nell and she got hysterical and…"

"What happened?"

"It seems Max Kohl found her. He was supposed to meet her in the lobby, but she didn't answer, so he slipped upstairs when the clerk wasn't looking, and she was dead. And the police called Warner's and…"

"So Max was in her room?"

"He called the police. They found drugs."

"Are they sure it's a suicide?" I said.

"What?"

"I mean, why did they say it was a suicide?" I thought of my earlier conversation with Lydia. Maybe it was an accidental overdose.

Tansi paused. "I don't know, Edna. That's what Jake just told me. He woke me up. Why?" Then, her voice shaky, "Oh my God, Edna, you don't think…no…it couldn't be murder." A deep intake of breath. "Could it?"

Chapter Sixteen

Late the next morning, dropped off at the Burbank studios by my driver, I sensed a shift in the atmosphere on the *Giant* sound-stage. A ripple of euphoria. Not that anyone *said* anything, to be sure. There was no uncontrolled laughter, not even a barely suppressed smile. This was the world of illusion—from Rock Hudson who strutted past with Chill Wills and smiled at me, to the woman who offered me coffee and pastry and told me how lovely I looked that morning. For a moment I thought I was imagining it, this hum of bliss that covered the studio like a gentle patina on valued wood. But I knew, in my heart of hearts, that I read human endeavor purposely, and accurately. That was my job, for all the many decades.

And I was sickened by it all. I wanted to get away, even though I had a tedious meeting scheduled with the very people who would feel safe now, secure, the impediment dislodged. Good God.

I'd listened to the radio over breakfast in my rooms, and one of the last news items mentioned the death of Lydia Plummer, Hollywood bit player. Her minor-league credits included the soon-to-be released *Rebel Without a Cause* and the film *Giant*, then finishing production. The announcer remarked that she'd died from a suspected drug overdose. Miss Plummer, he concluded, had died at the Studio Club for Women where Mary Pickford once lived during another era of Hollywood glory.

I wanted to talk about the death. I wanted details. Was Lydia's death a suicide or an accidental overdose? Or something more ominous? What did Max Kohl have to do with this? He'd been in her room—forbidden in the women's hotel. What about *his* rumored drug involvement? A needle in the arm? The brutish, powerful Max could easily overpower the zombie-like Lydia, then entering her narcotic heaven. But when I asked George Stevens what he thought, he skirted the subject. So, too, did one of the assistant directors; even the good soul who primed me for the dailies wouldn't answer.

I tracked down Jimmy, who'd finished a morning of shooting. Dressed as the older Jett Rink, still with the graying temples and dapper-Dan tuxedo, he waved to me, and then was at my side. I waited for him to say something about Lydia, but nothing. I'd have to bring it up, and that made me furious. For God's sake, what was with these people?

"Come with me," he said. "Get some coffee."

Outside, by the gate, was a new car watched by an admiring guard. "My Flat-four 547 Porsche Spyder Speedster," Jimmy said. "A masterpiece."

"Jimmy…"

"I'm having 'Little Bastard' stenciled on the back."

"Jimmy!"

"You know, Miss Edna," he mumbled, a faraway look in his eye, "the only time I feel whole is when I'm racing."

He's avoiding the subject, I thought. I sensed something in the eyes, cloudy behind those thick eyeglasses; the awkward movement of his body, the twisting of the head. His own mortality—that, he relishes. Another's, well, dismissed. I'll not have that, I told myself. I just won't. It filled me with rage. So I accepted the invitation, telling him I had to be back to meet Jake and Tansi within the hour. He nodded.

He was explaining the car to me. "I can go 120 miles per hour." I didn't listen. I knew nothing of cars. Years back, I'd driven roadsters, clumsy oversized Oldsmobiles and Buicks, especially when I owned my home in Connecticut. Cars were vehicles for getting from A to B, with an occasional side trip to C or D, depending on the richness of this foliage or that gushing mountain waterfall that had to be seen. Other than that, they were instruments of vanity and often folly. But I nodded now, dutifully, as Jimmy gave his enthusiastic oration, all the time running his hands over the steel metallic blue fender, the glistening chrome, the leather so new and supple it seemed just hours from the offering cow.

Over coffee at Hoyt's Restaurant near Hollywood and Vine, I tried to cut through the dense vehicular verbiage. What fascination do men have with grease and joints and pistons and carburetors?

"Lydia is dead, Jimmy."

The line stopped him cold, and I saw him bite his lip.

"I know!" he thundered, so loudly that other patrons glanced our way. He leaned into me. "I know." A whisper.

"Then why is everyone avoiding the subject?" I snarled. "And you, Jimmy, the one she mooned over, despaired over, probably ended her life over." The last line was cruel, I knew, but I didn't care.

"I'm not to blame. I was honest with her. She was troubled, Miss Edna. She and Carisa and Max—all the drug users. *That's* what killed her. Stuff she put in her body."

"But do you care?"

"Of course, I do. I'm not an animal, for Christ's sake."

I couldn't read him. Despite his words, which I suspected were heartfelt, his wiry, malleable body suggested something else: a cavalier demeanor, even a frivolous one. It was the way he sat, like a schoolboy ready to flee outside to recess; the way he flirted with the waitress, a momentary flicker of the eyelids, even the deprecating nod to an autograph seeker, his name scribbled on a napkin. Yes, he was bothered, genuinely so, but he was also relieved. That's the word, I realized: *relieved*. Out of danger, the prisoner released from his solitary confinement.

"Jimmy, do you think Detective Cotton will believe Lydia killed herself because of guilt over her killing Carisa?"

His eyes got wide with alarm. "My God, Miss Edna, you have a way of stating things in headline form."

"I'm always the girl reporter in Appleton, Wisconsin—who, what, where, when."

"You left out *why?*"

"That I can't answer yet."

"Look, Miss Edna. I really didn't *know* Lydia well. We dated, had a brief affair. So brief, it might only have happened in her imagination. She got *obsessed* with me. Like Carisa. Two women a little unhinged."

"Jimmy, why do you choose women who are ready to spiral out of control?"

"You know, I think it's the other way around. They choose *me*. I'm like a magnet. I'm, like, there, and I'm lost myself, and I'm down in the dumps. I'm moody, and they come to me—like I can fill the deep, black hole in their lives. It's like a paradox. Women seek the men who are the ones they should never go near. You know, like men who are mirror images of their own anguish. That's me. If I'm at a party, and there's one girl— sometimes even a guy—who should *never* seek my company, in a half hour they're up against me, eyes pleading, hands clutching, wanting me. It's like they're drowning, and they don't want to go under alone. So I run away, and they say, there, another man is cruel to me."

"Jimmy, you could say no the first time they approach you."

"You miss the point, Miss Edna. I'm at the same party, trying to find someone who will go under with *me*. I don't want to *drown* alone."

"All right, all right. But I sense gloating—maybe that's not the right word here—I sense satisfaction that she's dead. Nell told everyone, including Detective Cotton, that Lydia was most likely the murderer."

"Of course she wasn't. Lydia couldn't murder. She was so riddled with guilt for everything she did, she'd confess right away to the cops."

"Or," I said, flat out, "her guilt made her stick a needle in her arm, choose to die, either accidentally or on purpose."

Jimmy looked down at his hands, and said nothing.

"I have to go back." I looked at my watch.

Back on the studio lot, past the gate, Jimmy pulled into a space where, he maintained, he could periodically check on the car. "You have to admit it's a beauty," he beamed.

Enough, I thought. Enough.

Josh MacDowell rushed past, a few yards away, his arms filled with costumes. He never looked toward Jimmy and me, but Jimmy, spotting him, rolled his eyes and slunk deeper into the seat.

"You don't like him," I said. "And yet you used to be drinking buddies with him."

"I go out drinking with a lot of folks. Me, who has a low tolerance for alcohol. A couple whiskeys and I'm dancing on a table. But, well, Josh got too familiar." He turned to face me. "I'm uncomfortable around fem guys like that. I knew Carisa through him, in fact. But you know that. When he drinks, he gets, well, swishier. Is that a word? There's men, and then there's men."

"What does that mean?"

"I don't want to talk about this."

"I don't even know what we're talking about."

"You know, Miss Edna, Carisa used to sleep with dirt bags in the industry—to get small parts. Lots of people do it. You're gonna hear stories about me. There was this director Rogers Brackett, who I knew here and then in New York. I lived with him, I did things. I had to. Or he did things. You know. That's how I got on Broadway. It's what you *do*. Carisa liked to throw that in my face. She used to taunt me. When you're real famous, it'll all come out. Or, why are you denying *that* part of your life? I bet you hang out at Café Gale on Sunset, where *they* hang out. Well, I got all kinds of parts to my life. I'm not too sure what I am. You know? I mean…"

"What, Jimmy? Tell me."

He banged the steering wheel. "Nothing, Miss Edna. Nothing that has to do with nothing. It's just that Josh and Lydia *talked* about me—to people. And Josh has got his grip on the innocent Sal Mineo, a little boy, who stares at me with puppy eyes and doesn't understand that Josh is using him."

"How?"

"How does anyone use anyone else? You find their vulnerability, and then you mine it like precious ore." He bit his lip. "Miss Edna, I got things inside of me that scare me."

I touched him on the wrist. "Jimmy, you have to find what makes you happy." I paused. "And someone to make you happy, no matter *who* it is."

He looked at me. "What are you telling me?"

"I don't know much about these things, but I do know that you can't live your life by someone else's rules." I smiled. "But you already *know* that."

His eyes got wide. "You're something else, Miss Edna."

I started to answer, but he shook his head. "No more." He swung out of the car, opened my door, and walked me to the gate. "I'm going home."

"You're not on call?"

"Not today. I gotta meet Tommy and Polly for dinner tonight. They told me to ask you and Mercy."

"When were you planning on telling me?" I asked, smiling.

"Right about now. Polly'll call you later." He waved. "I'm going home to work on the sculpture of your head."

"You'll need a lot of clay."

He smiled. "I'll need a lot of nerve."

Coffee with Tansi and Jake guaranteed the day would move downward. Both were lively and talkative. I was used to it with Tansi, the resident Warner's booster child. Tansi's years in Hollywood, I now believed, had made her a little scatter-brained and twitchy. But Jake, with his crisp manner and supercilious haughtiness, seemed to have caught Tansi's exuberance. For two people who ostensibly hated each other, they exuded an unpleasant camaraderie when I joined them.

Lydia Plummer. Her shadow paradoxically hung over the day, allowing people suddenly to brighten up. How downright sad! Over and over I recalled my brief, scattered words with her on the phone. It broke my heart.

Of course, the conversation centered on Lydia. Originally Tansi had scheduled the meeting to outline my next few days of meetings, preparatory to my leaving within the week. But Jake had asked to join us. Interesting, this development. A day before Tansi would have been annoyed at his intrusion. Now they were the Bobbsey twins at the seashore. They said all the right things about Lydia: how sad, how tragic.

"Warner is preparing to have her body sent back home," Jake said.

"To where?"

"Lavonia, Michigan. A mother is there. We'll plan a little memorial tribute on the lot. She had friends…"

"Frankly, you two, I must say that everyone seems rather *relieved* at her dying."

"Nonsense." Tansi glanced over at Jake.

Jake frowned. "Miss Ferber, let me say this. No one wanted to see Lydia Plummer die like that, but she took her own life."

"How do we know it wasn't accidental?"

"She was playing with fire. Drugs, Miss Ferber."

"Or she could have been murdered," I said, staring at him.

Tansi nodded toward Jake. "I told you Edna thought that a possibility." She turned back to me. "Jake says that's absurd."

"Of course it is," he crowed. "She killed herself. And the fact of the matter is the whole James Dean thing is over with, Miss Ferber. Odds are she killed Carisa. They'd been friends, they fought, she was angry. Jimmy left her, and she blamed Carisa."

"So all the strings are conveniently tied."

"Exactly." He sat back in his chair, complacent, breezy.

I couldn't win. Tansi and Jake, two studio lackeys, one admittedly a decent old friend, but myopic, choosing the happy ending. America craves happy endings. In Hollywood even death is a happy ending.

Jake took out a pack of cigarettes and lit one. Like Jimmy, he smoked king-sized Chesterfields. I hadn't noticed that. I followed the wisp of smoke across the table and desired one. Tansi noticed me eye the cigarette. "Edna, another one?" She offered me one of her Camels, withdrawing her own pack and sliding it across the table. I shook my head. "Let me try a Chesterfield. That's what Jimmy smokes."

Jake wasn't happy, "Oh no," he groaned. "Another acolyte."

"Camels are better for your health," Tansi insisted, tapping the pack. She pushed it in front of me.

I took one of Jake's cigarettes, and Tansi lit it for me, striking the match with a flourish. "Tallulah Bankhead has nothing on me," I said, waving the cigarette dramatically. They laughed, and Jake told me to keep the pack. "Please."

Tansi placed her cigarettes back into her purse. "I love how Jimmy keeps his pack of cigarettes rolled up in the sleeve of his T-shirt with the matches tucked under the cellophane. He forces you to look at that bicep, at the sleeve with the crumpled pack tucked there. Imagine Cary Grant or Charles Boyer doing that. It's a whole new way of looking like a man…"

Jake lost his buoyant manner, turning sour. "He looks like a juvenile delinquent. A menace to society. And you two…" He stood up. "Women like you," he looked at Tansi and not at me, "would let a man like that get away with…"

He started to say *murder* but stopped. He fled the room, the sentence unfinished.

◇◇◇

Mercy and I walked into the Tick Tock Restaurant on North Cahuenga, where the sign in the window promised Home-Cooked Meals. "I have a feeling somebody wants to tell me something," I'd told Mercy earlier. Polly had phoned, telling me the name of the restaurant and the time. Now I spotted the back of Tommy's head, and for a second thought Jimmy had arrived: that sandy-colored hair, styled into a gentle pompadour, but, lamentably, the red jacket as well. The red badge of slavery, I thought. Hester Prynne wearing the symbol of sin—and, ironically, love. Tommy, suited up for servile fancy.

Polly, spotting us, waved. "Oh, I'm glad you came, Miss McCambridge." She turned to Tommy. "This is a pleasure. An Academy Award winner. A Pulitzer Prize winner. Both at our table." Tommy looked confused. "Awards, Tommy," she said, irritated. "At the top of their profession." Polly was dressed in a polka-dot dress with a lime-green sweater, buttoned at the collar. She looked cute-little-girl now, wandering from schoolyard hopscotch. She'd even styled her hair—not cinnamon tonight, but a sensible auburn—into a ponytail.

Of course, we talked about Lydia, and Tommy shared his inanity. "The wages of sin are death." He spoke in a preachy voice, didactic as all hell. Polly frowned at him and delivered her own practiced line: "I always felt sorry for her—she seemed to be always running into trouble."

Mercy asked, "Were you surprised at her death?"

A pause. Then Polly spoke in a small voice. "I don't think about people dying."

We delayed ordering because Jimmy hadn't arrived, and eventually Polly, glancing one last time at the doorway, drummed her index finger on the menu. "I don't think he's coming." That made everyone nervous, as though Jimmy were the glue that held everything together. His absence meant vacant lots of stalled conversation.

"Just like him," Polly griped.

"I sense that you asked me to dinner for a reason." I waited.

Polly and Tommy looked at each other, and Tommy cleared his throat. "That last dinner we had, you know, well, I…we… think that we left you with some wrong impressions. I said some things…"

"Or," I said, blithely, "you gave me some very clear impressions."

"No, the whole thing with Carisa," Tommy began.

Polly spoke over his words. "Miss Ferber, I know that Tommy slept with Carisa."

"I told her," Tommy said. "Detective Cotton told her my prints were there. We had a fight, and I confessed. I lied about going with Jimmy, there. I mean…you know…"

Polly leaned in, nodding. "It's a sickness." She sighed. "I sort of suspected it all along, you know."

"Tell me, Tommy," I began. "Did you go to Carisa's apartment the day she was murdered? That night, in fact?"

"Why?" Tommy looked at Polly, who seemed frozen in place.

"You see, the super's granddaughter said Jimmy was there twice that day, within minutes. Once, she sees him up close. A little later, riding on a bus, she sees him running out the door. Jimmy said he was there once. That second time was you, Tommy, right? Connie, the super's granddaughter, caught a glimpse of someone that looked like Jimmy—red jacket, the look…"

He nodded, unhappy. "Yes."

"You went *then?*" Polly blurted at Tommy.

Nervous, looking at Polly, he explained, "I lied to Detective Cotton. Told him I wasn't there."

"Why were you there?" Mercy asked.

"Well, she phoned me the day before. She was crazy, you know. She thought she could blackmail me. She was gonna tell Polly I slept with her. You know what she wanted from me? I mean, real crazy. She wanted me to talk to Jimmy—make *him* come to his senses. She wanted him to say he was the father of her baby. Real nutty. So I stupidly went there, you know, to plead my case."

"What happened?" I asked.

"Nothing. She came to the door, started yelling about Jimmy fighting with her, abusing her, calling her a whore, just minutes before, I guess, and if I thought I was gonna come and abuse her, well, I had another thing coming. She'd call the cops. I got real scared and ran away."

"Connie thought you ran to a woman waiting for you in a car."

That stopped him cold. He looked at Polly, nervous. "No," he stammered. "I parked around the corner."

"There was no woman?"

Tommy glanced at Polly again. "I just wanted to get away. I thought she'd call the cops. So I ran."

"Did you see a woman?"

He shrugged. He was starting to sweat.

"So you lied to Detective Cotton?" Mercy said.

"Are you going to tell him I was there?"

"No," I said. "You are."

"But he'll think I murdered her."

In the awful silence that followed, Polly spoke up, her voice laced with venom. "Well, did you?"

Chapter Seventeen

Irritable, suffering from the lack of a good night's sleep, I wandered the *Giant* soundstage aimlessly, avoiding entreaties by Warner's staff that I rest, read magazines, have coffee. When I spotted Detective Cotton, who was lolling near a stairwell, jotting something into a small loose-leaf notebook, I grunted, got his attention. I wasn't happy with my own attitude, to be sure. Certainly the law had no obligation to fill me in on every myriad detail of the case; certainly not. I was a civilian, an East Coast interloper no less; and, frankly, a little too nosy sometimes. Yet Cotton *had* confided, or seemed to. He *had* proffered information and seemed to respect me as a confidante. No, I told myself, I feared I'd misread him. I'd thought I might like him. But now I was back to disliking the self-assured, smug warden of the law. He nodded at me, still intent on his jottings.

"Sir," I said, drawing myself up to my imagined height. "Good morning."

"Miss Ferber, a pleasant surprise."

"I don't know what's pleasant about it."

He tucked the pad into a side pocket of his sports jacket. "Something wrong?"

"Frankly, yes. You see, Detective Cotton, when we had that little *tête-à-tête* in my suite, I thought we'd established a rapport that suggested trust and—" I stopped. The look on his face was slack-jawed, almost comical, a little like that of an excessively loose-flapped hound dog.

"Madam, I did share with you. Honestly."

"I sense that you mete out morsels of information to designated parties with the hope that one will spark some reaction."

He laughed. "Miss Ferber, I'm not that complicated."

"You deny it?"

He looked away, and then back at me. "All right, a little. It's a technique an old-timer taught me. But must I share every idle speculation I have or every trial balloon I send up?"

"Yes."

He laughed. "What are we really talking about here?"

I decided to shift the subject slightly. "I have information for you."

"That's why I'm here." He waited.

"I know you've been told that James Dean made two appearances at Carisa's apartment the evening she died, one just before the murder…"

"Or," he interrupted, smiling, "*during* the murder."

"I learned last night that you've been lied to. Tommy Dwyer, who, as you know, dresses like Jimmy, admitted to me that *he* made a visit to the apartment. It seems to me you would have garnered that information from him earlier."

Cotton laughed. "Miss Ferber, I must tell you that I just assumed all along Tommy was lying to me when he said he wasn't there. He's a shifty, unreliable man, not too bright, and he doesn't know how to lie persuasively. Given Connie Zuniga's spotty eyewitness account, I figured it was him running out of the building."

"And you did nothing about it?"

"Are you sure of that?"

"Well, no. But…"

"Look, it was just a matter of time before Tommy confessed. I've talked to him, and another investigator talked to him, and we were convinced the third go-round would crack that obvious lie."

"But this is a bit of evidence that suggests Jimmy is telling the truth."

"Yes, true. Jimmy was there earlier and not *then*. Tommy, maybe seven or so. But that doesn't mean he didn't return a little later—James Dean, that is." He paused. "Thank you."

I nodded. "And I take it you're not convinced that Lydia Plummer's death ends this case."

"Not a bit. That's a lot of baloney."

"Baloney?"

He smiled. "You don't like the word, Miss Ferber? I know everyone around here is ecstatic about her death. People in Jack Warner's office—not the head man, yet—are placing a large blotted period at the end of the sentence. That's why I'm here today. To remind everyone, including the killer who might be lurking here, that it ain't over till it's over. Let me say this. Lydia Plummer did not kill Carisa Krausse."

"You can say that with conviction?"

He touched his gut. "I know it here. Street savvy. Years of flatfooting it on L.A. streets, even Skid Row where Carisa lived— a place you seem to like to visit occasionally. Lydia's death is convenient, not only for the murderer, but for the studio. But it's not convenient for me. Look, Miss Ferber, Lydia, in her last weeks, was unfocused, a shambles, a weeper, a spurned lover, a bumbling soul, strung out on drugs. When I interviewed her—twice, in fact—she talked of James Dean, their affair, and she had a lot of vicious things to say about Carisa, vitriol I've rarely heard about a victim, frankly. And salty, too, a fishwife's harangue. It struck me as odd, that diatribe, because murderers usually try to temper their dislike of their victims to the police. She didn't."

"Really, sir," I began, "she was an actress. Remember that."

"Now ain't that a beautiful epitaph for her. You know, she would have appreciated the line." He stuffed his notebook into a side pocket. "Miss Ferber, the fact of the matter is my staff verified her somewhat lame alibi for that night. After she left the cocktail party. So, as of a couple days ago, I knew it was impossible that Lydia killed Carisa. She wasn't in two places at one time."

"Well…"

"I'm sorry. I suppose I should have phoned you."

"There's no need to be sarcastic, Detective."

"Sometimes there is." He smirked. "You know that."

I actually smiled. "At times there is. So what happens next? You're drawing in the wagons around Jimmy, no?"

He was ready to leave, but then paused, moved closer, an intimate's closeness. "So far he's the one with the motive."

"Think of it, Detective Cotton. Why would James Dean risk everything he's built up? He's not a stupid boy, truly. Killing Carisa would draw attention to him. He's the one who was the object of her madness, the target of her flood of letters—even to Jack Warner's office. He knew that. So he kills her, and you come swooping down, waving the letters like battle pennants. He had nothing to gain and everything to lose by killing her."

"Well, for one thing," he said, leaning back against the wall, "your boy seems to believe he has a charmed life. I know all the stories about his manic car racing in the hills. I know all about his nightlife. He's a risk taker. He lacks common sense. If Jack Warner wasn't on my back, he'd be making bail right around now. But so be it."

"He can be a foolish young man."

"Miss Ferber, I agree with you about something. He, or someone else, never *planned* the murder. No one went there with knife or gun or evil intent. This crime smacks of impulse, of anger. A quarrel, heated words hurled back and forth. Tempers flare. She'd a temper, we've been told. And Dean's temper is legendary. So they fight. In a moment of fury Dean, or someone else, hurls the Aztlan statue with such an impact that it knocks Carisa off balance. She trips and hits her head. She dies. Unplanned, unscripted. Anger, Miss Ferber. This is a scenario into which most people can fit themselves at one time or another. It's just that the person we fling things at usually doesn't die. And that's murder. Or, at least, manslaughter."

I was tired. Standing too long in that hallway, a pain in my shoulder blades; my feet ached. "True," I admitted.

"All I'm saying is that James Dean is suspect number one. That's a given. Murder by anger or murder by smugness. Take your pick. His touch is all over that apartment."

"Was Lydia Plummer murdered?"

"Not according to the Medical Examiner. She'd been dead a couple hours before Max Kohl found her. We documented that. He's not part of this." He turned to go. "Gotta run."

I thought of something. "One last thing. Lydia's letter to Carisa. The one in which she threatened her. You haven't mentioned *that* letter. When Lydia called me, she was frenzied about that letter. She regretted sending it, feared its contents were known."

Detective Cotton stopped moving. "What are you talking about?"

I explained what Lydia had said, how she was afraid of what would happen if anyone found the letter.

"Are you sure? Miss Ferber, we found no such letter. Jimmy's letter, yes. Are you sure she wasn't talking about that threatening letter?"

"Yes, I'm sure she said *she* wrote a letter, which, from what she said, I assumed you'd found and confronted her with. And I thought you purposely omitted mention of when you and I spoke."

He still looked baffled. "There was no such letter, Miss Ferber. I think you misunderstood her. She was hopped up, boozed up, incoherent, and slipping deeper into some narcotic bliss." He saw the look on my face. "I'm not withholding information from you. We found no threatening letter from Lydia. James Dean's letter was threatening enough."

But watching him leave, I was not so sure. I knew what I'd heard that fateful night. Lydia may have been rambling, but her words were clear.

I sat for an hour in the Blue Room with the producers and Stevens, nothing important, just idle time spent to make me feel important. Jake Geyser sat at my right hand, a little too close, leaning in, confiding, but looking cowed. Near the end, Tansi joined us, slipping Jake a sheaf of messages. When the room cleared, Tansi whispered, "A minute, Edna." I waited for Jake to leave, but he stayed at her side. "Edna," Tansi said, "you will not believe how that detective browbeat Jake."

"Why?"

Both Tansi and Jake seemed eager to relate the story. Cotton had come on like some gung-ho commando during an interview with Jake that morning. Detective Cotton had largely treated Jake with kid gloves in earlier interviews, Jake told me, as was just. After all, given his position as an assistant to Jack Warner himself, he deserved respect. His voice was high and whiny. "I announced I am a law-abiding citizen of this republic." Yes, I thought, a republic called Warner Bros. Studio. "He just kept yelling at me, hurling question after question. It was maddening."

"I walked in on it," Tansi said. "By mistake. I stood in the doorway and heard Cotton call Jake a bold-faced liar."

Jake blanched, perhaps as he had when Cotton threw the accusation his way. Now people didn't call Jake Geyser a liar. Behind his back, yes. His staff doubtless mocked his aristocratic demeanor, his overweening ego, his tweedy sartorial nonsense, and, more so, his unbalanced defense of all things Warner.

Tansi was shaking her head. "Imagine."

I turned to Jake. "Had you lied?"

Jake's careful voice broke. "I *had* to."

"What lie are we talking about?"

There was anger in his tone. "I misrepresented the times I went to Carisa's apartment. I was actually there—a bunch of times, negotiating a deal that she had no intention of accepting. It was like a game to her."

"That's hardly a grievous lie," I said, encouraging him.

Tansi touched my sleeve. "Wait."

"I lied when I said Carisa was contemplating an offer of money. The truth is, Warner gave her a lump sum the day before, but I was told to keep it a secret. But she didn't give me the signed paper guaranteeing silence. She tricked me. I'm not built for this stuff."

"Even I didn't know," noted Tansi.

"Why keep that a secret?" I stared into his pale face.

"Warner wanted to see how she'd react. Whether she'd follow up with more demands. More letters. Which she did—the morning she died. Another letter. I kept going there. She wouldn't pick up her phone most times, and I had to deliver a bag of cash."

"Good God," I said.

"I know, I know. I'm like an Al Capone runner."

"And Detective Cotton found out?"

He bit his lip. "The police found the money hidden under a pile of magazines. I lied about the money, said she was considering it."

"Well, this hardly seems the stuff of massive deception. Why would Cotton assault you today?"

Tansi and Jake looked at each other, conspiratorially. I didn't like the new linkage. I much more preferred Tansi as Jake's adversary and my own boon companion. In fact, I much more preferred the Tansi I knew years before, back in Manhattan days, Tansi at Barnard, spirited, fun-loving, cynical; not so wired and taut. And Jake, well, I never liked him and less so now, a man in authority with no moral center.

What he said next proved it. "He went crazy today because I stupidly lied to him again." He glanced at Tansi, and she half-smiled, encouraging. "I told him Lydia had confessed to me that she killed Carisa."

"What? My God. Why?"

"I know it was stupid. Tansi and I were talking about how everything was hunky-dory now, Jimmy free of accusation, but Cotton said he didn't believe Lydia killed Carisa. So I said, well, she had a last talk with me, and she hinted that she'd done it. It was dumb, and I regretted it immediately. But Cotton lost it, really. He said he'd have me up on charges, that I was a fool; that I could lose my job lying to a cop."

I was stunned. "Why would you even think to lie like that?"

"For a second I thought, why not? It's over anyway. She *did* do it. I'm respected here. They'll believe me."

I shook my head. Who in this glitter Hollywood had a brain?

"And besides," I added, "I agree with Detective Cotton. Lydia Plummer had nothing to do with Carisa's death."

Tansi gasped. "How can you say that?"

"I just did."

"Proof, Miss Ferber?" Jake asked.

"I don't have proof. But it's what I know."

"Edna, you're being…stubborn," Tansi said. And I almost laughed. Tansi seemed ready to say "ridiculous." It's a word I suspected Tansi used a lot. *Oh, this is ridiculous. Can anything be more ridiculous than this?*

I shrugged my shoulders. "I don't like the convenience of Lydia's death. Too many people are using her dying to forget the case."

"Maybe they have a reason." Jake defied me.

"Oh, I don't think so."

Tansi was not liking this exchange. "Edna, I know you got involved in this because of Jimmy. We *all* want to help Jimmy, but now he's *helped*. He had his army of supporters, and they came through beautifully. You, me, Jake, Mercy, Tommy, the others. The Warner office."

"Tansi, don't be a foolish woman." The words came out too harsh, too strident. Tansi looked hurt, and I considered apologizing, then changed my mind.

"Foolish? Edna, how could you?"

"I'm just trying to be truthful with you, Tansi. I'm your friend." But I looked at Jake, who was not an old friend, now glowering, his eyes dark with anger.

"That's hardly the way friends talk, Edna."

Jake smirked. "Don't you find it strange that you and Mercy McCambridge have spent a lot of wasted time running around and making fools of yourselves? Cotton told me you and Mercy visited the super. Even, I guess, harassed his granddaughter."

Tansi shook her head. "I can't believe you'd go *there*."

"It's not the black hole of Calcutta, Tansi. It's L.A., the dark side, the…"

"I wouldn't be caught dead there."

"No one is asking you to go there."

"You know," Jake said, "we do have a police force."

I smiled. "Which, I gather, you're not very fond of at the moment. Or have you changed your mind?"

"I have meetings." He stood. "James Dean is safe."

Tansi echoed, "Safe." She stood.

Jake headed toward the doorway. "You don't understand, Miss Ferber. James Dean is no longer a person. He's now a property." With that, he left the room.

Wildly, insanely, I flashed to Jett Rink, the helter-skelter wildcatter of *Giant*, that handsome, madcap boy who becomes so rich and powerful that he abandons his moral compass. Property, oil wells, ranches, Reata, Texas. A wasteland of black gold. Vast stretches of dried-out dead land, parched under crimson noon-time sun. Buffalo grass where no buffalo roam. Jett becomes the land and the oil under it: in the process he loses his soul. Jett Rink, James Dean: property.

Furious, I managed to stand, grab hold of the table's edge. "That's a cruel thing to say about anybody." But I was speaking to the door he'd closed behind him.

Chapter Eighteen

I sat in the blazing sunshine at a patio table at the Smoke House, staring across the street at the Warner Bros. Studio entrance. By myself, and comfortable. No, I told this person and that one, no; I want to be alone. Pursued by people—Rock Hudson, dressed as Bick, walked by with an assistant director, paused, debated joining me, but then kept moving—I'd fled the soundstage, slowly moving my way to the restaurant. An old woman in a gigantic red sun hat trimmed with garish bluebells, something I'd appropriated from wardrobe, thanks to Mercy's intervention. "Edna, you're going outside with no hat? This will have to do. Everyone will think you're a bit player. It's too hot out there." She positioned it on my head, chuckling in her gravelly, cigarette voice. So now I sipped a glass of minty iced tea slowly, meditating. I was happy being alone, despite the circus hat I had to wear.

I was bothered. Tansi's misguided pique, her rigid personality; and Jake, that weasel. And Jimmy, the luck of the roaring scamp, the boy wonder everyone wondered about. Jimmy and his cryptic talks with me. Who were these elusive, mysterious souls he favored in the long, long hours of night?

The waiter appeared, and I nodded. Yes, another iced tea. No, nothing to eat. I reached into my clutch and extracted one of Jake's cigarettes. I despised the man, and yet I joyfully, gladly appropriated his cigarettes. I struck a match, lit the cigarette, but barely inhaled the smoke. In the still California afternoon, the hum of unseen freeway traffic beyond some stucco-and-tile buildings, the presence of a single jagged cloud in the unblemished blue sky. I closed my eyes, and relaxed.

I heard a rumble near the studio gates, and, turning, spotted Jimmy tearing out, breakneck speed, on his motorcycle, turning the corner so fast he seemed momentarily parallel to the all-too-close asphalt pavement. A black leather bomber jacket, black boots, a pair of military style goggles on his eyes, doubtless covering those horn-rimmed eyeglasses he was always losing or breaking. He looked very militaristic, the red-blooded Eisenhower soldier liberating Europe.

As I watched him leave, I noted Alva and Alyce Strand on the sidewalk, looking after him. Bounding from a crouching position, they tottered after the disappearing bike, and I wondered whether Jimmy's crazed getaway was an attempt to ditch the pesky fans. Then, out of breath, the twins stopped, not far from my table, and stupidly waved after him.

I called to them. "Come here." They hurried over. I reminded them that I'd been at Googie's with Jimmy. "I'm Edna Ferber."

"We know you," Alva said, "because James knows you. He talks about you."

"You *talk* to Jimmy?"

They looked at each other. "No, but we hear things. We ask questions."

"Sit down." I motioned toward empty chairs.

They shook their heads. They were frightfully identical, the boy and the girl, with shocks of sandy blond hair, with gawky faces and marble eyes. Both clowns. That lamentable gene pool was starved and desolate. Their parents must have been brother and sister. I shivered at the thought.

Alyce glanced at her brother, her eyes panicky. "No, we have to go."

"Go where?"

She pointed, melodramatically. "We follow James."

"And where has he gone?"

They looked at each other. "We guess. Sometimes we're right, sometimes wrong."

The other picked up the thread. "Sometimes we sit for hours, waiting. And he never shows up."

Alva grinned, "Mostly we hang out near the studio."

"We think we know where he's going today."

"Yesterday for two hours he sat on his bike in front of the apartment of that girl who died?"

"Lydia Plummer?" I exclaimed.

They shook their heads: "No, Carisa Krausse. Just sat there. We sat far away and watched him sit there. He looked so sad. He never moved."

"How do you know he's going there now?"

"We don't, but he's headed like in that direction."

With that they scampered off to a battered car, fenders bent and antenna crumpled. In seconds they were lumbering past. A squeaky horn blew. Alva waved. They were deliriously happy. And decidedly insane. The by-product of a world of celluloid and ticket-stub heartache.

I wondered. Maybe. Just maybe.

At the studio gates, where a small gaggle of autograph-seeking tourists routinely gathered, a vender hawked Glamorland maps of the homes of the stars. I commandeered a yellow cab. I recalled Carisa's street, not the number, but figured, once there, I'd know where to go, though the driver looked none too happy with that destination. This was foolhardy, I told myself, and surely a waste of time. But I was not concerned with tracking Jimmy—no, I was curious about Alva and Alyce Strand. Simpletons maybe, but something one of them said—*Sometimes we sit for hours*—intrigued me. I needed to talk to the freakish pair. Perhaps they were the elusive, unexamined witnesses to some key evidence. Perhaps they were the truly bit players in the awful Hollywood caper.

The cab cruised to a stop at the corner of Carisa's block and I spotted Jimmy in front of Carisa's apartment, perched on his bike, just sitting there, arms folded, looking asleep, head bent. Surely, I wondered, he can't sit there for hours? An odd sight: the melancholy mourner, keeping watch. The last keener at the funeral. I paid the fare and got out, a matter of feet from Jimmy.

He was watching me, even though his head was bowed. I walked up to him, feeling especially foolish in the ungainly red sunbonnet, all those bluebells on it, an old lady carrying a purse and wearing a dress I actually bought to wear to the Bucks County summerhouse of Dick and Dorothy Rodgers. It was a frilly wide-skirted cotton smock, with redundant periwinkles aplenty. And here, in down-and-out Skid Row, the stench of greasy food from a hot dog stand, and nearby the burned-out shell of an old car, windows smashed and resting on axles—I looked stupendously out of place. It's the hat, I thought. Why am I wearing this horrible hat? Passersby might see me as a mad homeless woman who'd doubtless rifled through some abandoned chest of period finery and emerged on the street to scream at the endless flow of traffic.

"Jimmy."

He shook his head back and forth. "Miss Edna, you really do surprise a boy."

"It's you who surprises."

Quizzical, raised eyebrows, eyeglasses slipping down his nose, "Yeah?"

"Loitering here in front of Carisa's apartment. It's a little macabre, no?"

"I find it's a good place for me to think about things."

"What things?" I drew closer. I noticed he was sweating.

"Lydia."

"So you come here to mourn Lydia?"

"It all started here."

"What did?"

"Carisa dead, Lydia dead. Things happen in threes, you know. Am I going to be the third?" He stared up and down the street, as though watching for someone.

"Why do you say that?"

"What is the thread that goes from Carisa to Lydia to me?"

"Why does there have to be a thread?"

He sighed. "I don't want to talk about this." He stared up at Carisa's window. "Not here. This is where I come to be quiet." Abruptly, he started the bike, and a dissonant, coughing roar deafened me. I backed up and he raced away, pulling into traffic so abruptly a car slammed on brakes. A horn blared. The driver, a boy with sideburns and a duck's-ass haircut, screamed at me, "Your son's an asshole."

My son. My beloved son. "True," I answered, calmly, touching my eccentric hat. "This wasn't what his father and I hoped he'd become."

The driver, startled, gave me the finger and sped on.

I do so love L.A., I told myself.

"Can you believe that driver?" a voice yelled, and I jumped out of my skin. Alva and Alyce Strand were beside me, so close I could smell their garlicky breaths.

"Are you going to chase Jimmy now?" I didn't know which one to look at.

"Why?"

"Well, I want to talk to you." I spotted a restaurant across the street. "Can I buy you lunch, a soda, something?"

They looked at each other. "No." They turned away.

"I want to share stories about James with you."

Swiveling to face me, they beamed. I saw a bubble of drool at the corner of Alva's mouth. I feared they might hug me.

The restaurant was a seedy, dimly-lit eatery, more hash-house tavern than hamburger haven, with a weathered oak bar and a few rickety tables by the front window. In back, through a partition of suspended beads, was a dance room, with a jukebox. Empty now at midday, the place probably thrived at night, derelict though it was. I'd never know. It was called Ruth's Grill, and the daytime menu consisted of hot dogs and cheap Mexican food. The nighttime menu over the bar listed rib-eye steak and barbecued chicken. The Strands and I took a table by the window, and Alva said the hotdogs were wonderful, but suggested we skip the enchiladas. I had no desire to sample any of the offerings. They'd spent hours sitting there, they confessed, nursing lemon phosphates while waiting to see whether James Dean would show up to visit Carisa Krausse.

I ordered a coffee but its resemblance to the La Brea Tar Pits suggested I'd best leave it untouched.

It was easy to entertain the bubbly twins, at least for a few minutes, while they dipped and twisted in the chairs, constantly gazing out the grimy window, as though Jimmy might return. I regaled them with an innocent—and largely fictitious—take on Jimmy's horseplay, his zany life. No violation of privacy. I'd garnered all of it from the exaggerated press releases Warner's supplied to Hedda Hopper and others of her ilk. The Strand twins, though they probably already knew (and relished) every morsel, nevertheless begged for more. After all, here was a legitimate companion of James Dean, the novelist herself, authoress of *Giant* and other works they'd never heard of. And I called him Jimmy.

I, the veteran interviewer, with miles of soul-numbing Republican and Democratic Presidential Conventions under my younger belt, segued neatly into the events of the murder. After all, we sat across the street from the murder scene. So they chattered freely about their encounters with Jimmy, and nothing they offered was news to me. I was beginning to get depressed. For two inveterate watchers, they seemed to register very little. Days were blurs, times indefinite, hours merging daylight with evening; yes, that day, or was it…no…maybe…really, he was here twice…it's hard to keep track…but he had the station wagon not the…never the sports car…On and on. I got tired.

Sitting back, my head against the plate-glass window, I kept listening.

Alva asked for another drink. I ordered it. Alva said would I mind if he smoked. I nodded. Go ahead. He offered me one. I took it, fiddled with it, and the boy lit it for me, very gentlemanly, but then I realized it was stale, and put it out in the ashtray.

His sister Alyce was shaking her head. "What?" I asked. Alyce muttered something about ladies not smoking.

Ladies, I thought, need to smoke when the conversation bored so thoroughly, massively.

Alva blew smoke into my face. "That other guy is a pest, though," he said.

I sat up. "What other guy?"

"You know, from the studio." He described Jake Geyser, imperfectly. "He looks at you like you're a bug" and "He talks like he's a prince or something."

"What about him?"

"A couple times when we waited here, we'd see this guy. Like he was checking up on James."

"Did you talk to him?"

Alyce responded. "Yeah. He told us to get lost. He'd call the police if we kept hanging around James. He was here more than James. The guy would be around, like watching."

"He acted like he was his guardian or something," Alva noted.

"James has a right to go anywhere he wants."

Alva nodded. Alyce nodded.

I nodded.

"I mean," Alyce went on, "he looks angry a lot, like he was going to punish him."

Doubtless he wished he could. Puritan stockades on the town green; whippings; Chinese water torture; his face on the cutting room floor.

"What about Carisa Krausse? Did you talk to her?"

"No, we don't like James' girlfriends."

"Did you ever see Carisa with Jimmy?"

Alyce whispered, "No, but we knew he went to see her. We saw him walk in there. And we'd see her around the streets."

They looked at each other, confused. "The last time we saw her was here. Right here. In this restaurant. This table."

"You were in the restaurant?" I asked.

They shook their heads, no. "We were walking back and forth on the sidewalk and I looked in. She was sitting right where Alyce is, that seat, facing out to the street."

"Alone?"

"No, she was talking to some friend of hers, some girl."

"Are you sure it was Carisa?"

"Oh, yeah, she had that look, you know."

"What look?"

"Hollywood movie star, the makeup, the hands holding the cigarette in the air, the…the…chin up, the smile."

But Alva interrupted, "But she wasn't smiling, Alyce."

Alyce nodded. "That's right. She was angry about something."

"How could you tell from outside?"

"Because when I spotted her, I said to Alva—she's in there. And maybe James is with her, but it was just this woman with her. But she was waving her arms, and her face was all…" She stopped.

"Contorted." He finished.

"Contorted. You could tell she was yelling. And her girlfriend was yelling back. I could see her shaking her head back and forth, like no, no, no, no, no. You know."

"Then what happened?"

"Nothing. We left."

"Did you recognize the woman she was with?"

"No. It was Carisa Krausse I watched."

"Were you here on the day Carisa died?" I asked.

They looked at each other. They nodded.

"What did you see?"

They stiffened. "Nothing. We didn't stay. I mean, we came here because we thought we saw him driving this way, but everything was real quiet here. So we just left."

"We wanted to get back to the cocktail party in case he went back."

"So you saw him leave the party earlier?"

They nodded. Alyce said, "That's why we thought he was coming here."

Alva stood up. "We gotta go."

Alyce jumped up.

"You're making us nervous," Alva looked to the doorway. "What does this have to do with James Dean?"

"I don't know."

"I thought you were going to tell us stories."

"I did, didn't I?

They looked at each other. "We don't know if you like him the way we do."

"Of course I like him."

Alva, panicking, "We don't know if we believe you."

Chapter Nineteen

Jimmy invited some friends to his new apartment in Sherman Oaks. "It's not a party. I don't like parties," he told me on the phone. "But I got this cool new home." I had to attend, he insisted. "You got to, Miss Edna. My new place is where I hide away from the world."

"You're not exactly hiding if you throw a party."

"It's not a party."

He was making last-minute phone calls. He begged Liz Taylor until she said she'd stop in. She had another obligation. Mercy balked, but Jimmy persisted. I asked him if he'd invited Rock Hudson. "That famous star of *I Was a Shoplifter?*" To my bafflement, Jimmy explained, "One of his early classic roles." I kept saying no. Nighttime parties, unlike the serene afternoon luncheons and the genteel dinner parties I hosted, were for the young. But Tansi, all a-titter, finally convinced me; and so Mercy picked me up at the hotel and then Tansi at her apartment on Santa Monica Boulevard.

Tansi was waiting at the curb, and with her was Nell Meyers. That surprised me. Well, maybe this party was not so bad an idea after all.

Tansi was dressed in gold pedal-pushers I deemed too young for her; a white puffy blouse, cinched at the waist by a huge gold belt; and she wore a nail polish so loud it called attention to her bony, unlovely fingers.

I smiled at Nell, who didn't smile back. She fascinated me, this young girl new to Jimmy's world. Script girl to the stars, the Bohemian with her all-black outfits and her Garboesque makeup, both at odds with her squat, cast-iron stove build and that bobbed Anita Loos hairdo. Had Jimmy invited her? Or had Tansi convinced her to come along, acting as her protector since she'd engineered Nell's departure from the Studio Club?

"Jimmy said to bring Nell," Tansi told us. "At first she said no, but I told her she can't hide away in her room. This is Jimmy's new *apartment* we're going to see."

Nell said nothing, but looked bored, actually yawning and staring out the window.

Tansi talked as though Nell were not there: "Nell is part of the Beatnik crowd that hangs out at some café near Pershing Square.

Nell said nothing. Then, out of the blue, "Jimmy plays the bongos."

I stared, transfixed. I caught Mercy's eye. "Bongos?"

"He's very good." Mercy was savoring this.

"You've heard him?"

"I have," Nell answered.

I enjoyed the leisurely ride out of L.A. into the twisting lanes and woods of San Fernando Valley. It was a cool night, and the air seemed to hum. Once there, we trudged up a narrow lane to what struck me as a rustic hunter's lodge, hidden under dense shrubbery, wild eucalyptus, sagging palm trees. I smelled ripe lemons. Jimmy rushed down to greet us, dressed in tight jeans and a white T-shirt, a pack of cigarettes rolled up in the sleeve. He gallantly took my elbow, escorting me. "My hideaway," he said.

Inside, manic and bouncing around the huge room, Jimmy pointed to a balcony, where, he said, he slept on a mattress on the floor, where he could gaze down at a seven-foot rough-stone fireplace that covered one wall, above whose mantel was a gigantic bronzed eagle, grotesque and garish, wings extended, with menacing talons. "I've named him Irving," Jimmy said.

Scattered around were bongos—I feared a concert of discordant, horrible music—piles of hi-fi recordings, cameras, books, tape recorders. On one wall tacked-up bullfighting posters, frayed at the edges. This was a young man's room. Here and there were ungainly heaps of discarded clothing, underwear, rumpled trousers, all pushed into corners. There seemed to be packs of Chesterfields everywhere, all opened, all missing a few cigarettes, each one with a box of matches inserted under the cellophane. As we walked around the rooms, music blared from speakers suspended high on the walls. Mercy begged him to turn down the volume, which he did reluctantly.

I was drawn to a corner where an easel rested. He was in the middle of executing a lovely pen-and-ink drawing, a young girl's face, gentle and quiet: an amazingly calm visage in a room designed for chaos. And behind the easel a small, black walnut table, on which, to my abject horror, rested the incomplete (but recognizable) sculpture of my own granite head.

"For God's sake, Jimmy, throw a sheet over that. Would you have your guests flee into the night?"

He grinned.

The music still bothered me. "What is that?" I asked.

"African chants."

"Could you turn it off?" Tribal music, insistent, the drums beating mercilessly, the wails floating over reiterated beat; rawness, aching and sensual. Hardly party music. More appropriate for a soundtrack to a Johnny Weissmuller movie. Ape man, and boy. Swinging on vines.

Jimmy slipped on a recording of Doris Day. "For you." He bowed. Still inappropriate. Sappy, saccharine, painful.

Some guests sat on a threadbare sofa. I recognized Patsy D'Amore, owner of the Villa Capri. Three other men, waiters and kitchen staff, I was told, sat with him, in a line—thin, quiet men who sipped wine and stared straight ahead. They looked as unhappy to be there as I felt. Was this the party? The four men, silent, listening to an ebullient Jimmy, and four women, myself one of them—the venerable novelist.

This was hardly right, downright untoward, this freakish grouping. Nell, as short as a child but gaudy in her *danse macabre* makeup and shellacked Garboesque demeanor, was the sudden cynosure of the leering men, as she sat yoga-fashion on the floor. I wondered what her relationship was with Jimmy. Tansi had said she was not really part of his crowd. He had no interest in her. Yet Jimmy touched her on the shoulder when he walked by her, and she smiled at him. In the shadowy light of the room, she looked exotic, mysterious; and I supposed men might be caught by that allure. When, at one point, she wandered into the small kitchen—"Jimmy has the greatest lemon trees out back"—my suspicions were confirmed. Nell had been there before.

Polly and Tommy walked in. They'd obviously had yet another spat. Or, at least, Polly was the battler. Her face was flushed, the mouth set, the eyes hard. Tommy seemed non-chalant, spirited. He looked like he'd been drinking. I caught a few of Polly's spat-out words: "I warned you last time." But I'd come to expect the eternal warfare of those two sad souls. They seemed to crave it, thrive on it; battles royal, then making up, a dynamic that served as glue for an unhappy love story.

I sipped tepid white wine in a jelly glass. That seemed to be all Jimmy had available for his guests. Nothing to nibble on. The music came to an end. Silence in the room.

Sal Mineo appeared on the threshold, looking as if he'd come to the wrong address. Behind him, nudging him into the room, was a stocky man dressed in a lime-green shirt, a man with no neck and a spindletop wooly haircut. I couldn't remember his name though I'd met him a half-dozen times. An assistant director. Sal smiled at me, and then sat by himself in a corner, looking very much the misbehaved schoolboy, sans dunce cap. He spoke to no one, not even to his director-friend.

Tommy and Polly sat next to each other, up against each other, and didn't move. I watched the young couple, especially when Jimmy neared: Tommy getting tense, Polly softening her hard eyes. Jimmy whispered something to them and both smiled.

Jimmy got tipsy and climbed up the balcony, where he located and displayed Marcus the Siamese cat, who'd take shelter behind the mattress. "Performance time," he bellowed. He removed his horn-rimmed glasses. We're now all a blur, I thought, much the way he wants the world to be—blot out the harsh, linear lines, fog over the faces of people who can get to you. "The greatest poet in the world," he announced, "was from Indiana." I rolled my eyes: he couldn't mean—

Yes, he did, indeed. "James Whitcomb Riley, Hoosier hick like myself, an old geezer who never met me, but he wrote about me." And then, to my amazement, he recited verbatim Riley's lines:

I grow so weary, someway, of all things
That love and loving have vouchsafed to me.
Since now all dreamed-of sweets of ecstasy
Am I possessed of: The caress that clings—
The lips that mix with mine with murmurings
No language may interpret, and the free,
Unfettered brood of kisses, hungrily
Feasting on swarms of honeyed blossomings
Of passion's fullest flower—For yet I miss
The essence that alone makes love divine—
The subtle flavoring no tang of this
Weak wine of melody may here define:—
A something found and lost in the first kiss
A lover ever poured through lips of mine.

When he finished, the room was silent. I glanced at Tansi, who seemed to be weeping. Jimmy himself, hanging precariously over the balcony with a mewing kitten cradled in his arms, seemed suddenly embarrassed. Then, his lips trembling, his eyes closed, his free hand fluttering in the air, he said, "I don't know why I do things." He fell back onto the mattress, out of our sight.

We stood there, all of us, stunned, silent, heads inclined toward the balcony. Scraping sounds, gurgling noises, a faint meow, a raucous laugh. He stops time, I thought. He deliberately tilts the earth upward, bending the axis, dislocating longitude. In the stillness I could hear Tansi's labored breathing, a cigarette smoker's whistling squeak.

Suddenly, all our inclined heads swiveled as one to the doorway where Liz Taylor stood, bathed in the shrill honey-yellow glare of the outside light; just stood there, and in that moment seemed to take possession of the room. A statue, elegant really. And so dangerously perfumed and lipsticked and coifed that the line of dumbstruck men, positioned on the sofa, seemed frozen in a kind of saliva-drooling awe. Really, I mused, for God's sake. She wore a satiny black cocktail dress, clinging, sequined, with a diamond necklace and on that wrist a diamond bracelet. Jack Warner's bauble.

Behind her stood two paper-doll cutouts, an interchangeable young man and young woman, both in tweedy suits and horned-rimmed eyeglasses.

She spoke into the silence. "Where's Jimmy?"

From the balcony Jimmy, unseen, cried, "Liz, you came to my party."

Liz didn't know where to look. "I told you I would." A voice that was curiously Southern in texture, lilting, sweet.

Liz looked around and caught my eye. She nodded. But her look swept the room, and her eyes narrowed. "Jimmy, you lied to me."

A pause. Jimmy's drunken titter. "I lie to everyone. It's my job."

Liz fumed. "You said everyone from *Giant* would be here. George and Chill Wills…and…" She nodded over her shoulder. "I had them drive me here, knowing I'd be late for a house party an hour from here…" Her face closed up, furious, tears in her eyes. "Why do you do these things?" She drew her lips into a tight line.

At that moment one of the men on the sofa—one of the waiters from the Villa Capri—stood, dizzy with drink, emboldened, and sputtered, "Miss Taylor, I…" Suddenly, the room seemed to unloosen, relax. Mercy turned to me, Tansi took a step forward, Tommy and Polly walked away from each other. But it was all jerky, unsure movement, like a mechanical toy that wanted oil. It clearly alarmed Liz who, glaring one last time at the now-silent balcony, turned and fled the house, leaving a cloud of gardenia perfume that covered us like bedroom fantasy.

Silence. Then Tansi sputtered, "Well…"

Mercy whispered, "I love a woman who knows how to enter a room."

I whispered back, "Anyone can enter a room, Mercy. The secret is knowing that when you leave that room, you take all the oxygen with you."

No one moved. Jimmy clamored down and seemed surprised people were still there. "Was Liz actually here?" No one answered him.

I faced Mercy. "When can we leave?"

Tommy belched, made a drunken apology. He ricocheted his way to the bathroom, headed first in the wrong direction. So he'd never been there, I realized. On his way back, he carried a black-and-white photograph in a gold-gilt frame. Face flushed, hands shaking, he waved the photograph at Jimmy.

"What?" asked Jimmy.

"Why do you have this picture of you and Max Kohl on your wall?"

Jimmy squinted, pushed his glasses up his nose. "I dunno. At some bike race," he mumbled. "Like we raced in that competition outside of Salinas." It was a snapshot of Jimmy and Max, both on motorcycles, both staring into the camera with insolent, hardened glares, looking like twins in worn leather jackets. "It's me on my bike. It ain't nothing." He shrugged.

Tommy shook. "I don't see any pictures of high-school chums here, Jimmy." Sarcastic, sloppy. "Just that creep who scares everybody that bumps into him." Polly, holding his forearm, her nails into his sleeve, kept whispering, "Enough, for God's sake. Do you *know* how you're coming off?"

Quietly, almost to himself, Jimmy muttered, "Maybe because we never were high-school buddies."

Then Jimmy left the party. He simply did a half-bow, almost regal, and walked out his front door and didn't return. Tansi joined me and Mercy, so close I could smell her perfume.

"Mercy," I said, "let's leave."

Tommy was confessional now, hiccoughing his way through forbidden tales. "Max Kohl," he kept yelling, louder and louder. He spun tales of Jimmy's dark, clandestine life, a life squandered in the shadows of Hollywood valleys and hills. Polly couldn't shut him up, and I didn't want him to. Something was being said here. Tommy faced me. "You know why Carisa died?" He paused, looking from me to Tansi to Mercy. "It wasn't the money or even that baby. That baby could have been a dozen different guys' baby. Jimmy never *slept* with her, you know. The real reason was that she was going to expose his filthy sex life. That's why, I'm telling you." He went on. "It was Josh and Carisa who plotted revenge. Jimmy threatened Carisa. He got scared. Don't forget Fatty Arbuckle, for Christ's sake. Scandal's gonna kill him."

I broke into the rambling speech. "So you're saying Jimmy killed Carisa?"

Tommy, blurry eyed, "I ain't saying nothing. About *that*. I'm saying that Jimmy shouldn't have a picture of him and that... that...man Max on his wall. It's not..."

He stopped. Tansi began to move, and she was furious. She stood in front of Tommy. "This is a crock and you know it. How dare you call Jimmy one of...one of those people."

Tommy rolled his head back and forth. "I'm sorry to offend the head cheerleader of his fan club..."

He didn't finish because Tansi had slapped him full in the face.

◇◇◇

Weary, I stepped into the hotel lobby, after a mournful goodbye to Mercy whose parting words were, "Edna, you do know how to show a girl a good time." I smiled wistfully. On the drive back no one said a word, with Tansi and Nell silent in the back seat, Tansi still shaking and a little embarrassed. Neither she nor Nell said goodbye, just rushed out of the car.

Jimmy was sitting in the lobby. "Edna," he called to me. And I started. He'd never used just my first name before. Always Miss Edna. "I've been waiting."

I smiled. "For me? You could have found me where you left me. At your home."

"I had to get out of there. Everything got wrong there. I had things I wanted to share with you, but Tommy ruined everything."

"It's late."

"Can I talk to you in your room?"

"Not tonight. I'm tired."

"I…"

"Jimmy." I was irritated. "You'll just spend the time talking about yourself—your sad, hapless vision of your sad, hapless life."

"That's not fair," he said, loudly.

"I don't know what's fair with you. Just what are the rules? They're *your* rules in *your* universe. Meanwhile a young woman has been murdered…"

"And you think I don't care, that I'm *that* selfish?"

"Yes."

"I…" He stopped.

I sat down in a chair facing him and spoke quietly. "Tommy said some nasty things about you. About your life…your…" I stopped.

"I know, I know. I've heard it all before. Tommy gets drunk and always says the same old story. He thinks I'm supposed to be that hayseed kid on a tractor in Fairmount, the two of us ambling past the cemetery and stealing crab apples up the road. You know, I *wasn't* his friend in Fairmount."

"He's your shadow."

"And that's driving me crazy. Everybody is driving me crazy."

"What are you going to do about it?"

"Leave him behind. I have to." He took off his glasses, rubbed his eyes, then put them back on, pushing them up his nose. He looked around. "Yeah, I've done a lot of strange things. Hey, what can I say? It's me. But Tommy makes up a lot of it. You know, I tried to get him bigger roles in *Giant* and *Rebel*. But he's wooden, phony. He *acts*. It ain't my fault. He resents me. And I know when he's drunk it all comes out."

I stood, turned to go. "Good night, Jimmy."

"Wait." He reached into his pocket. "I wanted to give you this book."

I rolled my eyes. "Not James Whitcomb Riley, all that frost on the pumpkin and jingle, jingle bells and clippity clop, clop…"

He grinned. "No." He handed me Antoine de Saint-Exupéry's *The Little Prince*. "My favorite book. I give copies to everyone I respect." I took the volume from him. I'd read it a decade before, vaguely liked it—was oddly not surprised that he was attracted to it.

"It's a lovely story," I said.

He touched my sleeve. "It's me, Edna. A man is stranded in the Sahara after a plane crash, you know, and he meets this alien, the little prince who comes from a planet the size of a home, come to earth to find the secret of life. When I first read it, I found the greatest line: 'It is only with the heart that one can see clearly; what is essential is invisible to the eye.' Think about it, Edna. That's how to see the world: caring, love—all there inside you. You know, if you ever meet a little man with golden hair, he's the one, Edna. The little prince. Don't you see? The beautiful golden-haired prince has come onto Earth for a short time, the blink of an eye, and then…is gone. Don't you see, Edna? Briefly, and then gone."

I drew in my breath. "Jimmy."

"Me, Edna. Me."

I looked at him. Behind his thick eyeglasses those myopic eyes glistened with wetness.

◇◇◇

Late at night, alone in my rooms, I sat by the window staring into L.A. nighttime. One boulevard after another of shattered lifetimes, fragile lives silhouetted against spotlighted palm trees. The slender paperback of *The Little Prince* lay nearby, a talisman of supernatural power. Taken from Jimmy's hand, it seemed to possess energy. How foolish I am! A pleasant enough book, enchanting, really, but too simplistic, too ethereal. Nothing of the nuts-and-bolts of real people, my forte.

Unable to sleep, I'd ordered a pitcher of martinis, though I intended to sip but one. I sat there, the martini glass sweaty, and I made mental notes. The murder. The murder. The murder. Carisa and Lydia and Josh and Sal and Tommy and Polly and Nell and…and…Bit players suddenly writ large.

I thought about Jimmy and his gift of *The Little Prince*. Well, a step up from that Hoosier hack. But then I recalled Jimmy's recitation of that pivotal, theatrical line: "It is always in the heart that one can see clearly; what is essential is invisible to the eye."

Essential. Invisible to the eye. The heart. What was invisible to the eye here? What needed to be made visible, translated into the stuff of evidence? What compels a murderer? What? What?

I sipped my martini, finding it too warm now. I put down the glass and stared across the room at *The Little Prince*. James Dean. JD, the monogram of the disenchanted. Juvenile delinquent. The little prince. Lost star in the heavens. Lone star in the Marfa desert.

I reached over and extracted the last of the cigarettes I'd taken from Jake Geyser, idly flipped open the matchbook I'd stuck under the cellophane—My God! I'm imitating Jimmy now—struck a match and watched it burn against the black window before me, the heat touching my fingers. I finally lit the cigarette. The last in Jake's pack, the king-sized Chesterfields, so I crumpled and tossed it into the basket nearby. I sat there then, smoking, barely inhaling because I rarely did that anymore, and my mind suddenly focused, like reversing binoculars and seeing everything up close, etched, vivid; the distant almost invisible world now as big as a sun star. And there it was.

At that moment I knew.

Chapter Twenty

But the following morning I wasn't so sure. I had a theory, a reasonable idea of what happened, but the corners of my conclusions were ragged, shifting. I lingered over coffee, bit into the cinnamon toast I'd ordered, popped a strawberry into my mouth. I needed to talk to Mercy, who knew these people. No—not these people—this *world*. Hollywood beliefs, the cock-eyed value structure, hermetic and glass-enclosed, that conditioned these movie folk to move to dark and ugly extremes. Worlds on celluloid: worlds in real life. Blurring perhaps? Overlapping?

James Dean, his words to me one night. We come to believe what they write about us, and then we force the others around us to genuflect in agreement.

I got confused. The strawberries were tart to the taste, and I grimaced. How is it California, perpetual sunshine and acres of lush fields, can produce such bitterness out of brilliant light and bracing air and a paintbox blue sky?

Quite simply, it does.

I dialed Mercy's number and caught her at home. "Can we meet later to talk?"

"Edna, you sound so serious."

"I am. I have an idea."

I heard Mercy breathe in. "About the murder?"

"Yes."

I found a phone book in the desk drawer, leafed through it, and found what I was looking for. I dialed the number.

"Good morning," a deep, firm voice answered.

"Mr. Vega," I said. "I have more questions."

"Yes?"

"But not of you. I have a request." I wanted to talk to his granddaughter Connie.

"But she is not here, only weekends, you know. I believe I told you that. During the week she stays with her mother."

"Could you give her my number?"

Again, the hesitation. "My daughter works. And, well, it's summer. Connie stays with her cousins, the beach, the outdoors, friends…"

"I'd like to try."

"I need to reach my daughter first."

"Of course."

Fifteen minutes later, still sitting there, the phone rang, and I answered it on the first ring. Vega said his daughter, reached at work, deferred to his judgment. And he agreed. There was no guarantee Connie was home, though it was still early morning. Chances are she would still be in bed. "You know how young people are," Vega said. "And it's a hot summer."

Connie, groggily answering the phone, had already been awakened by her mother, who told her I would be calling. The girl seemed wary, perhaps unused to conversations with older strangers. A good thing, that I approved. Much of contemporary child rearing alarmed me; children in the post-war era were coddled, indulged, foolishly flattered. They would become insolent, demanding adults in a day soon after my death. They would be, the thought did not please me, James Dean.

Connie and I spoke for a few minutes, my questions this time more directed, less diffuse. Now, truly, I had a clearer vision of what I needed to know. So we reviewed the same story, and Connie seemed irritated when I brought up the woman she had seen waiting outside Carisa's apartment, the woman she thought was waiting for Jimmy/Tommy as he ran out of her building. I wanted Connie to describe the car. Not surprisingly, Connie was filled with details now. I smiled. Young folks know cars, especially in the car culture world of California. They might not look closely at people, perhaps, but at objects of desire, yes, indeed.

I thanked her and hung up.

Later on, sitting in the commissary waiting for Mercy, I fiddled with a napkin, jotting down words in a list, methodical, the way I take notes for my novels. My quick, inquisitive eye, scanning library archives, historical tracts, yellowing newspapers in dim, dust-choked rooms. I know how to grasp the salient point, that gold nugget of anecdote, some revelation of character. Now, pensive, I listed what I considered a concise rationale for my theory. Yes, I thought. Well, maybe.

Mercy surprised me, and I jumped. "Edna, the studio will provide you with reams of wonderful writing stationery," she said, grinning. "A napkin?"

"There was a time when I could remember the minutest details. These days, well…"

Mercy slipped into a chair. "I have gossip for you, Edna. I was weaving my way through the Byzantine maze of the back lot and there was little Nell Meyers, probably still with echoes of African chants in her ears and the resounding boom of Tansi's lovely slap against Tommy's face. And she's walking with a quaint cardboard box, prettily tied with a red string. Nell, it seems, is leaving her job. Today."

I started. "What? Why would she do that so suddenly?"

"I asked about that. She said she'd actually resigned two days ago, told her boss, but didn't tell us at Jimmy's."

"And why not? It seems the natural thing to do—to tell your friends."

"She said she wants to go away quietly. I guess Carisa and Lydia dying spooked her. She told me Hollywood's not right for her. She's going to a small hamlet in Pennsylvania, where her mom's from, I gather." She stopped. "Edna, what's that look on your face?"

I had blanched, shifted in the seat. "This is not good news, her leaving." Nell, fleeing with a cardboard box and a Greyhound ticket to some dirt road corner of civilization. Speaking rapidly,

I outlined my ideas to Mercy, who turned pale, but added, finally, a caveat. "Edna, these are random bits of information, compelling, I have to admit. But this notion about Nell. Well, isn't that a stretch?"

"What else have we got?" I asked. "We have to stop her. I mean, she's not leaving *today*, is she?"

Mercy nodded. "That's what I find strange. Yes, she is. Ticket in hand."

"We need to do two things," I said, staring at the ragged napkin before me, frayed and crumpled. "One, you find Nell. If need be, stall her from leaving. And I need to run this by Detective Cotton. I need his advice here. And," I added, eyebrows rising, "we may need him to get to Nell."

While I phoned Detective Cotton, Mercy went looking for Nell, who seemed to be making a sentimental round of goodbyes to people who scarcely knew her. Bustling down a hallway, I spotted Mercy. She shook her head as I approached, nodding toward a doorway where Nell lingered. She was with a make-up artist, chatting away, her cardboard box resting at her ankles. Nell said a hearty goodbye to the woman, and the woman looked annoyed. Nell, however, was smiling. "I will miss you people."

Mercy mumbled to me. "That's unfortunate."

"Could I have a minute of your time?" I said to her as she turned from the doorway, but Nell closed up, the smile gone. She looked nervous. "Why?"

"About Lydia."

Nell shook her head. "No. Don't you see? I don't want to be part of this any more."

But I persisted. Mercy joined in, speaking softly and even smiling, and Nell found herself sitting across from us in the commissary. I sat there, iron-willed, jaw set, eyes sharp and focused.

"Nell, I just need to ask you something."

Nell looked frightened. "Yes?"

"You probably knew Lydia better than most," I began. Nell nodded, nonstop. "But there is something I have to know. Mercy and I have been talking about the letters."

"The letters?" Nell actually gulped.

"You know, the letters. Not so much Carisa's stream of anger to Jimmy and Warner, but letters *to* Carisa."

"Jimmy never told me about his letter to her until later."

I made a clucking sound. "He didn't seem to tell anyone until he *had* to." I waited a second. "But no, Lydia's letter to Carisa."

"What about it?"

"You knew about it? You knew Lydia wrote a threatening letter to her?"

Nell waited a second, seemed to be thinking it through. "Not when she actually *wrote* it. I mean, I remember her, and even the others, bitching that they couldn't reach Carisa a lot of the time. She didn't answer the phone and even if you went there, as I did with Lydia once or twice, there was no guarantee she'd let you in. So I guess if you had to reach her, you, well, dropped her a note. It was..." She waved her hand.

"What?"

"Easier, I guess. But, you know, later on, after Carisa's death, that's when I learned about it. She told me she'd been hoping no one found out because it threatened her."

"But she was found out, no? Once the letter was found."

"Of course. And it scared her. She went nuts over it. She thought it would mean Detective Cotton would think she killed Carisa."

I timed my response. "But Detective Cotton never found that letter."

Her eyes got wide. "Of course he did."

"No."

Nell shuddered, looked around, nervous. "I mean, she *said* he...I assumed..."

"What did you assume?"

"Lydia said...I think she said...well, she was crying a lot... no, that was later...she..."

"Nell, I want you to tell me everything. You hear me. Step by step. Think back. Put things in order, please."

Nell looked around, again. The commissary was filling up with people, and getting noisy. She half-stood, as though ready to flee, then her arm hit the cardboard box she'd placed on a chair, and the string unraveled. The box toppled to the floor. Personal items—a photo in a cheap frame, a coffee mug, a Warner Bros. Studio paperweight, papers bound with elastic bands—spilled out, and, clumsily, frantically, she pushed everything into the box, and then closed the flaps.

Quietly: "This is important, Nell," I said.

She nodded.

◇◇◇

An hour later, in Mercy's dressing room, we sat with Detective Cotton. The detective listened to my terse summary, sitting there impassive and largely unblinking. He cleared his throat. "Not bad."

"Not bad?" I expected more. Backslapping, accolades, hip-hip-hurrahs.

"It makes sense…"

I broke in, impatient with his manner. "Of course it makes *sense*." You bumbling fool, I added, hopefully to myself.

Detective Cotton smiled, and I realized he was a man used to condescending to women—a man whose world—a downtown precinct of testosterone-jumpy cops—was a sanctified male preserve. A man who, had he the misfortune to be married, most likely treated the little missus like chattel, some Doris Doormat to do his bidding. I was very familiar with his ilk, frankly. And yet I'd thought him decent, a good cop. A man who seemed to entertain the idea that I might contribute to the investigation.

"You're a tough bird to read," I remarked.

"Why so?"

"I don't know if you value the ideas of women."

"I value a good idea."

"That's not answering my statement."

"I don't answer statements. I answer questions."

"You're playing games, sir."

"So, Miss Ferber, I do think you may be on to something here, and I'll not fault you for that. But I've been conducting my own investigation, you know, and this morning, finally, I convinced a judge—actually I convinced Jack Warner through his boy Jake Geyser—that the matter needs to go before a grand jury. It's time. And my case, I'll tell you frankly, is against James Dean. Warner isn't happy, and Dean has been forewarned. It's going to get messy, but this now has to leave the studio and go downtown. The case has languished too long…"

I felt my heart in my throat. "So you're going to name Jimmy as murderer."

"We're going to name him as number one suspect—not murderer. We'll couch the arrest in language the studio will tolerate. Means the same thing, just delays the inevitable."

"Give me twenty-four hours," I demanded, sharply.

"What?"

"I want to test my theory."

"I can't do that." He shook his head.

"Of course you can."

He looked surprised. "True, I can but…"

"If I'm right, I could save you some embarrassment."

"And if you're wrong, I seem the procrastinator."

"It's less embarrassing than mud in your face. Detective Cotton, you may be the detective in this case…"

"I'm glad you noticed."

"But it seems to me it's *my* detecting we're entertaining now."

"An amateur's luck."

"Sir, a veteran writer's keen eye."

"Miss Ferber…"

"Detective Cotton."

He had trouble smiling. All right, he nodded. "You have till midnight tonight."

I narrowed my eyes. "I'll be in bed by ten, sir."

A short time later, as Mercy and I were leaving the dressing room, I spotted Jimmy. He wasn't happy—agitated, jumpy, constantly pushing his eyeglasses up the bridge of his nose. "That goddamn

Cotton," he yelled. "He's here, and I said…you know what he said?…he…said…ah…don't leave town…like…"

"Jimmy." I took his arm. "Stop. Don't let this get to you this way."

He looked at me, almost uncomprehending, and then walked away. "Jimmy," I called after him, but he kept going.

Much later, walking out of the building, Mercy and I stopped, transfixed by an odd tableau on the sidewalk by the front gate: Jimmy, in animated conversation with Tommy and Polly, with Nell standing some ten feet away, nodding, that infernal cardboard box at her heels. For a minute the two women watched as Tommy seemed to become more and more agitated, swaying his body, still unfortunately clad in that red jacket, and spitting words at Jimmy. Jimmy, himself antsy, cupped his eyes, staring through the blinding sunshine at his friend. When we got near, the talk shifted, as Polly moved between the two men. "Stop this," she pleaded, one of her hands on Tommy's chest.

Tommy's face got closer, and a purplish color spread across his features. "You used Polly," he screamed.

Jimmy looked at Polly, tucked between them like a swaying lamppost, a woman taller than both men. She stepped back and held her hands up in the air. "Stop this."

Jimmy said nothing.

"You used Polly."

Jimmy looked at Nell, standing apart. "You *told* him?"

"I didn't know it was a secret."

Jimmy shook his head, grinned. "That was a bedroom confession, Nell."

Nell, filled with the confidence of a Greyhound ticket in her bag, yelled back, "What kind of man tells a girl he's sleeping with that he enjoyed sleeping with his good friend's girlfriend. Crowing about it."

Jimmy stared at her, confused. "I gotta stop getting drunk," he mumbled to himself. "I fall into bed with strangers."

Nell seemed ready to leave, twisting her body away, but at that moment she caught my eye. She folded her arms over her chest, reminding me of a sullen Buddha, and the look in her eyes was hard, deliberate. "I'm not sorry," she said, bluntly.

Jimmy spun around, looking helpless. He took a few steps back, glancing back at the studio entrance, then looked toward the parking lot. I realized he wanted to get away. He didn't want to be here, not because he disliked drama, certainly, but because this somehow no longer *mattered* to him. He'd already moved past this. Past Tommy. Past Polly.

"You don't deserve…" Tommy faltered. Then, in a swaggering gesture, he indicated the building behind him. "This."

Jimmy, quiet, swung his head around, following the direction of Tommy's arm, and started to walk back to the studio. But his face registered alarm, and I looked. There, in the doorway, stood Detective Cotton, watching. Jimmy's face got beet red, and he faced Tommy. "You're a small man, Tommy."

Polly reacted. "Jimmy, stop it."

"I mean it," Jimmy sputtered. "Small." And he actually laughed. "And that's the problem here. You know, you're tiny inside." He caught his breath, intoxicated with the new word. "Tiny." He stressed the word. Said, the word hung in the air like a curse, awful but true. I noticed him glance back at Cotton, and the look was different now: triumphant, sure.

Tommy's body shook. Jimmy stepped closer, waiting. Nell muttered something—to me it sounded like a grunt—and Tommy suddenly lunged forward, socked Jimmy in the jaw. Jimmy reddened, fell back, but then rushed forward, shoving Tommy back a few steps. In seconds the two were grappling with each other, wild, off balance; and with one calculated and powerful thrust of his muscled arm, Jimmy hit Tommy squarely on the side of his head. Tommy slumped to the ground and lay there, gasping for breath. Jimmy rubbed his still-clenched fist, contemplated his bruised knuckles, and, spotting Mercy and me, forced a thin, what-can-I-do smile, and walked away. Then he stopped, turned to face Cotton, who hadn't moved from the doorway. Facing the detective, he mumbled, "If I felt I belonged someplace."

Slowly, almost jauntily, he walked away.

Mystified, I looked to Mercy, who whispered, "His character in *Rebel* says that. Big scene, climax, really."

I shook my head. Hollywood: the place where people speak in someone else's lines.

Nell looked like she was going to follow Jimmy but then thought better of it. She saw me looking at her with censorious eyes, and, throwing back her shoulders in an arrogant gesture, grabbed her meager cardboard box, cradled it in her arms like a heavy child, and walked toward the parking lot.

I turned to Mercy, "Now that's an exit worthy of De Mille."

Stretched out on the ground, Tommy was moaning. Polly knelt down and cradled his head in her lap. She whispered, "You don't *need* him, Tommy. We'll leave Hollywood. He's always *used* you—us. He used *me*, too. You know that. He uses any girl. You know how he is. It didn't *mean* anything to me, what he did. It's you and me…" On and on, still cradling his head and rubbing his temples with her fingertips. She looked shattered, pale as dust; and she swayed back and forth, rocking Tommy.

I turned to walk away, and Mercy followed. Mercy whispered, "I'll never understand that relationship."

I muttered, "What relationship?"

When I glanced back, Polly was still holding onto a whimpering Tommy, whose eyes were closed now, but Polly was staring down toward the end of the lot. I followed her gaze. Jimmy stood there, leaning against a car, smoking a cigarette, his body rigid. From a distance, he could have been a young Jett Rink, surveying his worthless Texas acres, his Little Reata, God's forlorn land.

I looked back at Polly. She was rocking the sullen, immobile Tommy now, but she was looking at Jimmy—not with disgust or hated or even pique. No, I realized, the look was one of desperate longing.

Chapter Twenty-One

Mercy and I walked to the Smoke House across the street. Neither of us spoke, which was the way I wanted it. Echoes of Jimmy and Tommy's silly squabble still rang in my ears. But, more so, I was baffled by Polly and Nell. Why had Nell chosen to tell Tommy of Polly's one-time infidelity with Jimmy? Mercy was shaking her head. I was glad she was there—someone I could talk this out with, someone levelheaded, smart. A woman with fire in the soul, strength in her sinew. Luz Benedict herself, the strong-willed spinster of *Giant*.

But a noisy Tansi and Jake, both entering from the sidewalk, interrupted my reverie. Each carried accordion files bursting with papers, each in a hurry. "Edna," Tansi exclaimed, "don't forget your two o'clock meeting with Ginsburg and Stevens."

"I won't, Tansi."

Jake turned to Tansi, "We can't talk. We'll be late for Warner's meeting."

But Tansi hovered over me. "We just met Nell in the parking lot. She said Jimmy hit Tommy." Wonder, stupefaction; then an odd smile. "You'll have to tell me all about it." Jake made a *tsk*ing noise. He wouldn't look into my face and began to move away. Pulling her folder close to her chest, Tansi rushed after him.

Mercy and I still didn't talk, just sat there with coffee. Then Mercy broke the silence. "You look tired, Edna." A pause. "Don't forget your two o'clock meeting."

I groaned. "No, I'm skipping it. They don't know it yet."

Then, relaxing, we ordered sandwiches and more coffee, and we talked and talked. I posed an idea, and Mercy played off it. Yes, no, maybe; a possibility. At one point Mercy started to ask a question and then stopped. "You're right, Edna."

From my purse I withdrew the napkin I'd scribbled on, and spread it on the table. "Four points," I said, looking at it. "Indisputable. At least to me. Let's go over this again."

But we were interrupted by Tansi, who surprised us. "A reprieve. Warner is with some lawyers, so I get an early lunch." She waited for me to invite her to join us, but I said nothing. I drummed my fingers on the slip of paper before me, impatient. I wanted the time with Mercy. But Tansi, grinning nervously, uncomfortable with the silence, simply stood there. "I thought I'd join you for lunch, but, you know, if you're busy, well, then…" She waited.

I looked at Mercy, then nodded. "No, of course, Tansi, please join us." I picked up the napkin, carefully folded it, and tucked it back into my purse. "We just ordered."

"I want to hear all about the Jimmy/Tommy brawl."

"There's nothing to say Tansi. Those two just don't get along any more. The end of a friendship that was doomed from day one. And Tommy is angry so he strikes out. Jimmy is—well, Jimmy is just himself. It was an ugly, unpleasant moment, two wilderness bucks locking horns in front of two females. This Hollywood parking lot is, I guess, the last frontier."

"But…" Tansi started. "But is Jimmy hurt?"

"No," Mercy said. "Tommy suffered a bruise, though."

Tansi looked relieved. "As it is, Jimmy gives the makeup people a challenge, what with his sleepless nights, those bags under his eyes, the sloppy shaving…"

So we chatted idly throughout lunch, and Tansi lingered, even having a cigarette after the sandwich. Mercy kept looking at me.

"Edna?" Tansi offered me a cigarette.

"Remember when Jake gave me his pack of cigarettes?" I asked. Tansi shook her head. "Well, I just smoked the last of that pack, up in my room. Last night. I've also made a vow never to smoke another cigarette."

Mercy spoke up. "I'll never stop smoking. Sorry."

"Me, too," Tansi added.

I reached inside my purse, and withdrew something. Mercy watched as I dropped a matchbook onto the cluttered table, and all three of us watched it fall between a plate and a glass. It just lay there.

"I thought you didn't want a cigarette, Edna," Tansi said.

"I don't. I told you I'll never smoke again."

"Then…" She glanced down at the matchbook, and I saw color rise in her face. She looked at Mercy, who was staring at her, holding her breath.

"What?"

"I believe these are yours," I said.

"No, I don't think so…"

Emphatically, "Oh, yes." I breathed in. "I'm sorry, Tansi, I really am, but when Jake offered me a cigarette, you did, too. You even lit my cigarette. And you slipped your matchbook across the table at me. Later I recalled picking it up, dropping it in my purse. Last night, lighting the last of Jake's cigarettes, I reached for the matches, and I remembered. I had taken them from you."

"I don't remember that."

"Well, dear, I do. Sad to say. Do you see what they say?" All three of us glanced down at the matchbook, face up. Stamped in gold on the dull brown surface was Ruth's Grill. With a telephone exchange. And the slogan, "Cocktails and Steaks."

I pushed the matches across the table. "Take them, Tansi. They're yours."

"They're not."

"Tell me, Tansi, how did you happen to have matches from a restaurant across the street from Carisa's apartment? A place you said—more than once—you never went to. A neighborhood you studiously avoided. A neighborhood you insisted I stay out of—fear for my safety."

"I must have got them somehow—from Jimmy, maybe." Tansi stared into my face. "Or maybe from Jake. He went there a lot. He *told* you that."

"I sat in the same grubby restaurant one afternoon with Alyce and Alva Strand, in the same spot where Carisa sat when she was with another woman. And the two were arguing, Carisa yelling at her. They just saw the back of the other woman's head…"

"But you can't blame that on me. Really, Edna, that's impossible." She looked around the room, as though for a familiar face. When she looked back, she smiled. "I don't like this, Edna. We're friends, you know."

I sighed. "We are friends, Tansi. I've known you since you were a baby." My mind wandered a bit. "I remember…"

"Edna." Mercy touched my wrist, softly. "Maybe Tansi can explain."

Tansi, a little hysterical, "I just did. Didn't you hear me? I don't know how I have to explain such a trivial thing as…as a matchbook. I've had dozens over the years. From all over. I pick them up. Smokers pick them up. Just as *you* did. You said you picked mine up, no?"

I sucked in my breath. "Do you remember the afternoon you drove me to the hotel? You were in your new car and…"

"What does my car have to do with it?"

"Manuel Vega's granddaughter recalled seeing a woman sitting in a car in front of the apartment the night Carisa was killed. She was on a bus, but looked, and thought she saw Jimmy running out of the apartment building. Of course, we learned that it was Tommy, but she thought it was Jimmy. She thought he was joining a woman who was waiting in a car."

"That wasn't me. I've never gone there."

I rushed my words. "I asked Connie about the car. She couldn't describe the woman, but the car she recalled. Vividly. A brand-new Chevy Bel Air. Shiny turquoise with white top."

Tansi shook her head. "So? Do you know how many such cars there in L.A., Edna? Dozens. We're car people out here, and it's a popular car. We like our cars…"

"Yes," I interrupted. "That's why Connie mentioned it. She likes cars, too. And movie stars. Like Jimmy. But that got me to thinking. Tommy ran out—Carisa didn't let him in—but he was *not* joining the woman in the car, waiting there, watching. There had to be a reason Connie would notice, even if it didn't quite register with her. She obviously sensed someone waiting in front of the place where she lived. Like a lot of kids, she's in tune with street life. She spent her hours anticipating the visits of James Dean, her idol. So it stayed with her. Tansi, I think you were there that afternoon. I think you went there, for whatever reason, despite what you've said, and watched. You were watching for Jimmy, too. And you saw Tommy run out. And you went in to see Carisa..."

"No, for God's sake, no!" Tansi thundered. "This is preposterous. Really, Edna." A tinny laugh. "This is not one of your melodramatic fictions, you know."

I sighed. "I only wish, Tansi. But my instinct tells me..."

Tansi swirled around in her chair, then looked at Mercy, her eyes searching her face. "Mercy, tell her. Are you hearing this story? A matchbook and a car. A thousand of one of them, hundreds of the other. Circumstances."

Mercy looked down at her hands, and she seemed surprised they were shaking. There was sadness in her voice. "Edna."

I held up my hand. "You must have gone to the apartment after Tommy fled, somehow got inside, argued with Carisa— probably about the letters she sent Jimmy and Warner, including the horrible one that very day to Warner, the threat about *Confidential*; and I know you probably didn't want to go there. And the argument escalated and you threw that statue..."

"There!" Tansi thundered again. "Listen to yourself, Edna. Think about what you're saying."

I waited. Then: "You're going to say you were never in that apartment."

"Yes, I am saying that."

"But you went."

"Edna, talk to Detective Cotton. We've been through this, all of us. I was fingerprinted. We all were. Mercy—not you, but Jimmy's prints, Tommy's, even Nell's. Nell was there. That surprised me. Did you think about that? Jake, his prints were all over the place. Lydia. She's the one to look at. Jake, he'd paid Carisa off. He told me he went there a dozen times. He pleaded with her..." She stopped, out of breath.

"And so he did. And everyone liked to believe Lydia killed her. Nell believed the story. You finally got her to move out of Lydia's room and into your own place. Nell started telling everyone that Lydia did the crime."

"Everyone believed that."

"I didn't. Detective Cotton didn't."

"How do you know? Why didn't she...well, her prints... Edna, you know that Detective Cotton said...he told me, in fact...my prints were nowhere inside that apartment. Nowhere." She sat back, triumphant.

"That's right. Your prints were nowhere to be found," I sucked in my cheeks. "That got me to thinking. How is it possible that the statue had only one partial print of Jimmy's fingers, and a lot of smudges? And whoever rifled through her desk, messed up her letters, and probably absconded with a letter or two, left no prints there. None. A murder done in anger, unpremeditated, would mean that the frantic amateur would invariably leave telltale evidence behind. But nothing."

"I told you, Edna. I never *went* there."

"As I say, it got me to thinking. Then I remembered. Mercy and I went there right after leaving Warner's cocktail party. I remember how we went in our grand, rather elegant attire—our fancy dresses and, of course, our gloves. What women would go to a party like that without gloves? I had them, Mercy had them, and, I recall, you had them. All the women had them. It's what you do at such a party. If you left the party and went there, sat in your car waiting, you must have gone straight from the party. In your gloves, Tansi. No prints. Earlier that day Warner had got that last, horrible letter and his office was in an uproar. That panic punctuated the party, I recall, though largely undiscussed. But you were bothered. So you went there, rushing from the party..."

"No. Edna, please." Tansi's voice was lower now.

"I'm afraid so. But I have to admit—the matchbook, the car, even the gloves—all could be explained away by an adroit lawyer. The matchbook got me to thinking. But there was one point that finally convinced me." I paused, carefully planned my words. "The night Lydia died she called me, largely hysterical and crazy, but, through all the blather and nonsense, a couple things were clear. She was despairing Jimmy's leaving her, true—that probably led to her death, one way or another. But she was also bothered by Nell's moving out, at your prompting, even though that day you'd all enjoyed, at Nell's request, a reconciliation lunch. No hard feelings, you said Nell told you. Except that it left Lydia more maddened. She called me because you mentioned how helpful I was to you—and to Jimmy. Lydia probably misunderstood you. Certainly you never expected her to seek solace from me. But she called, rambled on and on, probably gave me clues to her impending death, which unfortunately I misread, and then she hung up. Later on, she overdosed. Probably on purpose, but maybe not. We'll never know. Max Kohl wandered in, and for a while seemed a perfect suspect. I also realized that he'd probably returned to Carisa's apartment the time I was there with Mercy in order to get the money he suspected Warner had paid to Carisa. She probably blabbed about it. The police would find it later. But that's another story. Anyway, I'm getting off track here."

I breathed in. "But Lydia said something curious to me. She was bothered by the discovery of a letter she'd stupidly written to Carisa, a letter that, like Jimmy's, made idle threats and dumb accusations. A letter written in anger. Lydia was afraid that its contents, revealed, would draw attention to her. Well, I mentioned that letter to Detective Cotton, thinking he was holding back information, but it surprised him. He'd not found such a letter. In fact, he just assumed Lydia, in her narcotic haze, was really talking about Jimmy's letter."

"She was...I know she was." Rapid, spat-out words.

"No, she wasn't. It was a moment of lucidity for the tragic girl. And that's why I had to talk to Nell. The three of you had lunch that day. The so-called reconciliation lunch that reconciled no one. And Nell, at my prodding, recalled that the subject of letters was brought up, Carisa's letters to Jimmy and Warner. The Jimmy letter, too. And then the subject turned to Lydia's letter—and its contents. It was all part of the conversation, and Nell thought little of it. She assumed you knew something from Cotton that she didn't. No one paid it any mind. But Lydia did. She thought that Cotton had found her letter. And then Nell told me that, in fact, *you* mentioned it at lunch. You brought it up. A few drinks, friendly chat, easy going, it just slipped out. No one knew about that letter. The only person, besides Lydia, was the person who probably took it from the apartment, either on purpose or by accident. You, Tansi, you."

A long silence, the three of us sitting there, with me staring across the table at the frozen, hardened face of the woman I knew as a child, a young girl, a young woman. Tansi, daughter of one of my oldest friends. Tansi, rigid now. Silent. Finally, she growled, ready to defend herself. But the lips quivered, the iron resolve shattered; the hands suddenly darted to her face, and she covered her eyes. When she removed her hands, her eyes were misty, frightened. She swallowed, then tossed her head back and forth, and sort of smiled.

"My God, Edna, my God."

"Tell me, Tansi."

"I *had* to do something. Don't you see?" She waited.

"Tell me, Tansi. I *don't* see. This is impossible for me to see."

Tansi's hands were shaking. Mercy reached across the table and touched the back of one wrist, a loving, comforting gesture. But Tansi recoiled, as from snakebite, and tucked her hands under her armpits.

"I had to. To protect Jimmy. Somebody had to. Nobody was doing anything. Jake was playing games, back and forth, going nowhere. Stupid, stupid, stupid. Those letters scared me. Warner kept telling Jake to take care of it. It drove me mad. Jimmy's so helpless, a boy, a child. He's...gentle. He's not built for this. I'd watch him and see the sadness, the hurt. You all see it, Edna. Everybody does. He can't help himself. He told me that story of his mother dying and how he couldn't do it alone, and my heart broke. And so I knew Carisa would do him dirt. I knew her, you know. I'd seen her in Marfa. She was all over him, just horrible. He couldn't stay away from her. It was me who got her fired. She had to go. And then the letters started arriving."

"But the studio was handling it, no?" Mercy said.

"No, they weren't. They didn't *understand* Carisa. Before she left Marfa, I talked to her, so I knew she was crazy. I knew what she was capable of. Not the money, not the baby. She wanted to *destroy* Jimmy Dean. The public James Dean. James Dean: the best thing that ever happened to Hollywood. Look at him—sensitive, moody, beautiful, talented. You know, I can't tell you how kind he was to me in Marfa. And here. Only a woman could understand the kind of hatred Carisa had for him after he left her. Warner, Jake, they thought cash and threats would do it..."

"So you went there?"

"It took all I could do to drive into that neighborhood. You can imagine. I was scared to death. Everyone in Hollywood always warns you about Skid Row. I'd never been there. But I went one afternoon, after the first letters, found the apartment, but she wasn't home. So I wrote a harsh letter and left it under her door—scribbled, dumb, angry. I said some dangerous things. But I said, Call me. I gave my number. Call me. We need to talk. And God, the stuff I said in anger. I just scribbled nonsense. Call me. And she did. She said my letter was sufficient for a lawsuit against Warner. It scared me. I went back there, and yes, we sat in that restaurant—that grimy bar and grill with the filthy tables and the greasy men, and she laughed at me, at first. She said I was one of Jimmy's patsies, some sex-starved spinster who he could wrap around his finger and she'd had enough of it. She knew things about him, she said, dirty things, things he'd done with...with people. I tried to talk sense to her. Why hurt him? He's on the verge of being one of the great actors of our time.

Like Cary Grant. The next Montgomery Clift. Brando. But she kept laughing, and I wanted to kill her. I realized I was in too deep now, pleading with her, but then she quoted from my letter. 'Wait till Warner hears about *this*,' she said. 'You'll be out of a job, baby.' And the more I pleaded the more she laughed. She said she was going to *Confidential* magazine. Then she got mad, wild, screaming at me. I had to run out of the place."

"The matchbook?"

"I never thought about it. I remember smoking cigarette after cigarette. Her, too. Both of us like furnaces."

"But why did you go after the cocktail party?"

"I knew Jimmy wanted you to go," she looked at Mercy, "and you said no. But I saw you were intrigued, Edna. That's why I said stay away. I didn't want Carisa telling you all those garbage stories, the filth about him. And I didn't want any mention of my stupid letter. Then that day that last letter came—the threat to talk to *Confidential*. After Jimmy ran out of the party, I decided to slip out, unnoticed. I figured he'd go there, to her. I sat there in front of her place, furious with Carisa, and I saw Tommy, that fool, running out. I hid my head but he wasn't looking. Then the Strand twins, like frantic cockroaches, ran by, looked up at the apartment, and then ran off. It seemed like everything was going crazy. I was so angry. I went in, up the stairs, pounded on the door. 'Oh, it's you,' she said, opening the door. 'The woman who will never get into his pants.' That's what she yelled at me. 'What is this—visit Carisa day at the Warner Bros. Studio? Am I on the bus tour?'"

For a moment Tansi's hands covered her face. "I pushed my way inside—yes, I was dressed for the party—and stormed around. She stood there laughing. 'Look at you, all gussied up from prancing around in a party dress that would be old on a fifteen-year-old girl.' Stuff like that. Then she said, 'It's no use. I got money from that eunuch Jake. Lots of money. Men are stupid. But money can't buy me. I have a story to tell!' Blindly, I swear I didn't know what I was doing, I picked up that statue and threw it. Somehow it slipped, hit her in the shoulder, and she fell and hit her head. You know, it happened so fast. I just stood there."

"She was unconscious?" From Mercy.

An awful silence. "I could see she was dead. All that blood. Just like that. It happened so fast. I, like, woke up, Edna. And I'm staring at a dead woman. I rushed around the apartment, thinking that no one knew I was there. All that clutter, that paper. A packrat. I remembered my letter, the things I said. I just panicked, opening drawers, and I found stacks of letters, one bunch in a rubber band. And on the top was my letter, folded inside the envelope I'd left it in. She'd scribbled on it in pencil, SAVE. In capital letters. That scared me. SAVE, she'd written. I grabbed that bunch of letters and put them into my purse. And then I left. No one was around. No one."

"And Lydia's letter was there?"

"That was stupid of me. I burned my letter, of course, and the others, one of them Lydia's, which I read first. And then, when we were having lunch, the subject of the letters came up, and I'm staring at Lydia who's been drinking, and I went on about the letters to Jimmy and Warner and talked of Jimmy's nasty letter. I said Carisa should have been used to getting threats by mail. After all, Lydia, I said, there was yours, your accusing letter. I said it right to her. I realized my mistake, I couldn't believe the words came out of my mouth, but I kept talking about Cotton and his investigation, and Lydia got drunker and then she went home. I could have slapped myself, but I thought—no one knows."

"Tansi, you should have come forward…"

"No," she said. "I couldn't."

"What if Jimmy had been arrested?" Mercy asked.

"Oh, I knew he wouldn't be. Warner would take care of that. It had to be Max Kohl or Lydia. Either one. When Lydia died, everyone was safe. I put the idea that it was Lydia in Nell's head earlier and that was that. Jimmy, well, the studio would never let him be charged with murder."

She stopped. The word "murder" stayed in the air, and she trembled. "Oh, Edna, what do I do? It was an accident. It just happened. She fell…"

"But you hid it from Detective Cotton."

"I know, I know, but I couldn't face it. Now what?" She sucked in her breath. "Somebody had to do something, for God's sake. Jimmy can't help himself. No one would ever *accuse* him because there was no reason for him to hurt her because it would *hurt* his career. And his career is who he is. He's an actor. You watched the dailies, Edna. Jett Rink. You wrote Rink before you knew Jimmy. Like a genius."

"What if Lydia had been arrested?" Mercy insisted, breaking into Tansi's ramble.

But Tansi wasn't listening. "You know what happened in Marfa? I'm running errands for Stevens, nonstop, but at night Jimmy'd sit with me, talk to me, tell me about his mother, Fairmount, his motorcycle, his nephew Marcus, his dreams. Just talk, talk, talk. The Little Koffee Kup, with two K's. The barbershop, the drug store. And then the stupid Carisa mess started. I'd warned him when he first started looking at her. She was playing a Mexican cook and goofing off. Stevens said get rid of her when I told him. I did, gladly. But she'd already started causing trouble for Jimmy. Tantrums, crying. Once she slapped him. He slapped her back. She said she'd kill him. Then we got her out of there, shipped her to El Paso, back to L.A. Jimmy was happy, but he told me that she would be a troublemaker. And do you know what I said to him? I'll take care of it. I had no idea what I was talking about, but I meant it. Being around him does that to people. You've seen it."

I watched her eyes get cloudy, dreamy. "The night she was gone, everyone was playing Monopoly or playing records or something, and Jimmy said let's go for a ride. He took your old rattletrap car, Mercy, since Stevens took away his car for speeding. And we drove out under the Texas night sky, way out among the brush and the jackrabbits, and we sat in the car and talked and talked and talked. For hours. I mean *he* talked—the way he does. I just sat there. I couldn't take my eyes off his face. And he had this six-pack of Lone Star beer, and we drank them all in Coca-Cola cups, there, under the stars, and munched on boxes of crackerjacks he got from someone. When I started to hiccough from that beer, he leaned over and kissed me on the mouth. He just did it. Once, quick. There I am hiccoughing like a fool, and he kisses me on the mouth. James Dean. Jimmy. And I smelled his stale tobacco breath, his beery breath, that raw smell, and then, you know, he just started up the car, glanced at me with a sliver of a smile, and he dropped me back to the hotel."

Chapter Twenty-Two

I'd been sitting at Mercy's kitchen table for hours, a lazy afternoon spent watching her make dinner. Outside it was raining, a drizzly L.A. rain, a foggy low-lying mist settling over the lemon grove I could see just beyond the kitchen door. I found it tremendously relaxing, this drifting afternoon, as Mercy deftly chopped glistening stalks of celery, garish carrots, red potatoes, overripe tomatoes, tossing the colorful piles into a large cast-iron pot, already simmering on the stove with crackling, diced onions in lemony butter. Mercy's soup—"my passion," she told me, "my love." A concoction to be blended with chunks of blood-red beef cubes, heated until the flavors merged, announced themselves to the small room, and served with a loaf of dark bread rising in the oven.

I started to cry. For three days, since the arrest, I'd been in a trance, airless, hidden away.

Mercy turned from the stove where she was dipping her nose to breathe in the oregano and garlic she'd just tossed in. "Edna."

I shook my head. "No, it's all right." And it was. It was all right because justice, though relentless, had been served.

How close Mercy and I had become! The company of women, I thought. How do men do it, with their distances, their reserves, their denials? Civilization needs forthright, strong women. How else to survive, to guarantee the passing on of feeling, caring, passion, decency? They do have madness to deal with, women do. I looked at Mercy: a woman half my age, with the throaty whiskey voice, a woman not beautiful but whose face held such character, such resonance. We understood each other. Tacitly. Deliberately. Exquisitely.

I smiled.

"Now what?" Mercy smiled herself.

"I'm feeling a bit melancholy. These past days have been so sad."

Yesterday I sat in the Blue Room, guarded by a nervous Jake who seemed lost without his feisty ally. I smiled at George Stevens who thanked me. He was happy. Jack Warner was away at a meeting but Jake handed me a note. *I told you there was nothing to worry about. In Hollywood there's always a happy ending.* Furious, I crumpled it up. There was a note from Rock, away at the same meeting with Jack. *I was wrong. I'm sorry.* That note I folded and tucked into my purse.

Liz Taylor, dressed in a puffy white linen dress with an apricot scarf around her neck, slipped into the room so softly she seemed a wispy summer cloud. Her violet eyes flickered, and she leaned in, touched me on the shoulder. "It wasn't supposed to end like this." I couldn't interpret the look on her face; the delicate corners of her mouth drooping melodramatically though her eyes—that almost unreal violet tint—seemed faraway. I said nothing. Was this the actress in one more final scene? I didn't understand Hollywood, never would, didn't want to. Not this world where lines were scripted for you, collectively rewritten: polished, deleted, giddily celebrated. Just like the people who spoke them. Who were the people who delivered them?

But Liz had a kindness about her, a bittersweet gentility. I sensed a decent human being here. She smiled wistfully, her salutation. Two men and a woman—their faces dull as cardboard—rushed in, as though they'd misplaced a precious jewel and now had found it, and immediately closed in on her, but never touching, whispering about appointments and obligations. She stared at them, her chin set, then moved seamlessly out of the room. Her perfume lingered.

I shook my head. "I'm thinking about Liz Taylor."

Mercy nodded. "A beautiful woman."

"There are always too many people around her. She's never alone."

Mercy tapped the ladle against the steaming pot. "Alone she might be forced to face the glossy eight-by-ten photograph they've turned her into."

"You know," I said, "one afternoon I was passing by the commissary, and I saw Rock Hudson sitting by himself, alone at a table, hunched over some papers."

"So?"

"He just sat there, this—this *presence*. All these people walked in, crew people, secretaries, best boys, worst boys, I don't know. And no one approached him."

"People don't dare."

"But why?" My voice was rising. "Over and over he looked up as folks neared, passed by, as though he were expecting someone. He's one more Jimmy Dean, hungry for attention and recognition, but scared of it. Because…maybe because…he doesn't quite know the rules he now has to play by. He looked so…so isolated there. He'd planted himself in the middle of the room, as conspicuous as a noonday sun, and he waited. He looked like a shy schoolboy waiting to be picked for sandlot baseball, but only if they made *him* the star player." I paused. "You know, Mercy, they're all up there on the screen and everyone embraces them, that frozen image, but then they sit in a cafeteria and begin to fall apart."

Mercy laughed. "Good God, Edna."

"This movie, my romantic story of Texas opulence and penury, has allowed them to avoid looking at themselves. One more chapter in avoiding the awful mirror. Here, in paradise, Jack Warner tells us that we shouldn't remember Carisa or Lydia. And even dear Tansi."

Mercy was silent a long time. "It's just Hollywood." Flat out. Final.

I nodded. "I was planning to convince Tansi to return to New York. Back there she was spirited, witty. The years in Hollywood made her high-strung, brittle, kowtowing to an ego-mad man like Jack Warner, who wields power like a fist in your face, or Jake Geyser, a toady who mimics his superiors. She lost her bearings here."

Mercy sighed. "So you really think she did all those things to serve the company? She really believed she was saving Jimmy's future?"

I shook my head. "No, not really. She told herself that. She did it out of some peculiar loneliness—some aloneness, maybe—that comes from living here among the cannibals. Mercy, she did it for her idea of love."

"What will happen to her?"

"Well, I've had one very angry phone call from her mother. She's quite the battalion of a woman, that one. She blames me. She's already lined up an army of high-priced New York and L.A. lawyers—funded by her ex-husband, Tansi's dipsomaniac father. His millions will save her. I can't imagine she'll ever do prison time. There's so much money there, and power. Probation, perhaps. Petrified Tansi need have no fear. She's already made bail, of course, and is nowhere to be found."

"I thought it peculiar that the newspaper talked of Detective Cotton solving the crime, 'following leads that culminated in the arrest,' and so forth. That struck me as duplicitous, a cavalier dismissal of your work."

"Septuagenarian spinsters, albeit with spunk and gumption, and a tiny withered Jewish lady at that, are not supposed to step into his bang-bang-you're-dead world. But Detective Cotton did assume control when I called him that afternoon, with Tansi sitting with you just ten feet away. In tears. Both of you."

"I go to sleep thinking of it. It haunts me, her shriveled, empty face."

"You know, Detective Cotton sent a dozen roses to my hotel. That was a surprise. Of course, each night they droop a little more, shedding perfumed petals. When I fly out tomorrow, I expect the carpet will be covered with browning petals."

"You're really anxious to get back home?"

"I am and I'm not. Alaska looms before me like a desolate wasteland. I'll be flying there again, stuck in snow drifts when it's a teeth-chattering one-hundred degrees below zero." I sighed. "L.A. will seem a paradise."

"Come back to visit."

"Of course. But I have to do *Ice Palace.*" I bit my lip. "I suppose it will be my last novel."

Mercy looked at me sideways. "Edna, you probably said that back in the twenties when you finished *Show Boat.*"

I grinned. For a moment I imagined myself back in Alaska, my vision colored by these last days in California. I knew my heart beat differently now.

Mercy pointed to a stack of books on a side table, all wearing glossy dust jackets, a tower of neatly stacked volumes. "Thank you," she said. Earlier I'd arrived with copies of my novels, and, a little sheepishly, had inscribed them to Mercy, each one with a different inscription. In *Giant* I'd written, "You did not fail him." That's all I wrote, and Mercy smiled.

"Did you hear from Jimmy?"

"No," I said. "They're shooting every day now—the last scene. He couldn't…"

"Still, he could have called you."

"There was a small drawing left in my hotel mailbox. It's a picture of a boy's face, and it looks, I suppose, as he did as a young boy: bony, intelligent face, the eyes, the lips—embryonic idol, that one. A boy in what looks like a confirmation suit, with slightly mischievous eyes. He signed it 'Jim (Brando Clift) Dean.' It's beautifully innocent and simple. I'm happy to have it." I thought of Rock and Liz. "What will happen to these young, beautiful people?" I said, suddenly. I looked into Mercy's face. "And you? Out here, among the cannibals."

"Me, I hide away, look at it all cynically, and probably will dissolve into booze and multiple marriages."

"Don't say that," I warned.

"We pay a price. We're a patchwork quilt of publicity shoots. Actors have a short shelf life."

"A lot of this scares me to death. You know, my novels have romantic characters, Mercy. Beautiful, willful women and gorgeous, though horribly flawed, men. But they're...creations. Here, they use real people who seem unaware that, well... the inevitable arc of rise-and-fall is built into this dreadful illusion."

"What's going to happen to *him?*" Mercy asked. "Could he end up lounging with other stars at the Beverly Hills Hotel swimming pool, waiting to be recognized?"

"I don't want to think about that. It scares me even worse."

"I'll never understand him."

I stood up, walked to the window. The rain was stopping. I saw a pale blue sky; the eucalyptus and lemon trees gleamed and shimmered in the yard's sudden light. "He's all that we think he is. Nothing more."

"Nothing more?"

I turned and faced her: "But that's enough."

Epilogue

I wake with a start, glance at the clock on the nightstand. Is it really five in the morning? An absurd hour to be startled awake, neither late night nor hazy morning; a limbo hour, the hour of desperate souls caught between lives. It's the new draperies, I decide, hung poorly, perhaps, so that watery early morning light, creeping over the Manhattan skyline, filters into the dim room.

But that's not it. I sit up, as panic floods me. But I'm more annoyed than frightened. I might be dying—but I know this isn't the case. I'll die when I'm damn good and ready, thank you. I'll pencil in my own death on a distant calendar. I have novels to write. Research. Travel. Notes to take, organize. In the dim light, my mind drifts to Alaska—all that cruel ice and bitter cold. *Ice Palace*: in the works. Death will have to wait.

What did my pesky sister Fanny say when the topic came up last year? "It's the one force of nature you can't control, Edna." We'll see about that.

My eyes dart around the shadowy bedroom, locating the shapes of the comfortable accoutrements I've placed here: the pen-and-ink sketch of me by James Montgomery Flagg, the Baccarat bud vase given to me by Heifetz, the gilt-framed letter from Teddy Roosevelt. Artifacts of my monumental and cherished success. On the small mahogany table by the window is a photograph I placed there yesterday, positioned so I can stare at it, smile, shake my head, grin. Now, suddenly, I want to avoid it, as if it holds a voodoo spell.

An hour later, dressed, I go into the kitchen, surprising Molly who stands at the stove, yawning. "I'll be back," I tell my house-keeper, who eyes me nervously. "I need to walk."

So I stroll down Park Avenue, but I'm dressed inappropriately in a coal-gray cashmere sweater and a jade-green cotton summer dress. I turn back, chilled. I stare into the autumn New York sky—that awful gunmetal gray, as dull as armor plate, yet pale and fuzzy in the far distance, with unlovely, sooty clouds hovering over New Jersey, where, of course, they belong.

As I enter the lobby, I tell myself, triumphantly, that the answer is obvious: I'm still covered with the glitzy fairy dust of Hollywood. July and August in California—well, that explains my uneasiness. All that brutal sun, that wispy late-afternoon fog, those cartoonish royal palms dotting the landscape like a cheap nightclub backdrop. That West Coast ambiance lingers, confuses.

New York in September—what is today's date? October the first?—is desolate and quiet, Manhattanites pulling themselves back, tucking in the corners of their summer lives, readying, like worm-white rodents, for the long numbing cold.

Dreadful Hollywood. All that smiling and bowing, that sycophantic obeisance. Miss Ferber this, Miss Ferber that. May I get you...How pleased we are...I must say you look stunning in those pearls...Your novel, well, let me tell you...And the heat. Dry, not humid really, but monotonous, deadly. There's too much space out there. People fall apart, become unhinged, jaws slack, bodies sagging. It takes too long to cross those endless boulevards.

It was such a comfort to return to New York. Emerging from the limo—ostentatiously provided by Jack Warner, no less—I stepped out onto litter on Park Avenue, a discarded half of a pastrami on rye, stuck to a piece of white butcher's paper. I was back home.

Molly is waiting with a pot of tea. "I forgot my coat," I say.

"Did you hear the phone ring late last night?" Molly's Irish brogue is rich and soft.

"Of course not." A full eight hours in my bed, requisite, solid puritanical sleep; that's what I demand of myself.

I scan *The New York Times*, placed so carefully on the breakfast table. I turn the pages aimlessly, refusing to stay on any one page. A wave of panic—again. Shaking, I flip the sheets quickly, driven, oddly understanding that I have no choice. By the time I get to page ten, the phone is ringing. I listen to Molly's greeting. I wait. Because now I know. For there—as piercing as a dagger to the heart—is the bold headline: "James Dean, Film Actor, Killed in Crash of Auto."

September 30, 1955. Yesterday. Already a lifetime away.

For a freakish second, I am relieved. It all makes sense: the disruption of my sleep, the edgy morning, the panic.

Henry Ginsburg, producer of *Giant*, tells me what I've just read. His exact words: "The boy is dead."

Those frenzied weeks in Hollywood make sense now, yet make no sense at all. As I left for the airport, he followed me out to the limo. Hovering, holding onto me, he whispered, "Edna, you've known me all your life."

At the time I smiled, used to his cryptic asides, inarticulate mumbling, and pebbles-in-the-mouth announcements. But that line stayed with me on the long flight back.

Now, reeling, I walk into my bedroom and find myself drawn to the black-and-white photo I'd propped up on the table, situated so that it caught the blaze of high noon, the afternoon light, the twilight shadows. Hunched over, gripping the table with trembling hands, I stare into the face of the dead boy. This exquisite photo arrived two days ago. Jimmy in his Jett Rink ranch-hand costume, the slouch, the ten-gallon hat shading his brow, the light-blue eyes almost absent, the cigarette insolently poised at the corner of his mouth—those sensual, impossible lips. He'd signed it: Jett Rink. Staring into that chiseled face that suggested so much raw emotion by the slightest movement, I touch the photo—my small, knobby fingers on the slick surface.

No flesh here, no dimension, no power. I want to tear it into shreds. This boy, this imp of the perverse.

The afternoon the photo arrived, I sent him a letter, a brief thank-you note really, in which I foolishly joked and vamped. Lord, how could a twenty-four-year-old boy make an aging novelist behave like a Victorian damsel in a revival of *Tempest and Sunshine*? Or like some simpering *ingénue* in a revival of my own *Show Boat*? I ended the note: "Your steely profile, which so reminds me of John Barrymore, a soul you've probably never heard of—well, Jimmy, you have *that* profile. But your hellfire car racing and tearing through the Hollywood Hills at breakneck speed will soon take care of that."

But he couldn't have gotten the letter. Nor will he.

As I turn away, my hand brushes the photograph onto the carpet, where it's lost in the shadows. I'm unable to pick it up. If I bend down, I will topple into his death.

A whispered voice, "Edna, you've known me all your life."

Yes, of course I have. I always have. The rebel, romantic fool, the afternoon of a faun, the soul in chains, the voice of the turtle.

But now that life is over.

To receive a free catalog of Poisoned Pen Press titles, please contact us in one of the following ways:

Phone: 1-800-421-3976
Facsimile: 1-480-949-1707
Email: info@poisonedpenpress.com
Website: www.poisonedpenpress.com

Poisoned Pen Press
6962 E. First Ave. Ste. 103
Scottsdale, AZ 85251